THE
PROPHET'S ALIBI

Timothy J. Korzep

iUniverse, Inc.
Bloomington

The Prophet's Alibi

iUniverse books may be ordered through booksellers or by contacting:

iUniverse
1663 Liberty Drive
Bloomington, IN 47403
www.iuniverse.com
1-800-Authors (1-800-288-4677)

ISBN: 978-1-4697-3701-0 (sc)
ISBN: 978-1-4697-3702-7 (hc)
ISBN: 978-1-4697-3703-4 (e)

Library of Congress Control Number: 2012900359

Printed in the United States of America

iUniverse rev. date: 3/2/2012

CHAPTER 1

Vienna, Austria, February 14, 11:27 a.m.

Eight shadowy men inside the abandoned industrial park located in the northwest outskirts of Vienna worked furiously against the clock. The obscure site was wedged between the Danube River on the north and the thickly wooded forest that buffered the Gewurztraminer wine district to the south. A paved road that led into the compound hugged the bank of the Danube for approximately three kilometers, while a poorly maintained dirt road skirted the southern edge of the dense forest beyond the complex.

Inside the loading bay of the second warehouse, the contingent all donned industrial uniforms splashed with logos that matched the two innocuous laundry vans parked just inside the rolling aluminum doors. The precise, all-male unit completed their last-minute synchronized drills—checking watches, loading clips into Berettas, and concealing combat knives. All but two of the men would leave the facility heavily armed.

On the floor next to the door, four black, hard plastic cases sat side by side, with their lids open. All were identical in dimension—two feet wide, two feet deep, and four feet long. In the first case there were two handheld surface-to-air rocket launchers strapped into its foam-rubber lined top tray of the box that was opened to a forty-five degree angle, exposing an ample cache of ammunition for their weapons. One of the men inspected its contents then closed the box, buckled its clamps, and moved to the second hard plastic box. This box contained twelve AK-74 assault rifles in its lower bay and its corresponding ammunition was strapped into the tray. The weapon was the newer version of its Russian-made predecessor, the AK-47. The third container included a digital television camera replete with all of the necessary audio-visual equipment for making a viable broadcast. The case was closed and locked, and the vigilant man moved to the final case. It contained three laptop computers loaded into mini-stabilizing bays within the larger lower bay itself, along with a considerable amount of network gear—wireless routers, T3s, etc. The final case was locked and all four cases were stored in the back of the second van. The lead van was inconspicuously loaded with an ample supply of clean laundry, all shrink-wrapped in clear plastic bundles.

At precisely 11:35 a.m., one of the men disengaged the two metal struts that locked the rolling aluminum door in place and yanked on the chain that hoisted the rolling door upward. Two of the men climbed into the first van, fastening their seatbelts. The remaining five men entered the second van—four sat in the back and the other got into the driver's seat. Both van's engines were started and the vehicles emerged slowly from the loading bay. The remaining man closed the rolling door, exited the warehouse through a separate door in front office area, and joined his five colleagues in the passenger seat of the rear van. Within seconds, the vehicles departed through the chain link fence gate and proceeded eastbound on the frontage road en route to central Vienna.

———————— ⊖ ————————

An armada of black limousines pulled up to the curb of the United Nations building in a precise formation, while chugging tailpipes puffed gentle plumes into the frigid February morning. A small flag on the antenna of each limousine identified the host country of its occupants. An efficient battalion of well-dressed Viennese security and Secret Service agents, as well as EU personnel assigned to greet the motorcade, was deployed. Some opened the limousine doors while others kept the small contingent of media personnel and well-wishers in check behind the designated chained together steel roadblocks opposite the drop-off curb. Access to the driveway entering the lower complex was immediately closed to all other traffic and fortified with an armed presence. Personal security agents assigned to their various leaders emerged from the limousines, flanking the ten leaders who followed them out of the vehicles. Out of the lead car emerged conservatively dressed EU president, Edgar Elliott. The distinguished fifty-six year-old Englishman was a staunch European Unionist despite recent troubles in Greece, creating somewhat of a personal rift with the British prime minister.

"Mr. Elliott!" one reporter shouted, while a multitude of cameras flashed. "What is the EU prepared to do about the continued strength of the dollar against the collapsing Euro?"

If the Euro was genuinely collapsing there might be dialogue about intervention, Elliott wanted to answer, but this wasn't a press conference. He turned his slender six-foot frame to acknowledge the question, and a modest lock of chestnut hair fell harmlessly upon his forehead. Instead of responding, he calmly brushed the hair away and nodded cordially in the direction of the steady flicker of cameras.

He was followed by recently elected Russian president, Alexander Nobakov, a fixture of and holdover from the former Soviet Union, who was now their freely elected president. His looks had changed little in nearly seventeen years of absence from the international community, with strands of thinning gray-blond hair combed over to the side of his forehead. He was a little huskier than during his earlier years—a result of the good life at his dacha on the Black Sea.

"Mr. Nobakov!" a journalist shouted from behind the barricade. "Mr. Nobakov, how does it feel to finally attend the G-10 meeting, having been on the outside for so many years?"

That question was also answered with a rehearsed nod, and the Russian leader turned stiffly toward the building's entrance. While several of the ten leaders had a reputation for their cordiality with the media, Nobakov was *not* one of them, and today was *not* that day. The morning briefing called for a quick photo-op, which was hustled to the high-speed elevators that whisked them to their secure meeting high above.

"What is your timeline for pullout of Georgia?" another journalist asked. It was the very salvo the newly elected American president had fired across the Atlantic just forty-eight hours earlier, setting the tone for an awkward meeting between the two super-power leaders.

The Russian leader turned intently to locate the source of the question. His disarming expression caused a small fissure in the pack of journalists, exposing just one reporter. Nobakov rubbed his chin while his eyes seemed to interrogate the young man, but he didn't say a word.

"No rest for the weary, is there Mr. Nobakov?" the Canadian prime minister, Scott Hammons said, while buttoning his suit jacket, jarring the Russian president from a visual water-boarding of the young reporter. Hammons himself had a short fuse with the media when they asked questions he considered out of line.

"Oh, they're really quite harmless, Mr. Hammons," Nobakov allowed, while the two leaders shared small talk.

Hammons was Canada's version of Teddy Roosevelt. The cane he used sparingly was the result of a curtailed hockey career and the ensuing abuse he'd put himself through as an amateur rodeo bull-rider. He hated relying on it from time to time, but there was no more cartilage left in his right knee to remove. Despite his misgivings, it augmented his appearance.

Marge Haydon emerged from a vehicle in a sharp navy blue suit surrounded by a small personal security entourage. She was the first American president ever to be elected from an independent party. In a rather unprecedented rise from near obscurity, the former moderate Republican senator from Montana had been on the job just over two weeks before being summoned to her first G-10 meeting. Her platform had caught the two conventional parties completely off guard, while catching the American voter in the sweet spot—implementing a flat tax and abolishing the IRS.

"President Haydon! President Haydon!" two journalists cried out. "President Haydon!" a third blurted out, wedging her thin frame between the other two.

Haydon turned to acknowledge the barrage of inquiries, and nodded toward the woman sandwiched between two men.

"President Haydon, do you really think your tax reform is possible?" the woman asked, with her head somewhat crowned by the armpit of the male reporter next to her, his offending arm thrusting a recording device in the president's direction.

"First of all, I hope the gentleman next to you is wearing deodorant," Haydon quipped, drawing a contained giggle from the press. Instantly, the female journalist's head was spared further affront as he switched the recorder into his other hand.

"Secondly, my constituents and I aren't here to discuss the U.S. tax code," Haydon continued. "But mark my words; we will roll out our strategy in the coming weeks. And the plan is both real *and* achievable."

"But President Haydon…"

"Well said, Madame President," a quiet but unmistakable voice said.

"Mr. Prime Minister," Haydon reacted, turning slightly to greet Britain's Robin Collinsworth. "What a treat to finally meet you!"

"Oh no, Madame, the pleasure's entirely mine," he countered, extending an arm to Haydon. His tone, compelling and disturbing, emanated from his thick barrel chest. His slightly hunched posture and thin wispy hair and eyebrows depicted more of a Charles Dickens character than a resident of Downing Street. But his engaging gray-blue eyes that peered through the round glasses perched at the end of his nose could entice anyone into dialogue. "Shall we?"

"We shall," she said, placing her right hand on his left forearm. The two hopped up onto the curb and turned to face a sea of flashes.

Just then Collinsworth caught a whiff of a very pleasant scent originating from the American. "What *are* you wearing?" he asked, recognizing the scent, but unable to place it.

"It's a secret," she replied, mischievously. Years earlier, she'd started wearing Issey Miyake for men. Just one spray of her husband Tyler's cologne was her subtle reminder of him when he was away on business. She was unable to break the habit.

They were followed by Japan's Yoshito Tanaka, a former Bank of Japan executive who'd run out of rungs to climb, and stepped into the lead role at the Japan's Central Bank. From there he was an easy choice for his country's premier.

"Mr. Tanaka," a well-known business journalist barked from the front of the media line. "It's Carlton Rose of CNBC."

Tanaka knew of the reporter, and simply nodded for him to continue.

"Sir, do you believe the carry trade has reached a potential international crisis?" Rose asked. The carry trade at one time had helped support global liquidity, but in recent years it had become somewhat of a speculative tsunami.

"Mr. Rose, as you well know, the carry trade is nothing new," Tanaka said. "The Yen just happens to be the least expensive currency available at the moment. The trade can be a very helpful tool when not abused. The mere fact that Japan's Central Bank is in a tightening cycle is not Japan's fault. Over-extended speculation is the culprit, not Japanese monetary policy."

"But Mr. Tanaka," Rose started to ask.

Tanaka shook his head just once, maintaining a tight smile, and rejoined the other leaders.

Germany's Chancellor Claudia Schmidt, a London School of Economics graduate, ascended the ranks as an economist at Deutsch Bank. Later she would sit at the helm of that global juggernaut for ten years. She knew finance and was a master of integration. Her tireless work ethic, charismatic personality, supportive constituents, and extraordinary ambition drove her into the political realm. In a meteoric ascent, she vaulted to the top of the heap and was elected as Germany's chancellor. She smiled professionally at the flicker of flashes.

Italy's trim leader Marco Veroni was a career politician in his second term as president, who seemed to enjoy his time in the tabloids as much as his time in office, causing his handlers nothing but grief. Whether he was skiing in Gstadt or gallivanting on his yacht in San Remo, the media was sure to find him.

Veroni was joined by France's President Didier Marceau, whose family had handed him a wine empire, and not too long thereafter France handed him the reins to the country. And yet, he was a worthy choice. Marceau was a combination of a myriad of things—class, elegance, hard-working, at times hard-nosed, but reasonable in diplomacy and logic when a viable counterpoint could overcome his position.

Marceau and his Italian counterpart shared a friendly rivalry over which country produced the best wine. The Frenchman also had an obsession with storied jewelry. He wore cufflinks he'd acquired through a very private Sotheby's auction. The two gorgeous 8-karat ruby nuggets mounted on 24-karat gold clasps were alleged to be from Napoleon Bonaparte's golden cloak that he'd worn in a famous 1818 portrait. It wasn't until recent years that he became active in politics as a result of affairs in the Middle East, which were also beginning to affect the landscape at home.

"Monsieur Marceau, can you tell us about the postal strike back in France?" a French speaking reporter asked.

"You are obviously French, and know our country's history of strikes. Like all of the other disputes before my presidency, we will resolve this one as well," Marceau responded coolly, as he and Veroni stepped onto the curb with the other leaders.

From the final limousine emerged China's Chen Zheng, the former silver medalist middleweight boxer from the 1980 Olympics who was a devout hard-liner, except when it came to foreign investment in China. As he joined the group of leaders he slipped his Ray-Ban Wayfarer sunglasses into his coat pocket and replaced them with a tight smile for the flashing cameras. A reporter started to ask a question, but the Chinese leader held up an open palm for the question to cease—and it did.

The ten leaders paused briefly for a group photo amidst an onslaught of flashing cameras, while questions continued to be hurled futilely in their direction. Special agent Sylvia Jensen and her small but polished Secret Service unit meshed seamlessly with the Viennese security agency. They meticulously cleared a path through the front entrance and toward the elevators, just to the right of the metal and explosive detectors which were temporarily disabled during the G-10 Summit. Anyone other than an invited guest courageous enough to try and gain entry to the premises would have to penetrate a wall-to-wall force of heavily armed UN police. The integrated unit quickly escorted the G-10 leaders and their personal attachés and distributed them equally into the four elevator cabs, and moments later the entire entourage began their ascent to the 47th floor, while building security locked all the bullet-proof glass entrance doors. All members of the international security contingent assigned to the conference had been required to check their communication devices in with the UN police on the ground floor due to a change in policy. Texting was an unacceptable distraction from duty.

In thirty-three seconds the four elevator doors to the conference center on the 47th floor opened almost simultaneously and its occupants were greeted by a maitre d' and his staff, all dressed in tuxedos. The maitre d' directed his staff to relieve the leaders of their overcoats, and gestured toward a set of stairs off to his right. "This way please," he said, leading the group of leaders from the black granite vestibule down the three steps to the carpeted main floor of the conference center across to the white table clothed buffet table on the opposite side of the room. Security personnel fanned out on either side of the main floor as a matter of prearranged protocol. There was a large round conference table featuring name placards denoting where everyone would sit to the left of the path where the leaders were taken.

Sylvia walked the perimeter of the conference center, stopping briefly to speak with a few members of her team. Two days earlier, she'd taken charge of the security detail and wound up as the alpha dog to oversee the G-10 security, consisting of Secret Service, Viennese Secret Police, and nine personal bodyguards assigned to the various leaders. She was the only female, and had already proven to be a competent leader for the same group of Secret Service agents back home. With their endorsement, there was no conflict here. She said a few words to the U.N. staff photographer assigned to cover the meeting and the lunch one floor above at the meeting's intermission.

Jensen was somewhat of a mystery to most insiders, including the president. The vice president had arranged her appointment to the president because of her background and his relationship with the woman's father, an Annapolis naval officer.

She had become a tactician in the Korean martial art of Hapkido by her seventeenth birthday, winning every competition she was entered in, and seemingly with lust for punishment to her opponent. Hapkido was the art of coordinated power, and was perhaps the best martial art for a woman because one could use all of the weight of a much heavier opponent and turn that into a weapon against the very opponent with that size advantage. From its origins the centerpiece spinning heel kick was designed to take down a horse to bring the soldier mounted on it down to ground level. Sylvia had eliminated every legitimate male or female opponent known in the United States like clockwork, and quit competing.

Still, her father pushed hard for officer's school at the Naval Academy, but his strong-arm tactics in the end backfired, and his defiant daughter found her way into an intense special forces training program on par with the Navy Seals. To date, women were still not permitted in the Seals, except in movies. She was an adept pupil, and her cool personality and religious physical regimen was a perfect marriage for the discipline necessary to become a stealth fighting machine for the Ranger's black-op program.

After her first tour of duty in the Serbian conflict, then a six-month stint in the Gulf War II, Sylvia had privately burned out, nearly imploding, as she struggled to define why a woman would ever choose the life she'd chosen instead of manicures and shopping. She found respite on the Cote D'Azur in the south of France, for years bouncing around between Nice and Lyon, and had a brief romance with a budding soccer star. He was a welcome reprieve from her otherwise cold and sterile world.

Eventually a certain intelligence group was taken with her assets, and lured her back into the inner circles long enough to deploy her regularly into tenuous global covert operations. Even Sylvia knew she was damaged goods in terms of life with a white picket fence. With every odds-defying insertion she was dropped into and extracted from, she came to realize there was no turning back. There were no tears. There was no emotion. She was what she was, and she was damn good at it.

At the request of a father who'd lost his wife and longed to know his daughter, a high-ranking retired admiral finally brought Sylvia back in from the cold to acknowledge his subordinate's request, *and* to put her tremendous skills to work in a civic capacity, to work alongside the Secret Service as a security consultant for Marge Haydon's presidential campaign.

Initially Sylvia fought defiantly to preserve her newfound identity in the south of France, where she could lie on the beach uninterrupted, read her Tolstoy, and masquerade as a human being. Finally, against her better judgment, she accepted the new role and her transition into a civic landscape was nearly seamless. Her reunion with her father, however, remained frigid. The family secret that'd tormented her as a teen had long been buried and conveniently forgotten by Rear Admiral Jensen, just as it was by Sylvia. In her case it was survival, and the layers of emotional scars served as both a buffer and honed her motivation. Hence, as much as a father wanted to know and love his daughter, they could barely get past hello. To unlock a vault tucked safely away in time might unleash a demon far worse than the one shackled away in both their hearts. Nevertheless somewhere in their yet-to-be-spoken words the admiral and his daughter's awkward fate remained precariously trapped.

Satisfied that the conference room was secured, Sylvia moved back to her station at the top of the black granite landing and spoke into her sleeve microphone and within seconds all but six agents vanished into the elevators and ascended to the restaurant on the floor above, according to plan.

On the 48th floor of the United Nations Building a small army of waiters and waitresses prepared Schaafhausen's dining room for its celebrated guests. For every server there were two security agents. With every pass of a server, placement of a napkin, fork, or spoon, it seemed there was a breach of security, seriously bogging down the preparations. That's when Chef Matthew Schaaf burst through the double aluminum doors from the kitchen, waving his arms wildly, demanding that the security measures be eased. "We have already been through this!" he shouted. "All week your people push us around. Now I push back. Enough! Allow us to feed our guests."

Sylvia was inspecting a fold of drapes nearby and stepped over to the ranting chef. "Calm down, Mr. Schaaf," she said coolly while grabbing his arm forcefully.

"How can I calm down if you do not let me do what I do best?" he continued, easing ever so slightly, while wiping a layer of kitchen steam and sweat from his face with his sleeve. "They shut down this floor two days ago, and the service elevator, and threw away the keys. The entire building has been X-rayed. Who or what could possibly get in here?"

"I understand," Sylvia said, coaxing the embroiled chef back into the kitchen. "What is your first name?" she asked, temporarily disarming the man.

"Matthew," he answered calmly.

"Show me the kitchen, Matthew."

Schaaf complied and proudly proceeded to show off the engine room of his masterpiece, his Schaafhausen Restaurant, stopping at each of the stations, giving helpful guidance to each member of his staff preparing the different courses of the dinner: seared salmon with shaved truffles, saddle of rabbit, duck mousse and wild mushroom timbale, the shredded zucchini salad, and a bouquet of exotic fruit and hand picked cheeses. The dessert was a surprise for the American president, a warm huckleberry pudding.

Schaaf had openly acknowledged Agent Jensen's cool but striking looks. "What is your name?" he asked.

"Sylvia," she accommodated him with a lukewarm response, merely trying to keep the frustrated artist at bay, while making small talk with him. He'd hardly realized she'd turned the interview around in no time at all, and now he was giving her a guided tour into the locked pantry, the kitchen washroom and broom closet. Once she was satisfied with her inspection, she abruptly terminated the conversation and rejoined her comrades in the dining room, leaving the chef entirely dumbfounded with her insincerity.

CHAPTER 2

Hong Kong, 5:51 p.m.

The view from the 72nd floor of One Colonial Center on Queen's Road Central had a special luster to Charles Li as he watched the sun edge closer to its resting place for the day beyond the Kowloon Peninsula. Streaks of crimson and gold painted the sails of boats returning to the harbor, as the Star Ferry dropped off another load of passengers at the Central Terminal. Li peered out from the empty brokerage offices of Pak-Li Global Assets and reflected for a moment on what tomorrow might bring for Hong Kong's largest precious metal and currency traders.

The financial markets had been overly frothy for quite awhile, reminiscent of the glory days of dot-com. And gold had participated modestly in the frenzy, but still was the best hedge against any sudden downturn. Pak-Li and their global consortium had quietly accumulated $110 billion U.S. mostly in gold and gold futures, amassing nearly one-and-a-half percent of the world's supply. All they needed now was a story to ride, or a small crisis.

───────○───────

The dining room at Schaafhausen was starting to reassume the look of a civilized restaurant, organization and tranquility once again reigning now that the security contingent's needs had been met. A nervous Matthew Schaaf glanced again and again at his Breitling wristwatch. In just two minutes the ten leaders and their entourage would pass through the elevator doors, and his long-awaited appointment with gastronomic destiny would finally be a reality. He pushed through the double aluminum doors to the dining room. Though he no longer barked his frantic orders, the accomplished chef was sweating profusely.

———————— ⊖ ————————

The drivers of the laundry vans eased the vehicles down the backside of the Reichsbrucke, idling through the early afternoon bridge traffic. The driver of the lead van glanced over to the left at the United Nations complex only three-hundred meters away.

"There it is," the driver sighed, annoyed with the traffic clogging the left turn lane. The light was green and no one was moving. He gave the horn on the vehicle three quick blasts.

The other van passed on their righthand side, the driver tapping his horn once while giving the thumbs up signal to his comrades, then proceeded down the backside of the Reichsbrucke and disappeared into traffic.

The passenger in the first van urged patience. "It's not every day the ten most powerful people come to Vienna for a visit," he said. "Everything will come in time."

Within minutes they passed the main entrance and pulled into the left turn lane leading to the loading bays, reserved for commercial vehicles.

———————— ⊖ ————————

As the first of the elevator doors opened to the 48th-floor restaurant, President Haydon emerged with the Russian president and the British PM just behind them, along with a few aides. Seconds later three more elevators delivered the remainder of the G-10 leaders and their entourages.

On the far wall fronting the kitchen the wait-staff stood at attention, arms at their sides, neatly attired in tuxedos. A beaming chef Matthew Schaaf was the centerpiece of his collective. Along the exterior wall in front of the recently-installed floor-to-ceiling bullet-proof windows, a line-up of black suited security personnel looked on with little or no emotion, temporarily obscuring a backdrop of outer Vienna and the wooded hills beyond. Sylvia stood at the end of the line-up closest to the kitchen.

President Haydon took a long whiff of the tantalizing collection of garlic, shallots, and other spices wafting over from the kitchen. "Smells delicious," she said to no one in particular.

"Indeed," the Russian and British leaders concurred, while an attentive waiter assisted the American president into her chair. Once the German Chancellor was seated, the other eight leaders took their seats at the round table according to their name placards. As it turned out, British luck prevailed, landing Collinsworth between the two ladies. Quietly and seamlessly the waiters removed the pristine white cloth napkins from the table, opened them, and placed them over the laps of their guests, while greeting them warmly. Centered above the dining table hung a magnificent crystal chandelier.

Schaaf and his staff waited for all to be seated as their cue to begin their service, while the chef nervously dabbed at the perspiration on his brow, once again glancing down at his wristwatch to check the time. When the seating was complete, the wait-staff proceeded with the pouring of wine and distribution of hors d'oeuvres, while the anxious chef returned to his galley. As was the case in many fine dining establishments, each leader would have his own personal waiter, assisted by a separate busing waiter who was responsible for bringing each course of a meal from the kitchen, as well as the removal of dirty plates. The main waiter was responsible for final placement of each dish as well as the initial extraction of a finished course. When not directly serving his guest he took three steps back and stood attentively with his hands folded in front of him.

The first van eased up to the guard station on the back side of the UN complex where all of the commercial vehicles were made to properly identify themselves and their deliveries. From the guard station on each side the perimeter was fenced in to the back side to the complex, with coils of razor-sharp barbed wire woven through the top of a chain-linked fence. There were two twelve-foot concrete columns the fence was mounted to on each side of the station. On the top of each, a surveillance camera referred the images back to the security center on the first floor of the building. The retractable chain-linked gate, which typically remained open during normal business hours, was closed today, locked into the guard station wall.

"Gruess gott!" the driver greeted with the typical Austrian greeting.

One of the two men in the guard station emerged recognizing the laundry van's logo, but had his orders. He nodded back with a distant hint of a smile. "No one goes through today," he said.

"But we have this delivery for Schaafhausen," the driver tried. "They said it was urgent."

"Sure it is," the guard said, with a weak laugh. "Your company and every other company who makes deliveries here have been given instructions a week ago. No deliveries today until four."

"But," the driver tried again, while the passenger adjusted his right hand which was hooked loosely onto his belt. His thumb found a small button next to the belt buckle and depressed it, sending a signal to a chip in the vehicle's computer, instantly shutting down the engine.

"What are you doing?" the guard asked, his expression immediately washed of its smile. "Turn on your engine and get this thing out of here, now!"

"Sorry," the driver said, trying to start the engine, but nothing happened. He pumped the gas repeatedly then tried to restart the engine again.

"Stop!" the guard commanded. "You're flooding it," he said, smelling the obvious odor of gasoline. "What are you doing? Have you never started a car before?"

"I'm trying, all right?" the driver said in as convincing a tone as he could muster.

"Get out of the van!" the guard commanded. He then spoke into the standard issue radio clipped to the shoulder strap on his uniform, strode back to the guard station and said something to his partner.

"All units available—possible security breach at the southeast guard station," the second guard barked into a handheld walkie-talkie.

Inside the loading dock, four of the six-man UN security detail assigned to watch over what went into and out of the entire main tower were dispatched to help defuse the disturbance outside. It was a pre-rehearsed exercise in the code three security measures currently in force on the building. The back end of the house including the security bay had been off limits to the public for nearly eighteen hours. Only six UN receiving officers were on duty until four o'clock, at which point the lockdown would be lifted and the workforce would double.

To the left of the four retractable aluminum doors to the loading bay, the four UN security officers emerged through a single door, quickly advancing toward the southeast guard station, fifty meters in front of them. The second guard now stood outside his station, his hand on the holstered firearm, and his eyes remained riveted on the commotion in front of him.

The first guard drew his firearm from his holster and waved it toward the driver who was experiencing a sudden case of the 'slows.' "Get the fuck out of the van, now!"

"All right, all right," the driver said, moving a little faster now.

"You too," the same guard motioned with his firearm to the passenger of the van. "Out of the van, now!"

"No problem," the passenger complied, slipping out of the elevated seat and walking around the front of the van to join the driver. "What have we done?"

"Hopefully nothing," the lead guard said, "and you'll be on your way in just a minute. But your car didn't start, and it ran perfectly when you drove up. I've got a problem with that," he said, while his eyes pierced right through the passenger. He ordered two of the UN police to search the van, while he climbed into the driver's seat and attempted to start the van, this time without depressing the gas pedal.

Simultaneously, the second of the two guards walked over to check the two detainees' identifications, and perform a standard body pat-down, while one of the two remaining UN policemen watched over the interrogation, firearms drawn. The final guard retrieved the extension handle with an attached mirror from the guard station, and explored the undercarriage of the vehicle, looking for explosives or anything else that didn't belong.

As the driver was being searched, the passenger stood, awaiting his turn, his thumbs hooked into his belt, while glancing down to his inexpensive wristwatch.

"Next!" the interrogating guard said, motioning for the passenger to assume the position against the side of the laundry van.

CHAPTER 3

Maldive Islands, 2:45 p.m.

Gregor Heinricke sat nervously on the edge of his beach lounger, his forty-four-year-old lanky but somewhat athletic frame slightly hunched over. He rose from his awkward perch and sauntered down toward the water. Sand nearly white as snow and fine as powder sloped down to greet the gentle blue waters of the warm Indian Ocean.

Heinricke immersed himself a few times, while his hands combed through his medium-length hair, then strolled back. On the towel next to Heinricke were a cellular phone and a laptop computer, both with GPS capabilities, and both with scrambled signals.

Palm trees lined the top of the beach, and just beyond was a small collection of cabanas that jutted out into the shallow water. He'd rented the entire island for the week, which consisted of half-dozen grass-thatched cabanas and a small, well-stocked open-air bar and cafe. The proprietor of the establishment was paid a handsome sum to vacate the island altogether.

On a blanket about twenty-five meters away his girlfriend Katia and her Japanese-Irish plaything Arisa snoozed in each other's arms after their amorous activities, pieces of their skimpy swimsuits scattered in the vicinity of their blanket. Heinricke looked over, wishing he could be with them. Soon, he thought to himself. Very soon this should all be over.

———○———

Schaafhausen's dining room was buzzing with activity, the wait-staff dutifully proffered hors d'oeuvres and removed dirty plates almost unnoticeably. The security contingent had dispersed around the dining room according to a predetermined format, allowing the daylight to infiltrate the room through the floor-to-ceiling windows, while they were subjected to endure the airborne concoction of tempting spices and savory flavors. The UN photographer quietly snapped photos of the leaders and their interactions, while off in the distance, the only two news teams which had been cleared to cover this event from the air hovered at a safe distance from the UN complex, in identical French-made Dauphin helicopters, typically used by news teams in Europe. Painted on the side of one of the all-white aircraft was the European Union's logo, the circle of stars, representing the members of the EU. On the side of the other were the letters W-I-E-N, representing Vienna's most popular news source. Though nothing really could be televised back from the mirrored exterior of the building, the two aircraft would hover in their current positions until the luncheon had ended. With the exception of the two aircraft, a ten-mile radius had been established as a no-fly zone until 8 p.m.

Maestro Schaaf bounced back and forth from kitchen to dining room, nervously making sure there wasn't a sour face in the house, constantly looking at his wristwatch, while a curious Sylvia analyzed the fidgety chef from afar. The chef disappeared once again beyond the aluminum double doors.

———○———

The smallest of the five black UN security vans remained parked indoors in the loading bay, where all of the vehicles typically remained when there wasn't a large international conference taking place. It was the equivalent of a passenger van, only bulletproof, used primarily for shuttling mid-level diplomats quickly around the complex.

The four other black vans were comparable to SWAT vehicles, also bulletproof and equipped with satellite surveillance stations and assault weaponry. They were deployed at four different posts on the exterior with half-dozen UN police in full body armor assigned to each detail.

Within the UN passenger van parked in the loading bay next to stacks of boxes, lay two men—one between the front and second row of seats, and another between the second and third row of seats, still as corpses, dressed in UN police uniforms.

In the first glass-encased office next to the loading dock one of the receiving personnel was doing some computer work on the spreadsheet format, while a remaining UN policeman walked by. They nodded at one another and the armed guard continued. Quickly the man working on spreadsheet dropped the program down to the toolbar, revealing another program on the computer's screen that he'd been trying to conceal with the spreadsheet program, simultaneously keeping an eye on the armed guard who'd just passed by. It appeared to be a floor plan of some sort, only much more detailed, like an electrician's schematic. He'd been trying to hack in to shut off power to the four security cameras at each corner of loading bay. The cameras were mounted approximately twenty feet off the ground, well out of the reach of anyone without a ladder.

All of the loading bay's six receiving personnel were attired in shin-length white lab coats, and with the exception of the two agents in the two glass offices, the remaining four held clipboards, performing some sort of inventory at four different locations of the elevated loading dock.

The second UN police officer stood stationary next to one of the men taking inventory, while they conversed. The man working on the schematic took his cursor and maneuvered around the detailed floor plan then left-clicked on the test button for the circuit that controlled the loading bay's electrical supply. In five seconds, the system would shut down for ten minutes while an unscheduled system-wide test was conducted. Everything would shut down—its lights, cameras, the keypad access back into the building, as well as the two other keypad entries to the loading bay. Moments after that, the emergency system would trigger, producing a dimmed version of the lighting and nothing else. The freight elevators down the hall ran on an entirely different circuit, even though they were not accessible today from anywhere on any floor unless someone had an override swipe key, and all of those were in a vault in the security center—a fortress unto itself.

In an instant the lights went off causing an immediate stir among the eight lone occupants of the loading bay, everyone shouting and feeling around for something to hold onto. It was black beyond dark. There were no windows—just a large roomful of sudden confusion. Obviously surprised, the two men in the glass offices stumbled and tripped from their domains shouting "Hey! What's going on?"

About the time the emergency lights came on, the guard making small-talk with his friend realized his friend had reached into his lab coat and pulled out a silenced nine-millimeter berretta and aimed it at his head.

"What the?" he started to ask. All he could think of was, "Krista" and then he saw a blue supernova that was the end of his life.

In an instant, the computer whiz ended the second guard's life with two silenced rounds through his temple. "Ffffft, ffffft," followed by blood spurting out of both sides of the guard's head.

Suddenly the side doors to the van burst open, and two new armed guards jumped out and helped stow the two corpses into the van, then closed and locked the van's side doors. Quickly they ascended the steps to the elevated loading platform and recovered the corpses' automatic weapons lying on the floor and now stood guard over the loading bay as if nothing had happened. Two of the other loading bay personnel quickly wiped up any traces of blood with several terry-cloth shop towels and discarded the dirty rags into the large metal trash bins below. In nine minutes, they would be back on the live video feed.

Moments later the six lab-coated personnel pulled eight large boxes from the first shelf on the second aisle of the twelve-foot high stacks of shelving, with the logo **Embellish** stenciled on their sides. Six of the boxes were a scheduled delivery for a clothing boutique on the promenade of the complex's small retail area. The men pulled six mannequins out of those boxes, dressed them in their lab coats, and found the appropriate shoes in each of the boxes. They left themselves in the standard issue under gear of black industrial trousers, black tee-shirts, and black industrial workboots. They positioned their new stand-ins at their appropriate stations—two of whom would be in the glass offices, seated at the desks and working on their respective computers.

In the seventh box were black knit sweaters and ski masks, as well as the obsolete but still-quite-effective first-generation liquid bulletproof vests, which solidified on contact with a round of ammunition from most handheld firearms, as well as some automatic rifles. The clothing and ordinance was distributed and quickly pulled on.

The eighth box contained a large black plastic case containing six AK-74s and an arsenal of the standard 30-round clips—enough ammunition to start a war. Each man grabbed a weapon, locked a clip into place, and strapped ammo-belts held a half-dozen extra clips apiece around their waists, while the two guards watched over the proceedings.

Quickly the six-man unit ran down the hall, then jogged left, made two quick rights, and stood in front of the freight elevator. The door to the left of the freight elevator contained the main power access that drove the lift. It still operated on a keyed entry. Standing at a safe distance from the door, the unit commander fired two quick blasts from his Beretta, freeing the locked door. He attached four C-4 packs to four of the cables that carried the lift to all forty-eight floors. On the concrete pillar next to the cables he attached a detonator with a digital timer, and then set the device for exactly seven minutes. In six minutes the test would be over, and security cameras would be recording live feed again.

———————— ⊖ ————————

Matthew Schaaf reached into a plastic container of peeled garlic cloves on the shelf adjacent to the burners, retrieved a white plastic card the size of a credit card and backed over to the off-limits freight elevator. He passed the white card in front of a sensor on the panel to the right of the door. Nothing happened, and Schaaf's heart sank. Nervously he turned the card over and tried again. The door opened and he slipped in unnoticed. Once inside his shaking hand passed the white card in front on another sensor then depressed the button marked LD, for loading dock as the elevator door closed him in. Schaaf's heart pounded as the carriage began its forty-eight floor decent.

Sylvia hadn't seen the fidgety chef in nearly eight minutes, and began to grow suspicious. She also had to use the ladies room. She cleared it with her colleagues to check in on the absentee-chef, and to use the facilities in the kitchen.

In under a minute the elevator would reach the ground floor. In just five minutes Matthew Schaaf's restaurant would be serving anything but fine food. Though never completely clear about his role, Schaaf knew he was for one minute the most important man on the planet. Time seemed to stand still for the young chef as his eyes watched the indicator lights telegraphing his descent as sweat rolled down his cheeks. His mind tried to find solace in the bank deposit made in a Zurich account the previous night which would be matched by an identical amount the moment the elevator door opened. Overnight he'd become a millionaire five times over, but he couldn't suppress his guilt. Judas, he thought dejectedly.

Sylvia sharply questioned everyone in the kitchen as to the chef's whereabouts, and though no one really knew the answer. The recurring theme was they thought he was in the employee restroom at the backside of the kitchen. Good, she thought. She could kill two birds with one stone.

Three-quarters of the way down Schaaf's heart felt like it was going to explode. He could stop this, he thought, as the elevator light signaled the passing of floor ten. He could turn back, he continued to tell himself, watching as the floors sailed by. They would kill me if I stopped, he drilled himself. They'll kill me anyway, Schaaf realized as the elevator hit the ground floor. He was drenched with sweat now, as the bell to the last floor rang. Schaaf realized he'd made a grave mistake and pressed the Schaafhausen button.

It was too late now. The elevator door cracked open as the chef tried to reverse the process, desperately pounding on the close button. The barrel of a weapon protruding through the crack quickly reshaped Schaaf's posture. "Welcome, my friends," he said unconvincingly, looking as though he'd just gone for a swim.

In an instant the six-man unit swarmed the elevator, shoving Schaaf away from the control panel and into the far corner. The unit commander pressed the Schaafhausen button with the extended nose of his silenced weapon. Quickly he turned and glared at the cowering chef who attempted to maintain his composure. The chef's weak smile gave way to a horrified look, as the leader raised his firearm to rest on Schaaf's forehead. The chef's already fragile state had been broken, whimpering and trying to reason that he was the only reason this was all possible.

"Precisely," the commander agreed. "That's why we don't need you anymore," he snarled, his grip tightening.

"I can help you get out if they shut down the elevator," Schaaf pleaded, not knowing the elevator would be permanently out of order in just minutes.

"Didn't we tell you?" the commander responded. "This is a one-way ticket."

One of the militants stepped between Schaaf and his captor and nudged the commander's gun arm upward, removing the weapon from the chef's head. The man reasoned in Farsi that the chef may be of some value later. Clearly frustrated, the commander sighed, wishing he could inflict death on the turncoat chef, but respected an old warrior's opinion so he lowered his weapon, never once taking his hard eyes off of Schaaf.

As Schaaf's teary eyes tried to convey his thanks, the man who spared his life knocked him unconscious with a surprisingly quick blow to the head with his firearm. "Tie him up," he said, speaking in Farsi.

There was a chilly efficiency amongst the occupants of the elevator cab as the cab ascended rapidly toward its destination. The bell rang, signaling the cab's arrival at Schaafhausen. In an instant the door opened and out poured the bloodthirsty unit, quickly moving through the kitchen, surgically ending the lives of the culinary crew that might interfere with their operation. The six who were savvy enough to turn around in time to acknowledge their predators were instantly snuffed out by a silenced bullet to the forehead. The other four had their larynxes opened up by serrated combat knives. The bodies that might get in the way were dragged over to the wall by the employee lounge. Quickly the team moved to the wall that fronted the dining room, knowing that some of the wait crew would trickle in one at a time looking for their next course. As they did their throats were slashed, without even a moment to react to the predators, while they were added to the mounting pile of corpses a few feet away.

The unit commander whispered to one of the men to go immediately to the elevator, and pull the unconscious chef out and handcuff him to anything secured, still not sure how much of an asset the cook might be. He could always kill him later, he thought.

Just as the militant pulled the chef to safety and cuffed him to the anchored stainless steel leg of the dishwashing station, the militant heard four ever-so-slight pops, sounding almost like a quick blast of popcorn. In an instant the elevator was free-falling forty-eight floors into an abyss of darkness, creating a vacuum and sucking a few of the folded white cloth napkins stacked on a shelf near the elevator into the emptiness left behind.

At the southeast guard station, the interrogation had run its course. Both the driver of the van and its passenger had checked out just fine. The passenger glanced again to his inexpensive watch, and then depressed the same button on his belt buckle that disengaged the ignition earlier and re-engaged it. The guard who'd been trying to start the vehicle while his colleagues interrogated the two delivery men, smiled as the vehicle belched a puff of exhaust into the cold. The van was running.

"There you go, gentlemen," he said, convinced it was *his* ability with motor vehicles that ended the stand-off. "Have a nice day! Don't return until tomorrow."

Suddenly, there was a radio dispatch for the four UN police to return to their station—something about a loss of camera surveillance in the loading bay.

The laundry van backed into the turn-around area and departed toward the Reichsbrucke where they would disappear into traffic. The passenger glanced again at his watch. "One more minute," he said to the driver, "and the test will be over."

When the video feed from the loading bay was re-established to the security command center, there were sighs of relief when the two UN police appeared to be walking from one lab coated personnel to the next, seemingly conversational with the men. All appeared to be in order in the loading bay. The downgraded alert was radioed to the four returning UN police as a false alarm.

As the four men re-entered through the secure door to the loading area, one spoke to the two UN police inside who were now next to that entry. "Everything okay?"

"Yeah, everything's good. We're going to have a smoke. See you in a minute," one answered back. Off in the distance behind them on the other side of the bay four mannequins in white lab coats continued to deceive the security personnel.

As the door closed behind the two officers exiting to have a smoke, one reached into his right pants pocket and retrieved a small remote. He depressed a single button that sent a signal to the computer in the glass office that was still on the electrical grid program. In an instant the grid was sent it into its test mode again, temporarily shutting down, with no lights, cameras, or access into or out of the loading bay.

———————◯———————

The distribution of loaded firearms to four lead waiters and two runner waiters had been stealthily carried out earlier in the day. While some of the kitchen staff had questioned two large fifty-pound sacks of rice delivered ten days earlier to a restaurant that served very few rice dishes, their inquiries were met with a scathing tongue-lashing from their somewhat emotional chef. The bulky sacks of grain made for a great concealed mode of transport for six Glock 40 weapons. The lightweight handguns used widely by the FBI were made of polymer—a plastic composite, which could be broken down in just over a minute. The undetectable body would go virtually unnoticed in the sacks of rice, while the few action pieces including the slide and barrel would enter the restaurant store room in cans of coffee or sardines, along with twenty-four fifteen-round magazines. Re-assembly was as expeditious as the break-down.

At a precise fixed time, the six waiters in possession of weapons all discreetly placed industrial-grade mini earplugs into their ears, and one of the runner waiters tossed a small object that rolled in the direction of the dining table. Simultaneously, two lead waiters flung similar shaped devices in the direction of the security detail and closed their eyes tightly. By the time anyone could react, the three separate homemade versions of M84 stun grenades detonated, causing a sound so earsplitting it completely disoriented anyone in the room not wearing earplugs. Upon detonation the devices emitted an intense bang and a blinding flash of more than one million candela and 180 decibels causing immediate but temporary flash blindness, deafness, and tinnitus. Everyone exposed in the dining room instantly suffered complete confusion and loss of coordination and balance, while the reverberating shockwaves shattered the heavy chandelier above the dining table, sending pieces and clusters of it crashing down onto the table and all over the leaders. Simultaneously, every piece of glassware on the table exploded, shooting shards of glass, water, and cabernet all over the stunned diners. Some of the bulletproof windows splintered but remained intact.

Almost perfectly in unison the six waiters wearing earplugs opened their eyes only to discover a roomful of delirious occupants—leaders, security, and unprotected wait staff alike, and began a circular wave of killing. From the center out, bodies started to drop onto the leaders who had all dove to the floor in the disarming confusion, not really sure of what was happening. The systematic assault leveled the wait staff in seconds, and quickly reduced the first wave of bewildered security to slumping flesh. The UN photographer had actually caught a few frames of the exploding chandelier and glassware before he dropped the camera and covered his ears from the shrilling noise, making him a helpless target like everyone else in the room. In seconds he joined the mounting pile of corpses. Suddenly the second wave of assailants charged through the kitchen's double aluminum doors and unleashed clusters of bullets, further surprising the overwhelmed security agents. The ill-fated retaliation ended almost as quickly as it had begun.

The element of complete and utter surprise fueled screaming and shouting as pandemonium reigned over the dining room. President Haydon had been shoved to floor in a near-tackle by the British prime minister in an effort to save her from the crossfire, in turn losing his own spectacles. Collinsworth's hands felt around on the floor desperately trying to find his glasses.

In the kitchen's employee restroom, Sylvia heard the commotion. As her adrenaline surged, she drew her MK40 firearm. Her eyes were as dilated as a cat's in the night as she tried to peer out the cracked door, partially blocked by the dead bodies. She pushed and shoved at the door, trying to squeeze through.

Sylvia heard a relentless wave of shooting echoing throughout the dining room, with bullets pinging and flying off of the bullet-proof windows, as screams and shouts augmented the chaos. Not seeing and not protecting her president and the others was poisoning her. She knew with every second she was trapped in the restroom, another of her comrades would fall. With that there was even less of a chance she could be effective in neutralizing her adversary. Still she pushed as hard as she could, widening the gap in the door ever so slightly. Right about now that damn iPhone would come in really handy, she thought.

The ferocious assault and the feeble retaliation stopped approximately forty seconds after it began—the same duration of the debilitating effects of the M84s. All the diplomats were on the floor, some covered with bloody corpses, making it nearly impossible to tell who had survived. There was an eerie silence in the former restaurant, a smoky layer of death hovering precariously in the air, whimpers and moans of pain scattered throughout the room.

Under the unit commander's direction, the surviving members of the assault-unit began to assess the damage. Two of the rogue waiters and one black-clad militant had perished. One militant was still unaccounted for. One other rogue waiter was close to death, squirming in pain.

The leader instructed two members of his team to remove the dead security personnel from on top of the remaining leaders of the G-10 and handcuff the world leaders behind their backs, all the while standing above the wounded waiter. The other militant was instructed to go to the kitchen and check for survivors. "Kill anyone who isn't already dead!" he commanded, in Farsi. "And bring me the chef!"

The last militant climbed out of a pile of dead security agents near the kitchen doors, bringing the total number of black-clad militant survivors to five, including the commander. They'd only lost one. The commander looked at him and then his wristwatch. "Welcome back, brother. You have two minutes to secure the entire area. If it moves, shoot it!" he shouted. Then he looked to the dying rogue waiter at his feet and assured him of better things to come and quickly put a bullet into the man's forehead.

First, the German Chancellor was hoisted to her feet, tears and blood trickling onto her cheeks. She stared in utter disbelief, frozen with shock, while shaking her head. Then President Haydon was yanked like a prisoner of war to her feet, her skirt and matching coat ripped and spattered with blood, cabernet, and water. She stood frozen as she witnessed the victims of the bloodbath scattered around the room. "What are you doing?" she tried, her eyes still in denial. Just two minutes earlier they were enjoying a sumptuous meal.

"Silence!" the commander barked in Farsi, then approached the woman. As his hard eyes met her grief-stricken eyes, he held his weapon to her forehead. "From now on you speak only when I tell you to. Do you understand?" he commanded in a coarse form of English.

There was no answer.

Didier Marceau, who still lay on the ground, used the tail end of the one-sided shouting match as an opportunity to guard a piece of history. He discreetly unclasped his treasured cufflinks and backed them out of their French cuffs then placed them in his left front pants pocket. Without warning he was yanked to his feet by what he assumed was one of the thieves. As he was being angrily handcuffed, his Italian counterpart was guarding his own piece of history, slipping his anointed sapphire ring into his right Ferragamo loafer.

In a split second a man hiding in a fold of drapes by the floor-to-ceiling windows emerged, half-dead already, firing wildly at the leader and militants tending to the leaders. They dove into evasive maneuvers, quickly firing a spray of bullets at the lone gunman, rattling his frame and driving him back into the bullet-proof window, making an instant corpse out of the man.

"Stop!" the American president cried, fighting back a reactionary well of tears.

The commander ordered the shooting to stop and directed his comrades to contain the room. "Now!"

"C'mon, man!" Collinsworth pleaded, completely disoriented without his glasses. "What are you doing here?"

"Silence!" the commander shouted even more emphatically now, accommodating the Brit with his coarse English, while forcing the nose of his firearm into the PM's mouth. "What did I tell the American president?"

Collinsworth's full mouth could only garble back.

"You will speak only when spoken to. Do I make myself clear?" the commander barked, and then quickly shoved the firearm abruptly further into the throat of his captive.

Collinsworth forced himself to swallow, and then nodded yes.

"Now, everyone get against wall by stairway!" he growled in broken English, motioning with his weapon toward the exit sign adjacent to the elevators. The five armed militants and waiters that he'd assigned to the world leaders barbarously enforced his command, shoving the barrels of their AKs and Glocks into the backs of anyone who even remotely resisted. Scott Hammons hobbled awkwardly into the end of the line-up, having lost his cane in the chaos, wincing at the persistent probe of an assault weapon.

In the far corner of the room opposite the kitchen the militant doing the reconnaissance mercifully fired a three-shot blast into the chest of a security agent clinging to life.

Sylvia finally managed to squeeze through the opening in the cracked restroom door, quickly assessing the damage in the kitchen as well as the unconscious chef, and then peeked into the dining room. She could see it was utter carnage everywhere. The human side of her heart sank for perhaps a half a second, before her *assess-and-counter attack* instincts kicked in. One of the militants was headed in her direction, more than likely to retrieve the chef in shackles. Quickly she retreated into a storage area adjacent the chef, and opposite the gaping hole where the elevator used to be, unknowingly tracking bloody female shoeprints back to her location, including the dot where the heel touched the floor. She inched her head forward, allowing just one eye to peer around the corner to observe the approaching militant. That's when she'd realized she'd left her own bloody trail. Shit, she thought.

As he entered the kitchen, Sylvia quickly pulled back to where she couldn't be seen. The chef had regained consciousness and focused on the vision of Sylvia, instantly shining a ray of hope for the desperate man. He started to open his mouth to speak and just as quickly Sylvia raised one finger to her lips, at the same time indicating in hand signals that his captor was returning. The chef nodded ever-so-slightly that he understood.

She knew that the only way she stood a chance of saving anyone, let alone the American president, was to become one of the captors. She couldn't kill the approaching militant, not with her firearm anyway. She had to have his uniform. And hopefully he wouldn't discover her bloody trail beforehand.

As the man approached he said something to Schaaf in a language the chef wouldn't understand, but the tone was clear and it was anything but pleasant. The militant stooped to grip Schaaf's face and glared into his eyes, shaking the chef's head, making sure his prisoner felt his disdain for him, and then shoved his head away.

About the time when the masked man inserted the key into the handcuff that secured the chef's right hand, a thunderous blow was delivered from the butt of a handgun to the back of his head, knocking him unconscious instantly.

"Quiet now," Sylvia whispered to Schaaf as she finished removing his handcuffs. "If you want a chance to live, help me get this man out of his clothes, and quickly."

"Of course," the chef said, clinging to any chance of survival, immediately helping Sylvia strip the militant down to his underwear only.

Once Sylvia had removed everything the militant was wearing, including his body armor, silenced Berretta, serrated knife, and AK-74, she pulled him over to the hole in the wall where there used to be an elevator, and discarded the body. "Bon voyage," she said, as his body sailed into the abyss of emptiness. Sylvia rapidly stripped down to just her panties and removed her bra, then hurled all of her garments into the shaft as the confused chef gazed at her near-naked figure. There could be no trace of a woman or her garments left behind. Under the veil of the dead militant's clothes she'd hoped she'd be lean and athletic enough to pass for one of them. She quietly ordered Schaaf to the employee restroom, helping him with the black knit clothing and weapons. All the while the petrified chef stood there, watching, waiting for his next set of instructions. Under any other circumstances this would be a jackpot for Schaaf, or any other heterosexual man for that matter. Now that it was a matter of basic survival, his male desires never entered the equation.

Sylvia knew they wouldn't have much time before someone would come looking for them and quickly pulled on the black oversized military fatigues and buttoned them, pulling the belt to the last hole and buckling it. Fortunately, the former occupant of the pair of pants was reasonably thin.

She'd located a roll of gauze in the first-aid kit on the wall behind them and pulled it from its metal case and unraveled it about five feet and started to tie down her moderately-sized breasts as best she could, not knowing what the bulletproof vest would conceal, then handed the roll of gauze to Schaaf. "Here, make yourself useful," she snapped. "Move quickly now!"

The chef frantically made short circles around Sylvia, tying down her breasts with the gauze, while she held one end down on her chest until it was secured on its own.

"Tighter! Tighter!" she urged. What a terrible time to have tits, she thought. Her breasts were just big enough to be a nuisance or call attention to her gender.

When Schaaf got to the end of the roll of gauze, he clumsily stalled in front of her, uncomfortable with where he should tie the knot.

"Give me that," she said impatiently, then tucked the end of the gauze down the center of what was once cleavage. She was almost flat now. The cinch-down straps on the rigid bulletproof vest would likely finish the job.

"Get in there," Sylvia commanded, pointing toward the toilet. "And pull your pants down and sit, if you want to live," she reiterated, while pulling on the protective vest, then the coarse knit sweater. Quickly she slipped on the black ski mask, making sure all of her hair was tucked up inside. She had just enough time to glance into the mirror to acknowledge her handiwork. On first glance, Sylvia had the appearance of a man.

The restroom door opened grudgingly while the militant sent to do reconnaissance anxiously squeezed through. "What the hell are you doing in here?" he blasted in Farsi. "And where the hell is the chef?"

"He's in there," Sylvia answered in a surprisingly convincing male Farsi voice. Her training had required her to become an accomplished linguist. "He's a fuckin' mess! He pissed his pants. He shit his pants. He stinks!"

"I don't care what he smells like," the recon man barked, apparently buying her act. "Let's go!"

Sylvia in turn passed the command on to the chef on the toilet, while kicking the stall door open. "Let's go!" she said in Farsi, but waved for Schaaf to get up, while exaggerating a wink to the chef.

The confused chef arose, zipping up his trousers and buttoning them, slowly emerging from the stall in front of the persistent nudge of Sylvia's AK-74. He was disoriented, disheveled and flushed, with blood still trickling from his right eye from the gun-butt he'd absorbed earlier. To add more uncertainty to Schaaf's already fragile state, Sylvia shoved him from behind toward her new comrade. She wanted nothing more than to take out the black-clad man right now, but couldn't. Whoever sent him in to retrieve them was expecting two militants and a chef in return. Patience was her only option, for the moment.

Out in the dining room the commander surveyed the room and assessed the success of the mission. In exactly five minutes, thirty-two security personnel and aides lay dead, but only five of his men had perished. Three waiters and five black-clad militants, including him, had passed the initial test. And in the process, ten perfectly healthy albeit terrified world leaders were taken as hostages.

The decision of a budding young chef to become an overnight millionaire, and the element of surprise, had rendered the outcome a virtual success so far.

One of the waiters had shared with the commander that among the slain victims was a staff photographer for the UN.

"Bring me the camera," the commander blasted.

The waiter complied and dug the camera and its telephoto lens out from between two slumped corpses wedged together. Just as quickly the commander grabbed it and threw it down, stomping it violently with his combat boot, until it shattered into quite a few inoperable pieces.

Then the commander pulled a black remote similar in dimension to a standard television remote from a protective canvas case strapped to his belt. On it there were two rows of four buttons each. He pressed the top button on the right-hand row detonating a C-4 pack down in the main elevator room, which was attached to the hydraulics that controlled the pulley systems that carried the four main elevators up and down the main tower. In an instant, access to all forty-eight floors was shut down from the elevators. Then the commander pressed the second button on the same side of the remote, detonating a cluster of C-4 packs placed earlier in the week by a maintenance worker in the thirtieth through thirty-third floor stairwells, destroying four floors of stairs and any hope of access through manual means. At this point no one could go up or down. The only direction left for the captors and their captives was up.

As the two militants barged back through the double aluminum kitchen doors and into the dining room with the terrified chef, the commander pressed the upper left-hand button on the remote. He and a few of those in his command glanced out the windows on the opposite wall. Off in the distance, the one helicopter displaying the letters W-I-E-N peeled off from its current holding pattern, and toward the United Nations complex. The commander ordered his team up to the roof. "Let's go!"

Quickly the two men dragging the chef joined the rest of the assault team as they charged through the exit-marked door, right behind the others, and ascended the stairs to the roof. All the while the building's emergency alarms pounded on their eardrums, reminding them of an imminent response and retaliation. The commander was the last to exit through the door and he charged up the stairs.

In just moments, ten leaders, eight militants, and one chef were on the roof, while the first of nearly two hundred heavily armed agents passed through stairwell twenty-three, on their way to the top of the building, or so they thought. For the moment Sylvia was helping to abduct the people she'd sworn to protect.

Outside, the security detail at the guard station was ordered to temporarily abandon its post and assist the unit inside the loading bay, while the two rogue guards who'd slipped out earlier to have a smoke jumped up and over the six-foot brick wall and disappeared into the Viennese afternoon.

CHAPTER 4

Maldive Islands

Gregor Heinricke's former associate from Düsseldorf, who'd relocated back to London some time ago, was second to none at creating a story and manipulating the media. They'd made a lot of money together throughout the years by cornering small obscure markets, then breaking huge market-driving stories only to watch their shares take off for the stratosphere. That's how it worked. Stories drove markets. They'd done it with the Dollar – Euro, with gold on the way down, then up, then down again. They had made Wall Street darlings out of not much more than fairy tales, and crushed legitimate entities long enough to buy their shares back cheaply, making a fortune in each direction. No one was better at creating a seemingly legitimate story than Heinricke's good friend Nabeel Ali-Khan, a London School of Economics graduate.

Heinricke had loaded a program on his laptop which tracked breaking stories around the world and sent him an alert every time something of relative importance was taking place. He glanced over at the breaking BBC feed coming in and his posture immediately stiffened. Heinricke turned up the volume as the reporter breaking the story said that there had been an explosion at the United Nations complex in Vienna, Austria—the same venue that was hosting this year's G-10 meeting. The magnitude of the blast was still unclear.

The whereabouts and condition of the ten leaders was unclear as well. The reporter covering the story stood at the entrance to the complex as the video feed showed people running out of the building.

Heinricke fell back in his beach lounger. "Oh my God!" he whispered, and then quickly reached for his sat-phone. As he did, it rang. "Hello," Heinricke answered softly.

"Gregor," the voice said. "It's Charles. What the hell is going on?"

"I don't know. Are you watching this? Where are you?"

"Yes! Of course I'm watching this," the voice said. "I'm here in Hong Kong, still at the office."

"This is pretty serious."

"I had no idea this is what you meant. London gold has spiked ten dollars an ounce," Charles Li said.

"It's *not* what I meant," Heinricke said. "The story I spoke of has nothing to do with Vienna or anything remotely close. But gold's going a lot higher if there's anything to this, *and* oil for that matter."

"Is this your friend?"

"Of course not, that's impossible!" Heinricke blasted back. "Nabeel's a family man. He loves life! He doesn't blow up buildings!" Heinricke's girls also watched the broadcast now, not sure what to make of the breaking story. "I have to call Nabeel. I'll call you back," he said, then hung up.

Vienna

The first of the Dauphin helicopters lifted off moments earlier with Zheng, Veroni, Elliott, Collinsworth, Nobakov, and four militants. It was packed far tighter than the aircraft was intended to be, so the copilot was left on the rooftop. These were after all what most news teams across Europe were using, and any last minute equipment changes would've sent up flags. The militants had performed the sardine can drill in their dress rehearsal and it barely worked, but it worked nonetheless. There would only be discomfort for a short while until the rendezvous at the drop coordinates.

Sylvia had observed two of the waiters speaking to each other in Austrian Deutsch. Just as quickly the commander snapped an order at both of them in Farsi. They both answered in Farsi. "Yes, sir, it won't happen again." Sylvia tried to comprehend the implication of the commander's order to *only* speak in Farsi from here on.

The second helicopter emblazoned with the EU's logo also carried a second crew member, like the first aircraft. The commander instructed him to get out of the aircraft and join the other copilot. It wasn't certain how many militants or leaders would survive, so the contingency plan called for an alternate escape plan for up to ten militants. The first helicopter had dropped two large boxes containing five winged-flight-suits each, used mostly by Norwegian thrill-seekers jumping off of fiords. The first copilot had already suited up, and the second was instructed to do the same. The commander didn't have time for the explanation why, but it meant the chef wasn't going to be making the short flight with them.

The commander shouted instructions over the chopper's rotary noise to load Haydon, Schmidt, Marceau, Tanaka, Hammons, along with the first militant. He then looked toward the expendable chef. "Sorry, Mr. Schaaf," he said in English. "Thanks for letting us into your restaurant." Then in Farsi he gave an order to the two militants holding the chef.

In an instant, Sylvia knew how any of this became possible.

"No! Wait!" Schaaf pleaded, crying desperately. "Please! Wait! No!"

The two militants backed Schaaf over to the ledge of the building, the chef kicking and screaming. "No! Please!" he fought for his life as best as one could with his hands cuffed. "Wait! I can help!"

Inside the helicopter, President Haydon watched and pleaded for them not to end the life of the chef. "No! Stop!" she shouted, inciting the other hostages.

The one militant in the aircraft didn't want to hear it. "Shut up!" he blasted in Farsi, striking the American president with the butt of his firearm, knocking her unconscious. The Canadian Prime Minister Scott Hammons made a futile attempt at valor and tried to shoulder tackle the militant, earning him the same butt of a firearm to his head. He fell unconscious as well.

Outside, the commander glanced at his wristwatch. "C'mon!" he shouted in his native tongue.

To Sylvia, there was no conflict of interest at all: the life of one turncoat chef for the chance to save her president and the others. She and her fellow militant shoved the frantic chef off the edge of the building to his death forty-nine floors below. For about a half-second, Schaaf's blue eyes locked on to Sylvia's as if to ask "How could you do this?" her direct gaze had no answer. "She's not one of you!" he shouted, but he was already too far away in his descent to be clearly understood.

Quickly the two executioners rejoined the commander and boarded the helicopter.

"All right, let's go!" the commander shouted to the pilot. In an instant, the helicopter was airborne. They would have ten minutes at best before all of Europe would be in pursuit. Simultaneously, the two winged copilots jumped horizontally off the edge of the building, accelerating rapidly. In just seconds they would reach speeds of up to 130 miles per hour, more than adequate to rendezvous with the two Dauphin aircraft at their drop coordinates on time.

The flight of the two aircraft would only last 5 minutes and 40 seconds until the point of drop, just beyond the Gewurztraminer wine district that bordered the dense forest on the northwest outskirts of Vienna.

In the planning stages, it was unclear whether there would be a timely response by air from the international community. The element of surprise was effective indeed, but the captors had hoped their opponent would be on their heels, numb and in shock, long enough to make their drop and disappear into a Viennese forest. Regardless, after the two aircraft were hijacked, for precautionary purposes they were outfitted with Russian-made anti-aircraft missiles, still the easiest black market artillery to acquire. The laundry van carrying the four black cases and its occupants was then ordered back to its point of dispatch. Plan B was no longer necessary. The van that had experienced engine trouble earlier outside the UN complex had long since been abandoned at an obscure location.

The commander shouted orders at the pilot, who in turn radioed the lead Dauphin aircraft as to the exact time and coordinates of the drop. All the while, most of the hostages who were still conscious tried to conceive of what had and still was taking place. Except for the hum of the rotaries, ragged breathing, and occasional soft sobs, there was silence.

As the first aircraft neared the drop coordinates, the commander glanced at his wristwatch, assessing the window of time. Four minutes, 42 seconds. Good, he thought.

The first helicopter set down in a clearing in the forest, as four Hummers emerged from the trees with just a driver in each. Within 30 seconds, the occupants from the helicopter were loaded into two of the Hummers, and those vehicles disappeared into the woods. The space constraints had improved slightly from the conditions in the helicopters. In an instant, the aircraft was airborne, off to another location.

The second Dauphin set down in the clearing, as the commander glanced again at his wristwatch. Five minutes, 28 seconds. Too slow, he thought, and then shouted, "Let's go! Let's go! Let's go!" Moments later the two winged copilots had pulled the parachutes on their flight suits and descended perfectly into the clearing, right on time. In seconds, they'd removed their gear and approached the remaining aircraft.

The American president was still groggy and was slapped on the cheek to help awaken her. The Canadian Prime Minister got the same treatment. They were the last two to be shoved into the Hummers, while the commander hollered at the pilot to lift off, hand-signaling in a circular motion the same instructions. His eyes locked onto the forestry station on the far side of the clearing for half a beat, well aware of its potential importance to their strategy.

As the second helicopter lifted off carrying the two jumpers, the two remaining Hummers joined the other vehicles in the thickly wooded forest. All four vehicles immediately sped up a dirt road. The commander nervously scratched his jaw as he glanced again at his wristwatch: Six minutes, 15 seconds had elapsed.

———————— ⊖ ————————

On the roof of the United Nations building, a UN helicopter dropped off a small contingent of armed soldiers and lifted off, making room for the next drop. The first group of soldiers descended the steps leading down to Schaafhausen. In seconds, the world would know the gravity of the situation.

CHAPTER 5

Washington, D.C., 8:15 a.m.

Adam Morrison rehearsed his speech at the Naval Observatory on Massachusetts Avenue, opposite Embassy Row, otherwise known as the vice presidential mansion. Many felt that his quarters were better digs than the White House, set on a significantly larger piece of real estate and considerably more private at that.

It had been a long time since he was first accepted to officer's school at the Naval Academy. Thoughts of those days of youth kept interrupting a speech rehearsal which was already drilled into his mind. His forty years of unwavering service in the Navy were quite an accomplishment for the Tennessee native, eventually earning him rank of Admiral.

A good old boy from Johnson City, Tennessee, Vice President Morrison wasn't necessarily a brilliant man, but he was a socially adept, hard working over-achiever and very likeable, which was more than enough in his case to carry him through the treacherous realm of politics. Marge Haydon recognized his magnetic personality and down-home charm, and calculated he would be a great asset to her prospective campaign. And because of those qualifications, she and her family genuinely liked him. She tagged Morrison early on in her career, mentally noting that he would be a potentially viable

VP candidate for her presidential run for office. He could help carry the South while she held court in the urban areas, as well as the North and West.

Over the years, just as Haydon's political clout grew and her handlers' dreams came to fruition, Adam Morrison also worked his way up through the ranks after his retirement from the Navy—first in local politics, then as a state senator.

When presidential hopeful Marge Haydon approached him just a year-and-a-half ago about joining her in the quest for the truth, he'd initially scoffed at the notion, citing his lack of qualifications and the fact that he was a staunch Republican. So was she, Haydon reminded him. She quickly convinced him otherwise about being qualified, citing her own political career, and the need to steer the "party of fiscal responsibility" back on course, though they could only do so by leaving it temporarily, and not as Tea Party pawns. After a brief courtship, Admiral Morrison agreed to join Marge Haydon and her cause. The rest was history: Tennessee native to vice president of the United States. Together, they were a most compatible fit—both internally and in the public eye.

Back home Vice President Morrison was unabashedly still one of the locals though, who never forgot his roots. Whenever he went back to his hometown, he would stroll into Dixie's BBQ with a couple of his hungriest friends. Offering seven different award-winning sauces, many thought it was the best rib joint in the nation, bar none. On some weekends, even the vaunted Tennessee Volunteers football team would eschew Knoxville's offerings and drive over one hundred miles to sit down to a table full of succulent dry-rubbed ribs there after a hard fought SEC game.

The gracious staff would close the place down for Adam Morrison and overwhelm him with their southern hospitality, their finest smoked ribs, grilled chicken, and brisket. The shack-like rib joint was not particularly appealing visually, but he had closed many a deal there with local politicians who imbibed in a cold beer, and rolled up their sleeves to dig into a slab of famous ribs. Seven squirt bottles of the trademark family recipe BBQ sauces at each table came elevated the delectable feast to another level. There was no mystery as to why Johnson City's locals tended to be a little on the heavy side.

The motorcade was already out front, due to depart at 0900 hours for the short trip over to Annapolis. Rebecca Morrison made some last minute finishing touches to her husband's pristine white uniform. She knew the drill. She'd been doing this for thirty-eight years. Her eyes glowed with pride as she prepared her warrior for battle one more time. "Look at you," she said. "You don't look a day older than when I met you."

"Becky, what did I tell you about overdoing the meds?" he quipped.

She chuckled at his harmless retort. "I'm so proud of you, Adam."

"I don't know," the decorated officer said, making sure his salt and pepper hair was in place. "You know, this *Gray Away* isn't doing such a good job."

"Nonsense," she scoffed. "Most sixty-two year olds don't even have hair."

Before the vice president could answer, there was a sudden cluster of rapid knocks at the bedroom door. He glanced at his wristwatch thinking, *it's too early.*

There were two more sudden bursts of knocks at the door.

"I'll get it," Rebecca said, already en route. The admiral wasn't too far behind.

As she opened the door, the vice president's aide nudged his way through, which was an absolute no-no—a knock and wait to be asked to enter was the appropriate protocol. "Mrs.," the aide started, seeing the admiral right behind his wife. "Mr. Vice President, there's been an emergency," he said, short of breath, and then whispered the news into Morrison's ear. "They've taken President Haydon and the rest of the G-10 hostage in Vienna, sir."

Morrison's face went ashen. There was no preparation for this. "Jesus, no," he could barely say. "Oh Jesus, no."

"What is it?" Rebecca asked, recognizing a once-every-ten-years expression on her husband's face.

Morrison looked at his wife, then back to his aide, almost looking for direction.

"You must go now, sir," his aide responded.

The Secret Service detail assigned to his motorcade rushed into the house and pushed past the VP's aide, while the lead agent reiterated the aide's order. "Mr. Vice President, we have to go."

"What is it, Adam?" Rebecca asked.

The vice president looked at his aide and asked, "How many know, David?"

"Sir, we must go now," the Secret Service alpha urged, gesturing toward the VP's elbow, but not touching it, while the remainder of the unit took positions in all perimeters of the room.

"BBC broke the story a few minutes ago in Europe," the aide blurted out frantically. "It's all over those networks already, sir."

"Adam?" Rebecca asked, her eyes pleading.

"They've taken President Haydon and the rest of the G-10 summit hostage."

Rebecca sighed and wilted, unable to conceal an instant welling of tears. She'd been through just about everything with her high-ranking husband, but no training could prepare her for this shockwave.

"Go to your sister's in Alexandria," Morrison said. "I'll call you as soon as I can." Then turning to his aide, he spoke firmly, "David, please make sure my wife gets to Virginia immediately, and safely."

"Of course, sir."

"Mr. Vice President, we must go now," the Secret Service alpha urged, while giving orders for half of his unit to accompany and guard Mrs. Morrison. "She'll take your limousine, sir, but we must go now. Marine One will pick you up on the back lawn in two minutes."

The vice president turned to his wife again and held her. "I love you, Becky."

"I love you too, Adam," she said, biting her clenched fist, fighting back her tide of emotions.

"Sir," the lead agent pestered more adamantly, now gently starting to lead the VP toward the back lawn.

The decorated admiral stared into his wife's eyes, comforting her and assuring her while back-peddling awkwardly. "Go now."

Swiftly Morrison followed the security detail down a short corridor and into the mahogany-paneled library, where'd he'd spent considerable time, then through the French doors out to the Japanese garden that he had just recently planted, and to the back lawn and the waiting helicopter, running through a gamut of procedural checklists along the way. "David, I need you get ahold of the First Gentleman, *and* the boys. Where are they, by the way?" Morrison shouted above the helicopter's powerful rumble, while everyone's hair and clothing blew about in the propeller-driven wind.

"I don't know, sir," the aide shouted back. "But I will find them as soon as possible, sir."

"Very well then," Morrison said, leaning into his aide so he could be heard above the noise. "I want to speak with Mr. Haydon as soon as possible, David,"

"Yes, sir."

"Sir," the Secret Service alpha shouted. "We have a unit with the Haydon party over at Reagan National right now. We will extract and airlift them to your destination as soon as possible. But we must go now, sir!"

"Very well then," Morrison shouted back and boarded the aircraft swiftly with the helpful nudge from the agent.

Just as quickly, the lead agent boarded Marine One while his second in command closed the hatch door and pounded on the on the side of the aircraft near the pilot's location with an open palm, then backed away while making a circular gesture with a raised arm. "Let's go! Let's go!" He shouted. Seconds later Marine One was airborne.

Hong Kong, 8:45 p.m.

The sun had set on Hong Kong an hour-and-a-half earlier, and the daytime buzz of Central's financial community was fast asleep. Charles Li and Minh Pak were very much at work however, high atop 1 Colonial Center. The cleaning crew had come and gone. Li and Pak were the only two left in their entire one-floor war room. They both had considerable offices of their own, but for now shared Li's, monitoring the events of Vienna on his flat screen T.V. mounted on the wall opposite the window, and London gold on the computer screen on his desk.

"Can you believe this?" Pak asked, a little bewildered. "We're up thirty-two dollars an ounce already."

"Yeah," Li replied, half-dazed and distantly excited. "It's only going higher once New York starts running, then Hong Kong tomorrow. But at what cost?"

"Stories are one thing," Pak said. "But this could be catastrophic."

"Any word from Gregor?" Li asked.

"No. Not since earlier."

"I sure hope this isn't what his associate had in mind," Li said.

"We don't do this," Minh Pak tried to remind his partner. "We invest. We work. We earn it. People from the financial world don't abduct world leaders and blow up buildings."

"I know, I know, I know," Li said weakly, observing the BBC coverage on his monitor. The report out of Vienna was that they had found two ditched helicopters near the Austria-Hungary border. "I can't believe they can't find these bastards."

"It's unbelievable!" Pak said.

With every ticking moment of news coverage and speculation as to the whereabouts of the ten leaders and their captors, or if the leaders were alive at all, the price of gold climbed higher, now up thirty-nine dollars an ounce. Oil was moving right in tandem, up $7.23 to $117.05 per barrel. Pak-Li and company were making a fortune.

Maldive Islands, 5:57 p.m.

The tropical sun's unyielding rays were still several hours away from dissipating into dusk, enshrouding the equatorial paradise and its visitors with soothing warmth. Winter was for the moment a distant memory. Gregor Heinricke had exhausted the keypad on his sat-phone, in his quest to locate Nabeel. With each dead end voicemail, he grew a little more intense, and ordered Katia and Arisa to go entertain each other so he could better focus. His laptop had split-screen capabilities, allowing him to monitor both the news and gold futures. The latter was doing everything it should be doing in a global crisis situation, lighting up the computer's right side like a generous slot machine.

He'd exhausted all of his options and finally called Ali-Khan's home in London, knowing it was a violation of protocol. There were rules. Business was business, and it didn't include associates' families. "Hi Vatsana, it is Gregor. Sorry to bother you."

"Ah, Gregor, it's no bother at all. How are you?"

"I'm fine. I'm just—I was wondering if you've heard from Nabeel."

"I haven't," Nabeel's wife said. "But I know he had a one-day trip to somewhere in Germany and said he'd be working a little late, and to not wait up. He had something to prepare for a global conference coming up. But you know he's been somewhere in Europe every day for the last week."

"Yes. Yes, I know," Heinricke replied, knowing that Nabeel and a very select group were meeting down in a very small town on the German-Swiss border, called Schaffhausen. Until now, it had never dawned on him that the leaders were abducted from a restaurant named Schaafhausen. Though spelled differently, the identical names of two separate locations blindsided him like a runaway locomotive. The eerie coincidence pounded into his brain to a point that it temporarily deafened his hearing. "Thanks, Vatsana. I've got to go. Please have him call me when he gets in," Heinricke said, and then hung up. He pondered just for a moment. Vatsana didn't mention a thing about the events unfolding in Vienna. Either she didn't know, or maybe half the world was still in the dark, even in the information age. How was this possible? With his mind now in turmoil, he punched in the two-number code for Hong Kong.

The Pentagon, 9:13 a.m.

The Joint Chiefs and their staff were gathered in the large war room, watching a wall of flat screen monitors, waiting to be conferenced in with Vice President Morrison from a bunker known only to a select few. Video links were established with the other G-10 interim leaders, and at precisely 9:15 EST each country's leader-by-proxy began to acknowledge their presence. And then, finally, Admiral Morrison's voice could be heard throughout the Pentagon's war room on the conference line.

"Hello. I'll spare the formalities."

"Good morning, good evening, good afternoon," a chorus of greetings replied.

"What do we have, General Meyers?"

"Not much yet, sir," Joint Chiefs' Chairman, General Gordon Meyers responded firmly.

The sixty-nine year old Meyers, a Vietnam Veteran, had cut his teeth when he and his small recon platoon went down in their AH-1 Cobra under heavy fire in the dank, harrowing jungle in the Mekong Delta. They'd spent weeks avoiding Charleys and the NVA. He had never been more shaken up than when he was when on patrol with a few of those surviving the helicopter crash—until now.

Approaching sundown, they'd realized something wasn't right. Usually one could hear a cacophony of frogs, crickets and various insects. But on this particular night there was a dead silence except for a dull hum. The jungle's animals were very skittish. Private Meyers felt a little click on his combat boot, looked down and saw that several finger-length red scorpions had bounced off of his shoe and were attempting to climb up his legs. He looked around and noticed the ground was alive with them.

Private Meyers scampered up the nearest tree, but his platoon-mates weren't so lucky. A rogue scorpion had climbed up a comrade's leg and stung him, causing him to scream in agony. The soldier doubled over and fell to the ground. Meyers could see the scorpions swarming all over the man like giant ants as he writhed in pain, screaming primally for perhaps one minute, and then he was motionless, still covered by a teeming mass of death. Soon the jungle was pierced with all manners of howls of anguish and death, as what appeared to be an unholy horde of hundreds of thousands or more scorpions stung every living thing in its path, both man and beast.

Anything that failed to climb a tree was not spared, and when Meyers was able to climb out of the tree after the rare two-day scorpion migration, everything he saw, soldiers, Charleys, water buffaloes, small animals, were all stone cold dead. Every one of them shared the same wide-eyed, frozen mask of terror.

The 48-hour nightmare haunted General Meyers for years. Until today, it was his most troubling war-time experience. But this unraveling crisis was a different kind of helplessness, made more frustrating because of its colossal global implications.

"Our Intel is thin at best right now, sir. What we know is this: A contingent of approximately twenty heavily armed, well-organized soldiers somehow gained access to a freight elevator at the UN complex in Vienna, and ascended to the 48th floor restaurant, Schaafhausen. With the element of surprise, we believe the unit infiltrated through the kitchen, dispersed themselves throughout the dining room dressed as waiters, we think, because there is initial evidence of several deceased waiters at that location with weapons still within their grasp. At which point they deployed enhanced versions of three separate M84 stun grenades, completely debilitating *everyone* in the restaurant, and surgically and methodically ending their lives, except for all of the G-10 leaders. I say enhanced versions, because both the inner aluminum and outer cast steel casings of those devices seemed to have been bored out, causing an even more intensified detonation, capable of even shattering glass. Quite frankly, sir, no one stood a chance under those conditions. It was a complete annihilation. We're cross-checking a detailed list of security personnel and aides assigned to the conference, to confirm the dead, or god knows, if someone miraculously escaped—but thus far that looks highly unlikely. Our CIA bureau in Berlin has tried to call the phone numbers registered to each member of the security team. Unfortunately, there was a change in policy, and all of the agents' communication devices are in the possession of the UN police on the ground floor. Separate explosions took out the main elevators in the tower as well as the freight elevator and four floors of stairs, buying them time to airlift the hostages and their captors to another location in two French-made Dauphin helicopters. The executive chef, Matthew Schaaf, after which the restaurant was named, either jumped to his death from the roof of the building or was pushed. He may have had a role in this. Our sources in Vienna are looking into it. The two helos were ditched near the Austria–Hungary border. That's it. That's all we know, sir."

"No communication with the captors, general?" queried Morrison.

"Not as of yet, sir," Meyers said, while an ever-so-slight twitch toyed with his right eye. To most, the twitch went unnoticed, but to those who'd spent time in the trenches with the general, this nervous tic manifestation wasn't good. "We have no idea what they want or who they are. NSA has a blanket over every transmission signal originating from Europe. If anyone so much as breathes into a mobile phone or any other device, we'll be up their ass with the Hubble telescope."

"All right, general," Morrison said. "I want to know as soon as you have anything. You understand me? Anything!"

"Yes, sir."

"These bastards want something. You don't just abscond with the G-10 leaders unless you want to trade up," the vice president reminded everyone, then was suddenly jarred away from his conversation by an aide persistently tapping on his shoulder. "Yes, what is it?"

"Sir, we've located the First Gentleman," the aide said. "We have him on the line."

"Thank you," Morrison acknowledged. He excused himself from Meyers and the various acting leaders that'd been conferenced in. "Gentlemen, I have to go. We've located Tyler Haydon."

"Roger that, Mr. Vice President," Meyers acknowledged, along with a few others.

"Tyler?" Morrison asked into the mobile sat-phone.

"Mr. Vice President?"

"Yes, Tyler, it's Adam," Morrison said. The two men had come to respect each other for a multitude of reasons, but also had become mutually comfortable on a first-name basis. "Have you heard the news?"

"What news?" Haydon asked, combing his left hand through his healthy, dark brown hair. "The boys and I are at Reagan, ready to take off for Montana on a ski trip, and the Secret Service has held us back at the gate but won't tell us why," he said. Haydon still maintained his corporate jet for convenience's sake, though it was initially a conflict of interest in the beginning of his wife's presidency.

"Tyler, do *not* get on that plane."

"Why?"

"Tyler, they've kidnapped Marge and the rest of the G-10 leaders in Vienna," Morrison said, almost not even believing his own words. In the coming hours he feared he would have to get used to them.

"What?" Haydon asked, dumbfounded and blindsided, completely stopping him in his tracks. About the time Morrison started to explain, both Kyle, who'd gotten his father's darker hair, and Keith, who'd gotten his mother's blonder locks, fast approached their father to share the breaking Vienna news received from incoming texts on their smart-phones. Their steel-blue eyes were like saucers—stunned in disbelief, but they could see their father must've gotten the same news from the disturbing expression on his face.

Tyler motioned toward his sons while he continued to receive instructions from the acting Commander-in-Chief. With one hand on his mobile phone, Haydon reached out for Kyle first with his free hand, only because Kyle was the closer of the two boys, then hugged him. Kyle reciprocated the gesture, but Keith remained an arm's length away, as was his nature. Both boys looked to their father's eyes for a glimmer of optimism. Their father, the hotel baron, had always been strong, rarely showing emotion. Only now he showed distant signs of cracking. The boys were pretty solid themselves when it came to breaking a leg from a missed 'helicopter' jump landing on a treacherous ski run and tears weren't an option. But this was their mom—the American President. No one had to explain the gravity of a situation of this magnitude. They struggled as well to contain their misty eyes.

"Yes, Mr. Vice President," Haydon answered. "We'll leave the jet here, and await Marine One. Where should we wait, sir?"

"Hold your position, Tyler," the VP said, aware of the Hayden's private access lounge over at Reagan. "The Secret Service detail assigned to you and the boys is being brought up to speed as we speak and will escort you to the aircraft as soon as it arrives. After that, you will be taken to a secure location."

"All right, we'll remain here and await instructions."

"Your helo should be there in less than two minutes."

"We're not going anywhere," Hayden replied, then ended the call. He took a deep breath and exhaled as he looked to the boys and filled them in on what little he knew thus far, which, as it turned out was pretty much what the boys had learned via their texts and emails. Kyle had already opened the CNN page on his I-phone and was following the breaking story, sharing bullet points of the report.

Hayden walked over to the window to where he could see his jet and speed-dialed his pilot. In seconds the trip to Montana had been canceled.

In minutes the Secret Service personnel received instructions and expeditiously escorted the Haydons out of their private lounge onto the tarmac where Marine One had just touched down. The First Family and the agents boarded and seconds later the aircraft lifted off without delay.

In Colorado, NORAD was placed on Def-Con 4, scrambling a nationwide blanket of F-15 fighters as a matter of procedure. The nation's docks, harbors, and waterways were also placed on high alert. Until the intentions and capabilities of the unidentified enemy were assessed, no security measure was left unchecked.

On the West Coast, only early morning commuters were being shocked with the news interruptions which now dominated most radio and television stations. Whoever wasn't awake yet would soon be jolted from their blissful dreams and soft pillows with the shocking realities of the unraveling nightmare.

In Washington, D.C., layers of heavily armed black helicopters were immediately deployed, dominating the gray skies. Just as quickly a fortified military presence could be seen stationed in front of key installations, as was standard procedure in a national security crisis.

In Vienna, all roads in or out of the city were closed. For that matter all major roads in Austria were air patrolled and dissected. No one was allowed to leave or enter the country. All neighboring countries fortified their borders, instantly stiffening entry policy, while scrambling their own air defense procedures. Interpol agencies frantically combed their databases for recent cell activity in the region and throughout Europe, but that was fruitless until the rogue group communicated.

The financial markets were closed for the day in Europe and Asia now. London gold had closed up thirty-eight dollars an ounce. Oil had spiked to $122 a barrel.

In New York, the Dow, NASDAQ, and S&P futures were all indicated lower, signaling a sell-off at the opening. Remarkably the financial markets were going to be allowed to open. New York gold futures were up almost $60 dollars an ounce from the previous day's close. Recently, the fluctuation in the price of precious metals, in particular gold, had come to resemble the price swings of dot-com, but never anything like this. New York crude had for the first time in months topped $120 dollars a barrel.

The four Hummers rumbled through the Viennese forest, bouncing off the pot-holes and imperfections consistent with a rough dirt road torn up by winter's elements. It was normally used by forestry vehicles on rare occasions, and occasionally by adventurous young lovers looking for sanctuary from the constraints of watchful eyes in the city. But even now, only a fool would brave the low double-digit temperatures currently gripping Austria and most of Europe.

The vehicles traversed steadily down the backside of the forest until they came to a 'T' in the road. The lead vehicle turned left and the other Hummers followed closely behind, moving efficiently through the tall pine trees, dodging patches of snow still left behind from last week's flurry.

The commander glanced repeatedly at his watch. Every detail of their synchronized drills of the past thirty days had been going according to schedule, give or take a few seconds. In just minutes, if not already, the skies would be full of airborne surveillance in search of the brazen madmen whom had absconded with the world's leaders.

The four vehicles squeezed through a tight hairpin turn banked by a steep hill on their right and a ravine on the left, while some of their captives held their collective breaths until all four Hummers passed through. It would be the last treacherous stretch of dirt road on their journey. Within seconds the road opened up into a clearing and suddenly joined the paved portion that backed up to an industrial complex that appeared to be deserted.

The vehicles turned to the left for about one hundred meters, then passed an opening in a chain-linked fenced off area on the right. The lead vehicle stopped about twenty meters past that opening. Then the next vehicle stopped behind the first, then the next behind that one, and finally the fourth stacked itself behind that one. Quickly the last vehicle proceeded in reverse through the opening in the fence, and then through an open rolling aluminum door into the interior loading bay of that particular unit, where it came to a stop next to a large industrial-sized van. Moments later the other three Hummers backed into the loading bay and came to a stop joining the first vehicle, in a perfectly synchronized move.

They plan to leave, Sylvia noted to herself.

Two men dressed in identical gear that the militants wore welcomed their brothers with their precious cargo. One of them dashed hastily out to the open chain-link fence and pulled the rolling gate portion mounted on four-inch hard rubber wheels, until it closed in the exterior bay, while another of the men manned the roll-up aluminum door. Once the exterior gate was shut and padlocked, that militant returned to the interior of the loading bay, and the man operating the aluminum door pulled aggressively on the thick chain that controlled the door, moving one hand rapidly after another until the door came crashing down, slamming into the concrete slab. Just as quickly he inserted the telescoping struts on either side of the door at waist level into their openings, securely locking down the building.

All of the militants quickly emerged from the Hummers and forcefully yanked their packed-in captives out and up a short set of steps onto a six-foot concrete landing; all the while the leaders continued to protest feebly this unthinkable and cowardly act. The emphatic jabs of assault rifles planted in their backs quickly reminded the shackled leaders how little regard their captors had for them, or their complaints.

The leaders were led down a wide barren hallway with offices on either side, its glass windows revealing work stations and computers in all of the offices. One by one the leaders all winced at the pungent aroma as they passed a restroom on the left. Mercifully, Sylvia closed the door to the unkempt facility. Based on the smell she'd figured it had probably been at least three to four weeks since the place was occupied.

She'd been recording everything in her mind, where each door was with respect to the next door, or where she might hide a body if she ever got the chance. It struck her as odd that from the hallway door forward, in a building that looked abandoned from the outside, the facilities were considerably warmer than the warehouse area. The building had electricity and was heated, she quickly surmised.

Through the doorway at the end of the hall they entered a large room approximately fifteen feet deep by twenty-five feet long. The center of the room featured a large, oval-shaped conference table, with an all wood, in-lay finish, probably pretty expensive in its day. Surrounding it were eleven evenly spaced chairs. The leaders were distributed around the conference table according to a plan. One by one their handcuffs were unlocked from behind their backs and re-cuffed in front of them so that they would be able to drink from the liter-sized bottles of water sitting on the table in front of them, perhaps the first act of humanity afforded to them since their abduction.

Quickly the three men dressed as waiters retreated to the loading bay and slipped into the same attire the rest of the unit was wearing and returned to the conference room. Each man carried a small suitcase containing silencers specially machined for the Glock 40 handguns and a supply of magazines adequate for a small war. The logic was if the unit had to mobilize and engage an adversary, they would do so as silently as possible, at the same time controlling as much of the flash from the fired weapon as possible. The operation's organizers were certain that satellite surveillance above all of Austria would be intensely scrutinized, and even the spark of a match would be spotted from the heavens.

The silencers were distributed to the militants throughout the room along with the ammunition. The cases were closed and stacked in the corner, and the militants dispersed at equal distances around the dimly lit room. Sylvia stood attentively next to the door to the hallway from which they'd all entered. In a moment, two men emerged from a doorway on the opposite side of the room, dressed in the identical combat-ready black-clad outfits just like their brothers. Sylvia could see they all were heavily armed, with the exception of the last man who'd just emerged through the same door. He was clearly not outfitted like the others. Regardless, her heart temporarily sank as her odds of success were just cut nearly in half. Now there were fifteen militants counting her. It also was the first time she'd actually had a moment to assess her opponents since the high-speed chaos of the abduction. These men were anything but flimsy. Most of them appeared to be quite fit. And now the Viennese waiters were among all of them.

The one man not outfitted like the others appeared to be in street clothes—rather nice street clothes, Sylvia noticed. She could see that the ensemble he wore was black like the others, but more refined. It was difficult to tell because he remained just out of direct light, but Sylvia thought he wore black slacks, shoes, and a nice polo shirt with its top button undone.

He remained at a short distance away from the conference table, just out of the soft beams of light shining down out of the eight ceiling canister lights, while he studied the occupants in the room for a moment. He then calmly approached the commander, who was a few steps away to his right, and kissed the commander on each cheek, while shaking his hand. "Welcome, my brother," he said, in Farsi. "Congratulations on the success of your mission."

Sylvia's ears scoured the otherwise quiet room, listening for any other information the man might share, while watchful eyes around the oval table assessed the man who appeared to trump all other authority. Sylvia's eyes focused intently across the room at the man, trying to recognize who he might be. Seconds later, that would be futile. The man turned toward the wall behind him and held out his left hand. In it the commander placed something the size of a small dark pouch.

Damn it! I can't see a thing, Sylvia thought, desperately demanding her inquisitive eyes to discern any clue of hope.

CHAPTER 6

Pentagon, 9:32 a.m.

Initially the broadcast quality was amateurish, its fuzzy images difficult to decipher. Then the signal was sharpened and the lights in the makeshift studio were brightened, while those producing the video continued to tinker. An additional four lights were added to help with the clarity of the broadcast, one in each corner of the room. The camera focused straight ahead on an unidentified man at the head of the table. He was dressed in the same color as every other captor in the room, but different clothes. He also wore a black knit ski mask.

The BBC and Al Jazeera networks were selected by the rogue cell to carry the coverage because of their strategic reach within their particular communities and as well as the broad scope of their global influence. They in turn would share the video-feed with their other global affiliates.

Within a half a minute the images were transmitted clearly, and the camera's focus was widened to include everyone at the oval table and almost everyone in the room. What the world had feared was now reality: The leaders of the G-10 were sitting around a conference table in a room, with their hands bound.

They all displayed some evidence of being in a struggle, wearing torn, blood-spattered clothes. In the background were images of militants, each holding what appeared to be assault rifles.

The armed man operating the camera signaled to the man at the head of the table with his fingers – three, two, one…

"Good afternoon," the spokesman began in British English, although that would only be noticeable to his captives. To the global community of viewers, the audio had been filtered into a rather generic garble. "My name is The Prophet. We represent no organization known to the West. Today we are conducting our Town Hall meeting with you the world, and your leaders. The reason for this dialogue is to discuss the ongoing suppression of the Middle Eastern countries, the villainous misrepresentation of the Muslim faith, and a general understanding of the events of the past decade, so that this audience might understand the struggles of the Arab nations of the past fifty years—and why we fight for our survival with the only means at our disposal, and for He whom we believe to be our God."

Vice President Morrison's expression hardened as he whispered something into an advisor's ear, and then returned his focus to the broadcast, riveted to every word, while code-crackers and NSA agencies urgently tried to pinpoint the source of the signal. In tandem EU specialists had blanketed the airwaves frantically attempting to track its origin.

Tyler Haydon and his two sons were escorted into the vice president's clandestine quarters. Morrison broke from the broadcast to greet the First Family, shaking the senior Haydon's hand with one hand and planting an earnest grip on his right shoulder with his other hand. It was an awkward moment for dialogue.

"Have you seen our mother?" Kyle asked.

"Yes, we have," the vice president replied, while gesturing in the direction of the large monitor for the Haydons to see. "Come watch. Their broadcast has just begun."

Tyler and the boys studied the monitor, observing the president as well as the others. Suddenly the reality of seeing his captive wife took Tyler's breath away.

The boys were never exactly bosom buddies. Kyle had chosen the path of the straight and narrow, lettering in two sports—basketball and football, and now was active in his father's business.

Both boys were outstanding athletes for that matter, whether on the slopes, riding dirt bikes, wrestling, or whatever else they'd attempted. But Keith tended to find trouble as a teenager. He briefly fell in with the wrong crowd, occasionally cutting class to drink beers and smoke cigarettes.

His grandfather on his mother's side provided a steadying influence, helping to guide the younger sibling through his troubled waters. But all of Grandpa Ray's sage wisdom could not prepare Keith to cope with the prospect of losing his mother. Shaken up by the surreal vision on the monitor he turned to his dad and asked, "Mom is going to be all right. They are going to get her out of there, aren't they?"

"Of course they are, son," Tyler replied firmly, while placing his arm around his son. But even he didn't know whether that was possible.

"Are mom's clothes ripped apart, Mr. Vice President?" Keith asked. "And is that blood on her?"

"I'm afraid so, son," he answered, "on both counts. Now listen up. The Prophet, as he calls himself, is speaking again."

"First of all, I *am* sorry to have inconvenienced all of you with the burden of uncertainty regarding your respective leaders," the voice of the captors continued. "It was the only way to get your attention. With any luck, you might see them again. I'm also confident you and your intelligence agencies are trying as I speak to unscramble the source of the signal of our broadcast. Good luck. We have access to advanced technology just as you do, but maybe even more advanced. But just in case you should get lucky, I would remind you we have your ten leaders here. Please be careful with your pursuit.

"Secondly, I have a remote control with five buttons remaining," the Prophet said, holding it so his television audience could see. "Each one of these buttons represents an explosive device planted in five different cities worldwide, which, for the moment shall remain nameless." He then handed the remote to the commander just behind him.

"You can't do this!" the Canadian president shouted, even though there wasn't much he could do under the circumstances.

"Silence!" the Prophet snapped back, head-gesturing for one of his guards to restore order. Just as quickly, the guard delivered a vicious blow to the head of Prime Minister Hammons with the butt of his AK, causing most of the hostages to wince. Militant-Sylvia bit her lip as Hammons just as quickly slumped in his chair, unconscious.

"I've decided I'm going to give the American portion of the audience something to keep you busy," the Prophet continued, "while we conduct our Town Hall meeting. There is a rather large bomb on a ship entering one of your busier ports. How, you ask? Simple. Everyone has their price. Taxi drivers, deckhands, chefs—everyone," he said, toying with his viewers. "I can tell you this. If it is detonated, that particular shipping lane will be shut down for a considerable period of time—and we're not talking days. And unlike

U.S. military policy of the past twenty years, *we* will try to keep civilian losses to a minimum. Good luck!"

Maldive Islands, 6:34 p.m.

Heinricke's heart sank as the numbing reality of watching these unknown militants hold court set in, threatening the stability of the world. It was equally disturbing not being able to see the face that hid under the Prophet's mask. He felt as uneasy as a young, inexperienced currency speculator who'd guessed wrong and didn't hedge his bet. Only this time, he had guessed right at the expense of humanity. Heinricke grimaced as he glanced to his laptop. New York gold was running wild.

———◯———

In Boston, New York, Miami, Seattle, Los Angeles, San Diego, and anywhere else in America with a port of importance, tense waves of Port Authority and Homeland security personnel, along with local FBI and police agencies, pored over docks and ships, tearing into containers, hulls of ships, oil tankers, and anything else that might be a viable threat to a shipping lane.

Bomb squads stood ready to dismantle anything from a single stick of dynamite to a container of fertilizer to the most intricate liquid crystal device. Without any description of the device or its possible whereabouts, the job was almost futile for the recently downsized Homeland security agency, even with assistance from local agencies. There were a lot of ships in a lot of shipyards across the country.

Conventional wisdom suggested the Middle East had been stabilized, hence the reduced Homeland security unit. The fascio-radical Islamic movement as the world knew it had clearly moderated when the leader of the group, Mohammed Bin Al Mir, was captured, tried, and imprisoned six months earlier. Cut off the head and the body would die, it was said.

———◯———

Next to the Prophet at the end of the table, one of the militants showed the leader some type of movement being tracked on his laptop computer screen. Someone or something was trying to crack the origin of their transmission's signal. The Prophet whispered something into the commander's ear, and then addressed the audience on the other end of the video camera.

"To those of you trying to unscramble our signal," the Prophet said slowly with a subtle smile. "Might I remind you, we see you. We see every move you make. For example, you've probably raided the home at 814 Linc Bahn Gasse by now, only to discover 70-year-old Frederick Hoffman and his wife Clara watching this very telecast. I do hope you haven't caused them any severe chest pain. They're older now and Frederick has a weak heart. I'll warn you again. Be careful."

Pentagon, 10:09 a.m.

General Meyers stiffened at the initial setback of his Intel being detected. "What the hell do ten or twenty uneducated militants have that can detect an advanced tracking system like ours?" he blurted out.

"Sir, if they're smart enough to abduct ten world leaders from under our noses, they're not uneducated," Paul Simonson, Director of Pentagon Intelligence replied. "Whoever they are, these guys have done their homework."

"I don't care what kind of homework they've done," the husky but fit Meyers barked back, trying to conceal the annoying twitch in his right eye into a squint. "Now Goddamn it, find them! Why can't NSA locate their signal? Our technology is supposed to be a helluva lot more sophisticated than theirs!"

"We're trying, sir," Simonson tried to reassure him. "We just need a little time. That's all."

"Time is what we don't have, Mr. Simonson. That's our president out there, along with some very important people. Do you understand?"

"Of course," Simonson said, knowing there wasn't a satisfactory answer at his disposal.

"General, I have the vice president on a secure line." An aide said, handing a headset speaking device to the general.

Meyers fumbled briefly with the device but managed, then stepped back from the console where two rows of twenty agents were monitoring their work stations. "Mr. Vice President?"

"General Meyers, why can't we locate this signal?"

"Apparently these militants have resources on par with ours, sir, and have bounced the signal off a satellite leading us to the residence of an elderly couple near the train station in Vienna," Meyers explained, embarrassed he didn't have a better answer.

"What kind of assets do we have in Vienna?" the vice president asked calmly.

"CIA. FBI. We're in contact with Interpol. They've deployed all of their available assets. The Austrian air force has scrambled an aerial dragnet with the help of EU aircraft available in the area. The Austrian army has locked down its borders, while the local police agencies are working inward from there. But even that is a crapshoot, since we don't have a traceable signal to isolate."

"Any word yet from the port searches?" the VP asked.

"No, sir, nothing yet."

"MI6 and the Austrian Intel, HNA, say they may have something," Morrison shared. "They've been following a sleeper cell's activity—a lot of money is exchanging hands but not much else. I'll keep you informed. Let me know as soon as your people make some headway with the signal, general."

"Roger that, sir," Meyers acknowledged evenly.

———————◯———————

"We will now formally begin our discussion," the prophet began. "President Haydon, after the events of 911, your country determined it was necessary to go into Afghanistan and rearrange the mountains, in search of Mohammed Bin Al Mir."

"We had clear evidence that—" Haydon tried, before being cut off.

"Uh-uh, quiet please! I'll tell you when you can speak," the Prophet said, a little more lenient to the American president than he was to the Canadian. "When you went in, the coalition forces had carte blanche to do pretty much anything they wanted to and needed to, to preserve the integrity of your country. The fact of the matter was that never before in the world community's history had U.S. sentiment been so high. There was even some Arab tolerance for what you were doing, so long as it remained justly regionalized. Am I accurate so far, Madame President?"

"The world in fact was united against the terrorist regime being harbored in Afghanistan. Yes, that's a fair assessment," Haydon replied.

"But when U.S. and British intelligence determined that they had concrete information indicating weapons of mass destruction in Iraq, it became necessary for a preemptive strike on that nation. Is that correct, Madame President?"

"Based on our intelligence at that time, we felt the evidence was conclusive to warrant a preemptive strike to protect our interests at home," Haydon agreed.

"Even though, Madame President, the United Nations clearly reiterated that you stand down from any such invasion, until the evidence was more conclusive? The very agency that the United States was instrumental in creating for the purpose of a logical and rational solution for a potential global conflict—so that no one country could act on its own against any country without the support of a coalition."

"We had evidence," Robin Collinsworth blurted out, unable to withhold comment.

"Silence!" the Prophet demanded. "You will have your moment to speak, Mr. Collinsworth, but only when I say to."

The flustered prime minister stiffened, but just as quickly withdrew from the dialogue, turning slightly to see if he was next to be smacked by a rifle butt to the head. One of the hooded militants hovered over him for a moment until he was waved off by the Prophet.

"In fact, Madame President, the Pope in Rome called it the most barbaric attack against humanity since Adolph Hitler—this from your own religious leader. Rather remarkable. Wouldn't you say?"

"I believe those words were manipulated by the media," Haydon tried, but knew in her gut that this was one of her rallying points in her campaign against her two presidential adversaries—in particular the Republican candidate.

"Regardless of which order the words were placed, Madame President, the message from the global and religious communities was loud and clear. 'Don't do it!'"

"We believe we had enough evidence and support for our cause, Mr. Prophet. Your country wasn't randomly attacked like ours was."

"Do you hear yourself?" the Town Hall anchor rebuked, seemingly in disbelief. "Is anyone in your country's leadership accountable? You all behave like puppets. You sound like your predecessor, the former president. Even up until his shameful last days, he still denied the facts. Is this what they teach you in the school of honor and integrity?"

"We did what we deemed necessary to protect our country," Haydon tried again. "And President Woodson left quite honorably—I can assure you. One man, even one man such as the President of the United States of America, cannot act alone. He could not order the attack on Iraq without the overwhelming consent of Congress. That's how it works, Mr. Prophet."

"Please!" the masked anchor blasted. "Please don't insult me. And please don't insult our viewers. Don't you dare insult me again! When a country acts in self-defense, it's usually done from within their borders, near their borders, or from the waters that surround that country. The fact of the matter, Madame President, is that your intelligence was not only inaccurate, but incredibly manipulated to create mobile WMDs that simply never existed. Your weak-at-best theory was followed by a coalition invasion of the Arab sovereign nation that consisted of ninety-nine percent U.S. forces, hardly a convincing display of world support. The fallout destroyed the social and economic balance that is so difficult to achieve in this region—all based on this far-fetched theory of WMDs that U.N. reports had already confirmed didn't exist. Just as quickly the term WMD was erased from your vernacular so that you could liberate Iraq, wasn't it?"

The American president tried to put up a fight, but she herself had raised these very issues in her campaign for the White House.

"Well I have news for you, Madame President, that nation never needed to be liberated. Its leadership was strong—perhaps unconventional at times; it's true, but for good reason. It is a delicate balance that holds this social structure together. The West questions a leader and his tactics. But it's the very leadership the U.S. empowered against his neighbors for U.S. interests in the region. Might I remind you Madame President, far more Iraqi civilians have died at the hands of the U.S. forces in your two campaigns than at the hands of the alleged Butcher of Baghdad," the Prophet explained, allowing for a long exhale while waiting for a response from the American. There was none.

"Let the truth be told, your military built twelve bases in the outlying desert areas to carry out ongoing military strikes in the region, while the coalition forces occupied Iraq, killing close to 200,000 innocent civilians. How different is that, Madame President, from the barbaric practices of the fallen Iraqi leader? And why don't your news agencies report the deaths of *mere Muslims*?"

"We never conducted genocide on the people of Iraq," Haydon tried. "We only fought on their behalf, for their liberation. Sometimes in war there is collateral damage."

"Collateral damage?!" the Prophet blasted. "How can you differentiate between genocide and invasion? Murder is murder."

"I understand, Mr. Prophet," the President attempted. "But if a group from San Francisco or New York or anywhere else in the United States disagrees with policy in Washington, we simply don't annihilate them."

"True. However, if that group, or an individual, attempts to take the life of you or any other high-ranking official, I suspect their days are numbered. And it was no different in Iraq. There were repeated attempts on the life of President Salaam Hassan. In each case justice was served. Time was not wasted in a court of law, when it was obvious that the court of law had no precedent to spare an assassin's life. Am I right, Madame President?"

"We have a judicial process they will go through," Haydon patiently explained. "When it is determined that they are guilty of their crime, then and only then will the appropriate sentence be handed down."

"Madame President, I know the Constitution as well as anyone," the anchor exhaled, growing tired of what he construed as a feeble denial. "What if I was to tell you I spent four years at a top American university? What an absolutely remarkable notion for an alleged Islamic extremist. Yes?" the

Prophet didn't wait for her answer. "Now please don't demean me with your rhetoric."

For a moment Haydon and the Prophet just stared at one another. The president tried to buy time with her answers. But at the same time her knowledgeable and articulate captor tried to get her to admit wrongdoing in global affairs before she was in power. Her predecessor's policy had long been scrutinized—she herself being one of the most outspoken critics from within her party's ranks.

While Haydon waited pensively for the next round of disarming questions, her mind clung dreamily to the hope of her bodyguard's survival. The vice president's lingering tales of Sylvia's Amazonian capabilities temporarily washed away the bloody visual images from the massacre at Schaafhausen. But just as quickly the sobering reality of that very bloodbath obliterated her daydream, knowing no human could've survived it. She took an exaggerated gulp of water, then wiped away at a growing bead of perspiration from her forehead.

In the back of the room one of the militants whispered into another militant's ear, stepped toward the door to the hallway, and caught the Prophet's attention.

"Where are you going?" he asked.

"Restroom," the man on the opposite side of the doorway from Sylvia answered.

The Prophet waved him on.

Sylvia's eyes grew with anticipation, while she assessed the potential opportunity. She was confident she could take control of the room if she pared the number of militants down, and was equally certain in her ability to move swiftly through half a dozen of these men, regardless of their training. But as long as the captors had the leaders, and the commander had the remote in his possession, the situation would remain dire. For now, Sylvia would have to settle for one adversary, and a split-second was all she needed.

As the Prophet turned for a brief moment to address the militant operating the laptop to his left, Sylvia retreated silently into the dimly lit hallway in pursuit of her prey. Then the Prophet resumed his dialogue with the American president.

Slowly Sylvia followed the footsteps of the militant back down the hall until she could see him enter through a door on the right. As she arrived at the partially opened door, she waited until she heard the sound of a man relieving himself. She removed her eight-inch serrated combat knife with her left hand, and nudged the open door ever so slightly with her right hand. Fortunately for her the mirror was on the righthand side of the bathroom, and out of the immediate and peripheral view of the soldier. There could be no hesitation.

She looked first back down the obscure hallway toward the conference room to make sure another militant hadn't been sent to pursue her, and once she was satisfied no one was coming she entered the room like a soft shadow, and quietly closed to within inches of the man's back. As he finished his business, his hands went down to zip up his pants. The second he started to zip up his zipper, Sylvia quickly drew her knife and ripped it across the man's throat, severing his esophagus in an instant.

The man gasped momentarily for a fleeting breath, then slumped into Sylvia's waiting arms. The blood from his torn throat spilled down the front of his black knit sweater. She quickly wiped her bloody knife off on his pant-leg while steadying the dead man against the wall with her left arm, careful not to get any of his blood on her or her knife's holster, then backed out of the bathroom, dragging her fallen prey down the hallway until she came to the door of the loading bay from which they'd all entered, still careful not to get any of his blood on herself or the floor. She deposited the corpse behind a row of boxes to her left opposite the short flight of stairs that led down to the vehicles, then quickly retraced her steps to the rank bathroom, making sure there wasn't any blood that might tip off future washroom visitors.

After a moment of house-cleaning, Sylvia noticed a thermostat on the wall opposite the bathroom door in the hallway. She turned the temperature up to thirty-seven degrees Celsius and returned ever so quietly to her post at the town hall meeting.

Now there were only thirteen obstacles between her and the liberation of her captives—her day was getting better already.

CHAPTER 7

Los Angeles, 8:07 a.m.

The immense Royal Sweden G Class tanker with Saudi registry glided into the San Pedro harbor under the draw-bridge en route to its mooring place with its load of LNG. On deck it was a balmy sixty-seven degrees. In several insulated containers, 135,000 cubic meters of liquefied natural gas was kept at a chilly minus 260 degrees. The ship was just one of a growing number in the fleet that carried some twelve million tons of LNG around the world every year, bridging the gap between places like Brunei, Oman, and Nigeria, with an abundance of natural gas, and markets with a rapidly rising demand like the U.S. and China. The development of LNG had been around for over forty years. But now the cleanest fossil fuel was running neck-and-neck with oil as the predominant source of energy.

The Los Angeles port, along with every other major shipping lane in the country, had been owned and operated by the global behemoth Halifax—a drilling and pipeline titan that had bought up all of the shipping lanes in America in 2008 to help facilitate its expanding distribution needs. Along with the U.S. ports, Halifax also owned and operated everything on both sides of the English Channel.

After the failed attempt by the Saudi pipeline and shipping giant, Baqqar Solutions, to buy up the same American ports in 2005, a parlance ensued between the two giants. Rumors had swirled around the world about a marriage between the two oil magnates for nearly fourteen months. Then finally at the beginning of the fourth quarter of 2009, the imminent deal was finally announced: Baqqar and Halifax were at last married, to the raves and adulation of Wall Street. The pundits had called it a match made in heaven. Though terms of the deal were initially unclear as to who would control whom, in early 2010 it was announced that the company would be headquartered in Bahrain. Most of the management from Baqqar would remain, while only key management from Halifax would be absorbed into the new company.

The Saudi giant, Baqqar, was suddenly the largest pipeline and shipping concern in the world, which soon controlled two-thirds of the ports in the world—including all of America's interests. The company was well aware of American sentiment and in early 2010 had renamed itself Global Solutions.

Ten minutes earlier the deck and hull of the supertanker were swarming with Homeland Security agents, Port Authority personnel, and a small pack of feisty bomb-sniffing dogs, just out of harm's way beyond the entrance to the harbor. The ship's captain was well aware of Port Authority protocol under normal circumstances, but today's beefed-up level of scrutiny left he and his crew feeling somewhat felonious. He tried to assure his stone-faced interrogators that there weren't many ports of interest out on the open sea to pick up an explosive device. Once it was determined that the ship was clean and paperwork was in order, the Pegasus was allowed into port.

With the help of a few tugs, the gigantic tanker eased up to the space reserved next to a massive holding container at the dock, where it would deliver its well-travelled payload. From there the gas would be pumped into rail containers and distributed throughout the western states. It was just a part of the immense Royal Sweden refinery of San Pedro that housed everything from crude oil to gasoline to LNG.

Maldive Islands, 8:19 p.m.

Heinricke anxiously paced the bleached white sands of his temporary domain, clutching his sat-phone, still unable to reach Ali-Khan. He and his colleagues in Hong Kong weighed the story that was propelling most commodities, and hoped that it wasn't Ali-Khan's evil doings that had transformed their well-rehearsed investments into overnight fortunes. Heinricke stared at his phone, praying a call from Nabeel would break the numbing silence of his tropical serenity and quell the demons of self-doubt, as a single bead of sweat dripped from his brow onto the keypad.

Austria, 5:21 p.m.

The Prophet rehashed the events of 911 with his Town Hall panel, while his global audience following attentively. He offered a level of sympathy to those lost on that tragic day, and condemned those who'd orchestrated the heinous acts against the innocents, briefly confounding those in the room and undoubtedly the analysts back in Washington.

"Where's he going with this?" they would undoubtedly ask.

"The fact of the matter is that ninety percent of the planet was on America's side that day," the anchor continued, then addressed the American. "So, while the rubble that was once the Twin Towers continued to smolder in the ensuing days, President Haydon, there was complete solidarity for your cause."

President Haydon didn't say anything as she studied her captor.

"What happened to Building Seven, Madame President?"

"It was hit in the attack, then burned to the ground," Haydon answered impatiently.

"Please. You're starting to bore me with your formulaic answers," the Prophet shot back and instructed the man next to him operating the laptop to transmit a video from his laptop to the broadcast signal. "We're going to show our viewers what really happened that day—what has been suppressed by the western media—what continues to astound many worldwide—what your government is willing to do to your own buildings to gain further support."

The militant with the laptop typed in a command, transmitting a video feed into the broadcast signal. All the while President Haydon and the others studied their adversary. In just a moment, the video began to play back into a split-screen broadcast worldwide, while the anchor narrated a pretty convincing display of what appeared to be explosive charges being detonated at twelve separate stress points on Building Seven, felling it perfectly without endangering any other buildings nearby "As you can see, building seven wasn't even near the Twin Towers. How is this possible? Why was it necessary to take out your building seven?" the Prophet demanded.

"What?" more than one leader asked in unison, while recoiling in disbelief.

"Was it because Building Seven housed all of those government documents? What are you covering up? How much do you need to lie to your people to sell them on a war that they never wanted—or a war that made no sense? You had Afghanistan. Why Iraq? They had nothing to do with the unfortunate events of 911. The leadership there wanted nothing to do with the Al-Qaeda terror network. And now look at the irreparable damage you've inflicted to that region! There was balance!"

"Mr. Prophet, please," President Haydon tried. "We've seen this video for years. It has been through every kind of forensic analysis available. It has been proven to be tampered with, just as the conspiracy theory surrounding the Twin Towers themselves. There were other video transcripts that showed similar blasts on both of the Twin Towers, that felled those two buildings perfectly as well. Every conspiracy theorist in America *and* abroad tampered with these video transcripts and then tried to convince their fellow questioners of self-sabotage. Mr. Prophet, what if these buildings and all of the other buildings in New York City built after a certain year were constructed to adhere to strict codes in the event of any such occurrence—so that they *would* implode into themselves? Furthermore, why would America sacrifice three such structures and the innocent people within those buildings?"

"Because Madame President, sometimes it's a necessary sacrifice to make to garner overwhelming support to go out and get the bad guy, as you say— and maybe even expand that search, on the wings of this new-found solidarity, into regions that never had anything at all to do with this heinous attack on all three of your buildings."

"It's a stretch, Mr. Prophet," Haydon tried to reason. "You're trying to sell us all here, *and* to the world, that the government of the United States would allow let alone orchestrate the demise of the very symbols of freedom and financial might, and to be willing to turn our backs on the innocent people showing up for work that day?" Haydon questioned, pausing to weigh her own words. "It's simply impossible."

"President Haydon, I wish I was the only one. I *wish* that I could be your lunatic for the day—that I've lost my marbles, as you say. I *so* wish that I was off my rocker. But I'm not. Even the American people question the morality and ethics of your U.S. policy makers," the anchor said in a surprisingly measured tone, convinced he was making a valid point. He subconsciously wiped at the sweat from his forehead, forgetting he was wearing the ski mask, and then continued. "The fact of the matter, President Haydon, is that America has a history of tolerating allowable levels of collateral damage to its own interests, to muster support for its global interventions. Even *after* your Pearl Harbor incident, I believe there was the questionable strategy of provocation involving your neighbors to the south—Cuba. I'm sure you've heard of Operation Northwoods?"

The president didn't say a word.

"The plan, written and designed by your Department of Defense and the Joint Chiefs of Staff in 1962 for the Kennedy Administration, called for American-led attacks on your own cities – primarily Miami and Washington D.C., in which commercial jetliners would be allegedly hijacked and flown into your own buildings. Innocent citizens were to be shot in your streets, while boatloads of refugees fleeing Cuba were to be sunk on the high seas.

Phony information would be assembled to implicate Castro, and alas, the American people would have no problem going "all in" on the invasion of Cuba. Madame President, I could elaborate further on the exact contents of the plan, but I don't think it's necessary. I think you get my drift…scary the similarities of that plan and the events of 911."

"The plan was never accepted, nor was any portion of the plan ever executed," Haydon tried, not sure how her captor would react. She'd heard all of these wild-eyed allegations before. In her mind, all of the conspiracy theorists' tirades surrounding 911, Pearl Harbor, as well as the alleged Kennedy-era blueprint for 911 were convincingly disproven. She grew frustrated and hot from her exchange with the Prophet. She wiped her brow with the tattered sleeve of her suit, and took a long swig of water.

In the Pentagon, an almost stunned General Meyers quietly mouthed the words, "What the hell are we dealing with?"

"Good God," Morrison added.

"It's all declassified information, gentlemen—has been since 1997," Simonson reminded. "Hell, I remember talk of painting our F-86s to look like a Cuban MIGs, as part of the plan."

Meyers grimaced at the Deputy Director and his knowledge the fifty-year old policy. As far as he was concerned, all of this belonged back inside the vault.

"Let me throw out another conspiracy theory, Madame President, since we're talking about so-called conspiracies," the Prophet continued. "What if, President Haydon, I was to tell you that after your dot-com bubble had finally burst, America had finally come to the end of an economic cycle of historical magnitude? Do you know that the American economy had clearly come to the end of a Kondratieff Wave? And maybe even eclipsed it by two years? History will also show that your economy had come to the end of another Elliott Wave."

The President and the other leaders looked at the Prophet with expressions ranging from skepticism to bewilderment. The alleged mercenary was now attempting to give a clinic on economic theory with those brought together to discuss global economic harmony. She was baffled. "Where are you going with this, Mr. Prophet?"

"I'm sorry. Have I lost you, Madame President?" the Prophet asked. "Have I lost all of you?"

"I confess," Haydon said. "You have."

"Me as well," Collinsworth added.

"Me too," several more chimed in.

In the Pentagon, General Meyers asked no one in particular the same question, "Where the *hell* is he going with this?"

"Well, Madame President," the Prophet began. "And the rest of you, bear with me for just a moment and hear me out. You might find this very interesting."

"Very well," Haydon obliged. "Please do explain."

"Right. Well, most economists and market historians believe that when the American economy had peaked in early 2000, your financial markets had peaked right along with it, forming a bubble, which in the ensuing months burst, as we all know by now. As you also know, your financial markets tried to rally in early 2001, which again was an historical blueprint of the last Kondratieff Wave. In fact all of this economic and financial marketplace behavior was a blueprint of the last 'bust-to-boom' cycle that burst with the 1929 stock market crash and the ensuing recession. People forget, however, that there was a two-and-a-half year bounce off the bottom before you entered the Great Depression."

In the Pentagon, General Meyers thought he was just thinking, but his mouth conveyed his thoughts. "Someone please tell me that we're not getting a lesson on global economics and market history from an uneducated militant."

"It looks like we are, sir," Director Simonson said, a little surprised as well. "Only I don't think he's unqualified at all, sir."

Meyers could only grumble back, while the vice president echoed the general's sentiment at the sophisticated nature of the masked man's words.

"Fast forward to 2001," the Prophet continued. "The United States was clearly in the early stages of a recession. Your housing markets had come to a screeching halt. Your commercial real estate markets were well into a pullback. By the way, all of these things that I've mentioned are some of the critical engines that work directly in concert with a normal business cycle, which in this case was losing steam fast.

"Now, suddenly the World Trade Center's Twin Towers get attacked and crumble to the ground. In American terms, this was Armageddon. In financial terms, this event broke the spine of the U.S. economy, overnight—both physically and psychologically—an unwitting home run for the terrorists of 911.

"While your president at the time was justifiably garnering the support of the world for an all-out attack on the sponsoring country, your Federal Reserve Chairman—a brilliant man I might add, and also a market historian—he had an even tougher job—save the American economy. It was *his* aggressive policy that was crucial in planting the seeds of hope," the Prophet explained to a riveted and dead-silent audience of world leaders.

"Now, here's where it gets interesting. We all know that, historically, at the beginning of a new economic cycle, i.e. Elliot Wave or Kondratieff Wave, whichever barometric measure you prefer, typically war is the cornerstone of an economic recovery. The problem though is that there was still a mountain of debt left from the dot-com debacle, and your country hadn't really paid its dues for that economic implosion, as well as quite a few other countries for that matter.

"Now, we all know it was critical to the Woodson administration and its marketing department, news agencies, propaganda machine, or whatever you chose to call the vehicles of information, to make 'fear of the unknown' the central reason for an all-out offensive on not just the country that sponsored the terrorists that attacked your nation, but *now* also against all of the nations of Islamic faith. At the same your government put out regular terror alerts—red, green, yellow, blue, etc.—creating fear—fear to live, fear to travel—and most importantly fear to fly, ladies and gentlemen.

"With an aggressive Federal Reserve policy there was cheap money everywhere. With fear of flying and fear of doing anything but buying a home and sitting in it, that mentality eventually became the new modus-operandi in America. With the easing of qualifications, everyone was in, and we were off to the races! The housing boom was on, and the economy looked like it might just survive the dot-com debacle. Now, fast-forward for a moment: waiters, librarians, and taxi-drivers are all now 'flipping', I think you call it. Everyone is making money hand over fist, and guess what else? The tax base is suddenly booming as well, fueling the flames of a war-based economy, while the engines of war are redefining the Middle East. People were saying "War? What war? Innocent Muslims are dying? We don't want to know about that. We just won't look at it for now. We're making an offer on our fifth house tomorrow. We'll buy it, and put a tenant in it."

"Anyone have any idea what I'm getting at yet?" the Prophet asked, but didn't wait long enough for an answer. "All right, then. Let's fast-forward again. Does the sub-prime crisis ring a bell? Thirty-five percent of U.S. homeowners who've bought homes after 2004 have lost or will lose their homes, and suddenly you'll lose your tax-base, and your country is saddled with a trillion dollars in debt. All the great work your Fed has done, both old and new, can't save you from your house of cards. The World Bank is even leery of you. *And now,* what you have is that dead-cat bounce after dot-com, and God forbid, the historical makings of the second Great Depression.

"Your Congress steps in at the eleventh hour and asks "How could this happen? Innocent people are losing their homes." Well the fact of the matter is those innocent people never deserved to own homes in the first place. In historical terms they couldn't qualify. They had no down payment, they had no means to make their payments, and therefore should never been a homeowner in the first place. *Until* all the rules and laws were changed to facilitate such a fiasco looking for a place to happen. Why didn't your Congress ask those questions while everyone was printing money from profits in homes that in reality didn't exist? In perception the profits existed, and your fine citizens kept sticking their hands in the cookie jar and pulling out the profits until the reality of this house of cards finally took hold. The perfect storm for the latest of our modern day pyramid schemes had finally run out of hot air.

"In a sense, America might have been better off paying the price for the sins of dot-com, and endured that recession. Your citizens might just have said no to a trillion-dollar war that over the course of it would take the lives of hundreds of thousands of Muslims—admittedly some bad, but most of them good people. Now, unfortunately, you have what you have—a multi-trillion dollar war debt, which in the short-term is quite difficult to finance. *And* you also have a world full of silent enemies," the Prophet finally finished, leaving a room full of silence.

After about a ten second interval to fully assimilate what she'd just heard President Haydon finally spoke. "Wow! Mr. Prophet, that *is* a truly a magnificent theory, how about just a housing bubble?" She spoke very softly and slowly, careful not to stir him, at the same time dumbfounded by the audacious theory. She had no idea whether every other face of a captive in the room shared the same bewildered look as her own.

The president had heard far-ranging versions of this conjecture before, but never anything this well-tailored to a militant's wild whim before. She realized she was gazing at her captor with astonishment etched into her expression, while her eyes interrogated him and her mouth remained agape. She quickly composed herself and made a conscious effort to display that 'Marge Haydon for President' smile back onto her face.

"Normally, I'd agree, Madame President," the Prophet responded. "Normally I'd agree. However, as I'd mentioned, it was the perfect necessary storm for an ill-conceived war that never should have been. Call it a diversion, or what you will. Hitler did it—he saved his country from economic doom and restored prosperity. The German people just looked the other way while their leader enslaved the Jews and beat on the drums of war. What did they care? Their country was great once again!"

"The war certainly had its doubters, Mr. Prophet," Haydon conceded for a moment. "But how could an entire Congress be so stupid and support such an ill-conceived war, and two very differing groups at that?"

"Madame President, if you break down the components of what I've just explained to you, historically you couldn't deny the basis for which all of this has taken place."

"To your point, Mr. Prophet. I've heard about these economic cycles— Elliot and Kondradi…"

"Kondratieff, Madame President," the Prophet corrected. "He was a very learned Russian economist whose theory has held up against every argument *against* economic-cyclicality—Nicolai Dmitri Kondratieff had proven his theory all the way back to the ancient Israelites."

"I can appreciate that, Mr. Prophet," the President responded patiently, not knowing if or when the Prophet might lose his temper again. "But my advisors have brought me up to speed on all of these theories, and how they might fit into today's world. While all of them agree that both Elliott and Kondratieff's waves *were* textbook during their time, they also share with me that these wave theories may have outgrown themselves. *And*, Mr. Prophet, does one live by yesterday's standards? Or does one forge forward and attempt to better the present, and by doing so alter the course of history and redefine these very barometers of yesterday's economic path? These very theories are perhaps no longer applicable," President Haydon suggested to an obviously very bright man—though slightly misguided, she thought, while moving forward, carefully hand-picking her words. "That in a time of global expansion, these theories simply don't apply, because you can't necessarily lay a regional economic template over the global landscape."

"Oh bullshit!" the Prophet screeched, suddenly fueled by the American's unwillingness to bend. "You're attempting to manipulate a set of circumstances that historically can't be denied, all for the peace of mind of America. Convenient denial, again!" the Prophet bellowed again, this time slamming his closed right fist down onto conference table. Then the Prophet barked a command at the two militants standing guard by the door that led down the hallway—one of those guards being militant-Sylvia. As he took a big gulp of his water, he was nudged again by the militant operating the computer next to him, showing him something flashing on his screen.

The guard opposite Sylvia signaled to her that they should go try to find the thermostat. She gladly obliged, but then she already knew its location. She understood the instructions just fine, but waited half a beat to follow her comrade down the hall.

"It seems you have not honored my requests," the Prophet said calmly toward the camera now. "I've warned you once, yet you still persist in trying to locate our signal."

There was no answer, for this was a one-way broadcast.

"In case you didn't believe that I was a man of my word," the Prophet said, pausing for a moment, then he whispered something into the commander's ear. "This should keep you busy for awhile."

The Commander started to depress a small device in his hand that appeared to be the remote.

Several Town Hall participants shouted, fearing for what uncertainty awaited the free world. Unconsciously, Hammons and Elliott lunged clumsily in the direction of the Prophet, since he was the only one among the enemy that wasn't armed, surprising him and knocking him out of his swivel chair. Unfortunately they'd also knocked President Haydon out of her chair and onto the floor in their futile attempt at valor, and Elliott accidentally trampled her left ankle in the process.

Just as quickly the American president pushed herself up onto her feet in an attempt to assist her constituents, who were both immediately swarmed and physically suppressed. She too was instantly neutralized by a brutal blast from the metal handle of a militant's weapon to her head, causing the ex-boxer from China to launch out of his chair in what was starting to resemble a domino-like series of chain-reactions. Zheng head-butted the militant who'd tried to control Haydon, knocking him over. Equally as fast, Zheng absorbed the butt of a weapon to his right eye opening a gash. Remarkably, he stood defiantly even as he was being restrained, while a healthy trickle of blood flowed from his eyebrow and down his cheek. He'd seen tougher days in the ring, and to him there was no honor in hitting a handcuffed woman. The militant struck him hard again, in the stomach this time with the same butt of his AK rifle, causing the Chinese leader to temporarily double over. His solar plexus muscles weren't quite what they used to be. The militant then viciously grabbed the Chinaman by his hair and yanked his head up and shoved the barrel of his weapon into his captive's mouth, before being called off by a surprisingly calm leader. "Return all of them to their seats," the Prophet said in Farsi. To those watching around the world, there were no words to describe what they were witnessing.

The commander hadn't depressed a button on his remote as it turned out. He was making a phone call on his scrambled sat-phone. On the other side of the planet, Captain Amir Hassan answered the call. He was still aboard his supertanker, going through some registry paperwork for the Los Angeles port authority.

Once order was restored in the room, the Prophet looked behind him to the commander, and asked him to terminate the call. "Now is not the time," he said, then gave his commander new instructions in Arabic. "Depress button four on the right side of your remote."

Without saying a further word, the commander terminated the call, and followed his instructions, depressing the designated button on his remote.

Command Center, Vice Presidential Bunker, 11:39 a.m.
Admiral Morrison's face went ashen at the chaos being broadcast, while Kyle and Keith were riveted to their mother's image on the oversized main monitor, trying in vain to somehow help her, but it was a video-gone-wrong

seven-thousand miles away. There was nothing they could do. Tyler cringed at the prospects of his wife, the American president, being trampled by her comrades trying to defuse a tragic situation. As the militants hit her and the others, his body tensed up. "Stop this now!" he raged at the monitor, while clenching his fists and vowing revenge.

Morrison continued to observe the president and other leaders being maliciously roughed up on the main monitor, while scanning the other flat-panel screens for any new news coverage alert. "This is outrageous," he hissed in disbelief. "This is the most powerful person in the free world! Do they know what they're doing?" he continued to rant as his tone intensified. "General Meyers, please give us some good news."

"Mr. Vice President, we're getting initial word out of Italy," Meyers started. "There's apparently been a significant explosion at the historic Opera House, Teatro La Scala, in Milan. We're waiting to confirm, sir," Meyers said, pausing for a moment. "Sir, our intel is informing us that it's MIFED in Milan right now—one of the three major film festivals that caters to the international film industry," Meyers continued, almost as if he was a two-second tape delay of the information that was rolling in to him. "Apparently, there was a gala being held at La Scala for all of the nominated directors at this year's festival," Meyers exhaled, as his techs finally patched through a BBC feed to the main monitor on the wall opposite his command post. The visual was horrific—the house that hosted such greats as Puccini, Caruso, Domingo, and Pavarotti was nearly gone, with flames roaring from the rubble and what was left of the historic structure. "Are you watching this, Mr. Vice President?"

"I am now," the vice president growled. His face turned noticeably red with anger and his breathing grew hoarse as he watched the footage on his monitor from the BBC affiliate in Milan, initially dispatched to cover the film festival.

Then Meyers and Morrison heard the words from the reporter that they both ultimately knew would be inevitable. "It doesn't appear anyone or anything could have survived such a horrific blast…"

CHAPTER 8

Sylvia accompanied her unsuspecting accomplice to the thermostat and a little further. In a matter of seconds she had sliced the life from him with the jagged edge of her knife in similar fashion to her first mark, and now they both lay in the loading area in the row of boxes, never to threaten a world leader again. There were now only twelve assailants remaining.

She returned to the conference room in the midst of all the commotion and immediately helped defuse the would-be rebellion. The Chinese leader was bleeding, the British prime minister looked disoriented, the Canadian was unconscious, and her president looked even more disheveled, with blood trickling from her left eye and the right corner of her mouth. The rest of the leaders just looked angry. And although they had no idea how much their blundered coup had helped Sylvia, it'd given her a perfect window to eliminate one more mark and slip back into the room unnoticed. Of equal importance, the Prophet and the commander hadn't yet discovered the discrepancy in the militants count.

The broadcast resumed with the Prophet apologizing for the harsh treatment of the captives. "It doesn't have to be this way. If everyone behaves themselves, then no one will be mistreated."

Sylvia studied the Prophet and his demeanor. He wasn't tense, nor was he barbaric. He'd never handled a firearm since he arrived on the scene. He was fluid in his delivery, and his hands were perfectly manicured. This was not a soldier but he knows his shit, she thought. What the hell is he doing here?

"We regret the incident in Milano," he said, taking a swig of his water, and realizing it was still pretty warm in the room. "I thought I told you to turn down the heat," he shouted to Sylvia in Farsi.

"I did," Sylvia answered in her trained male Farsi voice. "Give it a moment to turn off."

Marge Haydon didn't realize it had been a while since she'd used a restroom and asked permission to use the facilities. A chorus of additional requests followed the American president's request, temporarily stopping the Town Hall meeting, and frustrating the Prophet.

"Take her," he barked toward Sylvia to escort the president. "And be quick! There are nine more."

Sylvia obeyed the command, even grabbing the American roughly by the arm for show, pulling the president out of her chair, undoubtedly further aggravating onlookers from the free world.

The commander approached and handed Sylvia the key to the handcuffs. "You'll need this."

Sylvia just nodded back sharply, not staring at the commander any longer than she had to, for fear he might notice the bare minimum traces of mascara left on her Mediterranean eyes. She'd long since wiped the scant hint of lipstick and smudges from her mouth. She turned and jerked her prisoner, hauling her down the hallway toward the restroom. As the door to the hallway swung closed behind her, Sylvia pressed the president face first into the wall next to the restroom door and whispered into the confused leader's ear. "Madame President, it is Sylvia. Don't make any noise. Just know that I am with you."

In an instant, Marge Haydon's heart leapt for joy as Sylvia spun her around to remove the president's handcuffs. The hopeful captive squinted to confirm what her wanton ears had heard. Indeed, the person's eyes peering out of the black ski mask were familiar and warm. Sylvia winked with one eye, and the president's heart raced with hope. Her eyes welled up with sudden optimism. She wanted to speak, but knew better. Just the vision of Sylvia was enough. The fact that she'd endured the hellish attack back at the United Nations complex and lived, reincarnated as one of the mercenaries, sent chills up the president's spine.

Sylvia gestured for the president to use the facilities, her mouth allowing the hint of a smile. Marge Haydon tried to conceal her quivering smile and obeyed the command of her captor.

When Sylvia returned with her handcuffed prisoner, there was another one for her to escort—the German Chancellor. She strong-armed Schmidt back down the corridor, then shoved the German woman into the corridor wall, pinning her long enough to share her identity with Schmidt and free her hands, giving another leader hope where there once was none.

As Schmidt started to react, Sylvia held a single finger to her lips and whispered ever-so-quietly, "Shhh."

Still, Schmidt seemed insistent, and motioned Sylvia in closer. Sylvia glared at the woman but grudgingly complied. "What?" Sylvia whispered impatiently.

"I know the voice of their leader," Schmidt divulged, catching Sylvia completely off guard.

"What?" she whispered, recoiling slightly.

The German leader pulled Sylvia's head closer, and whispered again in her ear. "I know it sounds crazy, but I *know* that voice. I don't know where from, but I know it, and I know it well."

"Okay," Sylvia acknowledged, nodding affirmatively. "We'll talk later. Now get in there, or we'll both be in deep shit," Sylvia urged, gesturing with her head toward the open bathroom.

Schmidt complied and disappeared into the bathroom.

The commander, the Prophet, and the militant next to him were huddled around the laptop computer discussing the trace on their signal. The Prophet instructed the militant-techie to bounce the signal to another pre-determined location.

Sylvia had efficiently serviced ten leaders in twenty-three minutes—not bad by any standard. During that span, she got a bonus she'd hoped for but didn't count on. After she'd disclosed her identity to the Canadian leader in the same manner she'd done with the others, he was getting ready to step into the restroom when another militant made his way down the corridor, and shoved Hammons aside, telling his comrade to watch over him while he relieved himself. "Guard this meat of an ass."

"Of course," Sylvia obliged. In the moment the militant turned to enter the restroom, Sylvia stepped right up behind him with her serrated knife drawn, moving it higher and into position as the Canadian's eyes grew with anticipation. In a split second she severed the man's throat and he slumped into her arms.

Hammons was as rugged as they came, but this was no rodeo. Getting thrown off an angry bull was a walk in the park compared to this. What he'd just witnessed was something altogether different. In just over a second the American bodyguard had ended a man's life, seemingly with lust for the onerous task.

"Get over it, sir. He didn't think too much of you," Sylvia whispered to Hammons, motioning with her head for him to use the facilities, while she added the limp corpse to her growing collection out back. She was down to eleven combatants. Sylvia knew the others would be onto her soon. If she was lucky, she might get one or two more of them before they discovered there was a mole in the unit.

When all the captives were seated the broadcast resumed. "Welcome back to our show," the Prophet said with a somewhat curious smile. "It appears you'll very soon be discovering our location. You are to be commended."

Vice Presidential bunker, 11:59 a.m.

The staffs of Adam Morrison and General Meyers had analyzed the grim results out of Milan's Teatro Di La Scala. There were no survivors. The famous structure that had housed all of the greats was practically rubble. Attending the awards gala were all of the nominated directors for this year's top film presentation and celebration. Among them was the Iraqi-American writer/ director, Tariq Al-Tamr, who had won this year's film of the year for his docu-drama *In the Teeth of the Lion,* which provided a rare look into the other side of the unpopular US-led invasion of Iraq. Apparently, according to his film, there was considerable support from the Iraqi people, but his noble effort would permanently limit his time on the public stage.

Pentagon, 12:01 p.m.

General Meyers weighed the Prophet's words, confused by his nonchalance. "Mr. Vice President," he spoke in a very measured tone into his headset. "We're monitoring this son-of-a-bitch as we speak. We feel confident we'll have his location within minutes. Stand by, sir."

Meyers stood over his tracing team while they monitored the software program that was narrowing in on its target. The mapping program had determined the militant's location to be somewhere in the eastern portion of Vienna, tracking through the last edge of residential area and along each twist and turn of the Danube as it approached the Hungarian border. While the program navigated a map similar to an automobile's navigation system, only in fast forward, the screen next to it displayed satellite images of real time visual that confirmed the navigational software's accuracy.

In a moment, the satellite feed was playing a live video of a protest out in front of several abandoned warehouses out on the Danube near the Hungarian border. It seemed Greenpeace was livid over the construction of a dam project that was supposed to have been shelved because of its negative environmental impact.

The video also showed what looked like a local equivalent of a SWAT contingent of approximately twenty troops, surrounding what appeared to be a laundry van, weapons drawn.

Pentagon intel confirmed the team was Interpol. "Wasn't there a report of a stalled laundry van at the back of the UN?" Meyers asked, as his face hardened at the images of the van.

"Yes, sir," someone said.

In a moment, video images showed two members of the SWAT team storm through the vacated front of the van to throw some kind of canisters into the back of the van. As smoke bellowed out into the icy cold, just beyond the van and against the backdrop of the tattered warehouses, members of Greenpeace could hardly believe their eyes. Their protest had been stopped at gunpoint.

Seconds later the SWAT team opened the rear doors to the van. The rest of the smoke cleared out and one of the SWAT members indicated the van was empty.

"Son of a bitch!" Meyers blurted out, trying to suppress his frustration. "They're playing us for fools! How?" he glared at Director Simonson. Now the twitch in his right eye had become noticeable to anyone close by. "They're making us look like amateurs! How is this possible?"

"I told you before, general, these are not ignorant people. They are committed, and they have resources."

Meyers stiffened in the direction of Simonson, not wanting to hear why they were being outfoxed by advanced technology which more than likely had an American origin. Instead he confirmed to the vice president what the VP already knew. "False alarm, Mr. Vice President."

———————◯———————

"Just a reminder," the Prophet interrupted his international audience. "I really do expect you to honor my requests. Now, to keep you busy, I'm going to give you another quiz. What are the most dangerous bombs in the world?"

The captive leaders all studied the Prophet with their eyes, careful not to look to Sylvia for answers.

"Mr. Collinsworth," the Prophet began. "I'm told you are a man of values and a man of faith, unlike the characters you played years ago in those inexpensive B movies. Can you explain to me why America's God and Britain's God are so much more important than the God of Islam? Tell me why the blood of our children is expendable, and the blood of your children is worth going to war for? Do we not all bleed red? Isn't the loss of life the same for the both of us?"

"Of course," Collinsworth tried, but his words were quickly trampled.

"What if," the Prophet pondered for a moment, "and I realize this might just sound like blasphemy to someone from the West, but I'll ask it anyways. What if my God and your God is the same God?" the Prophet asked, gasping in mock-sacrilege while covering his mouth.

"I don't think that's blasphemy at all," Collinsworth began. "The Bible says there is one God, as does the Quran."

"How noble," the Prophet quipped. "Don't tell me about the Quran. What would you know about the Quran?"

"I'm trying to engage you in dialogue, sir. You asked a question. Please let me try to answer it," Collinsworth attempted. He knew the longer he dialogued with the Prophet, the better the chances were for the broadcast's signal to be located, or the better the chances were that this American masquerading as a mercenary might just pull off a miracle.

"Very well then," the Prophet allowed, flicking his wrist toward the Brit.

"The Bible is a model of a path to God, as is the Quran, allegedly. The Bible says forgive your enemy. Yet many of the followers of the Muslim faith all over the world subscribe to the belief that the Quran states all Christians must be eliminated. As you know, sir, The UK, as well as all of Europe has opened its doors to Muslims of all origins, and so has the U.S. for that matter."

"What is your point, Mr. Collinsworth?" the Prophet asked, seemingly disinterested in the Brit's alleged knowledge of the Quran.

"The point is, sir, what the West sees is that the religion of peace is perhaps not peaceful at all. The religion of peace could possibly be the breeding ground of bitter and contentious hatred with one mission: killing innocent civilians who might just be Christians. Fascio-radical-Islamic fundamentalists murdered over three-thousand people in the Twin Towers and the four airliners. Yet we continue to open our homelands to all of you."

"Silence!" the Prophet blasted. "What came first, the cart or the horse, as you say?"

"Innocent people in Bali. Innocent people in Spain. Innocent people in the Philippines. You tried to kill hundreds of innocent commuters in our subways. You attacked!" Collinsworth tried to reason.

"*You* attacked!" the Prophet exploded back. "The U.S.-led coalition attacked! You empowered a man to do your dirty work—a man who can be your balance of power in the region, without spilling a single drop of Western blood. And in a hushed piece of policy your ambassador gives permission to this allegedly barbarous dictator to invade its neighbor—a former province of that empire, while everyone looked the other way," the Prophet explained, calming himself now. "And then you demand that this leader vacate immediately the very province that you granted permission to invade."

"Mr. Prophet," Collinsworth pleaded. "You simply don't have your facts in order. That barbarous dictator had overnight become a threat to the region, as history will recount."

"Mr. Collinsworth," the Prophet calmly reasoned. "The world is aware of the facts leading up to that invasion, and in turn the counter-invasion. Where is the ambassador who brokered the deal to allow for such an invasion in the first place?"

There was silence. Everyone in the room knew the answer.

"That's right. She died mysteriously in a car crash, shortly after her removal from her commission in that region," the Prophet answered in lieu of the silence. "Strange how untimely accidents happen sometimes."

There was another moment of silence while every set of eyes in the room studied each other. The Prophet felt confident he was making valid points to those in captivity as he tried to do the same with his television audience. The way he saw it, the captives behaved as if they were all in denial, as if they'd all read the same script. "I have to use the restroom," he said, exhaling his frustration, while getting up.

For a brief moment, Sylvia's eyes grew with anticipation. Could this be it? She thought. Could this be the moment of opportunity? She would follow the Prophet down the hall and end him. No. She couldn't do that. He was the key to the commander, and the commander held the remote with all the buttons to the unknown.

The commander ended her hopes with a command in Farsi for everyone to sit tight while the Prophet used the facilities.

"Oh, I almost forgot," the Prophet said. "The quiz. What are the most dangerous kinds of bombs? Does anyone know?"

There was complete quiet while the Prophet circled the conference table, stopping first at President Haydon. "What about you, Madame President?"

There was no answer, and he continued his mischievous query, sauntering over to each leader. Everyone's eyes followed him with his slow, deliberate walk, daring anyone to answer.

"What about you, Monsieur Marceau?"

There was still no answer.

"What about you, Mr. Elliott? We haven't heard a peep out of you today."

When the Prophet returned to the head of the table, he answered. "The most dangerous kinds of bombs are the kind that don't go boom."

He smiled, and then nodded toward the commander who depressed one of the buttons on the remote.

CHAPTER 9

Vice Presidential Bunker, 12:37 p.m.

Vice President Morrison paced in his bunker while conversing with General Meyers. He'd abandoned his decorated admiral's coat some time earlier, and had since loosened his tie and rolled up his sleeves. Though there was sufficient air circulation and climate control in the bunker, there were spots of perspiration on his underarms as well as small beads forming above his brow which he continually swiped at with his handkerchief.

Meyers briefed the vice president on the tactical deployment throughout Europe. Legions of international military forces blanketed Austria. All airports had been shut down indefinitely, while the first layer of airspace was controlled by EU gunships. And above that a second layer of U.S. and coalition fighter jets had been scrambled out of nearby Rammstein AFB. The borders were sealed.

"This is not happening. We can climb up a gnat's ass two-thousand miles away," Morrison reasoned. "We've got a stranglehold on all of Austria, but we can't decipher this signal?"

"We are trying, sir."

"Well, get me something, Gordon. They've got our president over there. Do a door-to-door if you have to!"

"Yes, sir," Meyers replied, while being nudged by Director Simonson with a certain level of urgency. "Uh, Mr. Vice President, can you hold the line open for a second?"

"Of course."

"We're getting a report out of New York. Hold on," Meyers continued. "Sir, there's a story out of New York. It's early, but there's a report that says Wall Street's computer's are...on the blink."

"Clarify, please," Morrison demanded firmly.

"Our sources indicate the Dow was already down six-hundred-eighty points when apparently a huge wave of volume just hit, causing a four-hundred point down-spike. Traders say that investors are starting to panic and throw in the towel at any cost, because they can't control the sell-off. And apparently the derivatives market—which I know nothing about—is compounding the pressure to the downside."

"Spell it out for me, general," Morrison requested. "How bad is the sell-off?"

"Really bad, sir," Meyers informed. "Hold on," Meyers said, trying to listen in on the coverage in the background. "Sir, turn one of your monitors to CNBC," he exhaled.

"What now?"

"They've just shut it down."

"Net it out, general," the vice president demanded.

"They've just shut down the NYSE. Wait a minute. This thing, this virus, whatever it is apparently just hit the NASDAQ," Meyers explained.

Morrison's staff quickly tuned into CNBC and observed the correspondent reporting from the floor of the NYSE, where floor traders were still trying to assess the big downward spike, some walking back and forth and others staying in their pits, still unaware that the markets had closed. It had been chaos all day long. Before the opening bell rang, all futures were considerably lower in anticipation of the global uncertainty and the effect it would have on the market.

The three bright spots in the market had been precious metals, oil and defense stocks, which were expected to rally in the face of such turmoil. Gold futures closed up at the day's limit—the price of the bullion perched at $1,980 an ounce. Crude oil futures closed up at the limit as well, to over $125 a barrel. And defense-related securities always rallied in the face of war.

"Other than that, it was a bloodbath," the reporter said. "We're trying to get a sense of what happened with this down-spike which in turn set off the trading triggers, and shut down both indices. Early indications are a program was launched that interacts with the algorithms that drive shares up or down, similar to the software that program-traders use to set triggers to buy or sell. Traders are telling us that shortly after 1200 hours Eastern Standard Time six institutional sized blocs of shares hit the market, and apparently there was a delay in processing these orders simply because they were unprecedented; they were mammoth.

"When this rogue program caught the sales, it triggered a wave of selling, because out of nowhere the Dow was devalued by an extra four-hundred points. That was almost an additional eighty percent decline on the day relative to its earlier losses, in just seconds, bringing the current loss on the day to almost eleven-hundred points. I've asked the traders where the six large blocs came from and no one seemed to know. So it's still unclear if the rogue program was a precursor to the spike down, or the reaction to the spike, or worse yet—both. Many liken today's market behavior to the flash-crash of May, 2010, when the Dow dropped close to a thousand points in less than ten minutes.

"We're also getting a similar story out of the NASDAQ. As you might imagine, there was an initial rush to unload shares on all of the aftermarket exchanges as well, and the same thing happened there—triggers were hit and that exchange was closed just minutes ago.

"There's somewhat of a panic right now because no one seems to have any answers, consequently investors and traders alike don't want to go home with long positions on days like these, and it's still unclear if any of the exchanges are going to re-open today. We're being told the president of the NYSE will be down shortly to give a statement.

"Traders also tell us that shortly before these triggers hit, there was a rush of orders for gold and oil stocks that never got processed. When the markets finally re-open, look for those two commodities to spike higher again."

Hong Kong, 1:22 a.m.

Charles Li and Minh Pak hadn't budged from their posh leather chairs, with the exception of grabbing a snack from the office kitchen or having to use the restroom, still mesmerized by the uncertainty unfolding throughout the world. They'd exchanged several phone calls with their associate down in the tropics of the Indian Ocean, who was caught in a similar quandary. He was still unclear of the whereabouts of *his* associate who allegedly was going to be the driving force in some kind of market making event.

Li and Pak watched the split-screen monitor on Li's office wall set to CNN, BBC, and equally important CNBC-Asia. The latter was covering the Wall Street meltdown story which carried huge implications for the Asian markets, set to open in just eight-and-a-half hours. All the futures for the

Asian markets indicated lower openings, which was to be expected, and the question now was how much lower.

The reporter posed this analysis: "Would the Asian markets be the tail or the dog? Asian markets typically take their cue from U.S. markets and run from there. But in recent years, especially with the Shanghai composite's emergence and ensuing erratic behavior, in many cases the Asian markets have become the precursor to something worse. One thing for certain, regardless of the degree of the impending Asian declines; all of the precious metals futures are trading higher, as well as crude oil."

Li and Pak were well aware of the fortune they'd made for themselves and their clients. The computer on Li's desk was set to track all global activity, and already the New York numbers were beyond their wildest dreams, even for the planned five-day 'event' that was supposed to drive their holdings into the promised land. The additional pressure that their derivative holdings were putting on their overall portfolio had caused an exponential return with each milestone that was crossed. They could conceivably start to lighten up on their positions later that morning, even with knowing that this run still had legs on it.

It was a bittersweet moment in their storied rise in Hong Kong. They weren't quite sure how to react though. They didn't know if it was time to break out the Veuve Cliquot or to disinfect each other.

Maldive Islands, 10:37 p.m.

The sun had long since set on the island paradise and its three guests. The proprietor had simply walked home earlier in the day to the next island over—in some areas the water was sufficiently shallow that one could walk from island to island. Gregor Heinricke had given up his pursuit of finding his associate in the northern hemisphere. He'd figured Ali-Khan would resurface when he was good and ready. It wasn't his job to badger his friend or his family. And his gut told him that his friend was incapable of anything this unimaginable.

He'd moved his temporary office in from the beach, setting his laptop and the spent batteries on the bar-top just twenty meters up from the water, while plugging in the computer to an outlet normally used for a cocktail blender. The markets Henricke had been tracking on the laptop had all closed up shop for the evening, and New York was still closed as well. So he wasn't too concerned with watching so intently right now. He was acutely aware that he and his global alliances had made quite a bit of money in just one day, a banner year for that matter in just one day. And with the move upward, all of the trailing stops had automatically moved higher as well, meaning his hedged bet remained intact, adjusted to reflect today's gains.

Heinricke was mentally exhausted with speculating, both in the financial markets and with regard to who the rogue militants were. He grabbed himself a longneck beer out of the bar's refrigerator and took a long swig from it, then turned on the forty-two inch flat screen television that hung on the back wall of the open bar. He pressed the remote until he found BBC's ongoing coverage of the events in Austria, and the ensuing global reaction.

Off in the distance Heinricke could hear the playful laughter of Arisa and Katia coming from the direction of down the beach, temporarily breaking his half-hearted concentration on the BBC broadcast. He swiveled around on the bar stool and locked onto his companions' location about forty meters away, near the water. It seemed they too, had been enjoying several adult beverages.

Heinricke got up from his perch at the bar and sauntered down toward his ladies with an eased expression on his face, the bottle of beer loosely dangling from his right hand. Why not? he thought. It had been a long day at the office, and a good one at that. The time for unfounded remorse and guilt was over. He'd slayed the dragon and now it was time to play, he told himself.

Rural Austria, 7:59 p.m.

"Now, I have warned you to stop in this silly quest of trying to locate us," the Prophet gloated, having thwarted his relentless pursuers yet again. "It would be best if you just honored my request and watched and listened to the remainder of this broadcast, and no one else will get hurt.

"As I'd mentioned awhile ago, the biggest bombs don't necessarily go boom," the Prophet continued. "I would prefer not to take lives, but you've forced my hand to inflict a different kind of bloodshed, that of the financial type. By the time you get the U.S. financial markets open again there will be considerable losses. Now, my guess is if your leaders are capable of calming the uneasiness of individual investors, then this little ordeal will be short-lived. But we don't know yet how this will affect the Asian markets when they open in about eight hours, and you know that fear can be much greater an emotion than greed.

"Just so we make sure there is an understanding, please be warned the next time you attempt to decipher our signal there will be another blast. Now whether it's a conventional explosion or one similar to what the US is experiencing right now, make no mistake there will be carnage and it will be debilitating."

The Pentagon, 2:04 p.m.

"Son-of-a-bitch is toying with us," Meyers blurted out barely above a whisper, but loud enough for Simonson to hear.

Director Simonson stood three monitors away from the general with his arms folded while his right hand cradled his chin, careful not to obstruct his wireless mouthpiece. He continued to give commands to his various intelligence personnel, while pointing at some movement on the screen in front of the tech sitting at the station, and told the technician to pursue it, as Meyers approached.

"Mr. Simonson, let's try this some other way," the general said in a more measured tone. "You've got to give me something."

"We are trying, sir," Simonson said, stress etched into his face. "We are doing everything within our power, and then some."

"What kind of equipment is capable of this good of a broadcast?" Meyers asked, seemingly disinterested in the weak answer. "What kind of network gear do they need to transmit? What are they using to scramble their signal? Where does one acquire such equipment, black market or otherwise? And I realize Austria is a sophisticated country with a lot of cell phones. Can you put a trace on every cell phone call made from Austria in the last twenty-four hours?"

"That is like finding a needle in a haystack," Simonson said. "But our people here *and* there are working on it already."

"Good. Find me a needle then, and find it soon!" Meyers demanded impatiently.

"We're already trying to source their equipment," Simonson added.

"Thank you, Mr. Simonson," Meyers acknowledged, suddenly pulling away to answer the incoming voice on his Bluetooth. "Yes, Mr. Vice President?"

"I was just informed they are not going to re-open the markets today," the vice president said. "President Carlyle of the NYSE informed our people a moment ago to tell me that he met with the head of the NASDAQ and that they felt it was in the best interest of the stability of the overall marketplace, for the markets to remain closed until they can isolate this virus program, or whatever it is. They said they would have preferred to re-open the markets for the sake of market psychology, but at the risk of this thing creating sell-programs again, it wasn't worth it."

"I would have to agree, sir," Meyers said.

"They said they were pretty confident they could isolate and remedy the problem by the morning and open by 9:30, even if they had to handwrite orders like the old days."

"I'm not so sure those weren't better days anyhow, Mr. Vice President," Meyers said, irritated by the growing number of technical setbacks they were encountering.

"I couldn't agree more," Morrison said.

"General," the director interrupted somewhat frantically. "We have a rather peculiar development out of Milan."

"What is it, Mr. Simonson?" Meyers asked impatiently. "Stand by, Mr. Vice President."

"If this is true, then we're dealing with an entirely different animal," Simonson said again. Two of his assistants who'd been following the Milan incident were monitoring conflicting intermittent reports, while simultaneously feeding a condensed account back to the director.

"Our sources in Milan have a seriously incongruous version of the La Scala bombing," the director reported anxiously. "Sources on the ground are telling us La Scala is still standing."

"What?"

"Sir," one of the assistants interrupted. "Apparently hundreds of amateur smart-phone videos have been sent to local media outlets in Milan, with the images suggesting that the bombing never took place."

"How is this possible?" the general asked, half in denial and half-curious. "And why would it take so long to confirm or deny such a report?"

"Just a theory, sir," the other assistant jumped in. "But what if someone generated a completely professional, studio-grade digital video of the fictitious bombing in Milan and…"

"And simultaneously," the first assistant interrupted, continuing his co-worker's rant. "That person or entity hi-jacks the broadcast signal long enough to air their own broadcast."

"So how do you shut down an entire broadcast grid?" Meyers asked skeptically.

"Simple," the other assistant resumed. "NSA can scramble a signal anywhere. Why can't someone else? You walk by the Israeli Embassy or a number of any other security-sensitive locations here in DC and they shut down any network within a hundred feet. We've proven what we could do in Iraq by scrambling an entire city's radio and communications frequencies. It set the stage for a completely uncontested invasion."

"That was a highly sophisticated military-grade exercise, with an impenetrable overlapping twelve-layer security grid," Meyers interrupted. "It would be impossible to duplicate in the private sector."

"Who do you think developed the technology for the military?" Simonson asked back.

Meyers just glared at the director's disarming frankness.

"Sir," the other tech continued, chiseling away at the ice between the director and general. "What if their intention was to hijack the signal long enough to air a really believable situation that never happened, simultaneously holding that broadcast grid hostage for the necessary time to spread panic? At the same time the communications grid was scrambled…"

"So those civilians or otherwise who could observe and phone in a conflicting report were frustrated at every attempt," Simonson observed, finishing his tech's hypothesis for him.

"Yes, sir," the tech confirmed. "And who's to say that the intention of the Prophet wasn't just to sell uncertainty for fifteen minutes?"

"Brilliant," Simonson said, amused by his two assistants of just six months. Both of them were highly-recruited MIT grads, coveted by the darlings of Silicon Valley. The director was privately ecstatic to have landed them both.

"Who's brilliant?" Meyers asked.

"Obviously our adversary is, general. You and I both know that he who controls the flow of information, in most cases controls the outcome of the war.

"For now," Meyers allowed. "Gentlemen, I want to know the second we can confirm this explosion never took place."

"Yes, sir," both techs chorused back, then spun around in their respective swivel chairs to continue their work.

"Seriously, general," Simonson continued. "Did it ever dawn on you why the Prophet keeps asking, 'What are the most dangerous kinds of bombs?'"

"No it hasn't, Mr. Simonson. What I do know is that a rogue group of heavily-armed militants have killed thirty-two fine young men and women, not counting an additional half-dozen waiters yet to be profiled, and have forcefully abducted ten of the most important people in the world."

"Fair enough, general. But maybe the Prophet is a separate entity within the rogue unit, who doesn't want to see bloodshed or be responsible for it. Maybe he thinks he can accomplish everything he needs to with chaos and confusion. Think about it, general. Why does he ask, 'What are the most dangerous kinds of bombs?' And then almost as if he's sending us a message, he answers, 'The kind that don't go boom.' He's selling fear and buying himself time all at once."

"No argument there, Mr. Simonson," Meyers acknowledged. "Keep working on your theory. I need to share this information with the vice president. Please let me know just as soon as it becomes fact."

"Absolutely, sir."

"Mr. Vice President, I don't how much of my conversation with the director you heard but…"

"Most of it, Gordon. But connect the dots for me, would you?"

"Our intel has reason to believe the explosion in Milan might not have been real."

"Great," Morrison exhaled, somewhat cynically. "Is any of this real?"

"There are thirty-eight real corpses in Vienna. That for sure is real. And until I find ten world leaders, I'd say their abduction is real. We've just received confirmation from the FBI-Interpol unit on location at Schaafhausen that all security personnel assigned to the G-10 have been accounted for. No one survived. It doesn't get any more real than that, sir."

Morrison weighed the general's report for a two-second beat and probed further. "Gordon, there was a woman assigned to the president—not part of any agency or Secret Service detail. I know her personally. Her father and I served thirty years together in the navy. I had personally hand-picked her to guard our president's life because of her fearlessness and capabilities. She's a machine. Do you understand the ramifications?"

"Are you referring to Ms. Jensen, sir?"

"I am."

"It doesn't look good," Meyers answered reluctantly. "We haven't found her body yet, but there were quite a few bloody female shoeprints near a pile of corpses, and she was the only female assigned to the detail. Forensics at the location say the prints could be size 7 ½ to size 8. Ms. Jensen wears an 8. The prints start near the front of the kitchen and lead to the back of the kitchen—then they seem to form a tight pattern in between the storage area and the service-elevator shaft, which, by the way, no longer has an elevator cab. An explosion disintegrated the cables that carried it, and the cab itself fell forty-eight floors. The shoeprints drag through the blood, indicating some kind of struggle. But there's no sign of her shoes, her, or anything else. We believe that young lady fought valiantly, then was overwhelmed and thrown down the elevator shaft, forty-eight floors to her death."

Morrison exhaled slowly and somberly. "Is there anything else, Gordon? I have to inform this poor girl's father."

"Uh, yes," Meyers answered grudgingly. "They found her bra stuck in a crack between the threshold and the elevator doorframe. I uh…sir, I don't even want to speculate what those filthy animals did to her before they hurled her down that shaft."

Morrison stiffened at the general's somber account of the alleged violation and ensuing death, taking several moments to analyze the so-called struggle, then broke the awkward silence. "General, I know this might sound a little overly optimistic, but I have a theory. First of all, do you really think this group of well-organized, highly skilled combatants would deviate from a plan that undoubtedly was months or years in the making, just for a piece of tail? A plan I might add that unquestionably didn't allow for too many spare seconds for anything *but* the plan," Morrison suggested, slowly and deliberately. "That's highly unlikely."

"But…" Meyers tried.

"Secondly, I've read accounts of what Ms. Jensen has accomplished on more than one occasion, against significant numbers of well-trained men—physically fit opponents, Gordon. She's overcome insurmountable odds that you and I can't even fathom," Morrison recounted. "General, until you find that body, I'm going to believe that girl is alive and doing her job. Do you understand?"

"Yes, sir."

"I will *not* be calling her father quite yet. Now let's listen to this son-of-a-bitch in Vienna."

"So let's resume with you, Monsieur Marceau. You had protested to the empire's invasion from the beginning of the proposed campaign back in late 2002—perhaps the loudest of all. What happened?"

"Well, as you know," French President Didier Marceau began. "At that time the evidence was inconclusive. And then…"

"And then what, Mr. Marceau?" the Prophet interrupted. "What changed your mind?"

"Well, after those of us from the international community attending the emergency session at the United Nations in New York saw the evidence that was presented in a manner that was completely conclusive—that Iraq posed a great threat not just to their neighbors in the Gulf, but to their neighbors in all of Europe—that's when we changed our stance."

"Unbelievable," the Prophet interrupted. "I can't believe a man of your intelligence would bend so readily in the face of such a weak and contrived demonstration."

"On the contrary, Monsieur Prophet, the evidence was conclusive. And you know that France also has a large Arab and Muslim population. So it was not a particularly easy decision to make."

"You behave just as the others," the Prophet exhaled, flicking his wrist at Marceau. "You're just another puppet."

"I am sorry you think so," Marceau said.

But before he could continue, the Prophet held up his hand, directing the French president to stop speaking. The Prophet continued down the line at the conference table to the next leader, the Canadian Prime Minister Scott Hammons. "How are you feeling, Mr. Hammons?" the Prophet asked. "You've had a rather trying day."

"I'm fine," Hammons said, pretending to be impervious to being knocked unconscious twice in one day. As defiant as he intended to be, he knew he wasn't entirely lucid either. He had a lump on the back of his head as well as the front. The cut just above his blonde hair line had produced a small trickle of blood that ran down the right side of his face, occasionally interfering with his vision. Fortunately his captors had granted him some leniency and switched his handcuffed wrists back to in front of him, so he could drink from a water bottle like the rest, and swipe the trickle of blood away from his eye with his tattered sleeve.

"Again, we would prefer not treating you like we did earlier. Just behave like a world leader and not a ruffian," the Prophet offered.

"Elegant gentlemen such as you don't usually practice such bad table manners around women, let alone world leaders," Hammons offered back.

"Fair enough, Mr. Hammons. But desperate means sometimes require desperate measures. Now, shall we get back to business?"

"Let's," Hammons said, eager to share his two cents. "I was in New York during 911, and while I didn't see the planes actually flying into the Twin Towers, I've watched replays of it over and over and over again. And I have seen the videos of this conspiratorial spoof alleging that the former leaders of the United States had something to do with the destruction of their own buildings. It's ludicrous! It's utter insanity. It's inconceivable and so far-fetched that anyone who believes in God, or goodness, or simply humanity would destroy these buildings, or any other buildings in their own backyard, and the thousands of lives within, just to gain the support of most of the world which supported them and their stance to begin with."

"Another brainwashed puppet," the Prophet exhaled, shaking his head at what he perceived as another formulaic answer.

"Mr. Prophet, we simply don't operate like that here in the West," Hammons continued. "Our countries were founded on the belief in God, and the Judeo-Christian teachings in the Bible. While the Middle Eastern countries share a similar belief in God, or Allah, it is through Islam and the teachings of Mohammed that you base your Quran," the Canadian explained emphatically. "The Bible professes preserving lives, not taking them. From everything we could see not just from the West, but from most of the world's standpoint, was that the destruction of the World Trade center was the ultimate display of fascio-radical Muslim hatred of Christians and their desire to kill them…"

"Damn it!" the Prophet blasted while launching himself at the Canadian, cursing in Farsi. "Mr. Hammons, the West has been killing Muslims for decades—innocent Muslims!" he hissed. Two of the militants immediately came up from behind the Canadian, pressing their weapons into his back.

"Hey, I've had enough of your goons here," Hammons said respectfully, half-turning then cringing forward in anticipation of what he thought was another hunk of armor headed to the back of his head. "I give up. I don't want to fight with you anymore, Mr. Prophet. I'm just trying to give you an honest answer. We don't murder innocent people," the former college hockey player continued, never one to stand down when provoked. Still, he also hadn't quite recovered from the previous two blows to the head. But Hammons also knew in the back of his mind that there was a better-than-likely chance he wouldn't be alive much longer anyway, so he maintained his conviction.

"Tens of thousands of innocent Muslims murdered!" the Prophet blasted so angrily that he was unaware he was spitting at the same time. "And the people of the West never hear about our children—just your own!"

"We are not murderers!" Hammons growled, at first still hovering close to the conference table. Then he felt the hair on the back of his neck stand up, and he unconsciously moved in closer to the Prophet. They were now face-to-face. "It is no secret that Muslim extremists hate, and Muslim extremists kill!"

In an instant the two were heatedly exchanging words at close range with both parties convinced they held the truth, both of them completely losing all composure. But remarkably the Canadian kept his cuffed hands low enough so as not to be perceived as a threat. Still, one of the militants raised the butt of his assault rifle, ready to pound the back of the Canadian's head again.

The American president could hardly believe Hammons' voracity in the face of all of the firepower and urged him to back off. "Stand down, Scott!" Haydon cried out. "For the love of God, stop it!" Her plea was followed by the others attempting to restrain him.

The Pentagon, 2:24 p.m.

"Good God," Meyers mouthed the words, while gripping the top of his forehead with one hand. "What is he thinking?"

"What the hell is Hammons doing?" the VP blurted out.

"He's doing exactly what I would be doing, sir."

"We got it," a voice said from several feet away.

"General, we've got a lock on their signal," Director Simonson reiterated.

"Move on it, now!" Meyers barked. "Let's go people! Simonson, get our people over there on it. Put a blanket on these parasites, now!"

"We're on it, general," Simonson said firmly, then speed-dialed a number on his sat-phone. In a moment he was speaking to the FBI task force in Vienna, giving them exact coordinates of their point of interception. That information was immediately dispatched to every other law enforcement group in Austria, and the appropriate recon teams were immediately mobilized.

The two techs that'd been trying to authenticate the Milan bombing were simultaneously trying to get the director's attention. On one of the tech's monitors were images from an amateur video of La Scala and a crowd of people gathered in front of the famous opera house. Italian subtitles describing the situation moved from right-to-left in the small band at the bottom of the screen. The second monitor aired a network broadcast of a Milanese reporter also in front of the fabled structure—again Italian subtitles below the images. "Mr. Simonson," one of the techs persisted.

"Not now," Simonson said, holding up his hand, but quickly snuck a glance of the two monitors, then rejoined the general.

Meyers and the Pentagon's war room staff watched the broadcast on the main large screen monitor as the scene from somewhere in Austria intensified. The Canadian was insistent on making his point, temporarily forgetting he was about to incite a potentially horrific event. All the while, his constituents begged him to back down.

"God help us," the vice president mouthed the words from his secure location.

Austria, 8:45 p.m.

The militant monitoring the laptop's programs froze momentarily as he'd learned their signal had been discovered by an outside agent. He shouted for the Prophet to return but the commotion was still too loud. Instead he showed the commander just off of his left flank, who'd been observing the near-fracas but remained at the head of the table as instructed, anxiously clutching the remote. The commander observed the tracking agent, as the militant operating the computer explained to him what it meant exactly. His face grew rigid as he took a few steps toward the shouting match a few feet away, then he cried out to the Prophet, loudly enough for him to hear the interruption. "They've discovered our signal," he said in Farsi then returned to his post a few steps away.

The Prophet shouted at the Canadian to keep quiet. He was running out of patience though, and after one too many seconds of defiant chatter from Hammons, the Prophet ordered him to be physically quieted. Immediately the militant with a cocked and loaded butt of an assault weapon obliged, and Hammons slumped into his chair unconscious with what would very soon be a fresh lump on the back of his head.

The Prophet rejoined the militant operating the computer, and cursed as he was shown the tracking agent on the screen. He shoved aside the operator, as his fingertips danced across the keyboard like a professional stenographer, trying desperately to bounce their signal. Now he yelled at the commander in another language altogether, that no one in the room could recognize.

Sylvia, however, recognized the Arabic language immediately. The banks! The banks! The banks!

In an instant the commander depressed another button on the remote, while the captives and the world held its collective breath. There was nothing Sylvia could do.

CHAPTER 10

Boston, 2:51 p.m.

Colleen Quinn inserted her debit card into the ATM at the Yawkey Avenue branch of Bank of New England to get her daily twenty-dollar withdrawal. She'd performed this routine for nearly five years since getting a job at the sports memorabilia shop near Fenway Park. Every day she took the train in from Braintree where she grew up and currently still lived with her parents, then made her withdrawal. From there she'd get her tall café mocha and a bear claw at Starbucks, leaving her enough change for dinner and the T-line back home.

It was a typical, blistering cold winter day in Boston, as flakes of snow drifted down gently onto Colleen's navy blue-and-red-knit Red Sox cap, which covered just a portion of her long dark hair. She wore a pair of Levi's 501 jeans and a matching knee-length Red Sox down parka suitable for any of winter's elements, covering her fit figure. She removed one of her gloves to insert her card into the ATM and type in the code needed for the withdrawal, while her warm breath turned to steam as it met the frigid air. The ATM display said that there were insufficient funds to make the withdrawal. Colleen was a woman of limited means, but she was also well aware of what was in her account. And there was plenty left in there to make the withdrawal.

She removed her card then started over. The same message was displayed on the ATM screen. In the meantime several more patrons bundled up for winter's elements had formed a small line behind her, adding their smoky exhalations into the frigid air.

"Hey lady, come on already," one of the patrons said.

"Hey!" Quinn answered back, while turning briefly to assess the origin of the voice. The man issuing the impatient decree was exactly what she had envisioned, a short, thickly built roughneck who hadn't shaved in nearly a week. His face was nearly covered with his black knit cap. Ughh, she thought, and her mouth finished what she was thinking. "Put a cork in it, all right? The fuckin' thing doesn't work."

"Yeah, whatever. Ya probably got no money in there."

Colleen took her card out, grabbed her glove, and then walked by the man on her way into the bank. "See ya inside, pal," she said.

"I doubt it," he fired back.

Colleen walked into the bank and took her place in line. In a little over a minute a teller called her to come up to her window. "How can I help you?"

"Hi," Colleen said. "I tried to get money out of my account out at the ATM, and it said that there were insufficient funds in my account. And I know I've got money in there."

"Let's see what we can do about that," the teller said, then instructed Colleen to swipe her ATM card in the card reader on the countertop. She'd heard all of the excuses in the world from people who simply didn't record their withdrawals, then wonder why they didn't have sufficient funds to withdraw from. But at the same time it was her job to be pleasant. "Now type in your P.I.N. code."

"Is this gonna take long?" Colleen asked. "I have to be at work pretty soon."

"Hopefully not," the teller replied, while studying her computer screen for a moment. "It shows that you withdrew twenty dollars yesterday..."

"...And the day before," Colleen added, "and the day before that."

"Yes, I can see that," the teller said. "But I'm showing the one that you made yesterday left you with a zero balance."

"What are ya talkin' about here?" Colleen snapped, while fumbling around in her purse with one hand. "First of all, no one has a zero balance. You have three dollars and forty-seven cents, or seven hundred thirty-five dollars and sixty-eight cents. But ya don't have just zero dollars," Colleen explained, and then produced several ATM receipts, crumpled from a normal day's hand-entries into a purse.

"I understand," the teller replied calmly, trying to sooth her agitated customer.

When Colleen found the receipt with yesterday's date and withdrawal, she handed it to the teller. "See? I told ya," she said, pointing to the balance midway down on the receipt. It read "seven hundred thirty-five dollars and sixty-seven cents."

"That was close," the teller remarked, surprised at the accuracy of her customer's verbal estimate of what was in her own account. "And you're sure you didn't make a purchase yesterday or…"

"…For the exact amount of what's in the account?" Colleen quipped. "C'mon."

"All right," the teller said. "Let me speak with our manager. It'll be just a minute."

"Fine."

The teller got up, walked back to her manager's desk, and explained the situation. After a moment, the matronly manager returned with the teller, said her pleasantries to Colleen, and then viewed the computer screen. "Hmmm," she mused.

Suddenly the front door to the bank opened and the loud-mouthed man walked in from outside. "Hey, you took all of my money out of my account," he shouted, with a panicked look on his face.

A moment later another customer walked in and shouted, "Hey, where's my money?"

"Hey, what's goin' on here?" Colleen asked, suddenly a bit panicked herself. "I really do need some money!"

The branch manager tried to keep the handful of irritated customers calm, while scrambling for answers. Her fingers raced across the keypad of the teller's computer, attempting all of her manual override procedures. But with every minute that ticked off the clock, another disgruntled customer charged through the front door, inquiring where the bank's money had vanished to. In just a half an hour, the bank was boiling over, full of angry, frightened customers. Apparently, every customer in the bank's lobby was running a zero balance. Unbeknownst to *all* of the bank's customers, so was the Yawkey Avenue branch of the Bank of New England.

Word traveled quickly throughout the neighborhood of the local branch's problems. Unfortunately those customers who'd abandoned the Yawkey branch in pursuit of another branch quickly came to realize that more than one branch had no money to give out.

In fact every bank in the greater Boston area disclosed that their computers indicated that there was no money to be had by anyone. When it was discovered that *all* of New England's banks had run out of money, panic started to grip the region. Suddenly, there was a run on groceries, water and gasoline—everyday things that people had taken for granted but now they weren't sure if they'd be there tomorrow.

New England wasn't the only region in a cash crunch. The banking problem had since swept down the eastern seaboard through New York, the Carolinas, and all the way down to the tip of Florida. There were reports of similar problems starting to trickle in from the Midwest.

The obvious counter measure, using one's credit card to circumvent the banking debacle, was quickly rendered ineffective as every single swipe of a card at a store, restaurant, or gas station produced the same result; it was over the spending limit.

While local and regional leaders urged calm, this quickly gave way to fear and panic. It seemed a society accustomed to convenience couldn't overcome what it perceived as a sudden drought of food, gas, and alcohol, even *if* refrigerators and gas tanks were still full. At the moment, panic was the only possible emotion.

One thing became certain: Cash was paramount. If you had it, you'd be able to weather the fiscal storm, although you might have to isolate yourself from those who didn't have it for fear of the unknown. If you didn't have it, there were those who might resort to unfathomable measures to get it.

The barkeeper and his usual afternoon customers at Jimmy O'Reilly's tavern in Boston's south end watched the three new flat screens for the network coverage of the unfolding events occurring up and down the coast. There were isolated incidents of fistfights over a single dollar, near brawls at gas stations, and the breaking story out of Florida of a young mother who went on a rampage in front of her three young children in a grocery store because all of her credit cards and debit card were rejected at the checkout. She was set off when the store manager had informed the woman her twelve bags of groceries would have to remain until she could compensate the market for her wares.

Jimmy O'Reilly wasn't all that concerned about the panic though. The way he'd figured it, people always drank during a crisis, and that was good for business. All of his patrons were locals. If they didn't have cash, an IOU would do just fine. This banking thing couldn't last forever, he'd figured.

When word of the banking and credit card crisis reached the west coast, there was an initial surge in spending across the board in those regions as a preventive measure. It was probably another overreaction, but emotional people tend to gravitate toward the Armageddon theory, it was human nature after all. If the same militants who were holding the G-10 leaders hostage could strike our central nervous system—our banks—then in fact they could hit at anyplace, and perhaps at any time. Conventional wisdom suggested it didn't hurt to have a few extra groceries around the house.

Within two hours of the initial reports out of New England, the stranglehold on U.S. financial institutions and its customers blanketed the entire US grid. Financial institutions released sanitized statements nationwide urging calm in the face of what they were calling a system-wide glitch, and reminded everyone that the entire network was backed up. Trillions of dollars simply didn't just vanish, they reiterated. There were stopgap measures to ensure against any such fallout. It just would take time, they assured.

But later that afternoon the banking crisis had breached both the Canadian *and* Mexican borders. Any semblance of calm was suddenly in jeopardy on a national basis.

London, 9:01 p.m.

A similar horror story was unfolding in the greater London area, as ATMs were no longer dispensing Pounds or Euros. Pub crawlers and diners alike were suddenly placed on a cash-only basis, creating considerable embarrassment for those not carrying pockets full of the local tender, which in today's electronic society were most patrons. After all, wads of cash were bulky, attracted pickpockets, and didn't earn you miles.

London's story quickly became Brussels' story, and that spread to Paris, Munich, Zurich, Madrid, Lisbon and most of Europe. The inability to conduct commerce without cash quickly brought the continent to a standstill in a country that was already operating at half-speed due to the crisis in Austria.

Just a short while ago most Europeans were watching the televised coverage of America's banking fallout. Now they were joined at the hip. As was the case in America, international media centers recommended calm while authorities worked on the new crisis unfolding throughout Europe and America.

While anxious citizens on both sides of the Atlantic Ocean scrambled to find cold hard currency, London's gold futures were very quietly surging through the roof, shattering the crucial resistance mark of $2,000 an ounce. Brent North Sea crude oil futures were trading right in tandem, aggressively pushing through $130 a barrel. It would be just a matter of time before the gasoline futures would flirt with six dollars a gallon in America.

CHAPTER 11

Washington D.C., 4:09 p.m.

In the process of securing and mapping DNA evidence at Schaafhausen, the task force had located the UN staff photographer's camera that had been shattered to smithereens. Unfortunately for the kidnappers, the commander had failed to destroy the tiny wafer memory card that contained an account of all the afternoon's digital images, including the dozen eerie images snapped automatically by the photographer merely as a reaction to the earsplitting shock he was exposed to. The images were shared throughout the international intelligence community, revealing the grotesque contorted expressions on the faces of the G-10 leaders reacting to glass and crystal shrapnel, and showers of red wine and water. There wasn't a word spoken in the Pentagon war room or vice president's clandestine bunker as all who were present observed the disturbing sequence of images.

Austria, 10:13 p.m.

The Prophet's quick handiwork on the laptop enabled him to refract his signal's broadcast to another location and avert their discovery again, this time to a Graz based warehouse in southern Austria. It was a closer call than he'd expected, as he thought his tech was able to read the tracking program better and react more quickly. For a brief moment, sounds of air surveillance could be heard overhead. But there wasn't a shred of infrared light that could be seen from their remote abandoned location, and those aircraft just moved on.

The Prophet had asked the commander to deploy four of his militants to stand guard at the back of the warehouse in the event of a penetration. He'd speculated it would only be a matter of time before counter-intelligence would lock onto their signal again. There were counter-measures in place for just about every scenario, but careless mistakes would compromise everything they'd planned for.

The Prophet concluded the surrounding hills had to be swarming with highly skilled guerillas with infrared night vision goggles and every other enhancement for battle, or if not now, then very soon. Even though he held the world leaders captive and the commander had a remote with four unused buttons, a penetration of significant force by their opponent would be devastating.

Among the four selected to guard the underbelly of the fortress was Sylvia. Her hazel eyes riveted on her three adversaries, yearning for the opportunity to sever a larynx, or three—or just simply drill several slugs into their temples. Their method of death was inconsequential. She'd been handed a gift; three of the remaining eleven militants were hers for the taking, completely separated from the commander with the remote.

The four deployed militants quickly convened in the back of the warehouse where the four Hummers and laundry van were parked. They discussed an established plan to send half their unit up onto the roof, through the warehouse access stairs, which was a typical simple, forged metal rack strapped to the wall opposite the laundry van.

One of the militants opened the back of the laundry van to access several black cases in the rear of the van. He opened the first case and pulled out two thin black camouflaged down jumpsuits to protect the two volunteering militants from winter's brutal elements while they went to their respective posts up on the roof. After they slipped into the jumpsuits, they were each handed a pair of black insulated gloves.

Once they were fully dressed for the Arctic cold outside, both were outfitted with shoulder-strapped grenade launchers found in the second black case, and a considerable cache of ammunition. Each placed a pair of night vision goggles onto their heads just above their ski-mask covered hairline, and then strapped their AK-74s over the top of all of the other layers, and ascended the stairs. Attached to the night vision apparatus was a three-inch stemmed microphone with the coordinating earpiece, enabling the two militants headed up to the roof to communicate with the two remaining in the warehouse as well as the commander in the conference room.

At the top of the steps was a three-foot square metal access panel with a locking, oval-shaped hand lever. The lead militant tried to turn the knob but it was resistant. He clutched the top rung of the staircase with his left hand and delivered several forceful pops from the butt of his right palm, jarring the knob loose. He pushed the panel open and cautiously climbed up and onto the roof, still maintaining a low profile. In the event the thickly wooded forest just beyond was swarming with counter-agents, the slightest movement would surely compromise their location. Moments later the second militant, Sylvia, emerged up through the access panel and onto the roof, initially sitting on her haunches, quickly surveying a three-hundred-sixty degree view for potential predators. Just as quickly she closed the metal hatch and pounded it twice, signaling her two comrades below to lock them out.

The commercial complex abutted the icy Danube on the backside, and it was nearly twenty feet up the back face of the concrete wall of the building—a wall which was frozen and nearly impossible to scale. The two-man unit speculated that it was highly unlikely a counter-assault team would make an attempt to climb that side of the compound, at least not without making considerable noise, giving them the necessary window to counter such an assault.

On the side where they accessed the rooftop, they could see the dense forest from which they'd emerged with their vehicles earlier in the day. Down below was the caged-in parking area, locked off to the outside world. Their group occupied the second unit in a row of eight office-warehouses, all connected with a common concrete wall, typical construction for a complex such as this.

The location of the building was extremely remote which is why it had been abandoned by all except for one tenant, who rarely made office visits.

Except for the occasional breeze rustling through the pine trees opposite the complex, the night was still. The ominous cloud cover that threatened to blanket its white flurry over the region allowed occasional glimpses of light from the three-quarters moon.

The two militants lowered their night vision goggles and moved quickly over to the edge of the building that overlooked the thick forest just fifty meters away. From there, they could observe while using the one-foot cantilevered raised edge of the building for cover. They disengaged from their arsenal long enough to hit their bellies and assume the assault position, their AK-74s aimed at would-be assailants.

The Prophet went live once again, having launched chaos all over western society and managing to avert a near-miss on his own operation. The financial markets were closed, and institutions and individuals alike were frozen with their assets, if there were any assets at all. In the coming hours, any buying or selling of just about everything in Europe and North America would come to a screeching halt.

"Welcome back," he said, from the head of the conference table. "As I'd mentioned, beware of the silent bombs. I implore you to think long and hard about these ridiculous attempts to discover our location. You have so much to lose, not to mention the safety of your leaders. The next explosion might not be so nice," the Prophet said, and then gave an order to the commander, which made stomachs uneasy all over the world.

The commander in turn gave an order to two of the remaining militants. They quickly walked to the corner behind the Prophet's left flank to a large ice chest. One opened the chest and they both retrieved as many sandwiches wrapped in clear plastic-wrap as they could carry back to the table, distributing them to several of the ten leaders. They made two more visits to the chest to make sure the remainder of the occupants of the room, including their fellow militants had a sandwich and enough water to wash it down with. The four militants assigned to the back of the warehouse and roof had taken theirs with them.

It had been quite a while since anyone had eaten—both the captives and captors. At least the captors didn't suffer indigestion due to their presence at a massacre. Regardless, the day's tension had created a roomful of hungry occupants.

"You see," the Prophet said, in the direction of the camera. "We aren't monsters. We will take very good care of your leaders if everyone behaves themselves. Now we will take a ten-minute recess for dinner before we resume." The Prophet then took a small bite of his sandwich, dabbing at the corners of his mouth with a paper napkin.

Marge Haydon tore ravenously into the ham and Swiss cheese on a baguette, and then washed the first bite down with a swig of water. She had no idea how hungry one could get from being held hostage at gunpoint. It wasn't The Fifth Floor in San Francisco, but right now it tasted every bit as good.

"You have a spot of mustard at the corner of your mouth," Edgar Elliott said to Haydon, traces of a subtle smile etched into his expression. Then he took a moderate-sized bite from his baguette.

"Umm, sorry. I hope you'll forgive me," Haydon replied, while putting the finishing touches on her first bite of sandwich. "I didn't realize how hungry I was." Then she paused for a moment to wipe her mouth.

"Not a problem," Elliott said, in between nibbles of his sandwich.

"Mind you, the circumstances couldn't be any more sinister," Robin Collinsworth commented before taking a bite of his sandwich.

"This is heaven," Claudia Schmidt said, aggressively consuming her dinner.

"I don't know if I'd go that far," Scott Hammons offered. "But maybe it would be after another bump on my head? Perhaps," he added, winking with his blood-crusted eye at the Prophet, who remained stone-faced, as he chomped on the crunchy end of his sandwich. Then he deferred to the Chinese president. "What about you, Mr. Zheng?"

The Prophet didn't react to the Canadian's cynical quip. Even more oddly he allowed the leaders to continue their harmless dialogue.

"What about me?" Zheng asked.

"Do you consider this heaven?" Hammons repeated the German's assessment.

"No ," Zheng answered stoically. "And wouldn't it be a bit cliché of me to say that there's no fried rice, so how could this possibly be heaven?" the usually tight-lipped leader asked, while the others found his jibe humorous enough to laugh freely.

"I can do better," Zheng continued. "There is a place—somewhat of a whole in the wall—near the top of Lan Kwai Fong Road on Hong Kong Island. They make the most incredible Peking duck. I don't what they do but it's the best I've ever had. The skin is delicious and perfectly crisp, while the duck-breast inside is succulent and tender beyond belief," he explained, wondering if he'd ever get to revisit his old haunt again. "Right about now, it might just constitute heaven for me."

"It definitely sounds a little more heavenly than the current venue," Schmidt noted, glancing to the head of the table, "with all due respect, Mr. Prophet."

The Prophet had hardly heard her comment, as he was talking with the tech next to him; hence there was no acknowledgement.

"What about you, Monsieur Marceau?" Hammons asked the French president.

"Well, we have baguettes. That's a step in the right direction," he explained. "There is no brie, but there is hope for the world after all."

"And you, Signore Veroni?" Hammons asked the Italian leader.

"Perhaps they're serving the pasta dish next," Veroni retorted, then turned to the Russian president. "What about you, Mr. Nobakov? Can you do better than pasta for the next dish?"

"Of course," Alexander Nobakov answered awkwardly, because of his full mouth. First the husky-voiced Russian patted his napkin at the corners of his mouth while finishing the sizable bite of sandwich, then patted at the perspiration gathering on his forehead. "The next time we choose to have an intimate get-together like this, we will do so in my country, where I can make sure we start with the very best of Russian caviar."

"Ahhh, very nice," Didier Marceau said. "You are a man after my own heart."

"Yes, well," the Russian said, raising his water bottle. "Here's to French champagne and Russian caviar."

"Hear here!" Collinsworth chimed in, holding up his water bottle.

For a brief moment, the other world leaders raised their water bottles, joining in the toast, while easing just for an instant.

The Prophet observed the uneasy banter among of his captives, amused by their fanciful imaginations.

"And what would be your choice, Mr. Tanaka?" Nobakov asked. "What will you bring to the table?"

"If I may be permitted," Yoshito Tanaka started. "Only the finest Imperial Kobe Beef."

"Splendid main course," Elliott acknowledged.

"Indeed," Collinsworth added slowly, turning his head and shoulders toward Tanaka. "Well done, sir."

"I'll have mine medium-rare, thanks," President Haydon snapped, prodding a few weak laughs.

While the ten captives salivated over a meal that might never be, they each chomped away on their baguette, while slugging big gulps of water to wash it down. The room remained very warm, and with the rate of water consumption it was inevitable the restroom would need to be revisited by most, with or without the assistance of the American mercenary.

The Prophet did take notice of the Russian's sweaty brow, as well as some of the others. He too was warm, especially with the knit ski-mask he was forced to wear. He stood for a moment and whispered something into the commander's ear, while every set of eyes in the room followed him. In turn, the commander ordered one of the militants in the room to go out into the hallway, find the thermostat, and turn the temperature down.

On the top of roof of the office complex the two heavily armed militants also ate.

"What will your family do with your new earthly riches?" Sylvia asked the other militant, while chomping on the crunchy baguette hardened even more by the frigid air.

He had to think awhile about how to respond to this question. So many of these aspiring militants were easy recruiting targets for these sorts of well-financed terrorist cells organized by the likes of the Prophet and the commander. They had assembled clandestine homegrown networks of hungry and fierce Muslim loyalists training and operating in the arid mountainous regions of both Iran and Afghanistan. Conventional wisdom was when you had nothing, death as an option wasn't such a terrible alternative—especially when your family could be the beneficiary.

"I hope that they will find a better way," the second militant answered, pondering that very notion. "My two boys are smart, but they are limited in what they can achieve in my country. I would love for them to have the opportunity to go to school in the west somewhere, maybe even America. What about you, my brother? What will your family do?"

"Perhaps the same," Sylvia answered, still chewing on her baguette. "My wife and daughter have always said how much they would love to go live in London. We have relatives there in a nice neighborhood called Notting Hill."

"Tell me about Notting Hill," the second militant queried, while taking another bite of his meal.

"We were there once about five years ago. They live on a street called Portobello Road. On the weekends, they transform this entire street into an open market where you can get just about anything you can think of."

"Like what?"

"Like clothes, like music, like everything—there are fresh fruits and vegetables. There are butchers to cut any kind of meat you could want. Some will even barbeque it right there for you. There are old antiques of every type, and there are even rugs imported from our home country there."

"Really?"

"Yes, really," Sylvia explained, spinning her fanciful tale, then took another small bite from her sandwich. "And you can go to restaurants and have just about every kind of food."

"Like what?" the other asked.

"Anything—even Persian food. There are a lot of our people there."

"It's too bad I'll never get a chance to see London," the inquisitive militant said. "I would probably like it there."

"I'm sure you would. And don't say never, because you never know," Sylvia assured. "Anyhow, that's where I hope my family can end up. My son would go to school at Oxford, and become a great man one day I'm sure. And he's a big footballer. He loves a team called Manchester United, and wants to play for them one day. So he could play and study with the best."

"That would be nice," the second militant said, then pondered for a moment. "Isn't it funny how we're at war with those we wish to live amongst?"

"It is strange, isn't it?" Sylvia added, and then suddenly turned her head hard to the right, reacting to something, while dropping her baguette onto the roof.

"What is it?" the second militant asked, reacting to his comrade's sudden move.

"Shhh!" Sylvia said, placing her first finger to her lips, then thrusting herself to her haunches and swiveling toward the back of the building, her AK-74 pointing in the same direction. She signaled to her comrade to join him in pursuit of what lurked over the edge of the back of the building.

Quickly the second man was on his haunches as well, with his weapon drawn. He moved in unison with his comrade as both of them tracked down their respective sides of the roof, while keeping a low profile, advancing further into the black horizon while lowering their night-vision eyewear, until they could peep over the back edge of the building.

First Sylvia crept ever so slowly to the edge, ready to fire at anything that might disturb the fragile night, until she finally poked her nose over the edge of the building for a look, and just as quickly retreated from what would have been the view of any enemies. On the opposite side of the roof the second militant repeated his comrade's move, and then pulled back quickly as well.

Sylvia then repeated her initial surveillance over the edge but held her position this time for a few seconds to discover nothing ascending up the wall, and pulled back again—not necessarily concerned for her own life, but as a precaution to the preservation of the mission. The second man seemed to mirror every move of his comrade who was now holding position, looking out over the Danube's black waters. There was no watercraft in the immediate vicinity to indicate an amphibious assault, but the two militants dissected the calm waters for even a ripple that might be out of place.

After approximately two minutes of surveying every corner and shadow of the rooftops of all eight units, Sylvia finally conceded "False alarm," barely louder than a whisper, but loud enough to be heard by her comrade who she soon joined on the opposite corner.

"Sorry to spoil your dinner," she acknowledged, while easing her trigger finger from the weapon and onto his comrade's shoulder.

"It's fine," the second man offered. "It was just a sandwich."

"Yes," Sylvia agreed, while removing her hand from the other man's shoulder, and ever-so-carefully sliding it back to rest on her hip. "It was just a sandwich." But her hand didn't rest for long on her hip. It slipped into the back of her gear belt almost motionlessly while encouraging the other man to elaborate about moving his family to the west.

While one man shared his new vision for his family, Sylvia's fingers latched onto her silenced firearm and ever-so-smoothly retrieved it and positioned it down at her side. The other man's knit ski cap coupled with the head gear became his blind periphery. She added enough conversational fuel to keep the other militant describing a vivid dream of a better life for his family while she stealthily moved her gun hand up the middle of the talkative man's back at close range without touching him. As she eased the weapon to the point where she was comfortable with the element of surprise, her finger squeezed the trigger, discharging two quick rounds of ammunition into the back of the man's head.

In an instant the militant's body slumped into his assailant's arms, as a miniscule final exhale escaped from his lungs. The tap the round made on entry was similar in pitch to a bee-bee pellet bouncing off of a pane of glass. And although both of their mouthpieces were still in the up position, Sylvia had hoped desperately the noise went unnoticed downstairs. She couldn't waste any time positioning her fallen comrade.

She immediately stuffed the firearm back into her gear belt with one hand while propping up the limp corpse with her other arm and hip, then removed his headset and dragged him back toward the back edge of the building. She hurled his headset out into the blackened Danube and laid him down, positioning him into an assault posture, placing the AK-74 in his arms so that he had the appearance of a soldier guarding the back of their fortress.

"What's going on up there?" a voice from downstairs barked. "We haven't heard a word from you two in five minutes."

Sylvia then lowered her mouthpiece into talk position and spoke. "It's a beautiful night, my brother. We were enjoying our exquisite dinner under a romantic moon-lit sky. Won't you come and join us?"

"You have five more minutes until shift change," the voice said back gruffly.

Then Sylvia altered the octave of her voice to reflect her fallen comrade's voice as best she could. "It's very lonely up here without you two," she quipped and manufactured a weak laugh.

"Patience brothers," the voice said back. "Patience."

Sylvia needed only those five more minutes of patience before she could terminate two more targets. Until then she would have to wait in the chilly embrace of the silent Austrian night.

Chapter 12

Vice Presidential bunker, 5:14 p.m.

"Good evening, my fellow Americans and North Americans," Vice President Morrison began to address a continent desperate for the stabilizing hand of reason. "As you all know by now, our own President Marge Haydon along with the nine other leaders of the G-10, have been abducted and taken hostage by a group of militants in Vienna, Austria. Though their exact location is still unclear, we know that they are being held somewhere in Austria.

"As you also know, since you've more than likely been watching the same broadcast we've been watching, all of the leaders are alive and doing well at the moment. We thank the Prophet, as we have come to know him, *and* his constituents for the continuing humane treatment of these ten world leaders. We welcome an open dialogue with the Prophet, by means other than a one-way broadcast. We would like to know what we can do to help resolve this situation."

Pentagon, 5:16 p.m.

General Meyers recoiled at the vice president's words, but also knew that he had no choice. They'd discussed it and agreed that America had to take a leadership role in the attempt to calm the international community, while softening their rhetoric and try to entice these militants into dialogue.

MI6 and the German Intelligence Agency, BND, had come close to isolating the rogue unit's broadcast signal on several occasions, but their attempts were also thwarted by the evasive handiwork of their talented adversary.

Director Simonson had been brought up to speed with the alleged Milan bombing by the two assistants, and all indications were that the entire event was a hoax on a grand scale. The historic structure was intact, and all of the film festival's participants had been accounted for.

"Fear and uncertainty, general," the director conveyed.

"I should probably be elated that no one lost their lives, Mr. Simonson," Meyers explained. "And don't get me wrong, I am. But how do you think this makes us look? How were they able to hijack and manipulate a pretty significant network for as long as they did, wreaking near-term trepidation, followed by this banking fallout? These are no ordinary acts."

"Resources, sir, *and* technology. Put the two together and an entity has the ability to create illusions, or the perfect storm. And in this case they've crafted utter confusion. Can you imagine the uneasiness when the global community discovers that Milan was a hoax?"

"Initially, relief," Meyers pointed out. "But on the heels of the banking debacle and Wall Street, I'd imagine ambiguity and confusion."

"Exactly," Simonson agreed. "And I hate to be the bearer of bad news, but I think they know exactly how we look, general—vulnerable. That was the plan. Now whether we're really this porous or not remains to be answered. But if they have the kind of resources that it appears, and the know-how, we might not have seen anything yet."

"Why did I know you'd say something encouraging like that?"

"Look at the bright side, sir. Clearly the Prophet is the mastermind of the operation, and obviously much brighter than either one of us gave him credit for, but he doesn't appear to be the monster that some of his associates are."

"At least for now," Meyers allowed. "And time will tell if he's got a handle on his monsters."

"Indeed it will, general," Simonson said. At that moment, they both paused to acknowledge the vice president's words.

"Now to address the issues concerning the stock market, as well as our recent banking problems," Morrison continued. "I can say this with the highest confidence. I have been informed from the directors of all of our financial institutions that we *will* open all of the major indices tomorrow morning as normally scheduled. Our sources have informed us a virus of sorts was unleashed into the computer programs that created or exacerbated an already fragile situation on Wall Street.

"If you didn't liquidate your holdings, I urge you not to. Further selling will only fuel the panic. If you did sell your stocks, I am told that there is no better time to buy them back than right now. After all, nothing has changed fundamentally from yesterday to today, with the exception of our great leaders being abducted. And we *will* get them back.

"Now, with regard to this banking fiasco—rest assured that all of the banking systems throughout the United States are, and have always been, backed up. In other words every penny of information is stored and safe in secure storage locations," Morrison said firmly, trying to suppress his frustration caused by the day's events. "Rest assured, every penny of your hard-earned money is, and always has been, safely stored in the same bank that you left it in the day before. We have a legion of code crackers working on this problem as we speak.

"My fellow North Americans, I implore you not to panic," Morrison continued, inclusive of those from Canada and Mexico who were watching. "If you have food at home in your refrigerators, then go home and eat. Go home, hug your families, and try to stay involved in your normal activities as good citizens. And for God's sake, don't prey upon our vulnerable store owners for something that will be available tomorrow through conventional means. They are your fellow citizens after all. If you have gasoline in your cars, then don't feed the frenzy by joining the lines at the gas stations because you think you need to top off your fuel tanks. Please remember, we've seen worse crises in our time, and we *will* get through this trying moment as well.

"*If* for any reason we have not resolved these situations by tomorrow morning at seven a.m. Eastern Standard Time, then I have authorized an emergency act for a voucher system that will go into effect at that time. The system will work like this. All commercial vendors across the board will commence the government-backed sales of gasoline, groceries, prescriptions, or any other emergency ticket items, using simple, specially marked paper vouchers—in essence an I.O.U., which the individual will be responsible for paying with no interest once we've restored the banking system's financial records. The individual will be required to present two forms of identification—one picture I.D. and a credit or debit card. It may be slower than we're used to, but it *will* work.

"We're confident that we won't have to implement this plan, but in the event that we haven't repaired the network by the morning, then it will go into effect at that time. It is important that each and every American who has a job go to their job site tomorrow, and don't think that you should not continue your daily lives as if nothing is different today than it was yesterday. Mark my words, we will emerge from this as stronger, better, more unified nation. Please have faith in America, your fellow citizens, humanity, and above all, God. Good evening to all of you," Morrison said in closing with a strong, comforting expression chiseled into his face.

General Meyers dissected the vice president's message, confident it would temporarily assuage the overwrought nerves of citizens throughout North America. Still, the distant possibility calling for Marshall Law chipped away at his conscience.

"General Meyers," Director Simonson said, nudging the general to look over at the screen with the CNN broadcast. "Looks like the Brits have followed our lead."

CNN's London bureau had picked up coverage of the acting British Prime Minister, Michael Norcross' similar speech urging calm and civilized behavior in the face of their banking meltdown.

Shortly after the acting prime minister's speech, the other European leaders-by-proxy also followed suit, promising a new beginning in the morning, while encouraging panicked citizens to go home and relax.

Austria, 11:31 p.m.

Sylvia grew impatient with her tenure on the roof. It was cold and she had an agenda. "We're ready for the shift change, brothers," she said. "We've been up here for over an hour already."

"Yes, we know," a voice answered. "We're on our way up."

Sylvia removed her headset and set it down quietly, positioning herself next to the roof access door so that she could greet the first of the two militants replacing her and, if needed, help hoist him up through the opening with his equipment. They wouldn't be bringing as much firepower as the first two militants because the grenade launchers carried up with the first shift remained on the roof.

As the first man emerged from the opening saddled with his own cache of arsenal, Sylvia extended a hand to the man not expecting him to accept any help. As she'd guessed he shrugged her off, saying he didn't need assistance. She glanced beyond the first militant to see the second man already ascending the ladder, so she asked him to retrieve two more plastic bottles of water. "You will need it," she explained.

"We each have a bottle already," he answered, continuing his ascent.

Shit! Sylvia thought, while her mind scrambled for alternative plays.

The first militant hoisted himself to his feet, made small-talk with Sylvia for a few seconds then asked where her comrade was. She quickly pointed toward the far end of the roof facing the Danube. "He's over there," she said in her augmented voice, but this time her tone broke just for an instant. "Watching the back flank," she continued, her voice reversing to its more masculine pitch.

The militant snapped toward Sylvia and the sound of her inconsistent voice, as his interrogating eyes riveted on hers. Without her night vision headset, he saw something he hadn't seen before as a shard of moonlight pierced the cloudy sky and splashed across her masked face. Her eyes looked different than they had downstairs. Something wasn't right.

She tried hard to match his intense glare, her squinting eyes daring him to qualify his sudden turn on a brother. "What?

The militant didn't say a word, as his scowl intensified. Sylvia's eyes didn't quite have the appearance of a normal man's eyes, and he knew his team pretty well—at least without their black knit caps. Something dangling from her ski mask that wasn't there earlier caused him to reach up to grab at it. "What's *this?*" he asked, reaching out to grab a lock of silky hair straying from her knit cap. Sylvia reacted instantly, chopping down on his outstretched arm, temporarily knocking his hand off course. Immediately she leveled the silenced Glock in her other hand. Everything was a blur now as she sensed the other militant breathing down her neck from the blind side. As she'd raised her weapon to squeeze off a round at her assailant, she was tackled hard from behind by the second militant, sending two rounds harmlessly to the side of her mark. She was shoved into the mark's chest and they both tumbled to the ground. The second militant's momentum carried him into the dog-pile writhing on the ground.

Sylvia's mind worked overtime, anticipating a counter-assault from behind along with one she wrestled with. She would only have seconds to disable these two, while muting their would-be shouts for help. Quickly she raised her left hand still clutching the firearm while she toiled with the militant in front of her, and fired two quick rounds into his right temple. "Fffft. Fffft." Instantly the man fell limp.

She felt a strong blow to the side of her face, temporarily dazing her, and quickly rolled off of the lifeless man and into a defensive posture. A strong grip at her neck sent an instinctive warning that there would undoubtedly be a knife or firearm pointed at her in under a second. During the tussle she'd lost control of her firearm and it fell a few feet away from their heated struggle. As she rolled onto her back, the growling militant straddled her and pressed down hard with his knife toward Sylvia's throat. The glare from the man's eyes cut her in two. She'd noticed that the man's headset had been knocked nearly off in the wrestling match. She threw up her right forearm to deflect the angry militant's thrust just in time, but the knife also caught her arm. She winced at the sharp pain, but didn't make a peep, knowing any sign of a struggle would've been heard downstairs. In the same motion Sylvia reached for the militant's headset and threw it. As she did, it left her momentarily out of position and gave the militant a window of opportunity over his foe and he pressed viciously with his knife toward her throat with one hand. His other hand struggled to neutralize her other arm, all the while hissing Farsi obscenities. "You must die you fucking traitor!"

Sylvia suppressed the pain of her fresh laceration and focused on the man's eyes while fighting valiantly for her life. The man was quite strong and a formidable opponent. He pressed hard on his knife hand as Sylvia fought back. The man leaned in closer now, sensing he had the advantage, growling as the trembling knife came to within two centimeters of Sylvia's throat. Her squirming right hand somehow freed itself and she was able to shift his bodyweight just off the top of her chest, while throwing a nasty right cross to his jaw in the process. But the man still maintained possession of the knife, and scrambled to his feet. Sylvia also sprang to her feet. This was the circumstance she had hoped for, as she countered the crouching militant who flicked his knife whenever she came close.

She lured him in twice to see how far he'd commit to taking a swipe at her with his razor sharp knife by purposely thrust-kicking above his head. On the third pass the militant thought Sylvia had over committed herself and lunged forward with his knife, sure he would bury it in her torso. Instead he was the one left out of position. Sylvia crashed down hard on his forearm with an elbow and he dropped the knife, leaving him vulnerable to her wickedly fast hands. She unleashed a dozen bruising punches from her fists and elbows, and he finally dropped to his knees, as she finished the punishment with several kicks—first to the solar plexus then to the head.

Wheezing now the punch-drunk soldier fell over on his side, gasping for air, while Sylvia sized him up. She retrieved her firearm and swiftly re-approached her foe. She removed her ski mask to taunt the downed militant, unleashing her hair.

The fallen warrior wailed with anger as he discovered his opponent was a woman and cursed wildly. "You fucking whore!"

Just as quickly Sylvia raised her firearm and unloaded two rounds into his head. "Rest in peace, my friend," she hissed, then stuck her firearm into her belt. Quickly she wrapped her hair up in a tight bun and retrieved her ski mask, pulling it back over her head, careful none of her tendrils hung out from any of the sides. She scrambled back to retrieve her headset, sure that the commander would've grown suspicious by now. She replaced it carefully over her black wool cap, only to find a voice on the other end calling frantically for a response.

"Everything okay out there?" the commander's voice queried into Sylvia's headset. "I've been trying to reach you for several minutes."

"Sorry, commander. We'd removed our headsets while we ate," she replied, then lowered her voice an octave.

"I heard some kind of disturbance up there," the commander reiterated his suspicions. "Is everything okay?"

"Yes, everything is fine," her new voice said, and then she altered it again.

"All clear here," a third voice said, and then remarkably once again Sylvia changed it for the fourth time. "We were just kidding around. My comrade thought he could take me in a wrestling match."

"Stop playing around," the commander ordered. "We have unfinished business," he reminded them.

Sylvia turned her mouth piece one-hundred-eighty degrees upward so she could haul the two new corpses to the center of the roof without breathing too heavily into her microphone, but at the same time she could maintain audio-surveillance on whatever was taking place downstairs.

She dragged her second victim roughly halfway down the roof and set him down gently, so as not to cause too loud of a thud from his head hitting the asphalt and gravel rooftop. She noticed a trickle of blood from her right sleeve flowing out into her hand. She'd almost forgotten about the knife wound inflicted by the third militant. Briefly she pulled up her bloody sleeve to assess her wound. Her eyes grew slightly as she caught a glimpse of the two-inch laceration on the underside of her forearm. It wasn't life-threatening, she'd quickly surmised, but it was a bleeder and would need attention sooner than later or she could bleed to death. Now wasn't the time though.

Quickly she retreated to the third victim and grabbed him by his boots to haul him back to where the second corpse now rested. Then she darted over to the first corpse, perched in his staged assault posture on the cantilevered edge of the building facing the Danube, and dragged the dead man back to the center of the building and lay him down with the others. As quickly as she could, Sylvia arranged the three bodies in a triangle, face up with their arms touching and their legs spread-eagled. The distance between the three victims was as close to equidistant as she could manage, and they were triangularly asymmetrical. She stifled a brief wave of nausea, while dropping to one knee next to the foot of one of the corpses, quickly untying one of his boots and removing the bootlace. Sylvia wrapped the bootlace around her arm above the bicep as a tourniquet, using her teeth to help tie off a tight knot, hoping to staunch or slow the copious flow of blood.

She then ran back to the opening in the roof and lowered her head into the opening to see if there was any activity down below. Unfortunately the thickness of the roof did not permit any visual assessment of what might lurk below. What the hell am I thinking? Sylvia thought. They think I'm a fucking militant, like them.

Convinced it was safe to descend the crude metal stairs to uncertainty below, Sylvia cautiously began to lower herself, step by step, thinking through every counter-measure that came to mind, should someone below suspect her of being something other than a militant. As she descended to a point where she was low enough to see into the warehouse area, she let one arm dangle loose and turned one-hundred-eighty degrees and surveyed the entire area. Nothing moved. She waited one more second, and then turned back to the stairs, grabbing them with both hands now, and quickly descended the remainder of the way.

Once she was on the ground floor, Sylvia made her way to the tail end of the two rear Hummers and silently crept around the driver's side of the far vehicle in an attempt to remove the keys from the ignition, if they were still inserted. She peered in through the driver's side window and could see the keys had been removed, temporarily dashing her initial attempt at disabling the vehicle the easy way. She thought for a moment about the next logical attempt and before touching the door's handle, she peered in through the driver's side window and could see that the door was locked. Shit! She then quickly turned to the vehicle on her left. Its door locks were also locked. "Son-of-a-bitch," she silently mouthed the words, as her mind worked overtime on the next move.

Sylvia couldn't lift the door handle for fear the vehicle's alarm was engaged, and undoubtedly it had one. The vehicles were brand new and were loaded with every accessory and latest security option, and what good would it do but compromise everything she'd accomplished up to this point if the alarm went off? Regardless of the militants' reasoning, the vehicles were locked, and that was that. She had one last shot. Quickly, she dropped to all fours, rolled onto her back, and shoved herself under the front end of the first vehicle, hoping she could tug on some portion of the vehicle's electrical harness. Fuck! The vehicle's skid plate had completely covered the entire engine compartment. There was no access to anything mechanical and no more time to waste on trying to disable the vehicles. There was only enough time to complete her original objective … she hoped.

On the back of each of the Hummers was a three-gallon gasoline canister painted to match the color of the vehicle itself. She sized up the gas can on the first vehicle. It was strapped in to a simple black metal harness held closed by two wingnuts on the top hinging bracket. The first wingnut she tried was very snug in part due to the cold so she tried loosening the second one. That one came free immediately and she twisted it off the half-inch of screw threads on the protruding threaded stud, and put it on the vehicle's bumper. Then she jimmied the can and harness thinking that might take some pressure off of the first wingnut. Unfortunately it didn't. She resorted to brute force, hitting the right side of the wingnut with the butt of her tenacious hand. The wingnut budged but still wasn't finger loose, so she followed up with two more taps from the butt of her hand. Now the wingnut came loose as she unscrewed it the rest of the way, placing it on the bumper next to the other one.

Sylvia carefully peeled back the harness and removed the gas can. She was in luck this time. It was full. She peeked around the corner of the left side of the vehicles closest to the corridor that led to the conference room to make sure a second team wasn't sent out on reconnaissance, or if even a single militant had wandered further than the restroom to say hi to his comrades. Several drops of blood trickled out of her sleeve onto the floor.

It appeared no one had entered the warehouse area, so Sylvia cautiously ascended the steps back up to the roof as quickly as she could while carrying thirty pounds of gasoline, and set the gas can up on the ledge at the top. Sylvia then hoisted herself up the rest of the way. She hurried over to the first corpse and set the can down long enough to spin the sealed cap open, then drenched the man in fuel.

Sylvia repeated the process on every bit of the next corpse, and then stopped for a second before she doused the final corpse long enough to retrieve the lighter from his chest pocket. He had been her first mark and she knew he'd smoked, and where he'd kept his lighter.

Sylvia had hoped by igniting just the corpses in the triangular pattern she'd configured, they would burn long enough in an obvious pattern to send a pretty clear signal to anyone who might be conducting aerial surveillance, or infrared sat-surveillance.

She lit the gas-soaked bootstraps on the first militant and he quickly ignited into an angry ball of flames. In turn the flames jumped to the next corpse and quickly the inferno leapt to the third corpse—only this time the hot flame flared and it jumped to her right sleeve igniting its cuff. Sylvia shook her hand furiously, which only fanned the flames. Thinking quickly she tucked her inflamed sleeve under her left armpit and the small fire was extinguished in a matter of seconds, causing only a minor burn to top of her hand. That's why there are plastic surgeons, she thought while observing the burns to her flesh. She'd experienced a lot worse in her lifetime's collection of battles, but stuck it in a patch of snow to cool it off.

Then Sylvia turned to admire her handiwork. The flames were localized to the bodies, in a nice, neat triangle, almost like a sky-diving trio, making a clear signal if someone could only spot the flames in time. They would burn for perhaps a half an hour before the flesh would turn to charcoal, and the flames would smolder out. For now however the stench of burning flesh was carried into the sky, but suddenly an untimely gust of wind knocked the smoke into a hell-bound spiral over the edge of the building.

CHAPTER 13

Word of the non-event in Milan had reached every corner of the earth that had been fed the earlier bombing video. As Pentagon staffers had speculated, initial relief gave way to confusion and trepidation.

Maldive Islands, 2:52 a.m.

Gregor Heinricke's female companions had partied and fallen into blissful exhaustion, collapsing into one another's arms on the king-sized bed of the third grass-thatched cabana that jutted out onto stilts into the ankle-deep Indian Ocean. Heinricke himself was emotionally exhausted, but suffered a temporary bout of insomnia just the same. He sat at the bar while nursing a bottle of beer that'd been open for an hour it seemed, rendering it almost undrinkable. He'd turned down the volume of the flat screen with the remote so it wouldn't distract him from the charts he'd been studying on his laptop computer.

Tomorrow promised to be a great day in the financial markets for himself and his associates, but tomorrow was already here and he had to find a way to sleep.

Heinricke got up from the bar strewn with beer and champagne bottles left over from the evening's rigorous social agenda. His ladies were already dreamily counting sheep. He would join them soon. He walked down to the water and stood in its warmth, as the tides gently splashed harmless six-inch waves across his bare shins. He contemplated what would be tomorrow. After a moment of staring out at the luminous three-quarters moon bouncing off of the placid sea, he retreated from the water and walked around the tiny island not once but twice in just twenty minutes. Satisfied with the amount of stress he'd whittled away, Heinricke made his way to the cabana and ascended the wooden stairs to the deck before walking in through the front door. He took off his Khaki shorts and threw them along with his tank-top onto the chair in the corner of the room where the girls had also abandoned their clothes. Then he climbed into bed with his two sleeping beauties and in minutes he was asleep.

Hong Kong, 5:59 a.m.

Charles Li had nodded in and out of a light sleep for about the past two hours before getting up long enough to peel off his Oxford shoes and black slacks and climb back onto the black leather couch in his office. He'd removed his white cotton dress shirt some time ago, tossing it over his large black leather office chair, and wore just a ribbed-cotton tank top and boxer shorts. He pulled the inexpensive, fluffy blue blanket over himself, while his finger found the mute button on the remote to the flat screen in his office before resuming his ample snoring. The early morning rays of the sun in a little over an hour would serve as his alarm clock. Minh Pak engaged in a similar routine in the office next door.

Austria, 12:01 a.m.

The Prophet was ready to resume his town hall meeting. He felt he'd been more than humane with the dinner break. The ten minutes he'd promised everyone stretched into an hour and thirty minutes, after all of his captives were allowed another visit to the restroom. The militant he'd sent out to check the thermostat had returned, successful in his mission, the heat having been turned back to a palatable temperature. The water rations were also cut back and there would be no more restroom breaks until morning.

"Quiet everyone. You have had your meal. Now, President Haydon, we were talking about biblical references that called for the total elimination of the Islamic faith, which your predecessor had not-so-quietly professed. Can you expand upon those views?"

"Well first of all Mr. Prophet, I am not my predecessor," Haydon acknowledged, a little perplexed by the attempted association in policy. "And I don't believe my predecessor would openly engage in a campaign against all from the Islamic faith. It's not conducive to global relations. It's also not conducive to humanity."

"But then we both know your predecessor's concerns were never about global cooperation," the Prophet interrupted. "Were they, Mrs. President?"

"I cannot answer for someone else, Mr. Prophet."

"Very well then," the Prophet eased for a moment, while rethinking his question. He visually scanned the conference room, seemingly focusing on nothing, but something etched a grimace of concern into his masked face. He leaned back toward the commander, and whispered something into his ear.

In an instant the commander barked an order to three of his militants to follow him out back, leaving just six militants and the Prophet to watch over the captives.

"Madam President, it says in the Bible that anything other than the teachings of the Judeo-Christian beliefs must be crushed."

"Not exactly, Mr. Prophet," Haydon tried.

"No?" the Prophet drilled back. "Why then was your predecessor so intent on making this a religious conflict, one that alleges that biblically the members of Islam must be eliminated?"

Just as it says in the Quran that all infidels must be eliminated," the president boldly interrupted. "But that doesn't mean that all—"

"Silence!" the Prophet blasted. "We are not talking about the Quran!"

"But we must if you keep setting the tone for a religious battle to the end—"

"Silence I said!" the Prophet blasted again, barely allowing the president to make her point. "The point is, Madame President, your predecessor did more to annihilate the nation of Islam than any other world leader in history!"

"But—"

"And that includes the alleged butcher of Baghdad!" the Prophet bellowed. "How could you think that you could get away with this? Did your predecessor's regime do this to the Buddhists? Of course not!"

"But—"

"Silence!" the Prophet thundered. "I'm not done! The nation of Islam has been targeted by the West for decades. Do you think that members of that nation would just forget and go away? How long should we be expected to endure the humiliation and persecution of the recent past?"

"Mr. Prophet," Haydon answered timidly, not sure if she'd be trampled in another tirade. "An awful lot of Muslims are being murdered senselessly by factions within—"

"Those numbers are nothing compared with the numbers being wiped out by the West and its allies, *and*, I might add, an insurgency only running roughshod as a result of the imbalance created by the West. These areas were well-managed. You never saw this kind of chaos before the balance of power was interrupted."

"Of course not, Mr. Prophet," Haydon agreed, so that she might make another point. "That's because thousands of innocent Muslims were being buried alive in mass graves outside of the city."

"Quiet!" the Prophet blasted again. "I would advise you to stick to the subject that we're discussing," he said through his teeth in a much more measured tone.

Haydon knew better than to argue with such tunneled logic. She took a breath and started to speak. "Very well, Mr. Prophet, I implore you to recount the events that led to retaliation by the Western coalition," she said very calmly.

"And what events are those Madame President? And please don't tell me about the Twin Towers."

"Mr. Prophet, as you'll recall our airliners were hijacked and used as bombs against innocent civilians—mothers and babies were killed," Haydon explained. "Innocent people who were just going to work, or visiting loved ones were murdered in these aircraft as the aircraft were turned on other innocent victims in the World Trade Center, as well as the Pentagon. What were we to do? You yourself said we had the world's sympathy in our initial counter-attack on Afghanistan."

"That, Madame President, is the operative word," the Prophet said calmly now. "*Initially*, the U.S. *did* have the world's sympathy to retaliate where it was appropriate to retaliate—in Afghanistan. But America and the West has always maintained a presence in the Middle East. You are occupiers in a land where you do not belong, where you are not wanted. You covet our oil because we have more of what the West needs than the West does. Just buy it and go home. We don't set the price of oil. U.S., British, and Asian markets of speculation determine the price of oil. If you'll recall, Salaam Hassan only wanted twenty-five dollars a barrel. So who's the villain? Quit blaming the Middle East for the only commodity that we've been blessed with!"

The commander and his band of thugs sent out on reconnaissance had discovered something the Prophet had suspected and were now forced to confirm. The two guards who were supposed to be on the warehouse floor were nowhere in sight, and were no longer answering their headset radios. In fact none of the four guards put on first watch were in communication. The commander had initially whiffed the distant stench of something burning similar to a stewing caldron of molten viscous rubber only more alive, and visually scanned the warehouse looking for smoke, while ordering the other three militants to look around for anything smoldering. The repulsive odor seeping into the warehouse was a smell that the commander hadn't smelled in years, but clearly recognized as burning flesh. Only someone exposed to the charring flames of battle would carry that memory with him.

"I've found something," one of the militants called out from behind the row of boxes at the top of the loading dock and to the right of the hallway door. He'd discovered Sylvia's stash of three dead bodies. "Look!" he said, stunned at the sight of his fallen comrades.

The commander was only steps away and quickly stiffened at the sight of the corpses. "There's an infiltrator!" he said out loud, his eyes turning cold with anger. How could it happen? The plan was flawless. Or did one of his hand-picked disciples implode with fear and turn on his brothers? It was impossible, he told himself.

Immediately he ordered the three militants to line up in front of him and pull their ski masks off so he could identify them. As they did he'd recognized each of them instantly.

Briefly the commander knelt next to the three corpses and one by one he removed their bloody ski masks. He recognized these men as well. One of them was the former waiter at Schaafhausen.

The commander then stood, his face tightening with concerted anger as he looked up at the rooftop access panel on the opposite end of the room and noticed it was left open. That explained why the room was so cool, and where that God-forsaken odor was permeating from. Quickly, he descended the stairs from the loading platform to the main parking floor where the four Hummers and the laundry van were, and ordered two of his henchmen to abandon their warehouse search and climb up the stairs to check what was burning up on the roof. Of course, he already knew.

"Before your head ever gets above that opening, reach up with your weapon and empty its clip in the direction of whatever is up there," the commander instructed. "I want to know what or who is burning. And I need you alive."

"Ja Wohl," the first volunteer said, knowing immediately he'd breached the mission's strict protocol.

"What did I tell all of you back at Schaafhausen?" the commander blasted angrily through clenched teeth, his face just six inches away from his soldier. "You speak only in Farsi. Now get up there!"

"I'm sorry, but we're not even near the leaders," the militant tried, still in a Bavarian dialect.

"Neine!" the commander reiterated, pulling the man closer, a fiery rage burning in his eyes. "Schnell!"

The militant nodded a tight nod then shouldered his weapon and quickly ascended the forged metal stairs. As he approached the access panel opening, he steadied for a moment to retrieve his weapon that he'd shouldered prior to his ascent, then very slowly raised it to the same plane as the opening and continued silently until it was up to the roof line. Then without hesitation, he raised the weapon another two inches and opened fire. If his comrades were up there and still alive they would have answered the commander's calls. There was no reason to have concern for taking a life that had already been taken.

Then he began to spray bullets in a radius, covering a circular motion as insurance. He had a hundred-round canister-clip on his weapon, and intended to use all of it to be sure. When he'd turned a complete circle all the way up to the edge of the access panel door, his fuming weapon had sputtered to a halt.

Down the stairs and through the hallway the distant sound of bullets being sprayed at will echoed throughout the conference room, alarming the Prophet and the room's other occupants. He immediately halted the town hall meeting and spun around in his swivel chair to acknowledge the threat while his enforcers started to make a reactionary break toward the door leading to the chaos.

"Stop!" he said in Farsi. "I need you all here."

The guards immediately returned to their posts, as most of the G-10 leaders spun around in their chairs and several lunged for the floor. The militant sitting next to the Prophet, who'd been tracking anti-agents on his laptop, was also equipped with a headset and remained in contact with the commander. "What is going on, commander?"

"We have a breach," the commander answered. "One of our own has turned against us. We didn't want to warn you because he's on the same frequency. Now we will find him. And when we do, we will peel the skin from his testicles," the commander squealed with a controlled anger. "If you are listening, your children will rot on earth while your flesh burns in front of them, unless you give yourself up now. You are below the meat of an ass in Allah's eyes! Now come forward and die with honor."

While the conference room buzzed with tumultuous commotion, watchful eyes around the world dissected their televisions for the images of the ten leaders, not knowing what happened to some of them after they lunged from the perceived line of fire. The Prophet paced nervously at the end of the conference table, while his enforcers stood guard over the room, finally motioning for them to assist the leaders back into their chairs.

Collective sighs of relief were felt worldwide, as the handcuffed leaders who'd dove for cover were hoisted up off the floor and helped back into their chairs, seemingly alive and unhurt.

In the Pentagon, General Meyers tried to maintain composure while conferring with his staff, and simultaneously speaking to Vice President Morrison, subconsciously mangling the empty plastic water bottle in his right hand. Steps away Deputy Director Simonson retrieved the mauled former water bottle from the general and handed him a full replacement.

The first of the two militants doing reconnaissance disappeared through the opening and into the darkness of uncertainty beyond. The commander ordered the second commando up the stairs to watch his comrade's back. "May Allah guide you, my brother."

The first man crouched on the roof, while quickly loading another hundred-round canister-clip onto his automatic weapon, and proceeded swiftly into the back draft of smoldering stench. The sky was still black, as the cloud cover concealed the moon trying to shine through. He didn't have his night vision goggles. The rest of those were still packed away in the black case in the back of the third Hummer. With every step toward the flaming piles, he transmitted back to the commander. "There are three burning mounds of something, arranged perfectly in a triangle. I can't tell what they are. I will proceed."

He arrived at the flaming flesh, almost regurgitating at the sight and unbearable smell of what was obviously three of his fallen comrades. "The fire is clearly three of our men—their flesh is burning," he growled back to the commander, while the other headset-equipped militants listened in, including the one sitting next to the Prophet.

"Of course they are," the commander said, already knowing the answer. "I want you to survey the roof. Look around. What do you see?"

"It's very dark up here," the militant whispered, covering his nose with his bent left arm, shielding himself from a strong waft of well-done human flesh. He scanned the roof-top and cautiously proceeded with his finger tightly grasping the trigger on the firearm cradled in his right arm. "I can't see much further than twenty meters."

The second militant crouched on the roof next to the opening, his loaded weapon aimed in the direction beyond his comrade. He'd hardly had time to lock his vision onto the man when he heard the screaming whistle of something he couldn't see. In what seemed like just a fraction of a second, he watched as a mortar screeched through the darkness and exploded into and through the chest of his comrade—the blast setting off a reactionary burst of gunfire from the target's weapon into the night sky. The force of the propelled mortar blew him completely off of his feet and twenty feet backward as his feet caught the edge of the building, sending him into a headfirst tumble over the side to his death.

Simultaneously, the second soldier unleashed a ferocious assault on a fixed point where he'd speculated the mortar was launched from, relentlessly trying to empty his hundred-round magazine of raging firepower, all the while shouting into the darkness. "He is dead! He is dead!"

Amidst his unyielding assault the militant heard the unmistakable whistle of a fast-approaching mortar and dove to his belly for cover as the single round intended for him screeched dangerously close above and then beyond toward the forest. In a split second he'd realized he was no match for night vision eyewear and superior firepower and scrambled hastily for the opening in the roof and jumped onto the forged metal stairs, quickly reaching up to grab the roof-top access panel and pulling it closed and locking it, only to hear another round furiously passing overhead.

"He's dead! He's dead!" the militant shouted hysterically, turning the access handle to its locked position and scrambling down the steps as rapidly as he could, nearly out of breath. "He's dead!" he shouted again, jumping from the final step to the floor and turning to find the commander, his eyes bulging from his brush with death.

"Who is dead?" the commander asked as calmly as possible given the circumstance.

"Our brother," the militant answered, still breathing heavily from his near-record descent down the steps.

"There were five of our brothers up there," the commander said, his eyes demanding clarification.

"He was standing above the burning men, and I had just enough time to look over to see a grenade explode through his chest and blow him into the night sky," the militant said, still panting. "In an instant, he was vaporized."

"Very well then," the commander said, as his face tightened with anger. "You want war?" he growled into his headset. "I swear on my life, I will personally end you! You haven't seen anything yet. God help you!"

Only the taunting silence answered back.

Quickly, the commander gathered the two militants with him and asked for their headsets. They handed over the devices and the commander dropped them onto the floor and crushed them with his right combat boot, sending a crunching noise into the three active headsets—one of which was his. With a circular motion of his right hand and then a point, the commander directed his two disciples back to the conference room.

All three men burst into the conference room as anxious eyes from around the world watched the unfolding events being telecast from a tiny conference room in an obscure location in a land far away.

The earlier calm and composure of a town hall format had given in to frantic uncertainty as the commander and the Prophet held what appeared to be a heated discussion. Seconds later the commander emerged from their meeting, shouting into the camera's eye in Farsi, impassionedly waving his silenced handgun.

For a brief moment, the Prophet interrupted and interpreted for his angry associate. "You have been warned repeatedly not to try and interfere with our business. Now you will all pay!" he hissed. The Prophet then turned his head away from the camera as the commander's tirade resumed.

Pentagon, 6:47 p.m.

"In Allah's name someone now must pay for the senseless massacre of these soldiers of God," the commander ranted, still in Farsi, as the Pentagon staff interpreter deciphered the message. "All you had to do was abide by the laws of Allah," the interpreter continued. "Now a sacrifice of great magnitude must be made."

"What the...?" Meyers exhaled.

"What is he saying?" Vice President Morrison asked, as he watched the angry commander pace around the table, ranting and waving his weapon.

"Mr. Vice President, I believe something very terrible is about to happen," Meyers said, gripping his jaw.

"What the hell are they talking about?" Morrison asked. "Did any of our assets penetrate?"

"According to Intel, none have sir."

"What is this madman talking about then?"

"I don't know, sir," the general answered, cringing at the sudden, ominous silence from the commander as he came to a standstill behind the Canadian. "Why isn't the Prophet looking, or speaking? And where are the rest of the militants?" Meyers asked, loud enough only for himself and the vice president to hear.

"You're right, general," Morrison observed. "There were quite a few more militants earlier."

"Get up!" the commander shouted in Farsi to the Canadian. Hammons didn't respond, as he didn't speak Farsi. But an emphatic nudge of the commander's firearm to the ribs of Hammons seemed to act as a crash course in the current language being spoken. The Canadian popped out of his chair and onto his feet.

"No, no, no," President Haydon pleaded, sensing something horrible was about to happen. "You can't do this!"

The commander cursed at the American president, ordering two of his men to hold down Hammons as he defiantly scrapped and clawed as best he could while being slugged and pounded from fists and weapons. As the militants forcefully did what they were told, there was a host of pleas from the agitated leaders at the edge of their seats, led by Haydon. "Please!" she begged, while rising to her feet. "You can't do this!"

The commander shoved the American back into her chair, and physically opened the president's mouth and forced the muzzle of his firearm into the opening. The Canadian's chivalry was no longer an option. The mood in the room was intensely heated. No one else dared to move from their seat, not even the defiant Chinaman.

Haydon squirmed, trying to garble words but the firearm in her mouth made it impossible to speak. Tears welled up in her eyes, spilling onto her cheeks, as she could only plead now with her eyes. Sylvia's identity must have been discovered, she thought.

What happened next was almost surreal. The commander removed the muzzle from the president's mouth as she continued to whimper for the Canadian's life. He switched the weapon from his right hand to the left, and then petted Haydon's head. She seemed to temporarily calm to a quiet whimper as he spoke very condescendingly to her, half-crouching, as if to say everything would be okay.

Then the commander stood and stared straight at the camera and said "it is Allah's will." Then without hesitation he leaned into the pinned-down Canadian with his left hand still holding the weapon and fired two rounds into the back of his head. In a flash, Canadian Prime Minister Scott Hammons was dead.

The room went silent with shock, as every world leader in the room stared in disbelief, slumping back into their chairs, some with their mouths unknowingly gaped open. President Haydon's eyes didn't blink as just two feet away her friend and political ally slumped motionless across the conference table in a small pool of blood forming near his forehead, while his limp legs dangled off the edge of the table.

In war rooms worldwide an intensified resolve grew out of the silence, while speculation grew as to which country's leader was next. Time was of the essence.

"So much for your peaceful Prophet theory, Mr. Simonson," Meyers snarled somberly.

"But…" Simonson started.

The general firmly held up his hand for the director to stop. "Have your people rewind the broadcast feed to the beginning, and let's do a headcount on the militants. Maybe we're missing something here," Meyers said while he and his staff studied the commander standing back at his original position behind the seated Prophet at the head of the conference table. His handgun was temporarily wedged into his equipment belt, with both hands on his hips, while the Prophet still stared off to the right, almost as if he wanted nothing to do with the killing of the Canadian.

"We're on it, sir," Simonson complied.

"What the hell are these two up to?" Meyers asked, not really directing the question to anyone in particular. "Has there been a breach, or a shift in power?"

Before anyone could answer, the commander began to speak. The general's interpreter translated the decree from Farsi into English with about a one-and-a-half second delay of the commander's oratory. "You have been warned. And still you have taken the lives of seven of Allah's beloved soldiers."

"Who the hell is he talking to?" Meyers started, completely confused.

"I don't know, general," Morrison answered privately into the Bluetooth, equally lost.

"Shhhh!" Simonson urged the general, holding a single finger to his mouth to quiet the speculative chatter for his translator.

"In case you didn't know, the Canadian's death is on your hands," the commander hissed staring villainously at the camera, half-spitting his impassioned decree in the direction of the camera then hurling his headset microphone to the floor and stomping on it. "If any more of my men perish, two of your leaders will die for every one of them. You know our numbers. We are not afraid to die. We are committed to Allah's work. But you will run out of leaders before all of us go. Can you live with that? Can the West live with that? Can the world live with that?" the commander asked while tapping the computer operator on the head, and motioning for him to hand over his headset and close the computer.

The militant obliged, handing the headset over and began logging off the computer. The commander dropped the last active headset to the floor and stomped on it with the dense rubber heel of his boot. "Prepare to meet your death," the commander said, obliterating the last headset. The headsets were for internal communication only and that was no longer necessary.

Suddenly breaking his temporary moment of silence, the commander stared into the camera and said, "I will sever your head from your serpent's body." He then went ballistic, barking every obscenity he knew in Farsi and Arabic, completely puzzling the personnel in the global command centers. Suddenly, it became clear their captors were multi-nationals, but to what extent was still unclear. Farsi was spoken in only Iran, Afghanistan, and parts of Pakistan. The rest of the Arab nations spoke Arabic—meaning one or all of these militants were from various countries in the Middle East, or at the very least had spent time throughout the region.

But the burning question that still confounded every intelligence agency throughout the world undoubtedly had to be, whom or what was driving the commander to this boiling point?

The commander's tirade continued as he stormed around the conference room and ranted threats, brandishing his firearm, placing it at the temple of each of the leaders, maniacally threatening them one at a time.

Finally the Prophet stood up from his chair, and shouted, "Enough!" in Arabic, jolting the commander from his temporary spell. The two men stared at one another for several moments, and then the Prophet calmly urged the commander to return back to his post at the head of the table. "We don't have much time now," he whispered as the commander passed by. "Prepare everyone for our journey."

The Prophet then stared into the camera at the other end of the table and said "God help you bastards," in English. He stood from his perch at the head of the table, and made a slicing his hand-across-the-throat gesture toward the cameraman. At that point, all audio-visual coverage from the conference room was suddenly discontinued. In an instant the rest of the world was in complete darkness, the broadcast signal lost forever.

CHAPTER 14

Hong Kong, 6:29 a.m.

While Asia's financial markets slept, the Hang Seng, Nikkei, and Singapore's gold and oil futures had followed London's after-hours ascent with the continued geopolitical unrest. With the Canadian Prime Minister's assassination, the gold futures traded on London's FTSE spiked another twenty-eight dollars an ounce to $2,029. Oil futures were now trading at $133 a barrel for Brent North Sea crude, while U.S. gasoline futures were comfortably topping six dollars a gallon.

The Asian markets were merely tracking in concert with British and U.S. after-hour commodity prices for now while the eastern giant slept. In just a few hours the Asian traders would awaken and begin to assess the uncertainty gripping the world. With the entire planet in the dark as to the whereabouts of the remaining nine leaders and their captors, there was no limit to what the traders might do with the oil and precious metals markets.

The pace promised to be frenetic.

Pentagon, 6:36 p.m.

"Who the hell is responsible for the breach, Mr. Simonson?" Meyers asked calmly, as he directed Simonson and his staff to prepare all assets deployed in and around Vienna for what was likely the break they'd been waiting for. "For one, I want to shake this man's hand, or decorate the entire goddamm unit, whoever the hell it is!"

"It's being done as we speak, general," Simonson replied. "General, you'll recall some of the leaders dove for cover? Maybe they were reacting to gunfire. Maybe there were multiple rounds fired internally at the location, or better yet externally. In which case there might be sat or infrared images available to our local assets."

"Well get on it, Mr. Simonson," Meyers commanded, only now with a quarter of an ounce of warmth and optimism. "Time's a-wasting!"

"And sir, as you'd requested, the video logs confirm the seven fewer militants."

"Good work, Mr. Simonson," Meyers answered, a quiet confidence growing by the minute. The twitch in his right eye had slowed dramatically. "We might've just turned the damn corner."

"I'm right with you, general," the vice president said. "If we get them on the run, we've got a shot."

"Yes we do, sir."

"General, I have to make a statement on behalf of Prime Minister Hammons," Morrison said. "Please keep my staff apprised."

"Yes, sir. You will be second to know."

Austria, 1:27 a.m.

Sylvia had run the perimeter of the building in search of a set of metal stairs. However there was nothing on any of the four sides, including the backside that fronted the Danube. Very odd, she thought, unless the only rooftop access was interior access only. And in that case she had to get inside.

Quickly Sylvia doused the burning bodies with gasoline again to buy herself as much time as she could, given the rapidly disappearing flesh left on the corpses, careful to not get too close to the flames.

She had a decision to make. Sylvia knew the captors could not stay put knowing there was a lethal threat to their mission up on the roof. She also knew they were aware it was just a matter of time before aerial surveillance discovered the burning bodies, or satellite infrared if the cloud cover didn't break. But the ceiling was high, so either way Sylvia figured she would have help very soon and the militants down below would have to fly the coop.

She could remain on top of the roof and wait for the captors and their prisoners to emerge from the cargo bay, at which point she would have a top-level view of them speeding away into the blackened forest, or down the paved road out of the complex. Either way she wouldn't be able to capitalize on the clear target—the militants undoubtedly would split the captives up within the vehicles, using them as human shields. In a perfect world, she could just lock and load on the targets, vaporize them, then go get her wounds treated. It hadn't been a perfect world for some time however.

The best Sylvia could hope for was to wait for visual confirmation then blast her way through the locked rooftop access, and resume her pursuit into the forest.

Inside the cargo bay of the warehouse the nine remaining world leaders were led into three of the four Hummers, along with two armed militants in each of those three vehicles, while the Prophet and the commander formulated their final strategy.

"We know this is just one person up there," the Prophet said. "And we know this one person can't get off of the roof without coming through that access door right there," he continued, pointing to the ceiling panel. "And we also know that he can't shoot at us for the risk of killing one of the leaders. If we had the time we could storm the roof and take this detractor, even though he has a small arsenal at his disposal. But we don't. There are the fires up on the roof. And very soon this place will be swarming with every sharp-shooter in Europe. We will stick with our second plan."

"And you?" the commander asked. "When will you rejoin us?"

"I will be with you very soon, Anwar," the Prophet said. "First I will open this door. The second it opens, you will charge through the fence, then the second vehicle, then the third. I will be right behind the third vehicle, as planned. And we will rendezvous at our predetermined coordinates. But we must go now for they will come for us soon. If this friend of the infidels is stupid enough to take a shot at our motorcade, then it will be my vehicle that gets blown into the kingdom of God."

"All right then," the commander said, then embraced the Prophet, kissing him on each cheek.

"If in the event I don't make it, commander, you know the order in which we depress the buttons on the remote," the Prophet said, and then handed over the remote to the chaotically tempered commander. "Now go with Allah. I will see you soon. I promise."

The commander climbed into the first vehicle and secured the seatbelt, not so much for safety, but to stop the annoying noise it made reminding the driver to fasten their seatbelt. He fired up the engine, held his left arm out the driver's window and signaled for the other two vehicle's drivers to do the same. He nodded at the militant in the passenger seat, and reached up to adjust the rear view mirror to glance at the American president, the Italian leader, and the former Chinese boxer, who looked defiant and determined to be a hero.

That's why the third militant sat in the back of the vehicle though—to ensure against any such a move and remind him what the butt of a steel weapon to the shoulder blade felt like.

The Prophet reached into the fourth vehicle and turned the key, starting his vehicle as well, and then proceeded to the roll-up aluminum door. As he passed the commander's door, he knocked very lightly on the tinted window and gave a thumb up signal. He pulled back on the two hinging struts from the slots in the door's vertical track that locked the roll-up door into place. Then very quickly he started pulling on the chain that pulled the door up with one hand after the other as if climbing a rope.

The second the commander thought he had enough clearance he blasted through the opening, slightly scraping the roof of the vehicle, then the second vehicle screeched out with the third following closely behind. As the lead vehicle blasted through the chain-linked fence, veering immediately to the left, the Prophet was climbing into the fourth Hummer. Quickly he threw the gearshift into drive and screeched through the opening in the chain-linked fence, about two seconds behind his comrades. They had just turned to their right onto the dirt road that would lead them back into the snowy alpine forest.

Up on the roof of the building, Sylvia had prepared herself for this moment. Both of her grenade launchers were loaded. She simply wanted to obstruct the road into the forest for the four Hummers that had just emerged into view.

Laying down at the edge of the building, she steadied her first loaded weapon with her wounded arm on the concrete cantilevered edge and focused on a large pine tree that sat on the bank just to the left of the first turn in the road about two-hundred meters away. She waited for the motorcade to commit in the direction of the forest before she'd waste any rounds on a target that might not come into play. Sylvia told herself if she struck the base of the tree right it would fall right across the road and give her an additional few minutes of valuable pursuit time. But if aim was off at all, she could easily take out the one of the vehicles, killing all of its occupants.

She focused on her target—her trained eye zeroing in on a point of the tree just above a knotty bulge about three feet off of the ground, then squeezed the trigger, propelling the mortar across the sky in the direction of her mark. In just seconds the grenade exploded perfectly into the tree, severing the tree from its knotty stump and the tree started to fall across the road. Sylvia gauged the time of impact against the rapidly approaching motorcade. Her heart raced as fast as the vehicles advanced and wondered why the tree was falling so slowly. "Come on," she tried to coax the falling tree, loud enough for her own ears. But the top of the tree had snagged up in the branches of the surrounding trees, in part because the base of the broken tree was still slightly attached right at the knotty bulge that she'd tried to strike.

Quickly she grabbed for the other loaded grenade launcher, and steadied again on the concrete edge, and again squeezed off another round and watched the mortar fly as the motorcade bounced rapidly toward the point of what could be no return. "Come on!" Sylvia shouted, as again her second round exploded into the base of the tree, this time completely severing it from the stump. Now it would be free to fall, she thought.

The four Hummers raced toward the bend in the road, as Sylvia watched the base of the tree jump off of the knotty stump altogether and perch itself just to the left on the hillside that the tiny road wrapped around. Its top continued to fall, but not quickly enough. "Come on!" she shouted, urging the gods to help her.

One-by-one Sylvia watched helplessly as the four Hummers sped around the tightly banked turn, disappearing into the darkness. Now she would have to pursue them in the cumbersome laundry van down below.

She quickly rose to her feet, reloaded the launcher and stepped over to the roof-top access panel and blew the locking handle and most of the panel away, lifting what was left of it. She then strapped the launcher over her shoulder that was already strapped with an AK-74, and grabbed the canvas bag full of ammunition for both weapons.

Way off in the distance, Sylvia heard a noise she'd been yearning to hear for hours. She turned and her eyes searched the blackened sky-scape for what could only be the rumble of multiple Apache gun ships. Her eyes strained until they focused on the dim wing lights of not one, but two aerial fighting machines approaching out of the northern sky. They must've been two miles out. She could wait for their arrival, or pursue the Hummers into the forest on her own, knowing full well she might be mistaken as the enemy.

She opted for the latter, as her instinct told her the bodies still burning on the roof would be enough to garner the support of every military installation in all of Europe. Still, they would be useless if she couldn't locate the militants and their hostages. She had to move now.

Sylvia squeezed through the opening in the roof with all of her arsenal and rapidly descended the stairs. She hit the floor hard with her feet and dashed over to the driver's side of the laundry van. Her heart sank initially as the keys weren't dangling from the ignition, so she immediately glanced to the floor of the vehicle. There were no keys on the floor. She leaned in a little further to survey between the two front seats, and there on the floor between them was a keychain with two keys on it, sparkling like a ray of hope. She grabbed them and tried to force the first of the keys into the ignition. It didn't work. "Come on," she coaxed the second key into the ignition. It slid right in. She held her breath and turned the ignition—the vehicle started. "Yes!"

Sylvia slid the two shoulder-mounted weapons off and placed them on the floor along with the canvas bag full of ammunition, then climbed into the driver's seat. For a very brief moment, she thought about checking in on Prime Minister Scott Hammons. She'd heard the commander's entire tirade and dance of death, plus the ensuing gunshots on her headset and that was good enough for her. He undoubtedly was dead. That's what the commander said, and in her brief relationship with the militants' leader she'd surmised that he was a man of conviction who had no problem with taking lives. There was no need to confirm a corpse. That time might cost her a few more lives. Undoubtedly one of the gun ship's crew would be there in minutes and confirm it for themselves, or call for a medical back-up.

Sylvia threw the gearshift into drive and blasted out of the warehouse and through the broken chain-linked fence, then veered hard to the left. Fifty meters ahead she turned right onto the dirt road leading into the forest. As she neared the bend in the road with the partially felled tree, she assessed its position dangling above the road. It appeared the miss on the motorcade of Hummers might be the downfall to her larger vehicle and its prospects for passage. There was only one way to find out. When the laundry van was within five meters of the bend, Sylvia pressed the gas pedal to the floor and moved as far right onto the road as she could without sliding off into the thickly wooded ravine. She held her breath, certain she would hear some kind of scraping collision.

"Boom," was the initial sound, followed by an eerie twisting and scraping metallic noise. The vehicle dragged almost to a stop, but fought angrily against the fallen tree.

"Come on, dammit!" Sylvia shouted, forcefully pushing down on the gas pedal. The truck was hardly moving now, but if she stopped the fallen tree would surely settle, and her hope of getting through would be over. "Come on!"

In an instant the truck sprang free and started to advance up the road. Sylvia had enough time to look into her wing mirror and see the trunk of the tree hit the road behind her with a thud, along with half of the laundry van's roof. It was going to be a chilly night, she thought to herself.

The Pentagon, 7:58 p.m.

General Meyers shouted at the deputy director to quiet everyone down as the audio feed trickled in from the two Sikorsky SH-60s doing reconnaissance in the early hours of the Austrian morning. The two aircraft had been equipped with wings and Hellfire Missiles, as well as the mounted gun pods, basically turning the helicopters into fighting gunships, while capable of carrying a small crew. Apaches were fierce fighting machines but could only carry two crewmembers.

The volume to the news sources displayed on the war room's other monitors were also lowered as Meyers prepared the vice presidential bunker for what could be breaking news. MI6, the Mossad, the BND, and the French Intelligence Agency, DRM, were conferenced in.

"We're hovering above a warehouse—forty-seven degrees north-sixteen degrees east—the building sits on the Danube," Commander Miles Wainright of the United States Marine Corp reported. "There is a triangular configuration burning on the roof. And you're not going to believe this, but they appear to be human bodies. Can you confirm that, Captain Michaels?" Wainright asked.

"Roger that," a voice answered from the second gunship. "We'll drop a few men on deck to confirm."

Suddenly the video feed from the aircraft cameras was brought up on one of the main monitors at the Pentagon. General Meyers and his staff observed as the second of the gun ships dipped toward the roof, and two troops slid down the shortened cord to the roof-top. Both men spread out to observe two different fires.

"Uh, Captain," the first voice said. "That's a Roger on the triangle fire. It is, or it was…human. Jesus Christ this shit stinks."

"Roger that on the human sacrifice," the second troop reported. "Boy you ain't kiddin,' this stuff is nasty!"

In a moment one of the troops reporting back also confirmed an empty gas can in the vicinity of the third corpse. "Holy shit! Somebody had themselves a barbeque up here."

Captain Michaels ordered his two soldiers to go down into the building. "Get down in there. If it moves, shoot it. We're moving into position on each side of the building. We'll cover you. I'm sending in four more men to join you from the front side. Don't shoot them."

"Roger that," one of the troops answered back. As he and the second soldier advanced toward the hole in the roof, he observed the discarded grenade launcher and AK-74 lying over at the edge of the building. The camera in his headset fed the same images back into the main video feed in the mother ship. Quickly he descended the metal steps down into the warehouse. Right behind him was the second soldier.

Captain Michaels pulled up his aircraft and turned it around and descended to the ground in front of the complex near where the chain-linked fence was ripped open, and set it down long enough to let four additional soldiers out and assist in ground-recon, then went airborne again.

All of the men on the ground wore headgear with cameras, so the video feed was sent back to the mother ship and then to General Meyers and his staff. It was then converted into a split-screen with eight digital feeds.

Commander Wainright had already circled the building and discovered another corpse on the ground on the east side of the complex. One of his crew on board slid down a rope to assess the condition of the body down below, while Wainright continued his recon. His command had informed him and Michaels that they were now dispatched directly into the Pentagon, and General Meyers. "We believe we saw some kind of mortar fire coming from the top of the enemy compound just minutes ago, but we were two clicks out, so it's hard to confirm. Judging by the weapons we just discovered on the roof, chances are pretty good that's a Roger on the mortar fire. They can't be too far from here…requesting permission to apprehend."

"That's a negative," General Meyers answered back quickly. "Secure the building first."

"Roger that, sir," Wainright said, then listened for the soldiers in the hole to report back.

"Clear," the first soldier said, his camera telegraphing his every move into each crevice in the warehouse.

"Clear," another one said.

"Clear," still another one said. "It smells like car exhaust in here though."

"Requesting permission to intercept and apprehend," Wainright tried again. "There's fresh exhaust down there. That vehicle isn't far from here."

"That's a negative, commander," General Meyers barked back. "Secure the area!"

"But, sir, these bastards might get away," Wainright lobbied.

"I assure you, son, they will *not* get away. Hold your position. Your command center has already dispatched a dozen helos to join you," Meyers commanded. "Secure the building."

"Roger that, sir."

"Holy shit!" a voice said.

"What've ya got, soldier?" Wainright asked, taking a moment to match the voice with the troop.

"This guy's got a hole in his chest the size of a basketball," the soldier that Wainright had just dropped onto the ground reported back. He bent over and pulled the black ski mask from the corpse's head. "The mark appears to be of Middle Eastern descent." The video feed confirmed the soldier's words.

"We've got three more in here," an excited voice of a soldier inside the warehouse reported. "Ditto that on the M.O., except for one. This guy's got blond hair, and is quite Nordic."

The last corpse's description completely threw Pentagon intelligence for a loop, as well as every other intelligence service linked into the feed. Simonson scrambled to produce an answer for General Meyers.

Now the video feed showed four soldiers moving quickly down a narrow hallway, assault weapons drawn and leading their charge, while clearing the three offices and the smelly restroom. "Clear!"

Then the lead soldier crept up to the door that lead into the conference room, and peeked through the crack in the door, nudging it slightly with the barrel of his weapon to try and get a better glimpse into the room. As he continued to inch the door open his eyes came upon the limp, dangling legs of a body sprawled out on the center of the conference table. Those observing from the Pentagon had already seen this image approximately thirty minutes earlier, only from a different angle.

The lead soldier shoved his way into the conference room, his eyes dilated with anticipation. With his weapon drawn at eye level he charged into the room then quickly turned left to cover the left and rear flanks. The other soldiers charged into the room right on his heels. "Move! Move! Move!" he barked.

Finally the remaining two soldiers from the warehouse recon joined in and swept the conference room and the two offices on the far wall. "Clear!" was the final assessment from the battalion leader. "I think we've found your den of snakes. Only the snakes are on the run."

Another member of the recon team cautiously approached the corpse lying on the table in a pool of blood. His left hand came off of the barrel of the weapon as his right hand held it tightly, his trigger finger still locked and loaded. With his left hand he reached over to the limp Caucasian's neck and felt for a pulse, knowing the answer before he proceeded. "This one's toast."

Then he turned the corpse over and the video feed that was sent back to the Pentagon and its affiliates reminded everyone respectively why this was not anything close to a victory.

"We have a visual on a fleet of helos out of the north," Wainright reported from outside. "We've just had radio contact confirming they're three clicks out. Requesting permission, General Meyers, to intercept and apprehend the enemy."

General Meyers contemplated for about half a second, and then gave Wainright and his team permission. "That is affirmative, Commander Wainright. Proceed and intercept target. That order includes Captain Michaels and his crew. You boys go locate and isolate the enemy. Do not engage. I repeat. Do not engage! Wait for support!"

"Roger that," Wainright snapped back.

"I want your ground force at the warehouse location to remain and sweep for explosives—that includes the deceased Canadian President. You strip him down to his skivvies if you have to. For all we know, these bastards could've violated that poor son-of-a-bitch and booby trapped your location. Do you understand, commander? "

"Yes, sir," Wainright acknowledged, and then passed the order on to the ground troops. He pulled his aircraft up out of his hover position and proceeded quickly into the thickly wooded forest, buzzing the treetops that lined the only dirt road leading into the forest, while one of the aircraft's crew members shined a high-beam searchlight down below. Michaels and his crew followed the paved road out of the complex, while deploying their own searchlight. Within seconds Wainright's team discovered the former roof of a laundry van throwing off a significant reflection through the trees. They could see that the hunk of twisted metal had been crushed by a tree trunk on the dirt road down below. "Stay tight, Captain Michaels. We're on the trail of a nest of snakes."

"Roger that, sir! Gladly!" the voice said, and just as the quickly the second gunship peeled off to their right flank to rejoin the lead ship.

CHAPTER 15

Sylvia sped, traversing up the collection of hairpin turns, bouncing off of the crude dirt road lined with potholes, en route to the pinnacle of the mountain. Somehow the road hadn't seemed so difficult to navigate on the journey over to the warehouse, she recalled.

She speculated the militants couldn't descend out of the front side of the forest, for that side undoubtedly was swarming with a multi-national presence. Sylvia also knew that undoubtedly within minutes there would be a reconnaissance team in pursuit of the same target she was pursuing, which was both good and bad. Good because she'd been fighting the world's war all by herself for the last twelve hours and she could use a hand. But what if the recon team mistook her for the enemy? It was highly likely. But she couldn't risk abandoning her camouflaging attire quite yet either—she *was* still fighting this war alone. If she removed her ski mask to alert the recon team that she was a woman and one of the good guys, while the moon shone through a break in the cloudy sky, it could illuminate her face just long enough to compromise her position to the enemy. For now the ski mask would remain on.

At the top of the mountain the road came to a clearing. Sylvia's eyes scanned the field, sensing its familiarity. Quickly she recognized it as the drop point from just half day earlier in the French-made helicopters. She could only contemplate the militants would use the forestry station on the opposite side of the grassy knoll as their clandestine prison for the G-10 members, who now numbered just nine. It would make sense – if they presumed they weren't followed.

Sylvia eased up on the accelerator and parked the vehicle just shy of the clearing. She retrieved her two weapons off of the floor of the van, jumped out, and quickly followed the tree-line to the right of the van about three feet back from the clearing, advancing invisibly toward the side of the forestry station. She recalled the view earlier from the helicopter that the road to the clearing forked, with one of the forks ending behind the station, and the other in front. Clearly there were no vehicles in front.

Sylvia continued to serpentine through the trees, silently advancing toward the opposite side of the building, but there was still no sight of a Hummer.

Within a minute Sylvia had advanced all the way to the back side of the station and caught a glimpse of a rear bumper of one of the Hummers underneath the carport behind the building. Bingo, she thought.

Suddenly Sylvia heard the growl of the two gun-ships as they blasted into the blackened sky just above the clearing, then watched as they circled the area. Based on her angle, she was pretty sure the two aircraft couldn't see the vehicle under the carport out back. But she also knew she had to complete her initial surveillance before she could reveal her position to the recon-aircraft. She pushed further along the tree-line, remaining stealth to the aerial pursuit, while advancing all the way behind the complex until she could see the last of the captives being forcefully escorted into the building on the far side of the Hummer.

Sylvia discovered that there were only three Hummers. Where the hell is number four? She drilled her mind as her eyes tried to come up with that answer. She searched the adjacent areas, but couldn't find a thing.

Sylvia knew she'd only have a minute more at best before the two heavily armed aircraft vanished into the night if they didn't identify their primary target, so she quickly began to retreat back along the tree-line until she was out of the line of sight of anyone who might still be out back of the forestry station. And then, about fifty meters shy of her abandoned van Sylvia dashed out into the grassy opening, waving her arms wildly – one of her waving arms still was in possession of an AK-74.

But the aircraft seemed to be more intent on something on the far side of the clearing as both aircraft were hovering at the far tree-line where the dirt road forked. Sylvia continued to advance into the clearing almost as if she was going to run down the two gun-ships, still waving her arms wildly.

One of the crew members aboard Commander Wainright's aircraft caught a glimpse of the dark figure waving a weapon across the knoll and alerted the pilot. Wainright could hardly believe his eyes. "General Meyers, we have a visual on what appears to be an armed gunman. Attempting to neutralize."

About the time Commander Wainright reported to the Pentagon, the two air surveillance cameras sent streaming video back to central command.

General Meyers was being briefed by the command center just established at the former lair of the militants, but quickly excused himself because of the breaking situation not far away. "Stand by," he told the command at the warehouse then acknowledged Wainright. "Roger that. Approach with caution. It's a long shot, but this could be our friendly infiltrator."

"That is a Roger," Commander Wainright replied, directing his aircraft quickly to the front side of the militant, hovering about eight feet off the ground with its nose lowered like a predator in strike position just in front of the heavily armed man. Two armed crew members quickly descended a drop-rope into the field of long wispy blades of grass blowing about from the turbo-prop's wind all around the mark.

In seconds, Captain Michaels and his crew took up position on the backside of the militant in a complete mirror image of the sister gun-ship, its nose lowered and ready to strike while two crew members descended out of the gun-ship's belly into the field. The four soldiers took position now on the opposite sides of the two aircraft with two on either side of each other creating a perfect circle around the would-be militant.

"Put down your weapon and lie face-first on the ground," Wainright commanded unconsciously, and then quickly asked around to all of the crew members on both ships and on the ground if anyone spoke Farsi or Arabic. About the time the staggered answers came rolling in, the mark responded by first putting his AK-74 down, then removing the grenade launcher strapped to his shoulder. "Well I'll be God-damned! This son-of-a-bitch understands English," Wainright said, then quickly shouted another command. "Get on the ground—face first!"

"I am an American," the black-clad figure shouted back, hands high in the air.

"Get *on* the ground!"

"I am an American," the lone militant tried again.

The four soldiers on the ground intensified the grips on their weapons—one of the first two to drop into the field firing a three-round blast into the flowing grass next to the masked person.

Sylvia immediately dropped to her knees, shouting again. "I am an American!" Then she slowly reached for her ski mask, causing two of the soldiers to fire reactionary blasts into the ground around her. Sylvia froze.

"What's going on down there?" Wainright asked the field soldiers.

"The target says he's an American," the first of the trigger happy jacks replied. "I'll be damned if I'm gonna have my head blown off by a suicide bomber."

"Now how the **hell** do you boys think those seven other militants were killed at your previous location?" General Meyers bellowed from a land far away. "Now God damn it, let him take his ski mask off! Just maintain your distance and keep your weapons on him."

"Roger that," Wainright responded to the quarter-second delay command. "Let the mark remove his ski mask!" he ordered his ground troops. "I repeat. Let the mark remove his ski mask!"

"All right," the first shooter on the ground shouted through the commotion and the angry noise of the gunships' engines. "Take off your ski mask, slowly."

While everyone in the Pentagon war room held their collective breath, the dark figure slowly tugged at the knit cap.

"The mark is a woman," Wainright reported. "She appears to be Caucasian. Awaiting orders, General Meyers."

"Well I'll be damned," Meyers exhaled, his mind racing with speculation.

"General Meyers, this is the vice president," Morrison interrupted. "I want one of your field soldiers to address this woman—approach with caution—one soldier only. I want to get a closer look at this woman."

"Yes, sir, Mr. Vice President," Meyers said, and then reiterated the command. "Do not harm the mark. Do you understand, commander?"

"Yes, sir," Wainright answered. "Commencing order."

Slowly the first of the soldiers to fire his weapon advanced toward the mark kneeling in the field. Her hair was still blowing wildly in the crisp early morning breeze, while every command center around the world watched intently. The digital feed followed the barrel of the soldier's weapon and his slow approach until he had reached the woman with the flowing hair. "Awaiting orders, commander."

"General Meyers, have your commander ask the woman to pull her hair tight, up and away from her face," the vice president ordered.

"Yes, sir," Meyers acknowledged.

As the woman received her orders, she reached with two hands to gather her unleashed flowing hair, while looking down. When she had finally gathered enough of her hair to hold it out of the way of blocking the view of her face she looked up at the field soldier and into his head-cam.

"I don't believe my eyes," Morrison said excitedly. "That woman is Sylvia Jensen, the president's personal body guard. She's alive! General Meyers, you have that soldier lift her to her feet and hug her. She is to be treated like gold from here on out!"

"That is a Roger!" General Meyers said enthusiastically, and then barked the order to Wainright, while the occupants of both the Pentagon war room and the vice president's private bunker broke into a boisterous round of applause and cheers. "Help the woman to her feet. She is Sylvia Jensen—

President Haydon's personal bodyguard. Do you understand, Commander Wainright?"

"That is affirmative," Wainright said, then echoed the order to the field soldier who'd already heard General Meyers' decree, and was already helping up Sylvia.

"Ma'am," the soldier acknowledged, with his extended hand clutching Sylvia's.

"Thank you, soldier," Sylvia said, taking the man's helping hand up and not letting go of it. Once she stood face-to-face with the man, she managed a tight smile, still maintaining her grip while pulling him in close, then said "I was your prisoner because I chose to be, not because you dimwits hunted me down. I lit human fires so that you could find me. Don't ever stick that weapon in my face again."

"Calm down, ma'am," the soldier said, as the other three quickly closed in to investigate. "I'm just doing my job."

"So am I," Sylvia said. "Who's in charge?"

"Commander Wainright here," the soldier snapped back, motioning behind himself toward the lead gunship. "But we're taking direct orders from the Pentagon," the soldier added more respectfully.

"Good," Sylvia said. "Give me your headset. We have to act fast."

In the Pentagon, General Meyers quickly put the party plans on hold. "Okay people, this is very good news, but it's only one person. We still have nine world leaders to bring home. Now quiet please. We need to hear this information."

"Shhhh," Simonson reiterated.

"Commander Wainright?" Sylvia asked, peering over the shoulder of the ground soldier.

"At your service, ma'am," Wainright answered, dipping his right wing briefly to acknowledge the president's bodyguard, then just as quickly leveled off the wings again. "General Meyers, we have Sylvia Jensen on board. Stand by."

"General Meyers?" Sylvia asked, looking into the sky.

"Sylvia, this is General Meyers. Stand by for just a second. We're patching the vice president through."

"Yes, sir."

"Sylvia?" A voice asked.

"Yes."

"This is Vice President Morrison. First of all, thank God you're alive! I want to tell how proud you make me feel right now."

"Thank you, Mr. Vice President," Sylvia acknowledged, then took control of the dialogue. "Sir, we don't have much time right now for thank yous. Until our president is safe, as well as the other leaders, we need to move quickly."

"All right, Sylvia," Morrison acknowledged. "General Meyers, you give this lady whatever the hell she needs. And Sylvia, when this thing is over, you get yourself back to Washington. The president and I owe you one."

"Thank you, sir. I'll look forward to taking you up on that," Sylvia acknowledged, then began snapping orders. "First of all, General Meyers, we need to get these gun-ships out of here—and quickly! The enemy has grenade launchers and we don't need to give them a target they don't deserve. I'm confident they're aware of aerial surveillance, but if the helos leave quickly enough, we might get lucky and the enemy might not think we've discovered their location. The remaining five of us on the ground can hold the position for now. Order it now, general. Please, sir."

"Gentlemen, you heard the lady. Pull back out of visual range until further instructions," Meyers ordered.

"Roger that," Captain Michaels said, as he pulled his aircraft out of its hover position, and peeled back banking hard to the right, ascending quickly over the treetops and disappearing into the darkness. Commander Wainright was right behind the first gun-ship pulling his aircraft up and out of their hover, vanishing into the night sky.

"Awaiting orders, General Meyers," Wainright reported from a safe distance away.

"Stand by, gentlemen," Meyers replied. "What's next, Sylvia?"

"Stand by, general," Sylvia said, grabbing her grenade launcher and AK-74 while she and the other four soldiers retreated back into the tree-line. The three-quarter moon was still tucked behind a sky full of dark clouds, so the ground forces were difficult to detect.

General Meyers and his staff listened to the heavy breathing of the five soldiers, while the rough video transmission tracked the quick retreat into the forest.

"Okay, general, this is what I do know," Sylvia began, speaking much more softly now since she didn't have to compete with the aircraft and their engines. "There were eight militants still alive when I left the warehouse on the Danube—including the Prophet. There were nine healthy leaders as well. They were a little roughed up, but they were alive and fine. They're all aware that I'm alive and was masquerading as one of the militants, which may help in the event of a penetration. I don't know. They made the trip through the forest up to this location in four Hummers. There are unfortunately only three Hummers here now," Sylvia explained. "I need two things from you, general."

"You got it. What do you need?" Meyers complied.

"First of all, find me that fourth Hummer, general. Send some of your helos around the perimeter of the forest, or get us some sat-recon and locate that vehicle. I don't think that vehicle could make it out of the forest without being stopped. I would imagine we have a pretty heavy military dragnet on all sides. Right?"

"That is affirmative, Sylvia," Meyers acknowledged.

"I have a hunch whoever was in that vehicle wasn't all nine hostages and all eight captors. And I have already seen at least two militants at this location, and at least two captives. So my guess is that there's a higher probability that most if not all captors *and* captives are here at this location. But, I also have to tell you the leader of the group—he was very well-educated—civilized. I don't think he was a killer—just the conductor—maybe even the money. If he was the sole occupant in that vehicle; A) he more than likely has disappeared into the Viennese landscape, and; B) whoever was left behind with the hostages certainly doesn't mind dying, and doesn't mind taking every life in there with them. From the conversations I had with the militants that I terminated, I learned that the group is very well-funded. Every one of these militants and their families are set up for life whether they live *or* die. The chef back at the UN was also paid a handsome sum to sell his soul. For starters have your intel-people start working on the paper trail."

"Understood," Meyers said. "We're already on it."

"Oh, and general, I think some of the wait staff from Schaafhausen may be in on this. I know several waiters made the initial flight off the roof of the UN complex," Sylvia urged. "Scour the surveillance tapes from the restaurant."

"Unfortunately, they blasted the cameras off the walls almost as quickly as they murdered everyone in the restaurant," Meyers said, suddenly remembering the UN photographer's eerie series of photos, and the horrified grimaces of the leaders. Miraculously, in five of the images quite a few of the wait staff were visible. Oddly, a third of the waiters faced away from the blast, while the rest were exposed to the same mighty shock that the leaders were, Meyers recalled. "Simonson, pull the photographer's photos back up! I want the names of everyone in those photos—mothers, brothers, sisters, underwear size, everything. Now!"

"Yes, sir!" the director snapped back.

"General?" Sylvia asked.

"Sylvia, we found at least one very Caucasian corpse back at the warehouse with his head nearly cut off. I assume this was your work?"

"Uh, yes, sir," Sylvia answered somewhat tentatively.

"You did what you had to do. This waiter disclosure merely helps connect the dots."

"Perhaps," Sylvia agreed cautiously. "General, as far as the situation here is concerned, you need to put a thousand troops on the ground now—or whatever you can get me immediately—skilled guys—sewer rats though—guys that can squeeze through cracks if need be—guys that can climb the side of a building—guys that are *really* good with close-in work, hand-to-hand. Do you understand, sir?"

"Of course, Sylvia," Meyers replied. "I don't think I can get you a thousand of what you're looking for. But let me see what kind of assets we have in the area."

"Roger that, sir. Keep your air support out of sight. We don't need it. It won't help. Drop whatever ground troops and close-in guys you can come up with behind the tree-line," Sylvia acknowledged, then began unzipping her insulated camouflage arctic ski-wear, causing the four foot soldiers surrounding her to ask intermittently what she was doing. She didn't acknowledge their questions, but kept on stripping off the warm layers while discussing strategy with the general.

"These four soldiers and I will investigate potential cracks in the armor of this structure, and we will meet back here in thirty minutes, at exactly 0500 local time," she explained, glancing at her watch while the digital feed from three of the soldiers head-cams back to the Pentagon showed Sylvia continuing to peel off her outerwear exposing the black knit attire she and the other militants wore.

"What *are* you doing, Sylvia?" General Meyers asked. The images he was watching were indeed dark, but the general saw enough of the woman in dark clothing to get an idea of what she was up to.

"General Meyers, this is how your combat forces *must* be dressed. We could storm the complex and more than likely win a decisive shoot-out relatively quickly. Unfortunately we'd lose all or some of the leaders. And I'm not willing to take that risk."

"Point taken," Meyers said.

"But if we can somehow penetrate the fortress, and become one of them—even if it's for a half a second—the half-second element of surprise while they're trying to figure out which one of us is one of them—and the sharp shooters you send me are good and quick of hand—we could just pull off a miracle. It's *got* to be close-in work, general. It's the only shot we have. And even then there's no guarantee that we won't lose a leader or two."

"Given the circumstances, I think you're right, Sylvia," Meyers agreed. "We can't afford another loss of this magnitude."

"And General Meyers, your soldiers must be wearing these," Sylvia said, then removed her headset and pulled the black knit ski-mask over her head and stared into one of the soldier's head-cams. She reached for the headset that she just removed and handed to one of the soldiers, then placed it back on her head. "Are we clear, general?"

"Crystal," Meyers replied. "Let me get busy and get you some support."

"Thank you, general. I owe you one," Sylvia said.

"We'll talk about who owes whom another time."

"Oh, and general, unless it's absolutely necessary discontinue communication on this frequency until I or one of these men contact you."

"Roger that, Sylvia, breaking communication now. We'll talk to you at 0500 hours."

Sylvia asked one of the soldiers standing next to her to make sure all of her hair was tucked up under her ski-mask. As he complied and tucked the few renegade strands of brunette hair back under her knit cap, she gave the anxious soldiers orders, speaking a little louder than a whisper, gathering them all in close and staring into their eyes.

"Gentlemen, for your president, for your country, and for our world, we now have the honor and duty to circle this building and find its flaws. The shortest distance to both sides of the structure is along this side here," Sylvia said, motioning to her right. "All four of you traverse behind the tree-line about one or two meters in, along the back side of the complex. It's dark out. You should be fine behind the tree-line. Two of you stop at the northwest corner of the building, and you two continue to the southwest corner. At that point spread out and hit your bellies. I've been to the northwest corner already. You'll discover the three Hummers all parked under the carport out back. On my last visual I saw two militants and two leaders being taken inside. I doubt very seriously that anyone is still hanging around out back, but be careful just the same. These clowns thirst for blood, and I'd prefer not to give them yours. I want to see you all back home at a barbeque next summer. So be quiet, be stealth, and cover each other's asses. All right?"

"All right, check," they staggered their responses. "Yup, Roger that!"

"I'm going right up the middle, through this tall grass," Sylvia said, motioning with her head. "There are two windows on this side of the building, but I have the only ski mask and a hell of a lot of this tall grass to hide in, so I'll be fine. All right, does everyone understand their role?"

All four of the soldiers nodded back to Sylvia.

"All right, gentlemen. Let's synchronize our watches," Sylvia said, holding out her left wrist to show the men her chronographed wristwatch.

The four soldiers adjusted their time pieces to reflect the exact time on Sylvia's watch.

"See you in thirty minutes. Bring me some good news. And no radios *or* heroes. All right?"

CHAPTER 16

Hong Kong, 8:31 a.m.

Charles Li used the executive shower in his office to wash off some of the guilt he'd taken with him to bed on the couch just five hours earlier. He wasn't sure why he felt the way he did but an undercurrent of remorse would not subside. He and his financial constituents hadn't participated in anything conspicuously wrong. Nor had they done anything differently from in the past. They merely were momentum players in specialized markets. They took their time to accumulate significant positions then rode a story to riches. It didn't matter which way the market went, as long as they were on the right side of the story. There was nothing illegal about what they did. It was just doing battle on a battlefield afforded only a select few. The only blood being shed was that of someone sitting on the wrong side of the story, and the trade.

In Pak Li's case, it was a no-brainer. With the dollar no longer the reserve currency, precious metals were the immediate beneficiary, and had been for some time. However, any qualified chartist would tell you that the move the prized bullion had made was clearly parabolic, and was sure to break. With the two-session spike in prices, the premiums being added to the entire sector would surely have the effect of tectonic plates colliding. Many analysts felt that *when* the momentum broke, the waves of selling would have the ripple effects of a financial tsunami. But then that was the speculation dating all the way back to 2008.

Yet why did Charles Li still feel like he was a part of something very wrong? He stood and watched CNBC Asia to get a sense of how the Asian markets might behave this morning, while buttoning up a crisp, starched white shirt from the collection that hung in his private closet just steps away. He'd come to realize through the years that one always had to be prepared to take the battle home with him or in this case stay entrenched on the battlefield—his office. He wasn't married and didn't have children. His shares, his bullion, and his passion for the marketplace were his family. And so was Minh Pak, his partner of twenty years.

Most of the Hang Seng futures looked to open decidedly weaker from the previous day's close. As Li had expected, all of the precious metals futures were through the roof, as was the case with oil futures. Everything else that crossed the ticker on the bottom of the monitor was hemorrhaging in the red.

There was a knock on the door. Then just as quickly Li's partner stuck his head in. "Are you about ready?" Pak asked.

"Yes," Li answered. "In a few minutes, what's your hurry? The markets don't open for a while. Come on in."

Pak let himself in, then closed the door behind him, while Li walked over to his closet and retrieved a navy blue suit and hung it on the door knob of the closet-door. The inside of the door was a full-length mirror. Li pulled the matching navy slacks off of the hanger and slipped into them. "So now it's show time," he said to his partner, while buttoning his slacks and zipping up the zipper.

"Yep," Pak agreed. "Did you hear anything from Gregor?"

"Nope," Li answered, and then snuck back in to the closet to retrieve a belt. He ran the belt through the loops on his pants then buckled it. "It's four-thirty in the morning where he is. Undoubtedly he had a late night with his toys. We'll let him call us."

"Anything change in Vienna?" Pak asked.

Li emerged from the closet with a brilliant red tie and draped it around his raised collar. "Yes, as a matter of fact there was a change—a pretty big development at that," he answered while walking back over to his partner who was sitting on the sofa, half-watching the Asian pre-market data streaming across the bottom of the flat-screen monitor. "They still haven't found the hostages. But apparently there was a breach at their original location and half-dozen of the militants were killed by someone other than a militant, which is a good thing. The bad thing is they killed the Canadian President, execution style, on television for the world to see. Now they're on the run again and nowhere to be found. Speculation is that they might be really pissed off now and liable to do something really desperate, like kill more leaders, possibly even all of them."

"You'd think that the breach and the dead militants would have more of a positive effect on the markets, but uncertainty continues to weigh very heavily," Minh Pak said, while staring at the monitor.

"Yes it does," Li agreed, having just finished tying his tie. "But uncertainty is our greatest ally right now." He walked back to the closet door to retrieve his navy suit jacket and slipped into it, while buttoning two buttons, then gave a nod of approval toward the mirror. "Shall we go get ourselves a cup of coffee?"

"Indeed," Pak said, getting up from the leather sofa.

There was a Starbucks in the lobby of the building where a lot of the financial gurus tended to congregate every morning. The management had installed several flat-screens so that their patrons could observe the day's financial outlook.

Pak and Li went over their strategy for the day relative to where the precious metals futures were currently trading, trying to convince one another it was just another day. But they both knew it was anything but another day.

The two partners emerged from Li's office and strolled through the company's trading floor en route to the elevator. The mood from within was somewhat somber as the wait-and-see strategy counted down the remaining twenty-five minutes until opening bell. Most of the firm's traders acted in concert with Pak and Li's strategy. But there were a few rogue traders still trying to be cowboys.

"Good morning!" a few of them said heartily in the direction of their bosses.

"Good morning," Pak and Li answered in tandem, and then disappeared into the elevator.

Downstairs the Starbucks coffee house was buzzing with anticipation. It was just twenty-two minutes until most of Asia's markets would open. The Nikkei in Japan had been open for almost an hour now, and was getting absolutely clocked—down eighteen-hundred points, or just about ten percent. As expected, precious metals led by gold and platinum were shooting through the roof. Oil was also trading at historical highs.

Most of the patrons who were there were long on the markets, but they were also professionals, and therefore had hedged their positions. Still, the imminent bloodbath that was just minutes away would make for a very disconcerting morning for most.

Charles Li and Minh Pak ordered their lattes and stood off to the side while waiting for their orders to be filled. They made idle conversation with some of the regulars who pretended to be fine with a down market, but undoubtedly were already consuming a few more Rolaids than usual, and coincidentally disappearing before the opening bell. Most people don't like to die in public.

There was a British fund manager, Walter Grant that Pak and Li knew from the Scorpion Hedge Fund on the floor below them. Grant had paid his dues and had been running the fund for about three years now. He'd speculated that the Hang Seng as well as the Shanghai composite were extremely overbought and due for a significant correction—both exchanges' benchmark shares were trading at sixty times earnings—about three to four times the historical norm for the U.S. markets. He'd been shorting those two indices for about eleven months now. The way he saw it, it was the second coming of dot-com begging for a needle to pop it. And it was just a matter of time.

The problem up until now was that those markets would get rocked for a one-day one percent hit, then rally, fueled by the spike of buying from a new wave of Chinese investors—some 300,000 new accounts were being opened every day in China—and they merely bought the dips, an identical template of the dot-com philosophy.

Today promised to be different. Most of these new investors had never experienced pain or panic before. Everything on this side of the Pacific had gone almost straight up for years with few hitches, as investors took advantage of bullish sentiment and cheap interest rates, allowing them to buy more and more on margin. Grant could hardly contain himself—he was giddy with anticipation. If the Hang Seng and Shanghai were anywhere near the Nikkei indices level of disaster, he was about to hit the cover off the ball. Naturally the safety of kidnapped leaders was a big concern to Grant, but a home run was a home run.

Pak and Li took delivery of their coffee drinks and pastries and met with Grant back in the corner, where Grant had secured three oversized, burgundy colored velvet chairs and a small coffee table. Eleven minutes remained until the markets opened.

There was nothing Minh Pak and Charles Li could do now except let the markets play out their strategy. Their firm owned everything they were going to own, and all of the would-be sell-orders were tied to trailing stops. The more the gold markets rallied, the higher their trailing stops would be raised. This was just the end of a long run they'd been working on for about three years now. It was unfortunate that the world was teetering on the edge of psychological and structural disaster, but they were just businessmen who'd caught a break because they'd guessed correctly at the right time.

In just seven minutes the opening bell would ring. Walter Grant had never looked so confident, Pak and Li noted. Their acquaintance was about to add serious revenue to the Scorpion Fund based in the UK. Surely a significant bonus from the management would be in order, if all the dominos fell in their proper places. "You look like you're in a particularly good mood this morning, Walter," Charles Li said.

"Just another day on the battlefield," Grant replied, concealing a distant smirk. "Terrible about the G-10 guys, huh?"

"Horrific," Li answered, stern-faced. "It's absolutely horrific."

"Yes, it is," Grant agreed, trying to look for a silver lining. "But you guys should do okay today."

"We do well everyday," Minh Pak remarked. "We don't need good people dying to make us money."

"Yeah, of course," Grant said, a little miffed by the lecture in humanity. "Anyhow, good luck today just the same. Here we go."

Suddenly Starbucks grew quiet as the remaining patrons watched the flat-screen nearest them for the opening moments of the Hong Kong and Shanghai markets. Straight out of the gate the Hang Seng was down five-and-a-half percent—the Shanghai off about seven percent, as the same shares that were traded there were trading at a significant premium to the mother market of Hong Kong and its identical shares.

"Intriguing opening," Grant observed, raising his beverage to his mouth for a sip. "Somewhat predictable, but it's intriguing just the same."

"Give it some time," Li said, breaking off a corner of his brioche and dipping it into his coffee. "On your side of the market, investors haven't even begun to get hit with margin calls yet. They've never seen this sort of thing over here before. And if it gets bad, look out!"

"I know," Grant agreed. "I've got all kinds of time."

"These two markets have been running wild, untested, for far too long. We were due," Pak added.

"Oh, by the way, Minh, I have a confession," Li offered.

"What's that?"

"I bought a couple hundred February puts on each market, in my own account of course," Li said, somewhat mischievously.

"I uh," the usually conservative Pak started to say, having another sip of his beverage, while briefly hiding behind a hand to over his forehead. "I did the same—a little more than a hundred on each though."

"February's?" Li asked.

"Yep," Pak exhaled.

"Nice going, lads," Grant said. "You guys have got guts. There's only a week left before expiration. Did you know something?"

"We obviously knew what you knew," Pak said. "That these two markets were way over-bought. Like you said, it was just a matter of time."

"Yeah, c'mon! Hey, look at your gold there," Grant noted, observing the early spike in the hot commodity streaming across the bottom of the screen. "Not a bad start to your day—up thirty-four dollars an ounce."

"The day is young," Li said calmly and settled back in his oversized chair, while Grant and Pak made chit-chat for a while longer. "Short covering hasn't even kicked in yet. Gold should be flying down the stretch pretty soon."

The two markets fought valiantly, holding their current levels, while the Japanese market showed no signs of recovery. The three men hardly noticed that Starbucks was nearly empty now, most of the patrons having evacuated to their respective offices for cover ... or an abrupt change in strategy.

About forty-five minutes after the markets opened both the Hang Seng and the Shanghai composites started to deteriorate, initially very slowly. Then the momentum kicked in when a report from a CNN talk-show in America painted a very ominous report out of Vienna, questioning how the world's markets would react a day, a week, or a month from now, if the world leaders were never found, or worse yet if any or all of them were killed. The brazen report even went on to quantify which leader would carry more of a psychological or financial impact globally if they were to be killed.

"Unbelievable," Pak said. "Now they're putting a premium on the heads of world leaders. I've seen everything now."

"Can you believe this?" Li added.

"Hey fellas, this is nothing new, all right?" Grant added. "The blokes over in America love to speculate on this stuff. It's talk show heaven over there. Everyone's a world-renowned analyst when this shit comes up. What I want to know is what these guys do when they're not enjoying their fifteen minutes of world crisis."

"Yeah, no kidding," Pak said.

"Hey, not a bad day for you guys," Grant said, pointing up to the streaming ticker at the bottom of the screen. "Well I'll be gob-smacked! Up another fifty-three dollars an ounce. Splendid day! Good God, man! I think this is a new high—$2,053 an ounce."

"Yeah, not bad," Li said, subconsciously wondering why he still hadn't heard from his associate, Gregor. At the same time it was difficult to suppress his numbness from gold's mercurial ascent. "I'll be right back," he said, while getting up and heading for the exit. Li reached into his coat pocket and retrieved his phone while pushing the glass door to the street open. He speed-dialed his German associate while descending the three steps to the street. The line went straight to busy, so he dialed again. The same thing happened again.

"Hmmm," Li thought aloud, "that's weird." He tried one more time and the same thing happened. "What *are* you doing, my friend? Playing with your little girlfriends again?" Li then ended the call and placed his Blackberry back into his coat pocket, and rejoined his friends. "What's going on, guys?"

"You're making money," Grant said. "And the markets are coming apart."

"That means you're making money, Walter," Li said. "It took you a while. But it looks like you've finally got it right. Congratulations!"

"Thanks, mate," Grant acknowledged. "And same to you guys."

"Thanks," Li said, uninterested in a celebration, for a myriad of reasons. "C'mon, Minh. Let's go upstairs. I need to talk to you."

"Yeah, sure," Pak said, and stood up. "Good luck, Walter."

"Yeah, thanks! Maybe we'll celebrate later."

"Maybe," Pak replied, more as a cordial gesture than with any intention. Then the two partners left Starbucks.

Maldive Islands, 7:34 a.m.

Gregor Heinricke sat at the bar, half-slumped in his posture, wearing just his swimsuit—his basic wardrobe for the past several days, while he watched the flat-screen for the early Bloomberg coverage of the Asian markets. Thus far everything he and his global constituents had been planning for had come to fruition. His right hand played around on his laptop which still sat the bar, while he occasionally glanced at the interactive values of his various positions and the coordinating interactive charts. The buying interest in the precious metals sector was overwhelming and relentless, along with the associated precious metals stocks. From the opening bell, gold shot up like a rocket ship as if gravity didn't exist.

For a moment Heinricke almost forgot that there was a global crisis that was responsible for all of this. He'd also forgotten his mobile sat-phone somewhere, and knew he should confer with his associates, as a matter of protocol. He looked up from the laptop, trying to retrace his steps, still a little groggy from the lack of sleep. Coffee, he thought. "Need a cup of coffee," his mouth mumbled the words his head was thinking. The fresh brewed pot of coffee that he started ten minutes earlier was undoubtedly done, judging by the strong scent of Arabic blend wafting in his direction via the gentle morning breeze.

He got up out of his slumped perch at the bar and sauntered over to where the coffee pot sat, and poured a cup of the fresh brew. Lo and behold, there was his mobile phone in pieces. He'd taken the drained battery out to replace it with the recharged battery that sat in its charging cradle overnight, but never finished the job. "Shit!" he said, fumbling with the newly recharged battery until he finally got it into the battery compartment in the phone, then slipped its back cover back on to its locked position. He turned the phone over and pressed the *on* button, then walked back to his perch at the bar with his cup of steaming black coffee.

Heinricke resumed watching the Asian market's coverage while waiting for his phone to sync in. The girls undoubtedly would be out for a few more hours, after a long day of play and cocktailing. He had a weak but pleasant laugh at the thought of what comprised their busy agenda down here in the tropics, as his left hand softly wiped his two-day stubble. Suddenly the single ring on his mobile phone alerted him to an awaiting message, so he depressed the voicemail button and waited for the message.

"Hi, Gregor. It's Nabeel. I'm sorry, but my phone has been off..."

"Jesus Christ!" Heinricke reacted to the once familiar voice, almost falling off the bar stool. The call was so overdue it had the effect of a triple espresso, suddenly pumping a shot of adrenaline into the still-awaking currency trader. Heinricke pressed the replay button to validate that the call wasn't a figment of his imagination.

"Hi Gregor. It's Nabeel. I'm sorry, my phone has been off. I've been at a very small financial conference down in Schaafhausen, near the German-Swiss border," the British voice said. "These were some of the people that I'd been telling you about, with regard to a precious metals short squeeze and accompanying story. Well, as you might imagine, we were all stunned when we'd heard the news out of Vienna, so our conference was cut short. And I've been in my room at a friend's house most of the night, watching the coverage of these barbaric goons. It's just terrible. Anyhow, it's four in the morning here. I can't sleep and don't suspect I will be able to any time soon. So please call me any time."

Gregor terminated the call, not interested in finding out if there were any more messages, and immediately found the speed dial entry for Nabeel and pressed the call button.

The phone rang and rang and rang. Finally Nabeel's voicemail kicked in. Frustrated again, Heinricke left a message. Then his right hand minimized all of the open programs on his laptop, while his left hand found the cup of strong black coffee and raised it to his mouth to take a big swig. He set the cup down and both hands went to work on the laptop, opening up a new Google search window. It opened and he typed in the words "financial conference Schaafhausen," then clicked on search. While the Google search conducted its business, Heinricke lifted his head in the direction of the flat screen long enough to hear, "...gold has just hit $2,059 an ounce."

"Scheiss," Heinricke, said, half-dazed, while raising his hand to his mouth, subconsciously chewing on his first finger. He shook his head tightly almost as if to jar himself free of the news report's compelling trance, then fumbled for the remote and lowered the volume. He and his associates were rich beyond belief with the overnight windfall in the anointed bullion. They were in pretty good shape to begin with, but now Heinricke's group, which was overly leveraged in the various derivative vehicles they'd taken positions in, were silly rich as their multiples were in the hundreds. On the other hand, their hedge positions became worthless. But that was the cost of an insurance policy. It was money well spent.

Heinricke looked down at the screen and the search turned up zero results. "Hmmm," he thought, then typed in another variation of the search and clicked go.

His mind raced now as a combination of adrenaline from gold's ascent, caffeine, the phone call from Nabeel, the ensuing lack of response from Nabeel and the failed Google search, contributed to his sudden alertness. He tried one more variation of his original search. It turned up nothing as well. He inhaled slowly and deliberately and took a long swig from the cup of coffee, then got up and walked down to the water and immersed himself entirely. His mind did battle with itself as to why the Google search couldn't find a conference in Schaafhausen. All of these things should be publicized, he told himself, regardless of size. And wasn't that the name of the restaurant where all the killing and kidnapping took place? There were just too many unanswered questions.

Then he allowed the memory from just a few minutes earlier to penetrate his mind—gold has just hit $2,059 an ounce, bringing a subtle smile to his face. Then he let out a small giggle like a child, while his mind calculated the numbers that would be generated from all of his options. And it didn't matter if there was a correction, because everything that went up had the appropriate trailing sell-stops in place.

Except for Heinricke's sporadic giggles, the lapping sound from the six-inch waves of the Indian Ocean was the only noise around. Suddenly his ringing mobile phone on the bar jarred him from his playful solitude. He submerged himself quickly and squeezed his wet hair back with his hands and charged out of the water toward the sound of the ring. He arrived just in time to open his flip-phone and read its display, 'Voicemail.'

CHAPTER 17

Vienna, 4:48 a.m.

The posh Opera Plaza Palace sat just adjacent to the ornate Vienna Opera Plaza complex—hence its name. Like most of the finer buildings in Vienna, all of these were meticulously and regularly restored. Most of them were roughly two hundred years old, and looked like they did the day they were finished in the 1800s. Pristine white paint coated an unblemished set of bones, with brilliant gold trim on all of its case-work and arched entrances. The streetlights still sparkling in the wee hours of the crisp Austrian morning showcased the collection of storybook buildings—all of the gold trim in the Platz shining like a precious jewel in a highlighted jeweler's display case.

The frigid but gentle breeze passed through the street almost undetected because most of the trees had lost their leaves. Except for a handful of pedestrians tightening their scarves at the chilly gusts, very few felt winter's bitter elements.

In the center of the Platz stood a statue, as is the case all over Vienna. This one was a beautiful life-sized bronze replica of Vienna's own Johann Strauss, the famous writer and conductor from the nineteenth century. Strauss was perched proudly about six feet above the ground on a concrete base, with a bronze plaque mounted at eye level displaying a short history of the artist.

Vienna was very proud of its heroes, and its residents made sure their legacy lived on in earthly displays.

The Opera Plaza Palace was the only Mercedes five-star, five-diamond hotel on this side of Vienna. They were open for business 24/7. The inn was the quintessential benchmark in sheer elegance. Dignitaries from all around the world had graced the halls of this famous establishment for decades and centuries, wining and dining in the world-renowned restaurant just off the main lobby. After attending a gala or an opera across the street, patrons were only steps from a blissful night's sleep in a womb of thousand-thread-count sheets and goose down comforters and pillows. The hotel's patrons were royalty after all.

Earlier in the evening when the hotel had begun to experience what most of Europe and America had been experiencing with the banking and credit card fallout, they merely extended the courtesy to its guests to accept whatever charges were made during their stay. The way management saw it, there was no need to panic or indicate that panic was a concern at an establishment of this caliber. The least expensive room after all was listed at $900 U.S., while the suites ranged in the thousands of dollars per night.

Most of the hotel's guests were regulars and were pre-authorized upon check-in for an over-the-amount limit on their credit cards. That, coupled with the fact that a lot of older Europeans still carried cash, made for brisk business in the hotel's restaurant just a few hours earlier.

Upstairs on the sixth floor, a waiter pushed his rolling room-service cart down the nineteenth century corridor. Being careful not to steer into the gold-trimmed wainscot, he stopped at Suite 606. He knocked on the door and about twenty seconds later the hotel's guest opened it.

"Mr. Enghardt?" The waiter asked. The hotel's computer had indicated the guest had already been there for seven days, but protocol had called for him to *always* address the guest by name.

"Ah yes, please come in," the fair-skinned Klaus Enghardt said, somewhat with anticipation. The blond-haired, blue-eyed guest was draped in the oversized fluffy terrycloth bathrobe that sported the hotel's monogram on the left breast. "I'm absolutely famished."

The waiter pushed the cart in while the guest tried to hold the door open. "No it's okay," he said, stooping to place a rubber wedge under the door.

"Very well then," the hotel guest with a British accent said. "Over here is fine," Enghardt said, motioning to the side of the bureau where the flat-screen television sat. All of the furniture was from France's Louis XVI era.

The waiter parked the cart where the guest had requested, just in between the bureau and the matching chair with carved armrests and brass feet, indicative of that period. One by one the waiter elegantly rattled off the items that the guest had ordered, while an annoying mobile phone rang in the background. "Will there be anything else, sir?"

"No. Thanks very much," Enghardt replied. "Everything looks lovely."

"Then just your signature here, sir," the waiter said, producing a room service ticket.

"Very well then," Enghardt obliged, scribbling his signature on the voucher, then handing the waiter a twenty-Euro bill. "For your trouble."

"Thank you, sir!" the waiter said, very pleased with the tip, and then retreated to the front door to retrieve the rubber door stop and left. On the walk back to the service elevator the waiter thought about the Bavarian guest's name and a language that didn't quite match. He pressed the service elevator's call button, while reaching into his pants pocket to recover the twenty-Euro note. He smiled and returned the note into his pocket, as the elevator door opened. What the hell! He'd seen stranger things in his five years at the hotel than a voice that didn't match a name, he thought, then climbed into the lift and it slowly carted him downstairs to his work station.

Enghardt poured himself a cup of the Viennese coffee then added a dash of cream, a sprinkle of sugar and stirred it gently. He took a sip and retrieved his mobile phone from the bed. There was a message waiting, as he'd expected. He depressed the message button then returned to his coffee. The message was from his German associate, Gregor Heinricke.

The Englishman masquerading as a Bavarian listened to the short message while removing the plastic wrapping from the glass of fresh-squeezed orange juice and had a sip. The message was simply for Ali-Khan to return the call. He erased the message then speed-dialed his associate. In seconds, they were connected.

"Ah, Gregor, there you are, at long last. How are you, my friend?"

"I am fine," the German said with not much conviction. "I've been worried to death about you, since I haven't heard from you in nearly two days. And with all of this world chaos—"

"I'm sorry, Gregor," Ali-Khan interrupted. "But I as well have been worried about you, my family, the leaders, everyone! These are not normal times. No one in their wildest dreams could have drawn up something as unimaginable as this. My phone had been off because of the conference, and I simply forgot to turn it back on because of all of this chaos down in Vienna. I'm sure you can understand. I haven't budged from the television in eight hours. And after all, wasn't your own phone off for a while, when I called you a short while ago?"

"Yes," Heinricke admitted. "Yes, it was. I was recharging the batteries while I tried to get some sleep—I'm lucky if I got three hours."

"That's three more than I've had," Ali-Khan said. "I'll be living on caffeine until this thing is over."

"Nabeel, I have to ask you a question," Heinricke said, a little afraid to ask – but he still had to ask for his own peace of mind. "I don't mean to offend you, but…"

"You won't offend me. These are interesting times. Ask your question."

"All right," Heinricke started. "When I couldn't get hold of you, I was curious, and so I did a Google search on your conference held in Schaafhausen. I couldn't find a thing. What's going on?"

"Ohhhh, Gregor," Ali-Khan said, a little frustrated by what he considered to be somewhat of a sophomoric question, given the level of professional experience the two had shared throughout the years. "You know these things aren't always publicized. This one was off the radar, as it had to be given the nature of its content. I don't even think you've met any of these associates, even in your circles. This one was air-tight."

"Okay," Heinricke said, seemingly buying in, but still lacked total conviction in his tone.

"And besides," Ali-Khan continued. "We were about one hour into the conference, discussing our strategy to move the precious metals market decisively further along, when word got to us of this lunacy down in Vienna. We stopped our conference short because the world stage had very unfortunately done our work for us. As you can see, we all have done very well in our cumulative investments. Our plan couldn't have come anywhere near these results. In fact I've already liquidated most of our positions in the overseas markets, but we have a few things left in the London account that we still may move, or hang onto, I don't know. We'll just have to wait for the UK markets to open in four-and-a-half hours to liquidate the remainder, or perhaps not. For now though we need to get our leaders back."

"Why would you liquidate your position already, Nabeel?" Heinricke asked, very curious now why his friend might be so anxious to sell into what was obviously a continuing momentum swing to the upside—a significant one at that.

"Well, you and I both know that sometimes it's not a bad strategy to sell into breakouts. The price of gold exceeded my wildest dreams. So, what we sold is merely taking half our position off the market. Anything else would be sheer greed. And greed kills. You know that. We still maintain our UK and European positions. If gold runs further, we will realize further gains. And for those remaining positions we'll let our sell-stops take care of our work for us. I just don't think this world crisis and the ensuing consequences, as horrific as they are, will last forever."

Something went off like a debilitating time bomb in Heinricke's ears for just a moment, as he winced at what seemed like an obvious admission of insider information. Or had he suddenly become utterly conspiratorial? He questioned his own rationale and morality.

"Where've you been, really?" Heinricke asked, without weighing the consequences of that very question.

"I told you where—"

"No no no," Heinricke stopped him. "Where have you really been?"

"Ahhh, Gregor," Ali-Khan exhaled, finally realizing what his friend was getting at, artificially deflating himself while sitting back in the chair next to the room service cart. "You poor thing."

"Why?" Heinricke snapped back. "Why am I a poor thing?"

"You think that I am a part of this whole thing because I am of Arab descent. My God, Gregor, you've been my friend for twenty years. You know my family. You've stayed at my home. You've played with my children!" Ali-Khan said in disbelief, popping out of his chair and pacing the room. "I can't believe my friend of twenty years would say something like this. Are you reading spy novels or something?"

"No," Heinricke said calmly. "I'm not reading spy novels. There are just some things that don't add up."

"Like?"

"Your time horizon…not answering the phone…your undisclosed locations—"

"You know," Ali-Khan interrupted. "You're really pushing the envelope here. You are my friend first, then an esteemed colleague. Quit behaving like someone who's lost his marbles. Was I in Vienna conducting a raid on the United Nations building, with all that amazing weaponry? Of course not! Wake up, man! I've never fired a firearm in my life! You know that. How could I start now? You know what I do for a living. You know what I do for hobbies: I golf, I go to the gym. You're usually with me. I don't go to the shooting range, or even duck hunting. For God's sake, man, I don't take world leaders hostage. Quite frankly, I find this very notion appalling, Gregor. And I don't know why I'm even taking the time to engage you in this outrageous dialogue."

"Fine," Heinricke said, remaining calm. "Let me call you back in a few minutes at your hotel in Schaafhausen."

"Well first of all, you know the rules," Ali-Khan reminded his friend about the ground rules of communication that they'd set many years earlier: there were to be no land line calls, and all mobile-to-mobile calls were caller I.D. blocked. Their mobile numbers were only given out to 'insiders' anyway, with the less chance of a trace the better. It was a clandestine group that they belonged to which was three layers deep, and the ground rules were in place to keep it that way, though nothing in the structure in which they conducted business was devious or illegal. It was just protocol.

"Secondly, I'm staying at a friend's chalet and I really haven't the foggiest idea what the number is here, or where the bloody phone is for that matter. Now stop with this nonsensical tirade about me being something I am not—a terrorist, for God's sake! I'm done with this!" Ali-Khan snapped, and then ended the call. Sleep deprivation had started to take its effect.

Ali-Khan walked back over to the room service cart and set his mobile phone down on it next to the pot of coffee. He backtracked to the bureau and angled the flat screen back toward the cart so that he could watch the early version of CNBC-Europe, then sat down to enjoy his eggs Benedict and fresh fruit, still ruffled by his friend's cutting accusations.

Ali-Khan was famished, wolfing down everything on his plate while still managing proper British table etiquette, dabbing his cloth napkin at the corners of his mouth in between bites. CNBC took care of the rest, going back and forth in between Asian market coverage and European pre-markets.

He and his clandestine group had done well, with gold hitting $2,065 an ounce, then falling back to $2,060 and stabilizing in that area for the last half an hour. It was almost as if the world itself was now its own reality show, waiting for its own next move. Suddenly Ali-Khan's mobile phone rang. The caller I.D. indicated that it was his wife, Vatsana. What the heck is she doing up so early? He thought, and then pressed the answer button. "Hello, darling. What are you doing up so early?"

"Well I should ask the same of you," Vatsana said, in her sleepy Welsh accent. "I couldn't sleep. I've been worried sick about you, and haven't been able to reach you. Given the world's turmoil, I hope you can understand my concern."

"Of course, darling," Ali-Khan answered, rushing a sip of coffee. "I understand. As you knew, I was to be at the two-day conference in Schaafhausen, and we got about one hour into it before we collectively agreed to postpone it until after all of this craziness stops," he explained, sparing some of the details that he'd just shared with his German associate. His wife was very familiar with protocol when he went to these private conferences—they didn't usually talk until Nabeel called her. It was just that way. She didn't question it and she didn't need to. She knew her husband was a pretty important man in his circles. And as a result of his success, she and the children were provided with a pretty lavish lifestyle.

"Sorry, I'd forgotten to turn my mobile back on," Ali-Khan confessed.

"That's fine, darling," Vatsana said. "I'm just happy to hear your voice."

"And I, yours. How are the children?"

"They're fine," Vatsana answered. "We had a little bit of a scare with this banking situation. We were down at Harrod's and none of my credit cards worked, but I had enough cash on hand to get us through. As it turned out we just stayed in and ate at home and watched the tellie."

"This will all be over before we know it," Ali-Khan assured.

"Hurry home, darling," Vatsana pleaded softly.

"Of course," Ali-Khan complied. "I'll be on the first flight home. Though I suspect the airports will be a bit sticky for a few days. I will call you as soon as I know when I can return."

"All right then," Vatsana said through a yawn, suddenly allowing herself to feel the fatigue of being awake all night. "I'm going to sleep now. Oh, and by the way, Nabeel?"

"Yes?"

"Gregor called last night."

"Yes, that's fine. We spoke. Good night, darling. Or good morning, I should say," Ali-Khan said, and ended the call. He wished he could've just taken a pill and gone to sleep, but too many things still waited in the wings of flux. He would have plenty of time to sleep when this was all over. At some point he would have to call his friend, Gregor, and try to talk some sense into him if he didn't come to his *own* senses first. His mobile phone rang, shaking the scattered thoughts from his head. The caller I.D. was blocked so he pressed the answer button.

"Nabeel, I'm sorry," the unmistakably German voice said, exhaling slowly and deliberately. "I don't know what I was thinking. With all of these unthinkable events taking place in the world right now, I'm very confused. They're printing money in our respective accounts right now and I don't even care. And I know that sounds crazy, but it's true. In all of my professional years, I never wanted to profit from something like this. That's why I'm so confused. I don't know how to feel. But the bottom line is I don't know how I could have ever suspected you of anything but being my friend."

"It's okay, Gregor," Ali-Khan said, trying to reassure his friend. "These are trying times. I can forgive you for your vivid imagination."

CHAPTER 18

Viennese forest, 4:46 a.m.

On the northeast side of the forestry station, the separate two-man teams silently explored every crack in the exterior in their designated area, looking for any hint of entry. The first team explored in and around where the Hummers were parked, sliding on their bellies past the vehicles, silently creeping up to the structure itself. The lead soldier looked to his comrade, motioning with two fingers toward his eyes, and then pointing with one finger toward the window to the right of the door on the elevated back porch.

The second soldier took the directions and slowly ascended the steps to the elevated platform, without making a sound. He tried to stay close to the handrail on the right, reasoning that the old wooden steps would likely have some form of accumulated stress and weather fatigue in its middle, which might create a creaking noise that could compromise his position. Once at the top of the landing, he snuck under the glass window in the peeling and weathered wooden door.

The soldier quietly rose from his haunches and stood next to the door and quickly peeked into the uncertainty beyond. He could see nothing, but wasn't going to dwell long and leave himself open to be discovered. He started to reach for the door knob to check on whether it was locked, but decided against the move, figuring there had to be a sentry posted just on the inside or somewhere nearby. With his back to the wall he took two large steps to his left placing him at the edge of the window. Again he slowly peered around the blind edge and through the glass. There was nothing but darkness, but it was a quick glance. He peeked again, this time for a few seconds. The darkness was a void, but still he retreated back beyond what could have been someone's view. Very slowly he wedged his thumb up to the edge of the sliding window and gently pushed. Surprisingly, it budged. He pushed it ever-so-slowly to about two inches open to confirm that it was a legitimate crack in the structure's armor, and returned it to the closed position, exhaling silently a satisfied sigh of an immediate success. He then stealthily eased back down the steps to find sanctuary behind one of the Hummers.

On the opposite side of the carport area, the lead soldier quietly tried to detect any such similar opportunities, pushing on the two closed windows, one at a time, but with no luck. There was also an entrance at the ground level, with two crude wooden doors, approximately two feet by four feet, hinged together in the middle by a metal bracket and a closed padlock. He glanced up at his wristwatch and realized that they had seven minutes left until rendezvous at the original coordinates. His eyes combed the deck where his comrade had just been, only to find he wasn't there any longer. He didn't panic. Instead he followed what would've been the logical steps of retreat and his eyes locked onto his comrade at the back of the third Hummer, who was signaling at his wristwatch, and for him to join in the retreat.

On the far side of the building, the other two-man team had completed their mission, having found a possible way in through what looked like a door-within-a-door, somewhat like a doggie-door only larger. Their mission was to locate possible points of entry but not to enter. They withdrew into the dark forest behind them and continued further toward the rendezvous coordinates.

On the front side of the building, Sylvia had checked both of her windows to see if they were locked. Both were locked tightly. She had discovered a ground-level point of entry, identical to the two-door ground level entrance out back. This one however was hinged closed, but had no padlock securing the hinges, and she had very quietly penetrated the fortress, breaking her own rules of engagement.

Sylvia slithered down the steps, carefully navigating the blackened emptiness underground until she came into a tiny corridor with a hint of light originating from up a short flight of stairs. That's where the hostages must've been held, she figured. Her eyes strained to search her immediate surroundings for any motion or artificial light.

The sliver of light that barely trickled down the short staircase was enough to highlight two closed doors across from her. Sylvia didn't think the militants would separate themselves from their prized hostages, but had to be sure while she'd penetrated this far. She silently inched up to the first closed door, while her trained ear combed the silence for any detection of motion or irregularities.

She placed her ear on the first door, while her hand reached for the doorknob. In just a second, the door wedged open exposing nothing but darkness. Sylvia stood at the entrance to the darkened room, focused intently and listened for whatever messages the silence would reveal to her. She figured if the hostages were held in this room, then between nine of them someone would have to move a leg, an arm, or exhale in discomfort. After just five seconds, Sylvia was comfortable with her assessment that the room was empty, and closed the door.

She knew her time was very limited but couldn't vacate the premises until she had checked what was beyond the room next door. There were clearly no signs of light shining under or above the door, so Sylvia very quietly began to turn the door knob. She got the door opened about six inches and there was a sudden creaking noise. To her it was the shot that could've been heard around the world, and she just froze. Her eyes grew into shiny black buttons, figuring someone or everyone upstairs would've undoubtedly heard the earth-shattering noise and would be descending down the stairs to launch a full assault in just seconds.

Much to Sylvia's surprise, there was no immediate reaction from up above, and she used the silence to listen acutely to the void within the second room. After her standing five-count, she assessed the room was empty, consciously lowered her heartrate, and exhaled. She had determined all of the hostages were upstairs.

Suddenly the shard of light that shined down the stairs widened, and Sylvia quickly withdrew behind the twelve-inch wall next to door number two. Maybe someone did hear the obvious creaking sound of the door after all, she told herself, and she'd guessed that they'd opened the almost-closed door at the top of the stairs creating the significantly brighter light that spilled down the stairs. She again made a conscious effort to lower her heartrate so her ears could tell her what her eyes couldn't see.

Sylvia dissected the silence as she very calmly waited for any sign of a descent from what was at the top of the stairs. She heard what she thought was a light switch being switched on, but no additional light came on. She breathed a sigh of temporary relief. She was not afraid to kill what was a possible pursuer, but preferred to keep her presence unknown for the time being.

Suddenly Sylvia heard what she thought was that same switch being rapidly flicked up and down, followed by a Farsi version of "Shit! Why can't they replace the light bulbs around here?"

Her ears picked up what she thought were slow footsteps descending down the stairs. Sylvia removed her serrated combat knife from its leather holster and hoisted it up around shoulder height and waited. Her mind told her that whoever was at the top of the stairs *would* descend, and ultimately she'd have to do what was necessary. She speculated that her predator might be fragile. It had been a long night after all, and more than likely his nerves were fried. He'd had no sleep, minimal food, and was coping with a major change of course in a plan that was supposed to be airtight.

Sylvia was equally tired, but that kept her alert. She was trained for sleep deprivation, starvation, and every other tactic of warfare. She'd once completed a seventy-two hour covert stint deep inside of Iraq in the second campaign, when she didn't sleep and survived on just six ounces of beef jerky and one canteen of water.

She tried to anticipate the pace of the descent ratio, to which she'd have to thrust her combat knife up through her assailant's throat and into his brain, and it would be within one to one-and-a-half seconds, at most. Her heart began to race in anticipation when someone or something altered the light, temporarily darkening the stairs and lower landing. It was followed by a brash voice.

"What are you doing down here?" the voice asked in Farsi.

"I thought I heard something," the man half-way down the steps replied.

"C'mon, get up here! We've already swept this."

"But I really think I heard something," the pursuer answered.

"You heard a rat," the brash voice quipped. "Now get up here! We'll lock the door so your rat can't get in."

"All right," the militant halfway down the stairs said, and then turned to advance back up the stairs. He understood that death was what he'd signed up for, but at the same time he didn't mind staying alive to spend his riches. Half of his team had been eliminated by a ghost, and he had a strange hunch that the ghost lurked somewhere down below, unless he was now seeing ghosts. As he reached the upper landing, the militant turned and stared down below into the darkness and uttered the words, "Your day will come." Then he closed and locked the door.

Sylvia was now enshrouded in the comfort of the darkness. She exhaled her relief that she didn't have to kill the man right now, and then slowly stepped back through the small two-door hallway, feeling the walls for direction while retracing her steps from memory. She was convinced now that the hostages were all upstairs.

In just moments, she was at the base of the wooden steps to the two-door hatch that led up to the crisp outdoors. She climbed up and through, closing the doors quietly behind her, while her measured spurts of warm breath collided with the frigid air to create small puffs of fog. She would have to hold her breath long enough to disappear into the sanctuary of the overgrown field. Sylvia pressed a button on her timepiece, illuminating its face. She had two minutes to rendezvous. She crouched down and slid onto her belly, then slithered through the wispy, cold grass toward her objective.

On the other side of the grassy knoll, the two units had rejoined one another at the original point of departure, and shared their discoveries. They had agreed that they wouldn't initiate radio contact with the Pentagon until everyone had returned to these very coordinates. The only one missing was the woman in charge.

"Where the hell is she?" the senior-in-command asked aloud.

"Give her a break," another soldier said. "She's got another thirty seconds."

"Yeah, well, let's just hope she didn't compromise the mission," the lead said.

"With all due respect, sir," one of the other soldiers said. "She did single-handedly save the world, at least temporarily."

"Yeah, I guess you're right, corporal. That she did."

All of a sudden while the four men were discussing Sylvia's whereabouts, she emerged from the trees behind them. "Hello, boys! Did you miss me?"

"Holy shit, lady," the lead-in-command snapped in a tone a little louder than a whisper, jumping away from the intrusion. "No more surprises. All right?"

"No problem. Don't give up on me so easily," Sylvia said, and then turned toward the last defender of her honor. "Thanks for your defense, corporal, but we haven't quite saved the world yet."

"My money's on you," the soldier said, nodding with an affirmative, tight smile.

CHAPTER 19

Maldives Islands, 8:03 a.m.

Heinricke finally made contact with his associates, Li and Pak. He'd shared everything that he knew about the current crisis, and that he'd finally made contact with his long-time associate and architect of the supply-and-demand story that was going to catapult the gold markets into the stratosphere, but that the plan was never implemented.

"So what happened?" Charles Li asked into the speaker phone, peering out the window toward the Kowloon Peninsula, still trying to wash the blood off of his hands from the overnight windfall of profits.

"Apparently nothing," Heinricke explained. "My associate was at a very private conference somewhere in Switzerland, and he and his constituency were in the throes of implementing the strategy, when they were alerted to the events unfolding to the south of them and determined there was no immediate need to move forward, so they merely canceled the meeting. They had never hoped for this big of a move—at least not this quickly. So I've been informed that they've been actively selling into the rally."

"Why would they do that?" Minh Pak blurted out, sitting close enough to the speaker phone to be heard.

"For the simple reason that they feel this crisis can't last forever. The markets are historically very good at pricing in both greed and fear."

"What are *you* doing?" Pak asked quickly.

"I've peeled off half of my positions—the half that are actively trading in various Asian markets," Heinricke answered. "The rest I'll let run as long as they have momentum, and then wait to be stopped out."

"So we should begin to unload into the rally?" Li asked conversationally, not necessarily as someone looking for direction.

"That's your call my friend. It's always easier to unload into a rally—there are buyers everywhere, willing to pay just about anything. And you know, even if you have your stops in place, and there's a disorderly rush for the exits on the way back down, they might not hit your trigger until a few points later, but you'll get out. If it were me, I'd take some money off the table. Save some for the next guy. You have the luxury at the moment of the feeding the surge."

"Good idea," Li said.

"Okay, we have to get busy," Pak added. "Let's get together for dinner when this thing is over."

"Absolutely!" Heinricke agreed emphatically, noticing out of the corner of his eye that Katia was sleepily approaching from over by the grass-thatched hut that he'd left her and Arisa in just an hour earlier. "Listen, guys, I have to run. I have a needy child to tend to," he said, spinning around on his bar stool to observe the clumsy approach of the half-asleep, half-naked German girl.

"No problem, Gregor," Li said with a weak chuckle, aware of his German associate's reputation for alluring travel companions.

"Have a nice day, Gregor," Pak added. "We'll talk in a bit."

Katia arrived at the barstool where Heinricke sat and sleepily collapsed into his chest, while wrapping her arms around him. "Can't you come back to bed, Gregor?"

"In a little while, baby," Heinricke answered while wrapping his arms around her and letting one of his hands rest on her thonged derriere, then patting it lightly. Her warm, bare breasts on his chest felt very tempting. "I still have some work to do."

"That's what you said yesterday," Katia whined weakly to get her way, while letting one of her hands explore his right thigh.

"You're not making this very easy, Katia. Are you?" Heinrich exhaled a little heavier, reacting to Katia's wandering hand.

"C-mon, just for five minutes," she tried. Of course they both knew it wasn't five minutes she was after. It could take five hours with that look in her eye.

"I can't, baby," Heinricke tried again, but his hands didn't budge from Katia's soft skin as his right hand squeezed the right cheek on her silky rear end.

Katia allowed herself to slip out of Heinricke's weak grasp, falling to her knees right between his legs. Both of her hands were loosely holding his upper thighs. "All right—if you insist," she sighed very coyly, while looking up at him mischievously. She allowed her hands to wander, slowly massaging his upper thighs, clumsily stumbling over his private parts. "Whoops," she giggled.

"Katia," Heinricke fought feebly, knowing it wouldn't be the worst thing that could happen after a painfully stressful night.

"Yes?" she peeped, and then reached up for the zipper to his cargo shorts, while the other hand held him between his legs.

Gregor started to let out short spurts of breath, clearly becoming aroused. "But I…can't…"

"Can't what?" Katia asked, as she slid the zipper all the way down and slowly reached into his shorts with her right hand, while her left hand effortlessly unbuttoned the pants. As she did, and continued to massage with her right hand, he stood and his pants fell to the sandy floor. Suddenly the tables had turned, and Heinricke was now completely naked, and Katia was not.

He reached down behind her and slipped his hand into her skimpy undergarment, heatedly pulling it down now as Katia reached down with her left hand and helped him remove it the rest of the way. She kicked the last of the skimpy silk panties away with her right foot, while maintaining a grip on him with her right hand. She slowly kissed her way up his body until she finally stood and they kissed passionately, while she softly stroked him, still trying to help him erase any need to look at his computer, the flat screen, or fidget with his mobile phone.

Katia had been waiting for this for three days, and nothing would come between them now. Arisa was her alternate lover of two years, only when Gregor wasn't available. And in her mind, as much as she loved Arisa, there was still no replacement for her man. And she clearly had his attention now.

The two kissed heatedly, Heinricke forgetting logic and the stories that drove the markets and everything else that made him money. Completely committed to the moment now, he passionately forced her to one of the lower bar tables that fronted the brilliant white sand on the beach, while the two kissed and clumsily knocked over chairs until he laid her across just the right table—the one closest to the ocean. She didn't really care where he took her—she merely followed his lead. In his mind he painted a picture of how it was supposed to unfold. He kissed Katia, starting at her knees that bent naturally at the edge of the table, excited to get underway, but equally committed to making this moment last a lot longer than five minutes. He ran his hands up her smooth thighs, stroking gently, occasionally reaching up to her breasts, touching and caressing, feeling her nipples hardened with excitement. With every reach to her upper body, his mouth was pulled higher up Katia's legs, until he'd finally arrived at the forbidden fruit. He tasted her, causing her to squirm and arch her back in anticipation, while *she* now let out short pants of excitement, and then a soft moan.

Heinricke stayed with the routine, causing Katia's short breaths to grow into long exaggerated exhales until she couldn't take it anymore. She was about to burst, so she reached down and grabbed her lover by the back of the head and begged him to come up her body and kiss her and put himself inside her. "Please," she pleaded, while he continued to torture her with pleasure.

As Katia's beautifully proportioned body started to tremble, Heinricke finally did the humane thing and obliged, causing her to let out an immediate controlled squeal – her chest expanding and contracting with every long, slow deliberate stroke. He needed this as much as she did, maybe more so, because of the stressful weeks leading up to this moment. He stood above his canvas and admired the simplicity of her beauty, continuing to engage her. Then he rocked her up to a sitting position and held her closely. She was breathing heavily and sweating profusely, and he asked her to hold on. "Wrap your legs around me," he whispered.

"What?" Katia asked, barely loud enough for him to hear, almost hyperventilating in physical joy. "Okay," she said, wrapping her legs tightly around him.

Then Heinricke lifted Katia off of the table and held her tightly, never sacrificing the same motion they'd just had while they were laying down, only now he stood, while she squeezed every part of him. He turned toward the water and slowly navigated the short distance down the gentle slope to the shoreline, all the while the two of them carefully engaged in their bout of primitive gymnastics.

When he could feel his bare feet splashing into the shallow warmth of the water, Heinricke carefully lowered himself to his knees, still holding Katia. And there he laid her down in about one inch of peaceful water on the pristine white sand and now resumed what they'd started on the table, Katia once again arching her back tilting her head back, and allowing her mouth to drift open, completely consumed in pleasure.

Heinricke knew Katia was close to letting it all go, but quietly urged her to wait just a little while longer as he inched closer to a similar climactic moment. She initially protested, biting her lower lip in euphoric anguish. "I can't," she whimpered, her breath very uneven. "Please," she begged. "Hurry."

"I'm there, baby," he encouraged as he looked down upon her. She looked magnificent, he thought. She was completely wet, both outside and inside. "Hold on," he continued to coax, even though he was ready.

"I can't," she cried, her body trembling uncontrollably now, as she started to let out an eerie quiet moan of pleasure.

In seconds Heinricke joined in the hyperventilating joy, completely exploding inside of her, causing her to nearly cry in squirming bliss. Her shaking continued for another thirty seconds until her intense breathing gave way to long, relieved exhales of post-euphoria. Heinricke's hoarse breathing mirrored that of Katia's, winding down from perhaps an overreaction of stress overkill from the last few days. He finally collapsed into her chest, holding her and rolling slightly just off to the side of her, his right leg draped off of her lower torso. "God, I needed that," he confessed.

"You have no idea," Katia replied, barely able to focus on her man.

Heinricke rolled over completely lying on his back, while Katia followed his lead and draped herself over him now, as the warm three-inch waves peacefully surrounded them with their tranquil sounds, sending them into dreamland.

CHAPTER 20

Rural Viennese forest, 5:31 a.m.

Inside the forestry station there were three rooms upstairs just down the short corridor from the back entrance with one main room and a smaller office to either side of that room on the far wall, and a small restroom in the middle of a short hallway that led to the front door.

The hostages were split into two groups, mainly because the two smaller offices were working offices, with desks, several chairs, and filing cabinets, and there simply wasn't enough room for all nine of the leaders in one office. But the commander needed time and space to think, so he had four of the hostages placed in one of the smaller offices, and the other five in the other small office. They were all bound behind their backs and blindfolded, and the lights in the two rooms were switched off to keep them completely disoriented. Schmidt and Haydon sat in the only two chairs, one in each office, while the men either sat on the desks or leaned against a wall or filing cabinet.

There were two very small rooms just off the back entrance being used as storage facilities based on the miscellaneous boxes found in them on the initial sweep. That sweep ended at the bottom of the short flight of stairs accessing the subterranean portion of the complex, as there was no electricity in the lower section. The commander had given his cigarette lighter to one of the militants to do a walkthrough and make sure everything was secure just the same. The militant had gone into the two rooms at the bottom of the stairs, only to discover the rooms were full of boxes and file cabinets, so he closed the doors to those rooms and continued his lighter-assisted sweep into the next room over to the right. It was a much larger room, but completely unfinished. There were exposed wooden studs every sixteen inches with tarpaper lined in between, both on the walls and ceiling. It's also where the water heater was housed, though its pilot light was currently unlit, suggesting the facility hadn't been visited in a while. There was also a moderately pungent aroma from of an unkempt basement, with other life forms likely sharing the premises. On the far wall the militant could see a short set of crude wooden steps that led up to a two-door roof-top access. He ascended the steps in seconds and slammed both of the wooden doors with the butt of his hand. They budged a little, and that was good enough for him. He followed the light from his lighter out and up the stairs and rejoined the others.

The commander had been trying to formulate a plan to evacuate the premises. He'd figured the longer it was quiet, the better their chances were for an uncontested withdrawal. But he also knew that somewhere outside the rogue agent that had been masquerading as one of them for the last eighteen hours silently lay awake, waiting for his moment to pounce. It was only one, the commander reminded himself, but one who also had a small cache of weaponry.

They had just eight sandwiches left to share between the nine hostages and themselves, and enough bottled water to last for maybe another twelve hours. They had three all-terrain vehicles which could navigate the thickly wooded forest if necessary, but the commander was well aware that outside of the forest most of western civilization would be waiting for them if not sooner.

The commander weighed what might've happened to his colleague, the Prophet. Was he caught by the same person, or persons who'd fired the grenade launchers at their vehicles back at the other side of the forest? Or did he simply make a left turn at the fork when they'd all made the right, taking the path to an earthly escape while they were all left to face their doom alone?

No, he told himself. My friend wouldn't do that. He was equally committed to the cause. They shared similar origins after all—both being born in Arab nations. Still, both had integrated into western society and enjoyed lives that more than likely they couldn't enjoy in their mother countries. But the bottom line was that both were sons of a cause, and when the cause called, you went. It was an honor after all to be chosen.

Still the thoughts of an allegedly perfect plan being thwarted by just one person tormented the commander's mind. They were to have conducted their extraction flawlessly, then taken the world leaders to the clandestine location, and bedeviled the world with uncertainty and fear, as they had done. Then they would simply walk away, or just vanish back into their former lives. The Prophet would take care of the rest, making sure that everyone who participated in this effort would be taken care of for their remaining days on earth. But one, just one person had nearly ruined this flawless plan and seemingly altered the course of history—maybe even one of his own. Still, he couldn't allow the doubts to weaken him any longer. *He* remained in the driver's seat, he reminded himself.

The commander had the hostages. He also had the lethal remote with three unused buttons. He also had his son in a port far away, though his son had no idea of his father's drastic cause. His son loved his job and was proud of his title, Captain Amir Hassan, a former professional footballer.

There would be a steep price to pay for tampering with Allah's work, and the commander and his disciples were wholly committed at any cost.

Three-hundred meters across the grassy knoll, Sylvia broke the audio blackout and contacted the Pentagon. "General, we have established that there are two confirmed points of entry on the forestry station," she said, while the four soldiers huddled around her and listened in. "There's a possible third entrance on the front side of the building. Do you have the coordinates?"

"We do. We're looking at sat-images right now—though they're not much more than the cloudy ceiling above you."

"Good," she said. "Let's hope it stays that way—the darker the better. Sir, I've penetrated the building already, through the subterranean level. I've—"

"Stand by, Sylvia," Meyers said, getting a message from the vice president. "Vice President Morrison wants to know if you know the exact location of President Haydon and the other hostages." Morrison was juggling Bluetooths at this point, but didn't miss a word of Sylvia and the general's conversation.

"As I was saying, gentlemen, I've penetrated the building. I'm ninety-nine percent sure that all of the hostages are on the main level."

"How can you be sure?"

"Begging the general's pardon, sir," Sylvia responded aggressively, respectful of protocol, but growing tired of the interruptions, "because I am here, sir. You are there. I have lived with these animals for the last eighteen hours. I have spoken with them. I have eaten with them. I have drunk with them. And I have urinated with them. I have even killed them. The chef was mine. I am going to have a much better idea of their traits and tendencies than someone ten thousand miles away," she snapped, while the four soldiers reacted to her words.

"You what?" Meyers recoiled.

"General, listen to me please," Sylvia said firmly. "And let's not waste any more time. I merely obeyed the order of my commanding officer, as a militant in disguise, and shoved the chef off of the roof of the United Nations building—the same chef that compromised the integrity of the world leaders, and cost the lives of thirty-two security personnel. If I didn't do it, the militant next to me would have. And by doing so I got a free ride on that helo with my president—and with any kind of luck, sir, I intend to bring her home, along with the rest of the hostages."

Meyers didn't respond. There was a one second beat while he assessed the lecture he was receiving—by a woman no less. It had been a long night, and nerves were frayed. "What do you suggest we do, Sylvia?" he finally asked.

"We don't have much time, sir," Sylvia said. "This is what I do know. On your end, have your Intel guys follow the paper trails—there are a lot of them. Follow the chef and his money. Follow the two helos that did the extraction. Someone got a lot of money to swap out those helos. That should be an easy one. Follow the laundry vans, and who sold out. Follow the broadcast equipment trail back at the warehouse—I'm sure our people are all over that right now. Right?"

"Yes we are, Sylvia."

"These fucking swine think they're clever, but every door you open, you leave a roadmap. Get on it now, sir. With any kind of luck, we'll follow the path back to the leader."

"Roger that," the general acknowledged. He snapped orders at Simonson to broaden their search.

"All right, general, now, with regard to my dilemma here; there are seven militants, including the commander, guarding nine hostages. The militants are very willing to die. In fact, sir, they expect to die. The two at the top are quite smart as you probably have assessed by now. They are both of Arab descent. The rest are Iranian, Pakistani, Afghani, or who knows what. They're just minions, but dangerous minions at that.

"The ringleader is gone. He either deserted the main faction here, or somehow he will figure into their plan down the road. I don't know. But he's too financially adept to not figure in again. We have to assume he has enough resources to pose an ongoing threat. We have to try to source him out now, or we are sure to see him again in two years, or five years, or whenever. He's a lot more dangerous than al-Qaeda ever was. The commander inside is the key to him. We must try to take him alive. And that's going to be a significant challenge, because more than likely he's not going to want to be taken by an infidel, which makes him ten times more dangerous. It also means the likelihood of us losing one or more leaders is high. The rest of the militants are absolutely useless to us and they are expendable. Our best hope is complete and utter surprise.

"General, we have approximately one-and-a-half hours left of darkness,"

Sylvia continued. "And I think we should make our move sooner than later. And speaking of which, sir, where are those special ops you promised me?"

"Well, Sylvia, they should've been there awhile ago," Meyers said, a little confused.

"Begging the general's pardon, sir?"

There was a two-second pause. All of a sudden the forest surrounding Sylvia and the four soldiers came alive with slow movement as thirty-two black-clad special-ops soldiers emerged from the darkness. Sylvia had just been slapped in the face with one of her own tactics, and she loved it. "Uh, general, delivery of request confirmed. Thank you very much."

"Just trying to help, Sylvia," Meyers said. "You should have thirty-two of the best fighting machines under your command now, young lady. The command is Major Dominick Wilkinson."

"Dom?" Sylvia asked in disbelief.

"You know him?" Meyers asked.

"Hell yes, I know him! We served together in the second desert campaign."

"Well I'll be damned!" the general said. "It's a small world. Isn't it?"

"Yes, sir!" Sylvia agreed. "That it is!"

There were a handful of elite fighting machines in the Special Forces community, and as incredulous as the odds seemed, it wasn't impossible for two operatives to meet in another time and place—even after years apart.

In an instant, one of the special-ops troops tapped Sylvia on the right shoulder and as she spun around, he saluted her smartly. "Major Dominick Wilkinson is at your service, ma'am."

"Dom?" Sylvia asked, as she too saluted the masked man. "It IS you!"

Her old friend quickly removed his black knit mask, exposing his ruggedly handsome face. "Live and in person," he nodded. His short cropped brown hair looked identical to when Sylvia had last seen him seven years earlier, only now it appeared a few grays had begun to penetrate the sideburns. The face looked the same, tough and battle-tested, only a little more mature. Regardless, it was the face that brought back some fond memories.

"Holy shit!" Sylvia said, while removing her headset and ski-mask as well, allowing her shoulder-length brunette hair to drop freely. Her salute quickly gave way to a completely unprofessional hug in front of all of the others. "Man, you are a sight for sore eyes."

"And so are you," Wilkinson added. "But what happened to your face?"

"All right, smart ass," Sylvia glared. "My face has been bagged for the last eighteen hours. What's your excuse?" She snapped, noticing a new half-inch long scar under the left eye of her old friend.

"Caught a blade—an Iraqi got lucky and almost took my eye out."

"What'd you do to him?" Sylvia asked, knowing the reputation of her friend once he got angry.

"I cut both of his eyes out and shoved them down his throat and made him swallow them," Wilkinson said casually. "But I *did* let him live."

"How generous of you," Sylvia offered.

"Hey, he *did* ruin an otherwise perfect face."

"Ahhh, I see you haven't missed a beat since I last saw you," Sylvia observed. It had been some time since their last deployment behind enemy lines. And although a hostile desert was a very lonely place in the midst of two warriors' daily lives, they'd somehow managed a flicker of warmth in an otherwise frigid existence. After the war, they maintained an email relationship for about a year. Then it was over. He went covert to the next campaign and she went covert to Washington.

"In all seriousness, Sylvia," Wilkinson said. "I'm really proud of what you've done here."

"Wasn't my choosing," she said humbly. "I was just in the wrong place at the wrong time."

"Yeah, well, whatever timing it was, you're a fuckin' hero in my book," Wilkinson offered.

"Not yet I'm not," Sylvia confessed. "Let's go finish the job."

One of the soldiers let Sylvia know that the general was inquiring as to Sylvia's whereabouts, so she quickly slipped her headset back on. "I'm right here, general."

"I trust you and Major Wilkinson are done with your high school reunion?" Meyers asked.

"Yes, sir, we are," Sylvia replied, suddenly slipping back into pre-battle posture. "General, as I'd mentioned before Major Wilkinson's arrival, even with the best-case scenario of surprise tactics, we are likely to sustain casualties. Please understand that every one of these leaders is as important to their respective countries as President Haydon is to the United States and me. That said, we will do everything in our power to minimize those casualties, if not eliminate them altogether. All of the hostages are aware that I exist and have been on the inside as one of the militants, including our president, and that that is why they were all moved from the last location. I would think that they *all* know by now that it was also because of me that they were moved to this location, if they've had a chance to speculate with one another during their captivity. That could just make them assets in their own recovery, sir."

"Understood, Sylvia," Meyers acknowledged. "We're going to try and help level the playing field for you and your unit, by stealing a page from their script."

"How do you mean, sir?"

"This group was able to surprise and annihilate everyone at Schaafhausen because of the deployment of superior ordnance. They detonated three M84 stun grenades which rendered everyone there deaf and blind, Sylvia."

"Son-of-a-bitch," she exhaled. "So that's how they did it."

"That's how they did it. And that's how you're going to do it back to them. We've equipped Major Wilkinson with half a dozen of the very latest versions of the M84, and you should be able to neutralize their location long enough to defuse the stranglehold on the leaders."

"I love it, sir. Paybacks are a bitch."

"Let's hope so," Meyers said firmly. "Just don't forget to close and cover."

"Close and cover, sir?"

"Close your eyes, and cover your ears."

"Yes, of course," Sylvia replied. "There is another problem, general."

"What's that?" Meyers asked.

"The commander has a remote that, from what I understand, has three unused buttons. Those buttons, sir, are attached to three significant devices of doom—that could be anything from a major explosion in a highly vulnerable location, to some kind of financial disaster, like the banking meltdown the West suffered several hours ago. Did you neutralize that situation yet, general?"

"From what we understand, after consulting with a Northern California software firm named Bunker Hill which specializes in database security software, they're pretty sure it was a hardware malfunction of the external storage devices that caused the zero balance read-outs. The storage device manufacturers are fast-tracking technical crews and have new components, along with a rep from the firm, to deal with the problems as we speak. But in fact they tell us that every piece of the storage device's altered data has a footprint that can be retraced. In the end, Bunker Hill assures us that ultimately, all of the money is exactly where people left it."

"That's *great*, sir, whatever all that means," Sylvia acknowledged. "In any event, general, that remote could be an asset to us."

"I'm all ears," Meyers snapped, looking for clarification.

"Well, sir, the remote might be an awful lot to navigate in the split second of having one arm around the throat of a hostage and being surprised by thirty-three sharp-shooting throat-cutters," Sylvia explained. "Not to mention having your eardrums shattered, and being rendered legally blind in a split-second."

"General, he'll have about two seconds at the most to make a decision: Do I kill an American president? Or do I kill hundreds of thousands? Do

I start a financial catastrophe? But wait, I can't allow myself to be caught either, and subject myself to the same kind of torture I've undoubtedly dealt out in the past, like starvation, sleep deprivation, etc., and in turn give up my leader—the only one who can keep their cause alive. No, general, my guess is that no one can think that quickly with that many decisions of major magnitude before them. I'm guessing he'll freeze for about one-and-a-half seconds—maybe more. And that's all we'll need to neutralize him."

"You sound pretty sure of yourself, Sylvia," the general assessed.

"Think positively, general," she said. "That's what I do."

"I will," Meyers said, as the vice president spoke into his earpiece. "Yes, sir, Mr. Vice President," the general replied back to the VP.

"Sylvia, Vice President Morrison wishes to inform you that he has all the confidence in the world in you and your team, and that his and the world's prayers are with you as well—and to please tell you, God speed. He apologizes, but he's conferencing with the nine interim leaders right now."

"Thank the vice president, sir," Sylvia replied.

"Of course."

"Oh, and general?"

"Yes, Sylvia?" Meyers asked back.

"Sir, there are to be absolutely no helos—no air support of any kind anywhere near this location until you hear from me. It would be a death-blow to this mission's cover. Do you understand?"

"That's an affirmative, Sylvia."

"Now I'm just going to have a strategy meeting with my soldiers," Sylvia shared. "Then we'll be moving in to position. Feel free to listen in."

"Standing by," Meyers said.

"Okay, men, let's get in tight here," Sylvia said, motioning for everyone to gather around her, while maintaining a clear visual on the forestry station just three-hundred meters back across the grassy knoll. "All right, everyone, listen up. You four soldiers from my original recon-team—I need you guys on the outside. I need you watching our backs."

"Why can't *we*...?" one of them started to ask.

"Because, you will be as critical to this mission on the outside as we are on the inside," Sylvia reminded. "And I'm going to ask Major Wilkinson to add four of his men to your contingent, to help cover the perimeter."

That explanation seemed to satisfy the original four.

"Major?" Sylvia asked. "I need four of your best to assist these four fine soldiers here."

Wilkinson knew he wouldn't get a volunteer out of the lot. They had all signed up for the close-in work. "Okay," Wilkinson exhaled, as his eyes scanned the pack. "You guys don't make it easy. You...you...you...and you,"

Wilkinson said, as he pointed randomly into the multi-national unit, trying to be as arbitrary as possible.

"Sir, yes, sir," they replied sharply but quietly, trying not to show their disappointment at being left off what they undoubtedly considered the A-team.

"You four—this is in no way a reflection of your skill set. I've seen what every one of you can do. And I'm proud to have you watching my back, gentlemen," Wilkinson explained, then he singled out one of the four soldiers that would remain on the outside to quickly remove the upper portion of his uniform and give it to Sylvia. "She's gonna need it a helluva lot more than you are, soldier," Wilkinson explained.

"Yes, sir," the soldier complied, immediately removing his headset to peel off the vest with detachable sleeves, as well as the pair of gloves that went with the set. While the soldier extricated himself from the lifesaving clothing, Major Wilkinson asked Sylvia to quickly remove her black wool knit top and swap it out with the soldier.

"Sylvia, we're all wearing these—they're pretty neat," Wilkinson explained as the soldier handed him the vest and sleeves, knowing Sylvia had been familiar with its predecessor. "It's the new third generation bullet-proof liquid body armor—same as one and two. It still solidifies on contact, and it'll stop anything these guys will more than likely use for close-in work, I'm sure," Wilkinson explained, wondering why Sylvia hadn't begun to remove her black knit top yet. "What are you waiting for?"

Sylvia just smiled and started to pull off her top.

Major Wilkinson was very surprised to find Sylvia wearing a first generation vest under her sweater. "Where the *hell* did you find that? Better yet, tell me later—take it off anyways and put on this Gen-three. The sleeves are carbon-fiber micro-weave. You can't cut them. Suddenly Wilkinson caught a glimpse of Sylvia's forearm wound and asked "What the hell is that?"

"It's nothing," she replied, trying to conceal the wound from his sight while attempting to slip into the new vest. "Just a scratch."

"Like hell it is," Wilkinson said, while grabbing her forearm and examining the wound. The profuse bleeding had stopped, but the opening looked pretty bad. Most of the underside of her arm was coated in dark crusty blood. "Get me a field dressing!" Wilkinson ordered, a little irritated that one of his men with a field medical kit hadn't stepped forward yet.

"Dom, it's nothing," Sylvia tried again.

"Stop!" Wilkinson interrupted. "Where's my medic?"

"Right here, major," a soldier stepping forward said.

"Take care of this and do it quickly. Ninety seconds!" Wilkinson ordered firmly, while straightening out Sylvia's vest. He snapped his fingers at the partially defrocked soldier for him to hand over his gloves now. Wilkinson would attach her zip-on sleeves once her wounds were tended to.

The medic asked Sylvia whether she wanted a topical to numb the wound while he cleaned it out with peroxide, suggesting it might sting. She merely shoved one of the gloves into her mouth and bit down hard, nodding for him to continue.

He did and she winced at its cleansing effect, while Wilkinson continued. "By the time your mark starts carving on your arms unsuccessfully, I'm sure you will have thrust your knife up into his ribcage a couple of times."

"Not so fast, Dom," Sylvia snapped back. "If I was wearing a Gen-One, what do you think all these guys are wearing? That's right—the Gen-Ones. That's why they were so successful back at the Schaafhausen massacre. Our guys didn't stand a chance, but then again I'm sure they weren't expecting a shootout at OK Corral against a team of rogue agents with superior ordinance to ours. God knows I didn't. Anyhow, how the *hell* this shit got out, I'll never know," she said, while the medic dried her cleansed wound and applied six evenly spaced butterfly stitches.

"Just like new, ma'am," the medic said, finishing Sylvia's stitches.

"Thank you, soldier."

"Everything in life is for sale," Wilkinson reminded Sylvia, while attaching the sleeves to her vest.

"Yeah, I guess," she agreed half-heartedly, while shaking her head tightly. "How about you?"

Wilkinson didn't respond to Sylvia's sleep-deprived quip—he knew she'd been through a lot. "Anyhow, advantage goes to us in a knife fight," Wilkinson reminded her., "even if we never get into a shootout."

"Good point," Sylvia agreed, and then started to lay out the strategy for their counter-assault. "First of all, everyone speaks English, right?" she asked the soldiers from the multi-national force huddled around her. Wilkinson had shared the make-up of the unit earlier in their meeting. She'd never worked with Brits, Germans, Israelis, and Americans all in one unit before—separately, yes, but this unified effort would be a first.

"Of course. These guys are tight, Sylvia," Wilkinson assured, while most of his team either nodded or answered yes. "I've seen enough in the last thirteen hours to know we're both going to enjoy carving the turkeys with them."

"Okay, fine," Sylvia acknowledged. "I need you eight soldiers that we've chosen to circle the complex and watch our backs. If anything gets by us, I want you on it—and pin it down. I want these rodents alive if we can help it, but kill them if you have to. Do you understand?"

"Yes, ma'am!" they all snapped back.

"Okay. My guys," Sylvia said, looking at the original four soldiers. "I need one of each original two-man contingent to show our new guests the way into the fortress that you've just discovered.

"Roger that," the four men chorused back.

"Major Wilkinson, take two thirds of your men and follow these four to the two locations. I'll take the rest of you with me, and we'll go right up the belly of the snake," Sylvia said, motioning straight forward across the grassy knoll toward the structure. "Whoever goes with me, we may need to pick a lock. Does anyone possess such skills?"

In an instant six soldiers stepped forward and presented their wire-set lock-picking tools.

Sylvia nodded her approval at how competent Major Wilkinson' unit was, and then picked out two of the men. "Okay, you two come with me. Two of you go in the second unit. And two of you go in the third unit with Major Wilkinson. Do not attempt the doors until you've exhausted the first option," Sylvia instructed, then turned to her old friend. "Major, I won't lie to you. This is about as difficult a situation as you and I have ever faced. In essence we're trying to save the lives of ten people—nine great human beings, and one piece of human debris. I'm confident that all sixteen subjects are upstairs. I don't know if they've got the hostages in a separate room, or wired with explosives, or what. What I do know is that death is their ally. Our objective is clear though—when you have a shot, take it. I'm going to focus on the commander and his remote. Major, I want you there with me. If I take out the remote, I need you to stop him from killing a hostage. My guess is he'll have President Haydon somehow attached to himself, with a knife—with an explosive device, or whatever. But my hunch is this entire thing has ultimately been aimed *at* America and the UK. He's going to want to hang onto the ultimate prize himself. He'll be desperate if he loses the remote. He's liable to do anything. Whatever you do, don't kill him, and try to stop him from killing himself."

"Piece of cake," Wilkinson affirmed, wincing with pleasure at the prospect of such difficult odds.

"All right, everyone, let's make the world proud, and exterminate these serpents once and for all," Sylvia said, looking into the eyes of each and every man.

The men quietly chanted their approval, while Sylvia removed her headset and handed it to the soldier next to her. "Hold onto this for a second," she said, while handing her black knit cap to Major Wilkinson, and asked him to place it over her head while she gathered up her hair into a tight ball. "All right, let's go already, Dom," she said impatiently.

"Simmer down," Wilkinson shot back, slipping the cap onto her head and making sure no strands of hair were exposed. "In the old days you were a little less high-maintenance. What the hell do they do to you people in the civvies world?"

"Knock off the shit, major, or I might have to kick your ass," Sylvia snapped back, half-joking but wanting to remind the others of her leadership toughness. "Now put on your cap."

"I'll be looking forward to that," Wilkinson obliged, while quickly slipping his cap over his head, "after we save the good guys."

"That's a deal, major."

The men seemed to get a kick out the two commanding officers and their banter.

"Sergeant, dispense the six M84s to the lead commands," Wilkinson ordered one of his men.

"Yes, sir," the soldier replied, and distributed the ordnance.

"Thanks," Sylvia said, while grabbing her group's two stun grenades and stuffing them into a canvas pouch on her gear belt. "All right, gentlemen, let's synchronize," She ordered, while sharing her exact time with the unit. "It'll take you men on the far flank approximately five minutes to reach your location—a little less for the closer flank—and about five minutes for my unit to crawl on our bellies through this grass. We'll have approximately ten minutes to size up our respective locations. I *do* know that three or four of these men smoke, including the commander—smokers always smoke during times of tension. We might get lucky and pick one or two off if they pop outside for a ciggy. I doubt that they'd do it—they're probably already smokin' like chimneys inside, but you never know. Expect the unexpected. *If* for some reason we do get lucky and take out one or more of our targets, then I need to know about it immediately. At that point our timetable moves up and we move immediately. Otherwise, at exactly 0615 hours, I will give the radio command and we will move into position. I want to hear from each command post once we've penetrated the fortress and secured your location. At which point, I will give a command and we will strike fast and hard, gentlemen. There's going to be a lot of confusion in there once we commence and they start to react. The enemy looks a little like us, but their tops are a little different, so hopefully you won't be killing your fellow soldiers by mistake. Knives and Berettas only, all right?"

"Roger that," Wilkinson acknowledged, then gave the final command deploying his two units. "See you inside, Sylvia," he said, and then winked at her.

"Roger that. Take care of yourself, soldier."

CHAPTER 21

Hong Kong, 10:49 a.m.

Charles Li and Minh Pak had taken the advice of their German associate and visited their trading floor to give their various specialized traders orders on how and when to begin liquidating into the surging precious metals markets. Some dealt in commodities, others in options, and a few dealt in the bullion itself. Initially the co-owners of the firm were met with moderate resistance; some of the traders reasoned that you buy the breakouts, you don't sell into them. But Pak and Li had been doing this for a lot longer than most their traders, and simply reminded them where their paychecks came from. "Don't ask questions," they ordered. "Just do as we say."

With every incremental leap of ten dollars in gold's ascent past $2,050 an ounce, Pak, Li, and Co. were liquidating considerable positions into the surge, until the bullion had finally met resistance at $2,070 an ounce—its historical high. The commodity's price had been bouncing around like a lottery ball for some time now, after it made the new high of $2,077 an ounce. Of course, with every dollar past their strike price of $1,960 an ounce, the options went through the roof—and those too were being systematically liquidated into the upward momentum—the options with the closest expiration dates were sold first. Their previous near-term goal of $1,980 an ounce had been shattered, and their long-term price target of $2,025 had also been eclipsed. But these were price targets they didn't expect to see for another six months, and gold had run well over a hundred dollars in a day at the prospect of global collapse. Smart investors knew when to take a profit.

Charles Li and Minh Pak were having a career year, all in one day. In their wildest dreams they couldn't have hoped for anything this big. And now that their collective conscience was clear of any wrongdoing, the two grown men retreated to Charles Li's office down the hallway from their main trading floor so they could quarantine their giddiness from the professional world outside.

"Is it too early for champagne?" Li asked.

"No," Pak answered. "It's never too early, but I think I'll wait just the same. I want to see how this hostage situation plays out.

"All right," Li agreed. "We'll be out of just about all of our positions that we've accumulated in the past year shortly, with the exception of our core holdings. Do you think we should throw a couple dollars at shorting this thing—just for sport?"

"You're a crazy man. You know better than to stand in front of a runaway freight train," Pak scolded, half-kidding but his glare indicated it was anything but a joke. "Now turn up the volume on your TV."

"All right all right," Li surrendered, while reaching for the flat screen's remote on his desk. "Calm down, my friend. You know I was just kidding."

"Uh-huh, just kidding. You're a gambler," Pak grumbled. "Are you still playing the horses all over the world?"

"Oh, come on. That's a sport—not gambling," Li tried weakly. "Those are just beautiful animals."

Minh Pak just rolled his eyes and asked his partner to turn the volume up again.

Maldive Islands, 8:55 a.m.

Arisa sauntered out sleepily from the second cabana with nothing but a thin, see-through multi-colored sarong loosely draped around her hips, while her small but perky breasts remained uncovered, as they had been for the last three days. Her right hand reached up to rub the sleep from her eyes, as she tried to focus on a new day dawning. She looked over to the bar area and saw no familiar human sights, so she allowed her eyes to wander across the horizon until they finally fixed on two silhouettes lying naked in the warm waters down at the shoreline.

A serene expression pervaded her sleepy demeanor as she walked in the direction of the two motionless bodies. In moments Arisa stood above the two naked figures. "Damn!" she said. "I missed all the fun."

She turned and started to walk away toward the wafting scent of coffee drifting down from the bar, when Katia called out for her. "Good morning, baby."

Arisa turned and half-jealously addressed her friend. "Maybe for you, but some of us have been neglected."

"Ahhh, come on," Katia replied sympathetically. "You were asleep. We didn't want to wake you," she tried, but even she knew she wasn't going to share—at least not this time.

"Fine," Arisa responded half-pouting, then turned and walked up to the bar for a cup of coffee. She fumbled for a bar glass to pour the coffee into, then dug around in the mini-fridge behind the bar for some milk and concocted the perfect blend.

Down at the shoreline Katia rolled over on top of Gregor, quietly waking him from his deep sex-induced slumber. "Uhhhh," he exhaled, having absolutely no idea where he was, but knew it was one form or another of heaven. "Wuzza….."

"Good morning, baby," Katia said.

"Yes, good morning," Heinricke sleepily replied, while Katia playfully urged him to greet the day. "What time is it?" He asked.

"Who cares?" Katia replied, while maintaining her pretzel-like grip on him—her body softly weaving itself into his.

"I do," he replied calmly, but didn't rush to extricate himself from her soothing embrace.

In a moment Arisa returned with her doctored-up glass of coffee, sat down next to Katia, and offered her a swig. "Want some?" she asked, forgiving their selfish act of abandonment. Things surely could have been worse than running around naked on one of the Maldive Islands for seven days with your girlfriend and her man, so she forgave them.

"Sure," Katia replied, prying her right side off of Heinricke to grasp the coffee. "Danke."

Vienna, 6:02 a.m.

Nabeel Ali-Khan had finished everything on the breakfast cart that'd been delivered. He sat perched up on his bed in his bathrobe, with two of the four pillows supporting his back, while sipping a cup of Viennese coffee and watching the ongoing BBC coverage of the uncertainty in Austria. None of the reports had indicated that the authorities had moved any closer to resolving the hostage crisis. In fact, since the militant-hostage broadcasts had stopped, speculations of disaster were off the charts, further fueling financial market unrest around the world. Safe-haven bellweathers, like oil and precious metals, predictably were experiencing banner days.

Ali-Khan's right hand reached for the laptop on the bed next to him and his fingers dragged on the mouse pad revealing open trading and assets programs. While he studied his and his constituents' positions, a pleasant but controlled smile tugged at the corners of his mouth. He had never been an overly-emotional man.

Prior to his trip down to Bavaria, he'd integrated what remained of his asset management program which wasn't already held in the Asian accounts, into a fairly new program that allowed one to trade one's assets in any market in the world. It was all part of the global marketplace that came about with the mergers of various behemoths like the London Stock Exchange, the NYSE, the NASDAQ, the NIKEI, among others—one could literally trade their positions twenty-four hours a day in any market in the world. Efficiency was the word market pundits most commonly associated with the ongoing need to consolidate the global marketplace.

Ali-Khan was enjoying a very good day in the markets at the world's expense.

Rural Viennese forest, 6:11 a.m.

The first team, which included Major Wilkinson, reported from the nearside post behind the three Hummers. "Fox Trot One reporting—all quiet at location one," Wilkinson said quietly. "Standing by."

Immediately following, the second post reported. "Fox Trot Two—all quiet here—no smokers. We're open for business."

"Fox Trot Three reporting," Sylvia said, barely above a whisper from her position just at the top of the two open wooden doors to the ground access location. She'd just quietly let her eight men into the dark fortress and asked them to wait for her at the bottom of the steps while she crouched in the corner against the wall, well out of the vision of anyone inside the building. "I guess they gave up smoking for the New Year, gentlemen. Stand by. Perimeter guys, are you in position?"

"Roger that," the first soldier responded. One by one, all eight of the exterior positions reported back. "That's a Roger."

"All right," Sylvia calmly responded. "Stand by."

Inside the forestry station, 6:12 a.m.

President Haydon quietly tried to instill a flicker of hope into her fellow captives, while reminding them that her personal bodyguard was among them and that's why they were moved. "If she made it this far, she certainly has to be out there somewhere watching over us now," Haydon shared with Veroni, Marceau, Zheng and Nobakov.

"How do you know?" the French President asked, more to make dialogue than anything. "I mean, what are her credentials?"

"Didier, does it matter?" Haydon replied. "The vice president hand-picked her for me and I am told she's quite competent. Might I remind you she survived the massacre back at Schaafhausen, and eliminated half of their unit?"

"For now, she's our only hope," the Chinese president admitted. "She's gotten herself and us this far and that says a lot. More than likely these idiots will want to move us, I'm sure. It doesn't make a lot of sense to just sit here, but on the other hand I don't know how far they can run if the world is hunting them down. And I'll be ready to help, if this Sylvia resurfaces again," the former boxer warned.

"I wouldn't be so sure that these militants are idiots, Mr. Zheng," Russian president Nobakov reminded. "After all, you *did* get the education on Wall Street history and American foreign policy like the rest of us. Didn't you? These are anything but your run-of-the-mill militants. They are smart, educated, and beyond the likes of which any one of us has seen before. At least, their leader is."

"Good point," Zheng conceded. "Bad choice of words, I guess."

"Mr. Nobakov, you bring up a good point," Marco Veroni interrupted. "I haven't seen the Prophet since back at the warehouse location. Did any of you see him on the ride over?"

"Equally good point, Marco," President Haydon said, alert with curiosity. "I haven't, but I was in the lead Hummer. Did any of you gentlemen?"

"I haven't either," Nobakov answered.

"Nor I," Marceau chimed in.

"I haven't either," Zheng added. "These damn blindfolds aren't helping either."

"It's a longshot," Haydon pondered. "But maybe the brain of the operation is no longer on board—at least not here."

"Which makes the remainder of the group that much more dangerous," Nobakov pointed out.

"Very dangerous," Zheng agreed. "This is the 'idiot' element that I was referring to earlier."

"The commander isn't an idiot either," Nobakov once again reminded. "He's just a little more impassioned than the Prophet."

"You mean volatile?" Marceau volunteered. "He did after all murder our friend from Canada. Is that passion?"

"Absolutely!" Nobakov reiterated. "In its strongest form it is hatred! *And* he's willing to act on it."

"Well, regardless, these guys are dangerous," Veroni observed. "We need to expect the unexpected."

"I do. And I'm ready," Zheng said.

"Marco, I have a question," Haydon said. "Is there any truth to the rumor about that ring of yours?"

"Which one?" Veroni asked, forcing a stiff giggle, trying to ease his own tension. "I have a few."

"The one said to have been worn by the 16th century cardinal—the ancestor to the Medici family of Florence," Haydon explained. The sizable rectangular sapphire stone was said to be mounted on an 18-karat gold fleur d'lis set on all four corners by a weathered, small golden ball.

"Madame President, I slipped the ring into my shoe earlier during the melee at Schaafhausen. For what I paid, I hope it's the real deal. But at the moment, my hands are tied and you can't see. With any kind of luck, I will gladly show it to you later."

In the adjacent room Robin Collinsworth spun a theatrical tale about the journey of the American president's attaché, traces of his Shakespearean training inspiring his words. It was destiny, he insisted beyond hope that called back at the warehouse where they were held. It was almost criminal that the British cinema had never embraced the colorful character actor. Just as the Prophet had noted earlier in the day, his career never transcended the B movies.

"So what do you think the next move will be?" EU President Edgar Elliott asked quietly, after his countryman's oratory was done.

"I'd imagine our captors are discussing the matter as we speak," Collinsworth replied. "They must know that whomever caused them to abandon n extremely airtight plan at a perfectly clandestine location, is probably somewhere nearby—if not outside this building. Maybe our Sylvia stopped along the way to pick up a posse, and is about to ride in here with the cavalry to save the day."

"Is that our captor's thinking?" Elliott asked. "Or is that you hoping?"

"Perhaps it's a little of both," Collinsworth confessed. "Hope is all we have right now, and it starts and ends with that woman."

"Yes, but in here we're sitting ducks," Claudia Schmidt observed. "And they've got to know that out there."

"Maybe not," Yoshito Tanaka offered, playing the devil's advocate. "Maybe they might be thinking if the world around them isn't moving, then why make any motion?"

"My hunch is that the world *is* moving," Collinsworth countered. "They just can't see it moving, because they're under the spell of making the wrong decision, or *any* decision for that matter. Those decisions have always been made for them in the past, by the Prophet in this case, or someone else in the times before that. Not everyone can lead, as they're finding out now."

"Perhaps," Schmidt agreed. "But that's an awful lot of speculation."

"Maybe," Collinsworth allowed. "But I'm a firm believer in the strategy—cut off the head and the snake won't know which way to go."

"Maybe back into the forest?" Tanaka offered.

"Possibly, but I believe the trees are crawling with the good guys," Collinsworth replied optimistically.

"Let's hope so," Tanaka said. "Only time will tell."

Forestry station, main room, 6:13 a.m.

The commander had gone back and forth several times, trying to see the logic of leaving the compound versus staying put. On one hand it made sense to corral the hostages back into the three vehicles that sat out back, and navigate the Viennese forest to their undetected getaway. After all Italy was just three to four hours to the southwest of their current location.

That was only dreamer's logic, he reminded himself. He was an old warrior. And even he knew better than that. The West had limitless resources, air surveillance and every other kind of weapon that could neutralize an enemy on the run—an enemy exposed to winter's debilitating elements. Their water supply was still okay, but their food supply was dwindling fast. On the road it would only go faster. The original mission was supposed to be over in less than six hours, but that had all changed now.

On the other hand, the commander surmised, if they remained in their current location they might be able to wait it out for the next twelve hours until the cover of darkness returned. They could then try to mobilize into the western portion of the forest and slowly work themselves southward until they could reach the dormant vineyards near the Italian border.

This was just denial, he reminded himself. Whomever had caused them to leave the first location had to be lurking somewhere nearby. And this person was also an old and dangerous warrior, schooled in every tactic of warfare—they'd experienced that already. Most of the damage inflicted on them was from close-in work, done with just hands and a knife. What if this brave soul had that same opportunity to permeate their current location and do it all over again? On the other hand, imagine what this person would be capable of with weapons in the wide-open, the commander warned himself, as his mind battled with the plausible logic of a clever and faceless opponent. The commander finally determined his foe wouldn't threaten the lives of his precious hostages if they were mobilized. He needed them alive. Obviously the rogue soldier wasn't one of his brothers who'd turned on them, the commander concluded.

He finally realized his friend, the Prophet, was gone—never coming back. He was either dead, captured, or had flat-out abandoned them. He'd tried several times to reach him on his mobile phone, but no one ever answered. And no one ever returned the call. The answer was clear. They had to mobilize.

"Gather up the prisoners," the commander barked to his merciless militants, and they immediately responded to his request, popping out of their seats if they were sitting, or dropping a cigarette and stepping on the butt if they were smoking—then they crashed through the two closed doors to the smaller offices where the hostages were and flicked on the respective lights.

Outside the forestry station, 6:15 a.m.

"Commence penetration," Sylvia whispered into her headset. "Once again, gentlemen, I want to know the second you're in."

"Roger that," Major Wilkinson reported back from the first position, then gave the orders for his unit to ascend the back steps to the building. "Fox Trot One on the move."

"Fox Trot Two on the move," the second unit leader reported moments later. "Stand by for penetration."

"Fox Trot Three on the move," Sylvia followed suit, descending the creaky stairs into a dark and dangerous void.

CHAPTER 22

In Suite 606 at the Opera Plaza Palace, Nabeel Ali-Khan muted the volume
to the BBC news coverage that he'd been half-watching and tossed the
remote off to the side. Despite himself, his head buzzed with demons of self-
doubt, making it impossible to focus on the broadcast. He knew that the
plan six years in the making had failed—not due to anything they had done
wrong, but by an act of God. What they'd accomplished through discipline
and patience however, proved to them and the world that as long as there
were resources and faith, they would forever prove to be a formidable foe for
whomever they deemed their adversary.

Ali-Khan was sure his friend from so many years before would go out
like a hero in God's eyes—and he would do what was necessary to carry out
his work. And if God saw fit, then God would spare him from his earthly
martyrdom. If not, then he would soon be in the heavens with his maker,
forever protected in the comforting arms of peace. There was only one thing
left for Ali-Khan to do and that was to pray.

Ali-Khan removed his bathrobe, threw it over the foot of the bed, and
proceeded into the sprawling white marble bathroom in just his white briefs.
He passed the pristine porcelain antique tub with its four, polished silver claw
feet on the right and approached the pedestal sink. In a symbolic gesture,
Ali-Khan washed his hands in the sink and dried them with the hand towel
hanging from the chrome and marble stand that stood next to the sink. He
looked up briefly, making eye contact with himself, but just as quickly turned
away, uncomfortable with the vision in the mirror.

He then turned and walked toward the chrome towel bar with its white porcelain end-caps mounted on the marble wall to his right, just above the bath tub, and grabbed one of the large clean dry towels and laid it on the floor. He then dropped to his knees and began to chant his prayers in Arabic. He needed to be cleansed of his guilt for abandoning his friend and the other defenders of their cause, but in the end knew his friend would forgive him. After all, the plan had been broken, and Ali-Khan could serve his maker once again with his resources if he remained alive, somewhere down the road. Now was not *his* time to be a martyr.

Forestry station, 6:16 a.m.

All of the blindfolded hostages were gathered into a line-up in the center of the large room as the commander went over the extraction plans from the building with his men. Some of them stood behind the captives and others in front. The commander ordered every militant to stand behind a hostage, and his soldiers quickly conformed. They listened intently as he explained how each hostage would be handled, knowing the probability of a predator lurking on the outside was high.

"Each one of you will take a hostage," he explained in Farsi. "You will keep the hostage close to you, as if you were attached to their flesh. I want you all to draw your knives now," the commander ordered calmly but firmly. In an instant every militant had removed their knife from its leather holster. "Take a hostage now and hold the knife to the throat of your prisoner," the commander continued. As he did, he also grabbed a prisoner—President Haydon of the United States. In his mind she was the jackpot of all of the hostages. "Like this," he said, pulling her abruptly from the line-up, startling her from the darkness of her blindfolded world, and then turned her around to face the others.

The commander held the sharp edge of his serrated combat knife to the neck of his prisoner, causing Marge Haydon to squirm. She let out a tiny yelp—the only noise that could escape her throat pinched by a blade of death.

"Please," she peeped. "Please don't kill me," the American pleaded, as her eyes began to well up under her blindfold. She prayed silently for the return of her savior, Sylvia, and prayed aloud for this all to be over soon. "Please dear God in heaven; please stop this now," Haydon begged, as her mind raced. But for the first time since their abduction the president silently prepared herself for another option—death. She had a razor sharp knife held to her throat, and this wasn't a game.

"Like this!" the commander blasted, tightening the death-grip knife-hold on the American president's throat. "If these maggots outside try to take you, then you take the life of your hostage, and then try evasive protocol. Hide behind another hostage—hide behind the vehicle until we can join you. And if that doesn't work and you are still vulnerable, prepare to meet your maker in the kingdom of heaven, because there is more honor in death than there is in being taken alive. If the infidel gets lucky and somehow gets between you and your hostage then your grip on his throat with the knife hand will take the life of your hostage as you fall to the floor. Remember men, make God proud! Die with honor."

With the commander's words each militant tightened their grips on their respective hostages. The German chancellor also became emotional. She too, was unable to fathom a razor-sharp combat knife at her throat. Schmidt recalled the videos from the hostage crisis' during the 2005 wave of kidnappings in Iraq and beheadings, and that visual was eerily vivid in her mind right now, knowing the desperate mercenary holding a knife behind her could begin severing her head at any minute. Schmidt struggled to control her bladder.

The two extra leaders who didn't have a knife pressed to their throat, Elliott and Veroni, were held like dogs on a leash, by a tight rope around their throats by two of the militants who'd already squeezed a knife into another hostage's throat.

The male prisoners resisted as best they could without getting a shave. They knew ultimately their captors preferred death to life, so how much could one resist? Even the defiant Chinese leader knew his limitations.

"Now, men of honor, in just a few moments we will proceed to the vehicles out back and head west—to the Italian border. Remember, our foe can't afford to lose any of the hostages, so the advantage is ours. If we make it to Italy, then we may have more days on earth," the commander reminded.

Underneath the forestry station, 6:16 a.m.

Sylvia asked one of the soldiers in her detail who smoked for his inexpensive, disposable lighter, so that they would have enough light to navigate the short flight of steps up to the door to the main level without tripping or stumbling into a wall.

"I can do better," he whispered, then produced a mini-mag flashlight from a small Velcro holster on the opposite side of his belt. "I plan on enjoying a cigar when we're done," he whispered assuredly.

"Roger that, soldier," she whispered back, while reminding him and the others that any noise whatsoever would greatly compromise their mission, including old stairs. So Sylvia emphasized to step only on the edges of the steps, closest to either wall.

They quietly ascended the fifteen steps until they had arrived at the door that separated them from their appointment with utter chaos. Sylvia had guessed right—the door that separated them from doomsday was locked. She ordered one of the two lock-pickers up to the top step to begin his work, while she stood back on the second step shinning the tiny beam of light on the door knob.

The lock-picker continued to work on the archaic lock within the door knob, not necessarily needing light to see what his finger tips felt from the rods he'd inserted into the tumblers, while Sylvia waited impatiently just behind him. In just seconds the soldier had successfully picked the lock on the simple older door knob. Sylvia held her finger to her lips. "Shhh," she whispered quietly to her men gathered on the steps behind her. "Hold your position."

At the back of the building, the lead soldier ascended the edge of the ancient stairs clinging closely to the handrail, careful not to make a creak of sound. He slipped by the back door just under the window, and steadied his position next to the sliding glass window as he'd been instructed. Major Wilkinson was right behind him, followed by the rest of the assault squad, muted shadows of death swarming in anticipation of creating a graveyard.

Upon Major Wilkinson' order, the lead soldier slowly and carefully reached up to the metal frame of the window with his rugged, battle-tested hand, and with just his first two fingers he pushed on the frame. It started to open. He kept pushing while encountering no resistance. Wilkinson called for the soldier to his rear to circumvent his position, and prepare to make a human step ladder underneath the open window.

Once the window was opened as far as it could be, the soldier who'd opened it quickly withdrew his holstered knife with a nine-inch blade, and carefully placed the knife in the iron grip between his teeth, careful not to cut the corners of his mouth. The second soldier had hit a cat-like on-all-fours position right under the open window, while the soldier clamping on a knife stepped up onto his back and hoisted himself up into the open window. He took a very brief moment to assess his immediate surroundings. Satisfied that it was clear to proceed, he finished slipping through the opening, and landed silently on the floor inside. Then he too dropped to all-fours, while his head remained high and his eyes focused on what might walk through the door at any minute.

With a drawn combat knife wedged in his mouth, Major Wilkinson quickly duplicated the through-the-window move, enjoying the luxury of two human flights of stairs—one on each side.

Quickly and quietly the rest of the alert men followed their command through the opening, and into the abyss of danger.

On the front side of the building, the lead soldier of the third unit had quickly ascended the two steps to the small concrete porch, while his unit had one-by-one slipped through a clearing in the pines lining the dirt road next to the front of the building just behind him and to his right. Each and every one of them brandished a silenced nine-millimeter firearm or standard issue assault knife, his weapon of choice while navigating the outdoors. Some chose to carry both. When the soldiers had reached the wooden structure, they turned with their backs to the green exterior adjacent to the lead man, waiting for his signal to advance. A crisp breeze bristling through the pine needles was the only noise an otherwise silent, dark winter dawn had to offer.

After a quick assessment the lead soldier had determined that the door-within-a-door was no doggy-door after all—it was just a bad patch-job on a badly weathered door. After checking the doorknob to confirm that it was locked, the soldier signaled for one of the two lock-pickers assigned to the unit to begin working on the weathered doorknob.

The locksmith was next in the line-up on the wall and quickly holstered his weapon and ascended the steps, while removing the small kit from a separate compartment on his belt. The lead soldier stood guard with his drawn firearm over the lock-picker while shining his mini-mag flashlight on the doorknob so the soldier could see. Silently the picker removed two tiny, slightly angled rods from his sac, perhaps a sixteenth of an inch in diameter, inserted them into the key slot, and began working his way around the corrosion inside with two precision stems of metal. Just as quickly he realized the exposed lock needed a lubricant to help free the simple tumblers. He reached back into his packet and removed a small can of graphite lubricant and sprayed it into the key slot, then set the can down on the porch. The picker re-inserted the two metal rods and began working his magic, and in less than thirty seconds, the lock was picked.

The soldier with the firearm very slowly turned the knob and luckily the lubricant quelled any noise within the doorknob assembly. He pushed the front door open slowly for the armed and ready assault squad anxiously waiting behind him. On his signal, one by one the units passed quietly through the threshold.

"Fox Trot One inside the building," Wilkinson whispered into his headset from his position.

"Roger that," Sylvia whispered back. "Hold your position."

Seconds later, the second post reported. "Fox Trot Two inside the building."

"Hold your position," Sylvia whispered again, looked to her men and wished them well. "God speed, gentlemen. We're moving in. That *is* a go everyone."

Sylvia motioned for the locksmith to stand down and allow her to pass, as her right hand removed her silenced Berretta that she'd inherited from a corpse the day before. Her left hand quietly gripped the door knob and turned it slowly. It opened ever-so-slightly, instantly allowing a shard of diffused light to peek through the opening.

She was hoping for darkness to blend into, but that was a tall order considering the captors needed to see each other as well as the hostages they were guarding or getting ready to transport. She continued to inch the door open, until there was enough room to squeeze through. Sylvia stepped out into the partially lit hallway and approached the corner that she suspected led to a larger room. Now she could hear voices from out in that direction. Her ears strained as she could hear one man continue to give instructions to the others. She recognized the voice as the commander's, and determined that the militants were just seconds away from an exit strategy. In a moment, the second of her unit was at her heels. Sylvia whispered to Major Wilkinson to get ready. "Dom, they're coming out the back. Get ready. All units, prepare to deploy the M84s."

Wilkinson and his unit was every bit of ready for whatever might be advancing in their direction, as they'd just cleared the second storage room and stood adjacent to the back door at the corner that turned into the main area. He placed his combat knife back between his clenched teeth and very quietly removed both of the grenades, handing one to the soldier immediately to his left flank.

Sylvia peered around the corner and pulled back very quickly, not sure how long she wanted to leave herself visible, even though her mind told her she saw nothing. Just as quickly she looked around the corner and couldn't see anyone or anything, but still heard the clearly distinct voice of the commander. She stepped quietly down a short hallway toward that voice, her firearm out in front of her leading the way. She'd lusted for an appointment with this one-man death squad since his surprise annihilation back at Schaafhausen, but she had to be patient or she knew she would compromise the mission. The loss of the Canadian added fuel to her thirst for revenge.

Sylvia reached the end of the short corridor and in seconds all eight men in her unit were behind her, separated by approximately ten inches between each of them. She knew if she didn't arrive to the melee at exactly the right moment, Major Wilkinson and his unit would be vulnerable.

Sylvia readied one of the M84s, and handed the second stun grenade to the soldier immediately behind her. "The second I pull the clip and throw mine into the group, you do the same," she whispered emphatically. "You've got a two-second window from the time you pull the clip and detonation. "It's important to hold the grenade for a one-count before you throw. Detonation needs to take place right before it hits the floor, so you don't give these fucking rodents any warning whatsoever. Do you understand, soldier?"

"Yes ma'am," he whispered back.

Sylvia inched her way past the corner to see the commander with what appeared to be a stranglehold on one of the hostages standing in front of a line-up of militants and hostages. Sylvia immediately recognized the torn remnants of what was once a lovely Saint John's suit that her president had been wearing for over twenty-four hours. She could see that Haydon and the other hostages were blindfolded and handcuffed. She didn't retreat this time. She stood there silently as the commander ordered his unit to begin the exit strategy. She whispered through clenched teeth into her headset for all three units to move in. "On the count of three, we pull the pins on the grenades. Hold for a count of one – then throw. Don't forget, close and cover, gentlemen. Here we go. One, two…"

Pentagon, 12:18 a.m.

General Meyers' staff anxiously watched the various video feeds from Austria being played on the large split-screen monitor on the wall opposite the command post. The room was completely motionless and silent, and had been for some time. The broadcast images and the sporadic audio feeds revealed everything that needed to be said. Virtually all communication with the other command centers of the hostage nations had come to a halt, as they too were frozen by the surreal video and audio feed being shared with the Pentagon.

The general's right hand had become a cradle for his left elbow, allowing for his left fist to rest in the sometimes not-so-gentle clench of his teeth. He'd unconsciously chewed into the base of his left first finger drawing an ever-so-slight spot of blood. "Here we go, people," Meyers said, his eyes riveted on the figures holding their position for the imminent assault. The twitch in his right eye was back and had become a full blink.

In the vice presidential bunker, a hopeful First Family stood together, riveted to the figures on the large central monitor, praying for the liberation of their loved one and the others. This was the calm before the storm.

In just over a second there was a blinding flash displayed on all of the war room flat screen monitors, then a tremendous outcry of pain and confusion, while utter pandemonium had broken out.

Several silenced shots were barely audible and the blinding white screens went dark again, as murky images of bewildered figures writhing in pain stumbled about, some reaching to cover their ears. There was a rush from three separate units on the commander's unit in the middle of the chaos.

In the opening moments of the assault, two hooded figures fell to the ground. Then two male figures wearing blindfolds ran out of the digital feed.

"Mark terminated!" a voice cried out from in the middle of the blurred fracas.

"Mark terminated!" a second voice shouted.

"I want to know who those two were Mr. Simonson," Meyers demanded, while exhibiting a considerable amount of restraint. "Isolate the outside monitor and freeze-frame it and get me some answers."

"Yes, sir," Simonson complied anxiously, having already given orders to his video techs to identify the freed hostages. "We're working on it."

Neither of the freed hostages could see a thing, because they too were temporarily blinded, even though their blindfolds had restricted their eyes from being fully opened at the point of detonation. However, those conditions would allow for a much quicker recovery to their flash blindness. Their hands remained cuffed behind them, making it impossible to discern where to move—nor could they hear a command. If they wandered clumsily in the wrong direction, they'd be right back in the middle of the sure-death that they'd just escaped. Thinking quickly, the smaller and more agile Edgar Elliott dropped onto his back and tucked his legs through the handcuffs, so that they were now in front of him. Just as quickly he removed his blindfold, only to see a white fog and the hazy figure of the Russian president stumbling dangerously close to the melee he'd just been rescued from. Twice in one day he'd been blinded and deafened by something absolutely inconceivable, but knew from his earlier bout with both that in about thirty-five more seconds his vision and hearing would almost be restored. Elliott shouted for Nobakov to freeze, but he couldn't hear his own words, so how could the Russian?

General Meyers observed the two leaders stumbling carelessly back in the direction of something surely disastrous, and shouted a command to the penetration unit. "One of the two soldiers who killed his mark, retreat now, and get these two bloody leaders out of the building."

The frenetic pace of the intense assault would hold anyone's complete attention. If it didn't, one death awaited them. Unable to decipher and sense of direction or sound, Elliott and Nobakov traipsed precariously close to the melee.

"I repeat, this is General Meyers. I need one man to fall back and get those two leaders out of the building now. They're blind for Christ's sake! They can't hear!"

"I'm on it," someone shouted. Suddenly, one soldier peeled back from the furious encounter and clutched the two lost leaders just seconds before they'd stepped back into the fracas, and led them as best he could in the direction of the back door. But they resisted, not being able to make out who was clutching them so hard and possibly leading them to their earthly demise.

The soldier struggled to get them outside and physically forced them to sit on the splintery back porch, shouting at them, hoping they would be able to recognize he was one of the good guys. To someone observing the video feed at the Pentagon or vice president's bunker, the soldier looked like anything but a good guy, seemingly harassing the two leaders. Finally, Elliott squinted at the soldier, recognizing he was there to help. He held up his hands and shook his head affirmatively. "Okay okay, I understand," the Brit shouted, not knowing how loud he was speaking. "I can almost see again. What do you want us to do?"

"Don't move until you both can see clearly. Then get the hell out of here! There's a recon team back behind the tree-line. They'll take care of you. Do you understand?"

"Yes," Elliott said weakly, shaking his head, and then he placed a hand on the soldier's shoulder. "Thank you!"

Nobakov's vision had nearly come back all the way, and reached out to shake the soldier's hand. "Thank you, sir."

"No, thank you gentlemen for staying alive," the soldier shouted, not quite as loud as before. "I've got to get back in there now."

"Good luck!" Elliott said, but the soldier was already gone.

"Elliott and Nobakov!" Simonson shouted.

"That's two," Meyers acknowledged. "Seven to go."

The next ten seconds looked like open shark frenzy over bleeding flesh. It was almost impossible to decipher figures, and then one more hooded figure dropped to the ground—fortunately it was one of the captors holding two hostages. The soldier who just returned inside quickly helped escort two more somewhat defiant figures wearing blindfolds out of harm's way—one of them was wearing a skirt.

"Was that the president?" Meyers asked, frustrated by the confusion.

"President Haydon was wearing a different suit, general," Morrison reminded from afar.

"Roger that," Meyers exhaled.

The frenzy of close-in work continued, and then the video feed from the recon soldier closest to the Chinese leader had shown him somehow getting behind the militant holding the leader hostage and then warned that leader to think fast. "Stomp his feet!" he shouted, hoping the Asian man could at least partially hear his command—all this in the middle of shouting, screaming, and crying. The Chinese leader complied immediately, creating a very momentary slight gap between he and his captor, while instinctively trying to reach up to protect his throat, but his hands were cuffed behind his back.

The soldier reached up quickly and in an aerial motion ripped his knife across the throat of the militant guarding that leader. The captor fell into a motionless pile of death, as *his* knife slid across the neck of the Chinaman. Zheng too went down gasping for air. "Mark terminated," a voice yelled. "Chinese leader down!"

"Get him out of there!" Meyers commanded from half a world away. "Did you hear me, soldier?"

"Affirmative, sir!" the soldier shouted through the tense commotion, and pulled the motionless, profusely bleeding Chinese leader back away from the action, shoving his bloody knife into the grip of his clenched teeth. The soldier stooped down and lifted the badly wounded man, draping him over his shoulder, while speedily moving toward the exit. He could see the two new freed hostages were being forced to sit on the back porch, long enough to get their equilibrium back, while being advised by his fellow soldier. He laid the Chinese leader down next to the other two hostages. "I've got to go back inside," he told his comrade. "Keep pressure on his wound, and call for a medic."

General Meyers heard the request and ordered a team of medics to be dropped into the tree line. "We've got your back, soldier. Medics are on the way."

As the first two of the four freed hostages escaped into the perimeter out back of the forestry station and beyond the Hummers parked out back, they were immediately intercepted by two armed soldiers from the recon-team. "On the ground now!" both soldiers demanded from afar, but continued to advance on the first two fleeing men quickly. As the soldiers neared the two fleeing suspects, it was clear that they were bound behind their backs. Regardless, the soldiers had to be sure. It was still dark out, making it difficult to identify the two men. "On the ground. Now!"

The response was immediate from the first two hostages—they stopped dead in their tracks, and dropped to their knees.

"I am Alexander Nobakov," the first hostage said firmly into the barrels of two assault weapons. "I am the President of Russia."

"I am Edgar Elliott," the second freed prisoner immediately responded in kind, almost mixing up his words he was so excited. "I am the President of the European Union, and you fine gentlemen are a sight for sore eyes."

The two soldiers immediately recognized both leaders and lowered their weapons to a forty-five degree angle. "No, sir, the two of you are a sight for sore eyes," one of the soldiers said. "Are there any more?" he asked.

"There are two more hostages coming in your direction," General Meyers answered the recon soldier from his bird's nest, having had more current information than the two former prisoners. "There's one woman in the next group. Now please treat these people like world leaders," Meyers ordered.

"Roger that, general. Sorry, sir—just trying to be sure."

"And get one of your lock pickers to work on the handcuffs!" Meyers barked.

"Yes, sir."

In an instant, the two leaders fleeing from the building approached the soldiers and the first two former hostages. Nobakov and Elliott raced down the slight grade to meet them—Elliott raised his cuffed hands and wrapped his arms around the German Chancellor who was clearly rattled, while Nobakov verbally embraced the Japanese leader. "Welcome to freedom, Mr. Tanaka."

The recon soldiers ordered everyone back into the tree-line. Then they responded to a request of the soldier on the back porch to come down and remove the Chinese leader from the deck and get him into the safety of the trees. "He's still got a pulse, but barely," the soldier on the porch shouted. "I'm going back in. Get down here now!"

As the two soldiers descended down the very slight grade to retrieve the mortally wounded prisoner, Nobakov and Tanaka immediately retreated into the trees as instructed, while Elliott continued to assist the shaken German leader, a few paces behind the others. It had become apparent to Elliott that the chancellor had lost control of her bodily functions. He didn't even blink at the odor, as these were excruciating circumstances. "You're a hero, Claudia," Elliott encouraged the half-delirious woman.

Inside the fortress, the remaining militants had formed a shield around the commander to protect their leader. The recon team surrounded the outside of the remaining four militants and their hostages, outnumbering them twenty-nine to four. The situation had become dire for the militants, which made them that much more dangerous.

Somehow the relentless swarm of soldiers was able to penetrate and attach themselves, selflessly using their firearms or their own suddenly-exposed arms or hands, to temporarily stop the militants from digging their knives into the hostage's throats. The intense close-in hand-to-hand combat in some cases had caused the protective gloves to separate from the same protective shirt sleeves, briefly exposing a soldier's bare wrist or arm. There were screams of unearthly pain from several soldiers as their arms and hands were hacked up by the militants, but that was exactly the sacrifice they had to make to slow things down long enough to defuse the situation. Knives were thrust into the kidneys of any exposed militants, thwarting their attempts at digging their own knives into the throats of innocent leaders. Two more black-clad figures dropped to the floor, but it didn't appear any of the leaders dashed from the scene.

Sylvia had rushed the blind side of the commander but the still partially blind and deaf commander had turned immediately with his hostage, covering the opening that'd disappeared as fast as it'd opened. "Hang in there, Mrs. President," Sylvia screamed into the confusion, wanting her president to know she was not alone in this darkest hour, if she could hear at all.

"Sylvia?" the hysterical president asked, completely losing the ability to control her bladder now—the sheer anxiety and sudden excitement from an eleventh-hour chance at life had incapacitated her.

"Yes," Sylvia answered, quickly sizing up each and every move of the commander, who was darting back and forth rapidly to keep his assailants off balance. "It's me, Mrs. President." Sylvia then shouted for Major Wilkinson to abandon the others and join her. "Dom, I need you now!"

In an instant, Wilkinson freed himself from the melee just feet away, and locked his firearm on the commander. "I've got your back, Sylvia," he said calmly above the noise, staring into the wild eyes of the commander. "What do you need?"

The commander squeezed with his knife hand on the throat of his victim, knowing the situation was grave. He could no longer call on his brothers as they were being overwhelmed by the opposing forces—their numbers had dwindled to almost none. So he slowly backed himself and his hostage along the wall toward the open door to one of the smaller offices. The commander was running out of options and held up the remote with the three unused buttons, and warned the assailants in Farsi that there would be a great price to pay.

Sylvia shouted to Major Wilkinson, "Dom, neutralize that remote! I repeat, neutralize that remote! I've got no shot," she urged, as she stared down her two arms holding her firearm as it tracked the measured flight of the commander and his hostage. "Take it before he presses those buttons."

Sylvia then started to speak to the commander in Farsi, completely derailing him for just an instant as he'd never expected the words of brothers coming from the enemy. As an added deterrent, Sylvia quickly pulled her headset and removed her ski-mask, temporarily paralyzing the commander, as his eyes grew to the size of golf balls, fire and vehemence shooting out like shards of deadly lasers. The thought of a *woman* dressed as a man, and speaking to him like a man, drove him insane. Sylvia quickly replaced her headset while the commander cursed wildly now, vowing to end the woman's life. In an instant, the commander's head recoiled as he stared wildly at his female adversary, completely bewildered.

That split second was all Wilkinson needed, as his steady grip on the silenced weapon aimed at the screaming lunatic's remote hand as he inched toward the open door never wavered. As the commander reached the open doorway, his left index finger reached around the remote and started to make a downward motion toward one of the buttons, while still vehemently cursing at Sylvia in Farsi, then Arabic. As he did, Major Wilkinson coolly squeezed off two very quick rounds in the direction of the hand holding the remote. The first round exploded into and through the wrist of the commander and the remote flew into the air, as blood spurted profusely from the bleeding location. The commander wailed as the bullet nearly tore off his hand. It was unclear where the second round hit, but the president fell limp as the wounded commander dragged her into the small office behind him and locked the door, screaming and cursing wildly now.

"What's going on there?" General Meyers shouted, riveted to the visual uncertainty.

"Defusing a situation, sir," Sylvia answered, trying to keep the general off her back long enough to think.

"Is the president hit?" Meyers asked.

"I don't know, sir. Stand by," Sylvia replied. "Nice shooting, Dom."

"Nice what?" The general recoiled, again as a reflex.

"Quiet please, general!" Sylvia demanded as respectfully as one could who was trying to gain control of dire chaos.

Vice President Morrison intervened coolly, "Take it easy, Gordon."

"Thanks," Wilkinson reacted to Sylvia's compliment. "I didn't hit the president."

"I know," Sylvia said.

"My patterns are tight."

"I know, that's why I asked for you," Sylvia said again.

The melee next to them was over. All six of the militants were dead. All five badly shaken leaders were being assisted outside—the French president had sustained a pretty bad cut to just under his chin, but he would live. Two inches lower and he'd be lying on the floor with the pile of dead extremist martyrs.

"General, now would be a pretty good time to bring in those helos," Sylvia said, while motioning for Major Wilkinson to check and see if the doorknob to the small office containing the two biggest prizes was locked. "I'm sure these fine leaders could use a nice hot shower and a meal, maybe even a stitch or two. Wouldn't you say?" She could see that Wilkinson was unsuccessful with the locked door.

"Consider it done. Stand by," Meyers said, breathing a little easier now that eight of the surviving nine leaders were in the right hands, though the

Chinese president's status was still unclear. "Now let's go get our president," Meyers ordered, with an ever-so-slight tone of warmth. "Please."

"Yes, sir," Sylvia complied and turned to Major Wilkinson. "Dom, you heard the man. Let's go finish this."

"It would be a pleasure, ma'am."

"Hey!" Sylvia shouted in the direction of the other soldiers. "We don't need all you boys over there pickin' your noses! How about a little bit of help over here?"

In the Pentagon, Meyers and Simonson had an instantaneous chuckle at Sylvia's take-charge frankness. "God damn it all! I need a few of her working for me!"

"Yes, sir," Simonson agreed.

In an instant there were four soldiers standing off of Sylvia's right flank, firearms drawn. "At your service, ma'am," one of them said.

"Dom, blow the lock," Sylvia ordered, not sure how long the commander would let the president live now that he was out of bombs and martyrs.

"Gladly," Wilkinson obliged, firing two quick rounds into the simple tumbler chamber, and then hammering a very powerful combat boot into the door, blasting it open.

In an instant Sylvia charged through the still-swinging door—the door bouncing hard off of her right shoulder, as she moved to the left side of the small room, her firearm leading the way. Major Wilkinson was right on her heels, scrambling immediately to the right. Then two of the remaining soldiers squeezed into the room. That's all the room there was available without invading the immediate space of a now desperate militant commander so the other two soldiers remained outside.

The commander was propped up in the right corner of the room against a filing cabinet, with a limp, unconscious, or possibly dead president dangling from the iron death grip of his right arm still holding the serrated combat knife. His badly wounded left hand was rendered fairly useless from the blast to his wrist. Remarkably, it appeared that the commander was making a phone call of all things, while holding his mobile phone directly behind the president's head. He appeared to be teary-eyed but spoke in a controlled tone in Arabic. "My son, the time has come that I told you about many years ago, when we both would have to make the ultimate earthly sacrifice for our God."

"Father, I'm ready," a voice far far away answered. "What is it you ask of me?"

"Do you remember after the injury in the soccer game?" the commander asked, seemingly at peace with the recollection of the story they were revisiting.

"I took you to the best doctors in all of Paris. I so wanted for you to be a famous soccer star."

"Yes, father?"

"What the hell is he saying?" Major Wilkinson asked.

"Shhh," Sylvia hissed. She was the only one in the room who was fluid in both Farsi and Arabic. "I think he's saying good-bye to his son."

"Well, remember I told you before they gave you anesthesia for the operation that your greatest achievement would not be on the soccer field?"

"Yes, father, I do," the voice said.

Sylvia could only hear what the commander was saying, so she had to try to fill in the blanks of his conversation. What the *hell* soccer field was he talking about, she drilled her own mind, trying to grasp a desperate man's last thoughts while her hands subconsciously tightened on her firearm.

"Your moment is now, son," the commander said calmly, with an eerie state of peace flooding his face. He'd specifically withheld the information from his son that his shattered kneecap was replaced with a plastic kneecap—the plastic was explosive and had a tiny detonator rod implanted in it, which is why he always set off security alerts while passing through metal detectors at the airports. To security agents, it looked very much like a metal pin, which were very common in sports medicine, and the commander's son always carried a letter from his doctor when he flew. "I need for you depress the star button on your phone and hold it down for five seconds into your mobile phone right now, my son."

"Why, father?"

"After you do it, you will know," the commander explained calmly. "Please do it now."

Always the respectful son, Captain Amir Hassan pressed the button slowly on the keypad of his mobile phone. At that moment he stood in the cargo hold of the super tanker that was docked in Los Angeles' San Pedro Harbor, doing his normal round of checks before he took his shore leave to go visit family members in Encino. In an instant the former soccer standout was vaporized as the explosion was so intense that he never would've been aware of any sort of pain—he just had his one-way ticket punched to eternal nirvana. Equally as fast the human detonator ignited the vessel's various fuel cells which spread throughout the ships full load of LNG—Liquid Natural Gas.

The commander stayed on the line long enough to hear it go dead, then he simply let the mobile phone fall out of his hand to the floor. His expression was peaceful. His son had just made the ultimate sacrifice for God, and for the cause. And now he must do the same. The commander's thoughts had all turned to heaven and his maker—the thought of purity and cleansing open arms from above dominated his mind now, a peaceful serene smile tugged at the corners of his mouth. He hadn't felt this kind of warmth since his childhood. It was a beautiful feeling knowing he was going home now.

The commander knew he would bleed to death quickly enough, but couldn't risk his adversaries saving his life. He had enough time to kill the American president but probably not himself. And at the risk of his foe saving him only to torture him into giving up his sources, the commander's second choice was the clear choice: let the president live, if she was alive at all, and take his own life.

Sylvia sensed the commander's thoughts and warned Major Wilkinson and the other two soldiers to be ready to take the captor alive. "Don't let him die, gentlemen," she said softly, trying not to jar the commander from his peace. She then started to speak to the commander in Farsi, trying to coax him into a different ending than the one he'd committed himself to, slowly inching her way toward him. "It doesn't have to be this way, commander," she tried.

The commander seemed casually preoccupied with peaceful thoughts. His hazel-green eyes stared at Sylvia, as though he looked right through her, still smiling that eerie smile, almost seeing something else. "I have seen a photograph," he said calmly in his native Arabic now, barely above a whisper. "My son really did love you. You were his first and only love."

"What?" Sylvia shot back, her face contorting like a catcher's mitt while she tried to make sense out of the gibberish this madman was spewing forth. "What?!"

"What's he talking about, Sylvia?" Major Wilkinson asked, intensifying the grip on his own firearm.

"Hell if I know!"

"Surely you remember my son, Amir Hassaan?" the commander asked peacefully again in Arabic. This was between him and Sylvia. "He was a star with the Lyon Soccer Club."

"What?" Sylvia muttered in disbelief, her eyes widening and her mouth gaping open.

"Amir is with God now," the commander said dreamily, thinking about his son in the arms of his maker.

"What have you done to Amir?" Sylvia asked now in Arabic, a look of bewilderment and disbelief in her eyes, while losing the battle to emotion and charging her weakened opponent.

At the same time the commander acknowledged Sylvia's advance in his direction, and without a warning his knife hand which held the limp president let her fall, as he cursed his foe "Burn in hell!" In the same motion the upward thrust of his knife across his own throat ripped through his esophagus as

Wilkinson and the two other soldiers fired rounds into his arm holding the knife, attempting to disarm him before he could do harm to himself. All three rounds hit the designated pressure points on the militant's arm—one in the elbow, one in the bicep, and one in the shoulder—completely debilitating that arm, as the knife fell onto the fallen president. But it was too late for Wilkinson and his men to disable the commander before he could inflict mortal wounds upon himself, as he slumped to the floor next to the president.

"President down!" Sylvia shouted, rushing the fallen leader, not knowing the immediate impact of the fallen knife. "I repeat, president down! Get us a medic in here, general."

The Pentagon war room stiffened as grim uncertainty reigned. "There are two medics on the ground now, Sylvia. They're on their way in. Stand by!" Meyers shouted.

"Roger that, general," Sylvia shouted back through the confusion, running on pure adrenaline now while hitting her knees hard next to the fallen Haydon, and feeling the side of her neck with her left hand for a pulse. "I have a pulse, general!" Sylvia shouted, setting the firearm in her right hand down to find where the fallen knife had hit—if it had at all. The commander's knife, as it turned out, had fallen between the president's left forearm and her hip, sticking into the wooden floor. "It's weak but I've got a pulse!" Sylvia shouted, while exploring possible damage from the falling knife, rolling up Haydon's tattered suit and shirt sleeve and ripping away the untucked portion of her blouse.

In the Pentagon as well as the vice presidential bunker, there was a loud collective round of cheers.

"Let's not celebrate quite yet, general. President Haydon has been cut by the falling knife. Small surface lacerations to the left forearm and left oblique," Sylvia shouted, while tossing the serrated knife away from the commander's reach. "Where's the damned medic?" Sylvia demanded, her frayed nerves starting to show the signs of sleep deprivation.

In an instant, General Meyers shouted for his medics to respond. "Get the hell in there now!"

"I'm taking the president to some fresh air," she said, while stooping over to scoop up the woman who was a little heavier than herself. She'd carried men a lot heavier through battlefields before, but this was her president. Sylvia had vowed to die for if necessary, let alone carry fifty feet through a forestry station saturated with death.

Sylvia removed the commander's arm which had fallen onto the president when he fell to the floor, and noticed the eerie stare of the commander who was still alive—just barely though. He breathed unevenly and gasped for air from his torn esophagus, but his peaceful smile remained. "Don't even think about it," she said in Arabic. "It's not time for you to meet Allah yet." As she hoisted President Haydon up to her feet, Major Wilkinson tried to help her. "No thanks, Dom. One of your boys can help me. You try to save that bastard down there. We need him alive."

Wilkinson obliged, and dropped to his knees to put pressure on his enemy's oozing throat, while one of the two remaining soldiers stepped up to help Sylvia. They quickly navigated sideways out the narrow doorway, while Sylvia's helper ordered his comrades to move. "Step aside, boys! We've got ourselves an American president to deliver."

They whisked Haydon through the clutter of dead militants, as the president's head started to move around a little as she started to come to. "Where are?" Haydon tried to ask, but she was half-delirious and still half-blind.

"We're going home, Madame President," Sylvia said, as they stepped out onto the back porch, where they were greeted by the two medics General Meyers had promised. "We're going home."

"Home?" the president said weakly, and then Sylvia and her helper passed Haydon off to the welcoming and capable arms of the two medics, and returned to Major Wilkinson and the others.

Major Wilkinson tried futilely to stop the commander's wounds from bleeding. The tourniquet that he'd applied to the commander's left arm certainly slowed the bleeding from the left wrist that he'd blown to smithereens. And the bleeding from three strategic gun-blasts to the right arm was being tended to by two of the remaining soldiers. But the commander's lacerated throat was so severe, not even the major's battlefield expertise could save him. The commander had nearly cut off his own head—the insurance policy he had to take out against any combatant trying to compromise any future plans of *his* commander—the Prophet.

By the time Sylvia and her flank had returned to the tiny office riddled with the stench of blood and spent ordinance, it was too late. "Dom?" she asked Wilkinson, who was now standing.

"Not a chance, Sylvia," he said shaking his head. "He's got seconds, maybe a minute."

"All right," Sylvia said. "I want to be alone with this man for a minute. Major, organize a detail—gather up the bodies out there and whatever belongings, equipment, mobile phones, and whatever else you can find that is relevant. The Intel guys are gonna want to sweep this place for whatever clues or DNA that can help link us to Mr. Big. Now give me a minute."

"10-4," Wilkinson complied, and then directed his soldiers out to the larger main room.

After the men had left, Sylvia studied her adversary for a moment and she could see from the near-death squint in his eyes that he was just about lost. It appeared he was trying to say something, though his strength was nearly gone. She humanely dropped to her knees and lowered her right ear to his lips that were still trying to mouth a few words. Major Wilkinson had indicated that he'd already swept the room for weapons.

"Who are you?" the commander barely managed through a strained inhale and exhale.

"I am one who has lived among you, eaten with you, slept with you—in many ways I am you," Sylvia offered. "But I am different from you."

"How? We are both soldiers of God," the commander struggled to explain, barely legible now. "When you are called, you come."

"My God doesn't call upon me to murder the innocent people of the world," Sylvia tried, knowing there would be an equivocation for the commander's cause, but she could see he was barely clinging to his last few breaths on earth.

"That is what you believe," the commander squeaked, coughing now, while little spurts of blood squirted from the severed opening in his throat. He reached now for Sylvia's black knit sweater, trying to pull her down even closer to his mouth as he felt the remaining life draining from his lungs. "History will side with Allah's children. They will see that the infidels kill our babies in the name of Christianity, just as Napoleon, Ferdinand, Isabella, and the rest killed millions to spread the word of God. What is the difference?" the commander managed, now knowing he was just seconds from his long-awaited appointment with his maker. "I am going now to the kingdom of God," he said, as his loose grip on Sylvia's sweater finally relented, his hand falling to his own chest, showing barely a trace left of his weak smile.

"What did you do to Amir?" Sylvia tried again. "He wanted nothing to do with this struggle. He just wanted to play soccer."

"That is true," the commander exhaled weakly. "But there are greater causes than just soccer. Amir has now given his earthly life for Allah, and Allah will reward him with eternal peace."

Although visibly shaken, Sylvia quickly composed herself, turned and leaned into her foe and whispered into his ear. "There is an Allah—I agree—just not the kind of Allah who rewards a man for the murder of innocents, including your son. I hate to be the bearer of bad news, but there are no virgins, comrade, and you are below the meat of an ass. You've gravely misjudged *our* God." With that, Sylvia leaned back up and watched his last breath being sucked out of his chest. "May God *not* have mercy on your soul, commander," she said, shaking her head, then got up and dragged the corpse out to the pile of the others.

Wilkinson's unit had lined up all the deceased militants, shoulder-to-shoulder, with their faces up, and removed their ski masks. Even in the soft lighting the visual nearly blindsided Sylvia, causing her to do a double-take. "What the hell?" Sylvia asked, completely dumbfounded. "These guys are all…"

"Caucasian," Wilkinson finished her statement of bewilderment for her. "This is how they were able to infiltrate this high-profile Austrian restaurant over a period of time and remain undetected as normal waiters."

"Shit, Dom! But the language, everything…"

"You speak Arabic *and* Farsi," he interrupted again. "Anyone can take one of these fast-learn internet language courses. Hell, these guys are no more militants than we are. But they wanted the world to think they were. They're just fuckin' contractors though, and there's a ton of these guys for hire out on the open market."

The Pentagon team processed the unsettling discovery of the identities of the militants from afar via Wilkinson's headset. And although Sylvia had abandoned hers a short while ago in the chaos, she was close enough to the major that his highly sensitive microphone picked up her voice.

"What about all of the religious rhetoric by the Prophet?" she pondered.

"Pretty convincing, wasn't it?" Wilkinson reasoned. "And who's to say the Prophet wasn't of Middle Eastern descent, *and* committed to his cause? Maybe with the exception of him and his dead commander here, everyone else was a hired gun and didn't really give a damn about Allah or the seventy-two virgins. *They* were just in it for a truckload of cash."

"Why go to such lengths?" Sylvia asked, shaking her head.

Across the Atlantic, General Gordon Meyers found himself mouthing the same words.

"Why not, is more the question," Wilkinson reasoned. "If you're an unknown rogue group and want to remain that way, why not leave someone else's footprint? Why not finger the obvious—the usual suspects, Islamic extremists?"

"I've gotta get some fresh air. This is really fucked up, Dom," Sylvia exhaled. "I'm tired. Maybe I need some sleep."

"Everyone has their price, Sylvia. Remember?"

"I guess."

She walked outside, drained from what she'd just witnessed, as her mind still battled with itself over the pang of loss of a rare pleasant memory. For now she would have to tuck away any thoughts of Amir into her void of darkness.

Dawn had started to break and the immediate area was swarming now with vehicles and helicopters of all types. There was a fortified presence of troops as well as new command that'd arrived, though it was still too dark to decipher which was which.

Sylvia could see that the medics assigned to the president had bandaged up the wounded leader and were preparing to transport her. Haydon lay on a collapsible gurney with wheels, which sat on the ground level next to the back deck.

The medics were also outfitted with the standard issue audio-visual headsets making it easier for the Pentagon to follow the president's progress. They had just opened the gurney up to its fully expanded position, when one of them was asked by their chain of command to place her headset on the president's head.

"Madame President," the voice said. "This is General Gordon Meyers at the Pentagon."

"Yes, general," Haydon acknowledged in a drained but relieved voice.

"First of all, Madame President, I want to tell you how happy and thankful we are here at the Pentagon, that you are alive and well."

"Thank you, general," the president managed. "It's great to be back with the good guys."

"Yes, ma'am. You have an angel looking over you."

"General, I assume you're referring to a young lady by the name of Sylvia?"

"That I am, Madame President," the general agreed. "That I am."

The general's transmission with the president was being monitored by the vice president and he was anxiously awaiting his turn to speak to his boss, leaning pretty heavily on Meyers' Bluetooth to transfer him in. "Uh, Madame President, Vice President Morrison would like to speak with you now."

"Of course," Haydon responded weakly. "Please put him through!"

"Madame President," Morrison burst onto the line, unable to contain his exuberance.

"Adam?" Haydon asked.

"Yes, Marge. It's me," the vice president said. "I can't even begin to tell you how happy we are to have you and the others back."

"Well, Adam, I can't even tell you how happy I am to be back—and how very happy I am to have listened to you about Sylvia. One day I want to know the entire story about her."

"Marge, I can honestly tell you I knew she was good, but I had no idea she was *this* good," Morrison said. "Or that she had a direct pact with divine intervention. I'm very glad we listened to our recruiters. They hit a grand slam with Sylvia."

"Seriously, Adam, I want you to move for a Congressional medal for Sylvia—immediately. What she's done here is unprecedented," Haydon lobbied, though the mild sedative she was given seven minutes earlier was starting to take effect. She started to ramble, adding the fallen Canadian leader to her list candidates of honor.

"I will personally take care of it, Madame President," Morrison agreed, recognizing the president's deteriorating coherency, "on both accounts, Marge. You just get yourself home, Madam!"

"I will, Adam," Haydon complied, while being told by the medics that they needed to roll. "The doctors here say we have to go."

"Listen to your doctors, Marge. We'll talk again real soon."

"All right," Haydon agreed, but still had questions. "How are the others, Adam?"

"You'll see them soon enough, at Rammstein," Morrison replied, but couldn't say for sure which ones. "I have Tyler and the boys with me, Madame President. I'll put Tyler on now."

"Please!" she said, rapidly losing the battle with her sedatives.

"Margie?" Tyler asked excitedly.

"Oh, Tyler," she squeaked, unable to hold back her emotions. "I thought I'd never see you and the boys again. I love you so much."

"I love you too, Margie!" Tyler said, also at a loss, laughing and crying at the same time. Kyle and Keith clung to their father, joyfully studying his rare display of emotion—to them it was a convincing happy ending. They themselves would have to wait a while longer for their own chance to speak with their mother. For now, they were content with the reassuring joy in their father's eyes.

Suddenly though, Tyler's questions were no longer getting answered, so he and the boys turned and watched the monitor again to find out why.

As the medics started to wheel the president to a pre-designated helicopter, her eyes locked onto Sylvia. "Wait!" she shouted weakly to one of the medics while holding her forearm. "I need to talk to that woman, please."

The two medics stopped momentarily and turned to see who the president was talking about. Sylvia had already jetted down the stairs and stood by the president's side by the time they figured out who Haydon had requested to see.

"Madame President," Sylvia started, reaching out to hold the outstretched hand of the president.

"Sylvia," Haydon started. "I can't even begin to tell you, how indebted I am to you—how indebted the world is to you," Haydon shared, fighting her medication. "Do you have *any* idea where we'd all be right now if...?"

"I'm sorry I let you down, Madame President," Sylvia offered, while critiquing her own performance. In her own mind she wasn't to allow so much as a scratch to the woman she vowed to protect.

"Stop!" Haydon interrupted. "*You,* are a hero, young lady."

"Thank you, Madame President, but…," Sylvia tried again, still unsettled by the commander's course of action in his last moments on earth.

"But nothing!" Haydon interrupted again. "When you are done out here, you get yourself back to Washington. We need to talk."

"Yes, ma'am," Sylvia complied with a hint of reservation. "But…"

The president just held up one finger at her bodyguard, for her to stop. "Enough," she said, weakly. The sedative was clearly winning the battle with the president's coherency though, and the medics had their orders.

"Ma'am, we have to roll," one of the medics said, while handing the president's headset to Sylvia.

Los Angeles, 9:56 p.m.

The popular Korean-born traffic reporter Sheila Kim and her crew in Chopper 1 were doing their nightly traffic report, hovering above the 710 and 405 interstate freeways. Things weren't that different from night to night—traffic was traffic after all. And in LA there was always lots of it.

The pilot had seen the fireball first, but only by a split-second. It started as a spectacular blast from this location, but in seconds grew to something none of the traffic crew could imagine. Without missing a beat, the pilot turned west toward the San Pedro harbor as Kim tried to explain what she saw to her faithful audience, in between reports back to her NBC affiliate trying to get any feedback on the inferno's origin. In just over one-and-a-half minutes the pilot and his crew were hovering above what could only be described as hell on earth.

On camera, the sight was bad enough. In person, hovering above the five-hundred foot flames, the visual was nothing short of Armageddon. It appeared that six former oil tankers were burning out of control while the white hot flames had angrily jumped onto three adjacent storage tanks, enshrouding them in molten fuel which was yet to be identified.

"We're hovering above an enormous fire that erupted apparently just minutes ago," Sheila Kim began, trying to maintain a journalist's point of view, but the traffic reporter never expected this when she punched her time card today. Opportunity didn't always knock at the most convenient time.

"We're told that witnesses on the ground saw an explosion on or near that super-tanker furthest to the left, creating flames so intense the fire jumped ship to the tanker next to it—then the one next to it caught fire, and so on, like dominos. No one knows exactly what the initial tanker was carrying, chemicals, crude oil, or liquid natural gas, but whatever it was, it was under tremendous pressure and obviously extremely flammable. We're told that the initial blast was so forceful that it fired shards of white-hot shrapnel across the harbor, igniting anything it came in contact with, while sending flames as high as five-hundred feet in the air. The explosion was said to have blown out windows three blocks away."

Kim paused for a moment, clearly taken with the disaster down below her crew's hovering helicopter. She wasn't quite prepared for this, and took the tone of the report to a not necessarily unprofessional level—just personal. "Guys, this is weird. It's like Pearl Harbor down there all over again—only no planes. I don't think anything is getting into or out of San Pedro for a while," Kim said, turning silent for a moment. "One after another of the ships in the harbor seems to ignite or have some kind of debilitating explosion, and God only knows what will happen when those storage tanks blow."

Plumes of white and black smoke billowed into the sky, the flames angrily pushing higher and higher. Suddenly and without warning there was a titanic blast below from the first of the storage tanks—flames spiking higher than ever, piggybacking themselves like a stairway to the heavens. "Oh my God!" Kim screamed. "Pull up! Pull up! Pull up!"

In an instant, panic reigned as the broadcast was lost.

CHAPTER 23

Major Dominic Wilkinson and the rest of his team that didn't require immediate medical attention had gathered on the back porch just a few feet away from Sylvia, while she spoke with the brass in Washington. Four men from his unit who were cut on their hands or wrists from the close-in work with the militants, first received field attention, a local anesthesia if they wanted it, and then were airlifted to Vienna National Hospital to get stitched up.

By now, all of the soldiers who remained had removed their ski masks, and several of the men smoked cigarettes and congratulated one another while recounting each other's roles in the counter-assault on the militants. It wasn't every day that they could say they saved the world. And this really was a global effort. The multi-national special ops program had been in effect for some time, but up until now it had been relatively untested. And considering these guys were assembled under Major Wilkinson just seventeen hours earlier, it was indeed remarkable how seamlessly the makeshift elite unit had meshed.

The debilitating effects of the M84s and swarming surprise tactics were almost flawless. Of the nine world leaders they'd been sent in to recover, all nine were alive, though Chinese President Chen Zheng was clinging precariously to life. The cuts to his throat were a little deeper than originally thought. He'd received field treatment and was immediately whisked off to Vienna National Hospital for the finest medical care available.

French President, Didier Marceau, was luckier than his Chinese counterpart. His throat very easily could have been cut, surely making death a probability. But thanks to one of the wounded special ops guys sacrificing his own hand as a cutting board long enough to end the life of that militant holding him hostage, Marceau would only have two small incisions just under his chin—nothing a beard or goatee couldn't fix, or, a world-renowned French plastic surgeon.

The rest of the world leaders with the exception of the American president, were simply shaken and shocked by eighteen hours of barbaric mistreatment in captivity, and two bouts of blindness and tinnitus. After a hot shower and a decent meal, they would all recover in due time, likely with the assistance of a counselor to help debrief their harrowing experiences.

Major Wilkinson sat down on the edge of the back porch and reached into a pocket down around his thigh on his black cargo-type fatigues, and retrieved a can of Skoal chewing tobacco, and waited until he was sure Sylvia was watching. He then dug into the can with the thick first finger on his right hand and loaded up a pretty significant wad of tobacco and stuck it between his left cheek and gum. She used to give him a pretty hard time about chewing, always asking "What woman would kiss you?"

"*You* did," was always his answer.

Sylvia shook her head at the major and his habit then turned to resume her conversation with General Meyers.

With a bulging left cheek, Wilkinson grinned back at Sylvia, and blew a kiss at her even though she wasn't looking.

"I can't even begin to express my gratitude to you, Sylvia," General Meyers said. "You have done your country a great service, as well as the world. I look very forward to meeting you."

"Thank you, general. I really couldn't have done it without your assets here," Sylvia replied, moving closer to her old comrade sitting just a few feet away. "Major Wilkinson and his team were amazing, sir. I didn't really do anything. They deserve the credit."

Wilkinson shook his head at the humble antics of his old friend. He was grateful for her compliments, but wasn't really in the game for adulation. He was well aware of his own reputation, but could never really go for the footlights. He was just comfortable being the go-to guy in times of crisis. But Wilkinson also knew Sylvia's diversion to himself and his unit was entirely far-fetched, since none of them would be having this conversation if his old flame hadn't survived the massacre back at Schaafhausen in the first place.

Sylvia was still very concerned about the commander's last order, and asked the general if there was anything in their conversation he was withholding, either classified or otherwise. He insisted that there wasn't. Deputy Director Simonson alerted the general to the breaking news now being put up on the large main monitor in the Pentagon war room, replacing the split-screen images from the Austrian forest.

"Will this ever end?" the general exhaled slowly, in utter disbelief as the graphic details being displayed on the main monitor temporarily froze him. He'd just had enough time to unwind from an eighteen-hour global crisis, and now this.

"What is it, general?" Sylvia asked, suddenly rigid.

Her reaction was immediately mirrored by Major Wilkinson whose posture stiffened as his eyes queried Sylvia for more information. His men were having entirely too much fun with their conversation and he asked them to contain it. "Shhh!"

"Sylvia, the NBC affiliate has just broken a story out of Los Angeles. They've just blown the port of San Pedro."

"Fuck!" Sylvia exploded, instantaneously becoming furious as her mind questioned what she could have done differently to help avert this disaster, or what she could have done better. Her reaction caused Major Wilkinson to jump down from the back deck and empty his mouth of both spit and chew. Again his eyes queried his friend for more information.

"How bad, general?" Sylvia asked, not really wanting to hear about another world crisis.

Those weren't good words for Wilkinson.

"It's bad," the general replied, trying to communicate with Sylvia as rapidly as the story was unfolding, reading the text on the silenced monitor. "The port of San Pedro looks like Pearl Harbor—there are fifteen fully loaded super tankers with crude, or LNG, burning out of control as we speak. There are six fully loaded storage tanks burning out of control," the general explained. "It's...oh god..."

"What, sir?" Sylvia interrupted the cryptic answer.

"Apparently the initial reporters who were covering the story got too close to the flames when there was a massive explosion, and it blew their helicopter out of the air. They were all vaporized on live TV."

"Fuck!" Sylvia reacted again, barely above a whisper and shared what she could with Wilkinson. "They've blown the port of San Pedro in L.A."

"Sylvia, the report says the entire shipping lane into and out of L.A. could be shut down indefinitely," the general explained rapidly, hoping privately this event could also have been another Milan hoax. "I've got to go! I've got the vice president on the line. You get your ass to Washington and look me up. You hear?"

"Yes, sir," Sylvia replied, but the general was already gone.

Vice Presidential bunker, 1:15 a.m.

Adam Morrison and his staff barely had enough time to savor the news of the freed captives in Austria, when he'd been informed of the breaking horror story in Los Angeles.

Tyler and the boys were already being airlifted in Marine One, back to the White House, with a pretty significant security detail. For security reasons, the news of the freed hostages hadn't been released yet. After all, it hadn't yet been determined if the rogue cell responsible for the UN abduction had been fully contained. For that same matter the ill-fated demise of their contingent in the Viennese forest was also withheld, so as not to leak an indication either way to the sponsor cell.

But now there was another risk at hand—one of equal or greater importance—the threat of a global financial market meltdown. The markets that *were* already open were getting crushed. The European markets were all due to open in two hours, and their futures were all headed markedly southward across the board, with the exception of oil and precious metals futures. The American markets, both north and south, wouldn't open for another eight hours, but they could ill-afford another debilitating setback.

Then the news of the attacks in Los Angeles had jumped the Pacific as if it was a swimming pool, completely disintegrating the Asian markets attempting to stabilize themselves. Their shares almost immediately spiraled precipitously downward like falling swords. Only a market newcomer would try to reach out and grab something cheap on the way down, more than likely on margin, only to get sliced up some more. The bottom line was, panic was panic in any language—it didn't need an interpreter. All investors were getting annihilated.

While the price of crude oil shot up to just north of $149 a barrel, gold had no problem taking out its near-term resistance of $2,077 an ounce—it had spiked to just over $2,099 an ounce immediately on the heels of the LA story.

General Meyers and his staff listened in on the emergency conference call with the vice president and the leader-by-proxy of each of the victimized nations, while images of the escalating disaster in Los Angeles continued to play on the wall opposite him. Pentagon officials and the Joint Chiefs orchestrated military strategy and execution, but these decisions were of an entirely different nature and in the hands of the vice president and his constituency, as result of a clause in the Emergency War Powers Act.

After a twenty-two minute conference call between the ten representatives of their respective nations, it was determined that there would be a greater benefit to releasing news of the nine freed world leaders, while withholding their secure locations.

The temporary leaders also assessed that while the gravity of the Los Angeles disaster was indeed prolific, at the end of the day it might have had a fraction of the global impact than if the three remaining buttons on the remote had been activated, conceivably landing the world on the precipice of extinction.

After another two minutes to determine who would share the titanic news of the hostages and their release, it was decided unanimously that the American vice president would deliver the oratory to the world. It was a relatively new political landscape across the board globally, and with the exception of the captured Russian president, Admiral Morrison was seen as one of few remaining old guard—a rock the international community would relish seeing.

There wasn't time to hire polished speech writers or powder noses. And there certainly wasn't enough time to airlift Morrison to an immediately recognizable Washington, D.C. location. Still, his emergency bunker was adequately equipped with a humble but professional theater for such events, complete with the Presidential emblem emblazoned on a navy-colored draped backdrop.

This would be an ad lib presentation from a gentleman who'd had to do this countless times during his previous trials as a military leader. The fact that he'd already prepared for a different appearance eighteen hours earlier, still wearing his pristine regalia of an admiral decorated with badges of honor, made him a little more camera friendly, as well as an iconic image of stability to a shell-shocked world clamoring for just that. His personal assistant straightened his collar and tie while all of the major broadcast networks were given a five-minute advance warning of the emergency speech that was about to be delivered.

At exactly 1:44 a.m. Eastern Standard Time, the vice president's impromptu speech began; "Good morning or good evening, my fellow Americans, wherever you are; I would also like to say good day to all of our global community's citizens. As you know, for the last eighteen hours, we've all been at the mercy of a ruthless group of international mercenaries who had abducted our great leaders, then tortured them. As you also know, we've lost a true hero in Canadian Prime Minister Scott Hammons. We will forever remember him as a friend.

"In the last two hours, we discovered that there was a possible breach in the stronghold at the militants' compound somewhere in Austria. We had closely monitored that situation as it played out. Once we were able to confirm that breach, a team of multi-national special anti-assault agents were deployed into the cell's covert location. Approximately seventy-five minutes ago we were successful in recovering all nine living captive leaders, while capturing the remainder of the militants responsible for these terrible acts against humanity," the vice president explained, while leading the global audience to believe that the rogue militants were still alive.

He and the other leaders strategized that this was the best tactic that they could employ in the hopes of keeping the ringleader of this cell second-guessing and off-balance while he was still at large. Whatever they could do to plant the seed of doubt in his mind, might just cause him to make a move or a mistake sooner or later. "We are confident in our ability to obtain the necessary information from our detainees, and get to the nucleus of their organization that carried out this dastardly attack on the civilized world.

"We expect that, after a thirty-six hour debriefing and medical evaluation period for security purposes, all of the leaders will return to their respective countries. It is at that time that each and every one of them will be seen and heard from in their respective countries. That is all for now. God bless all of you. And God bless America," Morrison closed as quickly as he began, and then waited for his cameraman's signal across his throat that he was off the air.

As expected, in the minutes following the close of the American vice president's speech, reaction in the financial communities was immediate and relentless. All of the Asian markets, as well as Australia's All-Ordinaries, rallied furiously off of their historic lows. In many cases short-covering began to gain traction, further fueling the tepid rallies. As would also be expected in such a scenario, the safe-haven benchmarks of oil and precious metals began to erode while the welcome news of the world leaders' freedom could be processed. Once the financial communities could assess the impact of such events, the giddy reality began to take hold: Global stability would reign once again, and with that the deterioration in those hallmark commodities gathered steam. Their prices fell apart quickly.

CHAPTER 24

In the ensuing days following the eighteen-hour global crisis, relative calm slowly pervaded the daily lives of the world's community. The banking and commerce crisis that had frozen most of North America and Europe had been resolved. Bunker Hill, the small upstart database security consultancy out of Silicon Valley, had ridden in on a large white thoroughbred and saved the day, restoring all of the data that was suspected lost prior to the panic that'd swept two continents just days earlier. Unfortunately for the CEO of that firm, he had to be debriefed in a very private and intense twelve-hour session with the sub-committee assigned to the task force investigating the banking debacle.

The company's CEO explained to his interrogators after examining the databases on the storage devices it was determined the data was intact, and concluded the zero readings were a hardware problem, which satisfied no one.

After putting some high-tech equipment to the task, they determined that a magnetic charge was somehow imposed on the read heads of all the external storage devices. This infinitesimal magnetic field caused the heads to return all zeroes instead of what was actually written on the disk. The company's engineers determined that the magnetic charge would have dissipated in a matter of time anyway. The initial assumption however, became extremely confusing because the infestation had spread like a virus—therefore the assumption was it was a virus, and hence, a software problem.

While the CEO's interrogators acknowledged they had understood the explanation, they looked at him as if he was from another planet. Experts from his field were brought in to validate his seemingly preposterous explanations. Bunker Hill's main man said they could only isolate the means of altering the data up to this point, but went as far as to suggest that with enough time and resources the perpetrator's footsteps could be traced all the way back to the source itself.

Not-so-surprisingly, Bunker Hill had become the new darling of the federal government's IT department, as well as every major bank on either side of the Atlantic. All relevant parties had stepped in line to employ the services of Bunker Hill as a devil's advocate consultant.

The horrific Los Angeles firestorm that had raged furiously out of control was very real, unlike the Milan deception. It had finally been reduced to a handful of small bonfires, but not before it'd consumed nearly six square miles of shipping lanes and residential neighborhoods. The main bridge that had crossed from one side of the harbor to the other had collapsed, as an intense fire on the terminal side rendered its support structure into molten jelly. Just the riveted steel cross-members could be seen sticking out of the water now, as well as the concrete support that sat out in the middle of the channel.

Every Los Angeles fire company from Santa Barbara to Cucamonga was brought in to battle the hellish blaze, as well as the departments stretching from San Francisco to San Diego. But in the end, all of the battalion chiefs had conceded that one simply couldn't fight anything that intensely hot. It was self-perpetuating fuel and fire that had to run its course until it could be battled with their beefed-up assets.

Instead they evacuated a ten-mile radius around the immediate heart of the blaze where they set their defensive perimeter and did battle. It took the flames nearly sixteen hours to angrily devour its initial fuel source—crude oil, chemicals, and a bounty of LNG. Once that source was exhausted though, the firefighter's valiant stand commenced, and in another seventeen hours ninety-nine percent of the flames had been mercifully extinguished.

In the end however, just over nineteen billion dollars of cargo, infrastructure, and real estate had been lost to such an unprecedented blaze—not to mention the thirteen brave souls who'd given their lives to do battle with the raging inferno. Remarkably, only two hundred thirty-seven dock hands and crew members had perished in the instantaneous firestorm, as well as about a half-dozen homeless drifters. That number could have quadrupled if the fire had taken place during the day when the shipyard was operating at its normal full staff levels.

Estimates to rebuild the massive shipping lane ranged from twelve to eighteen months, while continued cargo shipments would be displaced to Seattle, the San Francisco Bay area, as well as the port of San Diego.

Officials at every level tried to assure that the fallout would be absorbed by the other shipping centers with little or no consequence to the Los Angeles area. Still, even the most optimistic analysts knew that was a pipedream. President Haydon immediately declared it a national disaster area, and announced she had already scheduled a trip out to Los Angeles to comfort the fire-torn city, and vowed to rebuild their critical port.

———————◯———————

In Washington, D.C., an immense parade was planned to celebrate the return of President Haydon. Well over a million people were expected to jam the streets of the nation's capitol in the near-freezing February afternoon for a shot at the parade route that started at Capitol Hill and ran up Pennsylvania Avenue to the White House.

Similar parades were planned in Milan, Paris, Tokyo, London, Moscow, and Munich, to celebrate the lives of those leaders, and the optimistic outlook for those countries' futures.

On a more somber note, Beijing was planning a parade as well—a funeral procession for its great leader, President Chen Zheng, who never recovered from his injuries. The procession and celebration of his new life would culminate in Tiananmen Square. Beijing had agreed to their procession being delayed by an additional thirty-six hours so that the American president and French president could be cleared to travel with their injuries.

One thing was clear however, every surviving leader who had been held hostage with the fallen Chinese and Canadian leaders insisted on being by their sides in their time of passing. They'd all come to respect them both for their defiant courage in the face of such impossible odds. The leaders had all become so close in a remarkable way, and in most cases not a lifetime's worth of politicking would have accomplished this. They'd hoped together, sweated together, cried together, prayed together, and bled together. And in the case of these two courageous heroes, they paid the ultimate price for global freedom with their lives.

Canada was to hold two parades for its deceased hero: one in Montreal, and the funeral procession with casket in his native Calgary. All eight remaining leaders committed themselves to attending both venues on the same day without hesitation.

———————◯———————

The financial markets continued to mend themselves in the aftermath of uncertainty. And equally as important as their wholesale recovery was that their volatility continued to subside, as stability took hold on a global basis. It wasn't necessarily a good thing for traders, but proved to be extremely beneficial to the restoration of the harmonious balance of investors worldwide.

Crude oil in the ensuing days had settled all the way back to its support level of $100 a barrel. The precious metals markets had also settled back to near where they were when the turmoil had all begun. Gold was back trading around $1,880 an ounce—all of the fluff had been taken out of its once-lofty price.

In Hong Kong, Charles Li and Minh Pak continued to squabble over whether they'd gotten out of their various gold positions too soon.

"We could've made a lot more!" Li argued, half-joking and always half-serious when it came to speculation.

"Greed is going to kill you yet," the more conservative partner, Minh Pak said. "We did well. Quit crying over spilled milk."

"Yes, we did. And you are right," Li conceded, but he was unable to hold back a snicker. "Did I tell you I bought two hundred March $2,000 puts, just for sport?" He shared with his partner, betting that the price of gold would be *at* or less than $2,000 an ounce by the third Friday in March, when those options expired. "It was in my own account of course; I know how you feel about these things."

"You didn't?!" Pak asked incredulously, as his jaw dropped. "You see what I mean? You're sick! Certifiably ill! You need therapy!"

"I know, I know. Again, you're right," Li conceded again. "You know what's even better?"

"What's that, sicko?"

"I bought them when gold had spiked to $2,099. I got them just about at the top—stole them basically. I threw a ridiculous bid out there, and got lucky. I had to do it," Li explained, unable to restrain his giggling.

The conservative Pak couldn't even respond. He just shook his head at his partner.

"Hey, I just made a $178,000 U.S. in three days—just for sport."

"You're sick," were the only words Minh Pak could muster up for his partner. Of course, they'd had these arguments before for the better part of their twenty years, together as partners and traders before that. Aggressive and conservative—it was a match made in heaven. They'd made each other a lot of money because of those traits. They'd also just racked up over twenty-five billion dollars in profits for themselves and their clients, not bad for a strategy which had taken about a year to implement and carry out *and*, more importantly, they'd done it all with a clear conscience.

———————◯———————

In the Maldives, Gregor Heinricke and his playmates boarded a motorboat large enough for the three of them and the boat's pilot, along with their small collection of suitcases they'd brought ashore just six days earlier. Since clothing wasn't really a necessity for this trip, even the girls had packed only a small carry-on each, as had Heinricke.

"Gregor, what happened to your laptop and the other stuff?" Katia asked, noticing her former boss didn't have his computer bag next to him. He *never* traveled without his computer, she thought.

"Ahhh it's not important," he exhaled while kicking back with both elbows propped up on the edge of the boat. After confirming all of his closed positions earlier that morning and tallying the profits from those trades, Heinricke had walked around to the other side of the small island, and hurled his laptop out into the warm waters of the Indian Ocean like a Frisbee. In an instant all of whatever was on his box was lost at sea. He removed the CDs from a side pouch on the computer bag and then tossed them one-at-a-time a hundred feet out to sea. Then he filled the black leather computer bag with fine white sand from the beach and zipped up the bag and walked it out twenty steps or so and hurled it as well. Seconds later his mobile satellite phone went airborne along with the rest of his goodies.

"I'll get a new one, Katia," he offered nonchalantly and rolled over, laying his head in her lap. With the one-point-six billion dollar nest egg he'd just amassed in his personal account while on vacation in the Maldive Islands with two beautiful ladies, he felt confident he could afford a new one.

London Heathrow Airport, 2:55 p.m.

The passengers from British Airways Flight 94 from Vienna were among the first from that country that had been cleared to fly after the embargo had been lifted. Once they'd met the intense security measures implemented at Vienna International Airport, it had been a quick one-hour hop up to the UK.

Passenger Klaus Eingardt stood in line with his sole carry-on suitcase by his side and his black leather computer bag slung over his shoulder, waiting to clear customs, impeccably dressed in a suit and tie, with mid-length, neatly groomed blond hair. Atop his head rested a pair of fashionable black sunglasses. He was next to being called up to the window. Eingardt was of medium build and looked like any other Bavarian.

He'd been having a very bothersome time with his left contact lens throughout the flight and it still persisted in bothering him, so he reached into his pants pocket to retrieve a small bottle of wetting solution which he had to buy inside of customs, and tilted his head back to drop a few drops into both of his irritated blue eyes for relief. Then he dabbed away the excess fluid with his handkerchief.

"Next," the thickly-built English agent with the shaved head called out, waving the passenger up to his station with his right hand. Passenger Eingardt was still dabbing away the wetting solution, and didn't respond to the request quickly enough. "Next!" The agent snapped, a little more emphatically this time. To him, everyone was the enemy today—no one was getting by him on his shift without going under the microscope.

Eingardt quickly moved up to the window and greeted the seemingly-hostile agent, while handing over his Austrian passport. Still, he also understood why the agent might not be so friendly in the wake of the recent events. "Good afternoon!" he said in English with an obvious German accent, while noticing the agent's name tag, "Agent Mallory," he completed his greeting.

"Purpose of visit," the agent snapped back.

"Yes, right," Eingardt responded. "I'm here for the SAP software convention."

The agent didn't verbally acknowledge the passenger. Instead he looked at him while conducting a visual strip-search, just as he'd done with the previous passenger, and the one before that. While his two hands deftly leafed through the passport, the agent squinted and locked his eyes onto Eingardt's in such a way, that even an innocent man would break down and confess to murder. It didn't help matters that Eingardt's left eye had started to twitch as a result of the spontaneous interrogation and pre-existing condition with his contact lens. "What's wrong with your eye?" Agent Mallory pressed.

"Contact lens," the Bavarian passenger answered. "They're satoric lenses— for blind people with astigmatisms like me," Eingardt tried to explain.

"Do you need time to fix it?" the agent asked, not really trying to accommodate the passenger, but more looking for cracks in his armor. It was a time of heightened security, and Heathrow had put their best out on the front line.

"No, thanks. I just put some drops in. It should be okay in a minute," Eingardt responded, but his contact lens continued to act up. "They always dry out when I fly."

"All right," the agent allowed, still holding his stare at the man with a twitching left eye. Then Agent Mallory's eyes finally joined his hands and checked the Austrian passport, as well as the customs document, and both the arrival and departure cards. After about one minute the agent seemed satisfied with the paperwork and passport, and stamped each accordingly. "Have a nice stay," the agent said, not necessarily meaning it, then handed the passenger his passport.

"Danke," Eingardt said, while reaching out for his passport and placing it in the side pocket of his computer bag. "Thanks," he said again in English this time, then turned and walked away, rolling his carry-on behind him. His contact lens was seriously misbehaving now, and he simply reached up and carefully squeezed the contact with two fingers and removed it. He was immediately relieved of the bothersome nuisance of the tiny piece of plastic in his eye that he was unaccustomed to wearing, and tossed the blue lens to the ground.

The actual reason he'd chosen to wear satoric lenses was not for his astigmatism, which is what these lenses were for designed for because they were made out of a more rigid plastic than the common soft plastic lenses that most people wore, and their denser construction design they could control the changing shape of an astigmatic pupil. The reason passenger Eingardt wore them is because they were the only lens large enough to cover the entire corneal area—completely concealing the true color of his eyes.

"Wait!" an emphatic voice barked out from behind.

Eingardt turned to see the husky customs agent waving at him to return. Shit! He thought, knowing that he now had one blue eye and one exposed brown eye. His heart raced, as he did the only thing he could do, and lowered the black sunglasses from on top of his head to down onto the bridge of his nose, covering his exposed alibi. Then he returned to the customs window that he'd just cleared—petrified inside, but still hiding his frayed nerves on the outside.

"You can't leave without this," the agent said, handing Klaus Eingardt the departure card that he'd forgotten to staple into his passport seconds earlier.

Trying not to show his obvious relief, the passenger thanked the agent and tucked the document into the side pocket on his computer bag. "Have a nice day," he said quickly, then turned and followed the signs indicating the taxi-stand's location, once again wheeling his carry-on behind him. Walking briskly toward the nearest exit, he reached up under his black sunglasses and pinched the remaining contact lens out of his right eye, and tossed it onto the ground.

On his way outside to hail a taxi, Nabeel Ali-Khan stopped to use the restroom. After using the facilities, he set his sunglasses on the stainless steel shelf above the sink next to the trash receptacle and washed his hands, while looking into the mirror to see how many occupants there were, then allowing his eyes to wander as inconspicuously as possible to double-check if there were any new security cameras in this particular facility. He was in and out of Heathrow three days a week and was well aware of the placement of each and every security camera in every restroom on the way out to the taxi stand, as well as the heavily watched public areas. It didn't get any easier on the outside of the airport either. This was London after all—the city of Big Brother.

Ali-Khan had quickly surmised that the restroom was free of occupants and there were no new cameras installed since he used this facility six days earlier—at least not visually. He dried his hands and discarded the crumpled wet paper towels into the trash can next to him, and then replaced his sunglasses over his eyes. He shouldered his computer bag again then walked toward the exit pulling his small carry-on behind him, well aware of the security camera in the upper left-hand corner right in front of him. Directly under the camera was another trash container. From that point the narrow gray tiled corridor took a hard right-hand turn then emptied out into the public area two meters further on the left.

As Ali-Khan arrived at the elbow-turn directly under the security camera, he paused momentarily, practically hugging the wall and taking his hand off of the carry-on's handle. Quickly he slipped the blond wig off of his head and discarded it into the trash container, digging around for a moment to cover it up with the other trash, then just as quickly ran both of his hands through his silky black hair. In seconds he emerged from the restroom, a new man, where he'd blend into hundreds of other arriving passengers proceeding to the exit.

In minutes Nabeel Ali-Khan stepped into a frigid winter afternoon, exhaling his warm breath into the chilly London air, emitting a foggy blast of his pent-up, long anticipated relief. He'd done it! He'd proven to himself and the world that with enough discipline and assets anything was possible in the battle for his cause. It was likely he had lost a good brother in the commander's noble stand-off. But if it was the case, his brother was in God's arms now. The remaining members of the commander's unit were either wealthy men now or casualties of their own cause.

During the time of captivity and its ensuing events, Ali-Khan had made himself and his international network of clients just over thirty billion dollars—but the plan was long in the making and had cost many lives. For his part, Ali-Khan's take was just under five billion dollars, all of which had already been distributed into various global accounts. There were more than enough new resources for him to ascend from obscurity and fight once again. When Allah chose that time of destiny was up to Him—if in fact it was Allah's wish at all.

"Twenty-six Hornton Street please," Ali-Khan told the cabby.

"Yes, sir!" the cabby chirped back, and they sped away into the blissful afternoon.

CHAPTER 25

Three days later: 14ᵗʰ and Meridian, Washington D.C. NW, 1:32 a.m.

Sylvia leaned casually on the cantilevered edge of the mahogany bar at Columbia Social, feigning an occasional sip of a very dirty Grey Goose martini, while her companion, Dom verbally flailed—again and again attempting to deliver the punch-line to one of his asinine jokes. His admitted comedic ineptitude and the forced laughter between them quietly grew into something resembling the genuine article—or perhaps it was just the nervous laughter of relief that comes naturally after the sort of ordeal they'd been through.

"Don't quit your day job, Dom" she chided.

"Thanks for the vote of confidence," Wilkinson said, shaking his head. "Ya know, you're funny. You're the only woman I know who doesn't get buzzed from a really strong martini."

"I told you a long time ago—it's like priming an engine for me. One martini and I get all fired up," Sylvia replied, focusing on the one remaining olive in her glass, while her mind chased the blur of the last three days, knowing full well it wasn't over yet.

"I guess," Wilkinson acknowledged, sipping his watered-down Jack and Coke, noticing the shift in Sylvia's interest. "Is that anything like having an espresso right before bedtime?"

She didn't answer. Preoccupied, she leaned forward ever-so-slightly to glance past the hunched over six-foot two-inch, muscular frame of Wilkinson and through the hip gathering of late-night patrons clinging to the wee hours for a last chance at companionship for the night, or perhaps just a meaty, whiskey-induced political discourse that seemed so common among aspiring D.C. politicos. Sylvia peered through a thick layer of tobacco smoke that hovered like an eerie fog just under the four equally spaced aluminum canister lights hanging above the bar top. Something or someone at the far end of the bar slightly under the forty-inch flat screen featuring a muted ESPN Sports-center broadcast caught her attention, while alluring tunes from the house iPod swirled throughout like an addicting aphrodisiac. She winked subtly then gracefully returned to her previous position. "Huh?" she asked, having no idea what Dom's last question was.

"How's he look?" Wilkinson asked, while twirling the ice cubes in his glass.

"Not as good as you, even with your new scar," Sylvia scoffed.

"Gee, thanks," Wilkinson sneered, while subconsciously reaching to conceal a scar just between his left eye and receding military haircut. "I work hard for my souvenirs."

"I'm sure you do, major. So did I," Sylvia reminded him, while pulling up her right sleeve just far enough to reveal the sixteen stitches that bound a very fresh laceration on her forearm.

"Touché," Wilkinson acknowledged.

"The mark will be easy as pie," she said confidently.

"I'll bet you say that about every guy you drag out of a bar."

"Nah, not everyone; you weren't so easy."

"Of course not," Wilkinson assured. "But then again, you didn't drag me out of a bar, did you? It was the cold desert if I recall. And we didn't have tumblers full of booze, either."

"If I order another, do you think your chances would get any better?" Sylvia asked, staring at her half-empty martini glass.

"God I hope so! But knowing you I'm guessing my desirability meter may require three more stiff ones to get the deal done, and we're not here to get that deal done. Are we?"

"Nice try, major. One and done. Remember?" Sylvia scoffed mischievously, while turning to lean back casually onto her elbows. The motion tugged her black knit, long sleeve turtleneck top away from her worn out Levi's 501s, exposing about two inches of her tight lower abdomen and a small diamond hoop pierced through her navel.

The two had had a short and meaningless affair years earlier in the midst of a seventeen day insertion behind Iraqi lines, their fourth such deployment together during that particular campaign. While they both acknowledged that the tryst was entirely stress relief, Wilkinson had to remind himself when they worked together, that it was just that—work. However, no man, including himself would be faulted for taking a second glance at Sylvia. And in his case, the memories of past pleasures subconsciously tormented him now, as he tried to suppress the recollection of the sweet fragrant smell of her hair, or her tantalizing taste. She had a body that would drop most jaws, mostly from regimen, and he was among the blessed few that'd seen it unclothed. He'd hardly realized his tight black ribbed turtleneck sweater had nearly inflated to the next size.

"Down boy," Sylvia calmly reminded him, sensing she'd been undressed by her companion's eyes. "I think you've been out in the jungle too long."

"That obvious, huh?"

Sylvia nodded back, while fanning herself.

"Last call," the raspy-voiced, thickly-built bartender shouted through all the commotion. He was brusque but charming as hell, and had a rolodex of bar jokes dating back to the 50s, and had used every one of them in the last seven hours while pouring close to two thousand drinks. "Yo, beautiful," he chirped at Sylvia. "You and crew cut here need a cocktail?"

"Nah, we're good, just the check," Wilkinson answered, amused at the coarse demeanor of Columbia Heights' version of Don Rickles. No one was safe.

"I like the new nickname," Sylvia chided, shaking out her silky brunette hair, strands of it camouflaging some the scrapes she'd acquired while masquerading as one of *them* just seventy-two hours earlier. After an abbreviated debriefing back at the Ramstein Air Force Base, she, Dom, and a small but efficient team were just as quickly deployed back on to the murky trail of a suspected disciple of the Prophet—the mastermind of the rogue organization that had threatened to knock the earth off of its axis. Any plans to accept President Haydon's invitation to the much-ballyhooed Washington D.C. parade and gala would be put on hold until the unit's mark was neutralized. For Sylvia, there couldn't be a better alternative. The thought of an awkward reunion with her father amid a collection of Washington highbrows made crawling into a sewer with disease-infested rats seem like a day at the beach.

Sylvia never forgave her father, the decorated admiral, or her mother, the elegant Spanish-born woman who'd taken the Washington society by storm. The model family from Annapolis had a secret, and their only child's existence hung precariously on the fragile wings of confidentiality.

What had and should have always been a storybook life, changed in a resounding ill-timed instant. It was only when Sylvia's mother lost her struggle with breast cancer that the unstable teenager slipped quietly into solitude, sweeping the disturbing anger in her heart under the rug. It was this secret and the ensuing vault of darkness however that ultimately transformed her into who she was today.

As she toyed with Wilkinson, Sylvia's motion allowed her to observe a lanky, somewhat-disheveled man at the other end of the bar that she'd been monitoring for awhile. Thin strands of dirty blonde hair fell carelessly across his forehead as he leaned forward. His nicotine-stained fingers crushed another cigarette butt into an ashtray that he'd managed to fill in a short period of time, only this time he didn't fire up another one. Instead he reached into his pants pocket and retrieved a significant stack of bills and peeled off three twenties and tossed them onto the bar. Sylvia reached up with her left arm and spoke into a concealed device in the sleeve. "Mark is on the move."

Wilkinson's smile stiffened into a slight smirk as he faced Sylvia with his back toward the mark. His eyes squinted at hers as if to ask for the next move, while he reached for his near empty tumbler and sipped the remaining watered down contents along with a few ice cubes.

As the man passed behind Wilkinson, Sylvia threw her arms around Dom and reeled him in closer, whispering into his right ear: "Ready to have some fun, cowboy?"

"Giddy-up," Wilkinson whispered back, as he shared in the friendly bear hug. "I could seriously get used to this."

"Oh yeah? Maybe until I stick my fangs in your neck," Sylvia retorted playfully while two other men passed behind Wilkinson moving toward the exit. The second man winked at Sylvia as he passed and then followed his companion out into the frigid D.C. night, both slipping into their heavy winter coats.

"Anyone ever tell you you're a total buzz-kill?" Dom asked.

"No, never," Sylvia snapped back coolly, disengaging from Wilkinson to grab her coat and retrieve some cash. "I'll get this one."

"Like hell you will!" Wilkinson replied, quickly throwing twenty dollars on the bar for their cocktails. "Let's go."

He snatched his coat from under the bar and they ascended the short flight of steps and exited to the right, pausing briefly at the top of the landing, their short puffs of warm breath piercing a gentle flurry of snowflakes. The man who'd winked at Sylvia moments earlier inside leaned against the enormous barren oak tree in front of the swanky new establishment. He gestured with a head nod to their right, and then lit a cigarette. Dom and Sylvia acknowledged the gesture, turning right onto 14th Street and assumed their rehearsed roles of a completely smitten couple who'd had entirely too much to drink, meandering down the right side of the street occasionally bouncing off of the stone walled buildings that lined the dimly lit street. Sylvia buried herself into Dom's body as if she'd had some experience at this sort of thing before, while his left arm corralled her shoulder, enjoying a role neither one of them would experience again for awhile. They giggled carelessly about an alcohol-induced scenario that never was, and then tried to suppress their artificial laughter.

About thirty meters ahead of them on the same side of the street strode the first of the two men who trailed the mark. Directly across the street from him the mark strolled efficiently, bundled up into his winter wear, exhaling sporadic puffs of cigarette smoke. The point man by the tree was now walking at a measured pace a safe distance behind the smitten couple on the same side of the street.

The mark stopped in front of a very nice four story brownstone building, flicked his cigarette into the street and reached into his pants pocket for his keys. Sylvia and Dom picked up their pace a bit, still carrying on like drunken lovers, as an elderly African-American couple passed by. The man ahead of them started to cross the street at a forty-five degree angle that would overshoot the mark, stopping briefly to allow an older model Mercedes to pass on an otherwise quiet street. Then he waded through a steady trail of warm exhaust from the car as it dissipated into the night.

The mark climbed the six steps to the entrance door and let himself into the building, as the man crossing the street dashed rapidly now toward the open door, needing to close the ten meter gap quickly before the heavy front door operating with a typical scissor hydraulic arm allowed the door to close. Sylvia and Dom also dashed at a forty-five degree angle toward the building the mark had just entered, no longer carrying on like inebriated lovers. The trailing agent behind them maintained his pace until he'd passed the elderly couple opposite him.

The lead agent raced hard toward the slightly gapped front door while retrieving a small piece of magnetic metal from his coat pocket, approximately one inch wide by two inches long. He quickly ascended the steps pretending to fumble for his keys, and noticed the elevator door on the inside of the lobby had nearly closed. The agent grabbed the door knob just before the door could close and applied his makeshift magnetic strap over the female portion of door locking assembly just behind the wooden frame, so that the male portion from the door would be blocked from locking. Then just as quickly he descended the stairs into a dark shadow just back from the base of the steps, while awaiting the fast-approaching couple.

Sylvia and Dom arrived in seconds. Moments later the trailing agent trotted up and tossed his smoldering cigarette out into the street. Dom instructed both men to wait ten seconds from the time he and Sylvia began their ascent up the stairs to the fourth floor, before they pressed the elevator call button. "Stay back until we enter the mark's apartment."

"Apartment 415," Sylvia reminded them, "fourth door on the left."

Both men nodded tightly that they understood.

"Romeo and Juliet to base—we're on our way in," Sylvia said into her raised sleeve microphone. "Let's go, major."

Two blocks away in a surveillance van, a voice confirmed the penetration. "Affirmative—that's a go."

Special agent Jensen and Major Wilkinson ascended the short flight of exterior stairs and pushed the door open. On the left side of the lobby there was a two-step entry into the steep carpeted stairwell. Sylvia hit the first two steps and turned hard to the right, charging aggressively up the steps, while Wilkinson duplicated her ascent as if they were doing synchronized stadiums. Quickly they'd passed the first floor landing, and charged toward the second floor. They'd practiced this drill repeatedly at a facility near the base in Ramstein. In twenty-eight seconds they would arrive on the fourth floor, hopefully in time to make a non-invasive entry into the mark's base of operations. Downstairs the two men waited patiently in the shadows while the necessary seconds ticked away.

The elevator door opened on the fourth floor and out stepped the bundled-up Ronald Bierschtadt. Down below Sylvia and Dom charged up the third floor stairwell, two and three steps at a time. In the ground floor lobby, one of the two trailing agents pressed the call button for the elevator.

Bierschtadt sauntered down the hall with no particular sense of urgency, reaching with his right hand into his pocket for his house keys. Sylvia and Dom were mere steps away from the fourth floor landing now. A second later they arrived at the opening, stopping ever-so-briefly to allow their own heartbeats to steady. In the lobby, the two agents stepped into the elevator and headed to the fourth floor.

Sylvia peeked around the corner and to her left, and could see the mark standing in front of his door, fumbling just a little to insert the key into its slot. Finally, Bierschtadt got the key inserted and turned the knob. The instant Sylvia could see his left foot penetrate the plane of the door way, she and Dom launched themselves down the softly lit corridor with weapons drawn. Bierschtadt quickly vanished from sight beyond the door. In just over one and a half seconds Sylvia and Dom closed the gap to Bierschtadt's door, and as it was about to close, Sylvia thrust her right boot into it, crashing the heavy wooden door open and into the stunned occupant of the apartment.

"Was ist das?" the German immigrant shouted, as he was knocked to the floor.

Just as quickly Sylvia hurled herself on top of him, swiftly embedding her Kahr MK40 firearm into his cheek. "Hello, Ronny," Sylvia scoffed, as she quickly pinned Bierschtadt's flailing arms under her knees. "How've you been?"

"Was, what, who are…" Bierschtadt struggled to comprehend what was taking place, while his language quickly transitioned to that of his assailant. The alcohol he'd consumed didn't help with his bewilderment either, a victim of absolute surprise.

Major Wilkinson closed the front door to just a crack, knowing he and Sylvia's flank would arrive any moment. After Sylvia confirmed she had contained their mark, Dom moved quickly to secure the remainder of the dark one bedroom apartment, following his firearm into each and every crevice and doorway he saw. "Clear," he whispered emphatically each time a new location met his approval.

Bierschtadt made the mistake of assuming his captor's gender meant weakness. With every attempt at wiggling free and trying to manage a punch, Sylvia thrust her free hand into his solar plexus. "You'd better relax, Ronnie. It doesn't have to be this way." It only took two such attempts.

"Who are you?" he asked both times, gasping for breath.

"I'm your conscience," Sylvia answered, half-smiling and half-sneering. "And you've been a bad boy."

Seconds later, the two trailing agents pushed their way in through the cracked front door with their drawn firearms and locked it behind them.

"Help the major secure the perimeter," Sylvia ordered quietly, still straddling her shaken captive, gripping his throat with her left hand, squeezing him tightly between her thighs, while emphatically shoving the nose of her firearm into his cheek with her right hand.

The two agents quickly complied, following all of Major Wilkinson's footsteps, closing all window blinds while turning on the lights in the areas as they were cleared.

Bierschtadt's posture slumped as reality began to set in. Cooperation was the only option now. Sylvia sensed as much, and loosened the death grip on his throat. "You ready to play ball, Ronnie?"

"Yah, yah."

Sylvia quickly zip-tied Bierschtadt's hands in front of him, knowing he was no more a physical threat than an angry ballerina, at least not to her. She pulled him to his feet, and then forcefully shoved him down on the living room couch.

In seconds, Major Wilkinson returned to the living room along with the other two men. "The room is secured," Dom said firmly, and then shoved his firearm between his sweater and trousers. Just as quickly he pulled the wooden coffee table out from in front of Bierschtadt, retrieved one of the metal chairs from the kitchen, brought it back into the living room and faced it backwards toward his prisoner, practically brushing up against his knees. Dom removed his weapon and pointed it at Bierschtadt's head, and sat down. "Now, start talking, scheisskopf!"

"About what?" Bierschtadt tried weakly, having trouble looking Wilkinson in the eyes.

Wilkinson simply removed the safety from his firearm, causing Bierschtadt to cringe backward. "I'm a delicate tulip compared to this young lady over here," Dom said, glaring down the barrel of his weapon. "Don't make me turn her loose on you!"

"What the major's asking is what did you do with the banks?" Sylvia started, standing over the top of Bierschtadt. "What did you do to Wall Street?"

"I don't know what you're talking about," the prisoner attempted.

Instantly, Sylvia hit Bierschtadt with a right cross, dazing him and knocking him over. "I've had a bad week," she spoke through clenched teeth, motioning for Dom to get up out of the chair.

"Uh-oh," Wilkinson scoffed, obliging Sylvia. "I warned you."

Sylvia picked the stunned prisoner up by the hair and sat him straight up on the couch, while taking Dom's place in the chair and leaning in hard, pressing into the prisoner's kneecaps. He winced with new pain and just as quickly she slapped his face with her left hand, getting his attention now, while her weapon did the rest of the coaxing. "Best case scenario? You talk, and you live. Worst case scenario, you don't, and you disappear. Mom and dad down in Munich never see sonny-boy again. Bye-bye," Sylvia reasoned "We take all your CDs, hard drives, computers, etc. We erase any trace that you were ever alive and we fix all of this on our own."

"It's a pretty good deal really," Wilkinson added, while the other two agents pressured the captive, inching closer. Just as quickly Wilkinson waved them off.

"So what's it gonna be, Ronnie?" Sylvia asked, pressing her weapon to Bierschtadt's forehead, while caving the metal rods of the chair-back into his knees even harder. Her face was maybe ten inches away from his now. "God you stink, shit-breath!"

He winced at the sharp pain and a second later his contorted expression lobbied for leniency. "Please," he begged. "I will tell you what you need to know. Please don't hurt me."

Sylvia eased off the pressure on Bierschtadt's knees and backed slightly away as he started to whimper, burying his face into his nicotine stained hands for a moment, then collapsed backwards, awkwardly combing his bound hands through his thin hair. "I'm so sorry. I didn't know…"

"A lot of babies couldn't eat, Ronnie," Sylvia prodded, slapping the German's cheek hard with an open palm. "Children, you scheisskopf! Now talk!"

THE END